MEMPHIS LEGEND

BRIAN CRAWFORD

MAVERICK BOOKWORKS

MEMPHIS LEGEND

This book is a work of fiction. Names, characters, businesses, organizations, places, events and incidents either are the product of the author's imagination or are used fictitiously. Any resemblance to actual persons, living or dead, events, or locales is entirely coincidental.

For information contact:
Maverick.BookWorks@gmail.com

ISBN-13: 978-1541353022

First Edition: December 2016

10 9 8 7 6 5 4 3 2 1

This book is dedicated to Miranda. If I listed all the ways you help me, this dedication would be longer than the book itself. So I'll just say: Thank you for your patience, support, belief and inspiration.

Acknowledgments

I almost skipped writing this page for fear of overlooking one of the many people that deserve thanks in helping me bring my story to life. I could not have done it without the help of supportive friends and family.

First, I'd like to thank my wife, Miranda, for putting up with me through the entire process. You never seemed to get tired of me despite reading each draft and being my tireless sounding board. Thanks to my Mom. Your support has been truly immeasurable. David Crawford, I thank you for being the best darn beta reader a big brother could ask for. You took the task to heart, and your input was invaluable. It would not have been the same book without you. Thank you to Jay Salmon. Your early constructive criticism and advice are much appreciated. (Now let's get your books out there, buddy). Lee Witte, thank you for making me rewrite the first scene with Dr. Lowe so many times. You successfully drove home the point that writing is rewriting. Amy Zilko, if not for your help with the editing process, I might still be working on my final draft. Thanks.

I know I forget someone, so let me say thanks to all of you that had to listen to me go on and on about my book, for telling me you can't wait to read it, and then being forced to wait as I went through the lengthy process. (It took longer than I expected as well).

Finally, I want to thank YOU, the reader, for taking a chance on my endeavor. I thoroughly enjoyed writing this story, and I hope that L.T. and Boyd and the rest of the crew have managed to entertain you as much as creating them did me. If so, I hope you will consider returning to Amazon and leaving a review. I am an indie author, so I rely on reviews and word-of-mouth. Thank you in advance for your consideration.

If you would like to be notified of new book releases or want to send me a message, you can contact me at Maverick.BookWorks@gmail.com. I also have a website, briancrawfordauthor.wordpress.com. However, I will admit in advance that I am a happily married man, father of four daughters, and still practicing chiropractor, so please set your expectations low on the website. (I know I have).

"When bad men combine, the good must associate; else they will fall one by one, an unpitied sacrifice in a contemptible struggle."

– Edmund Burke, 1770.

CHAPTER 1

It was 6:55 a.m. on a hot Tuesday in July when the man furtively entered Memphis Memorial Hospital through a seldom-used side entrance. His crisp, clean, dark blue denim jeans looked as though they had never been worn and were a strong contrast to the worn work boots and dirty windbreaker. The man was sweating, yet his discomfort appeared to be more than just physical; he looked uncomfortable in his surroundings.

Thousands of people come into the hospital each day, from all walks of life, yet instinctively I was transfixed by this man's peculiar behavior and appearance. His cold, hard stare was unnerving, and I was confident he was using the jacket to disguise something underneath. He was secretively gripping a formless mass through the jacket, not in the pocket, but something on the inside of the jacket. My inner voice, usually more subtle in its urging, was yelling at me to stay vigilant.

The man continued down the long hallway, stopping to look at the directory on the wall. It was obvious he didn't know where he was going, but he did know where to look. He read the names on the board, tracing the names on the board with his fingers, and stopped at Dr. Witmer's information while tapping the board affirmatively. His heavily tanned hands and wrists, absent of any noticeable tan lines, were evidence of a considerable amount of time spent outdoors without wearing a jacket or long sleeves.

I glanced at my watch. 6:57 a.m. My respiration increased as the first stirring of adrenaline entered my body; it was mildly unsettling. I was unsure if my suspicions were the cause, or that my shift started in three minutes and I hated to be late. It was not my style.

The man lingered in front of the directory for another 30 seconds, nearly immobile, staring, then abruptly turned and headed down the hall towards the elevator. Dirt fell from his work boots onto the clean, white tile floor. A result of the man's quick, determined gait. He was a Caucasian male, 5'10", 170, maybe 175 pounds, yet other people in the hallway gave the man a wide berth. Maybe they also felt something was amiss with the stranger, even if it was subconscious.

Reluctantly, I trailed him to the elevator, which the stranger entered with three other passengers, all women. One was a middle-aged woman, pretty, with a teenage girl who was obviously her daughter. It was easy to see she would be a real heart breaker when the teenage complexion cleared up. The other was a nurse I recognized from podiatry but did not know personally.

"Second floor please," he said in a pleasant Southern accent to the pretty middle-aged woman standing near the elevator buttons. When he made eye contact with me in the elevator, he gave a salutatory nod and smiled.

I relaxed my clenched fists as a feeling of relief encompassed me. Maybe my instincts had gotten rusty with disuse. Maybe I had been too quick to judge. The stranger was probably a courier clutching at papers under his jacket. Maybe even a process server feeling nervous about his current job. Feeling foolish, I decided to get off the elevator on the second floor and take the stairs back to my previous destination on the first floor. 6:59 a.m. I would be a little late. No one would even notice, although I would know.

The elevator door opened. The scent of sour, vinegary acetic acid mixed with dirt and toothpaste remained as an echo as the man exited the elevator in front of me. He furtively glanced around before walking to the directory near the elevator as I headed for the stairway. He was studying the directory, reading it with his fingers again. Even at the increased distance, it was obvious the man had stopped on Dr. Witmer's name again.

Pausing at the stairway door, I contemplated the suspicious odor of the stranger, reminiscent of a frat boy trying to disguise his smell after a long night of drinking. He was talking to himself and bouncing up and down feverishly.

The stranger abruptly turned and nearly jumped into a different open elevator.

Great, not again.

My heart rate quickened as the unmistakable surge of adrenaline entered my body. I welcomed the familiar rush while quickly formulating that my previous assertion was correct. The stranger was up to no good. He seemed to be psyching himself up to do something horrible, something so horrible that he needed to be psyched up to continue, and he was planning on doing it at Dr. Witmer's office.

The increase in strength and speed caused by the adrenaline had its advantages on stairs as I went up them three at a time, burst through the stairwell door two floors up and looked down the hall to the right. The stranger had exited the elevator and already turned to his right. I was looking at his back. He was walking at a vigorous pace, leaning forward in an effort to walk faster.

The first thread of indecision entered my mind. I was not entirely sure my hunch, my inner voice, was right. But it usually was, and that worried me. My internal mental struggle created a pause in my action while I decided whether to run or walk.

The stranger reached the end of the hallway and turned to his left, his profile revealing he was again gripping the formless mass under his jacket. Then he was out of sight.

My inner voice yelled at me to run. I had ground to make up.

I did not work in this part of the hospital, but I had been at the hospital for over three years and was reasonably sure I knew the floor plan. Dr. Witmer was a pediatrician, and her office was just around the corner. She shared a waiting area with Dr. Trueblood, an ear, nose and throat guy. Her reception area was on the left; Dr. Trueblood's was on the right. A person had to walk through the waiting room to reach the reception counter. To the left of the counter was the entrance to the treatment rooms. I also remembered a children's play area with a little Lego table and a fish tank.

The screams reached my ears before I turned left at the end of the hallway. Female screams. Worried mothers' screams. Scared screams. I slowed my pace as I reached the waiting room and was met with a tide of frightened mothers running my direction, pulling, or pushing, or dragging their children out of the area, out of danger. They were all scared. They were also all unhurt.

There was little time to mentally register my relief that no one was hurt before spotting the man standing just inside the door of the reception area. A young, small blonde receptionist fearfully sat a few feet from the stranger. He was menacingly pointing a gun in her direction.

"I said where the hell is Dr. Witmer?" He was waving the gun around erratically.

"She's in one of the treatment rooms." The girl was almost in tears.

"Then get her the hell out here right now!"

She was nearly paralyzed with fear, cowering, not wanting to make eye contact with the adversary. The tears started to flow.

"Get the hell over here and show me where the damn doctor is. Now!"

He grabbed the small woman by the arm, pulling her to her feet. He pushed her towards the entrance to the treatment rooms as the other receptionist was staring intently at the man, frozen in place, yet she looked more angry than frightened. One mother remained in the waiting room, prone on the floor behind the row of waiting room chairs, covering her small son. He looked about eight, and the wide-eyed look of excitement on his face made it obvious he did not share his mother's fear.

Observe. Orient. Decide. Act.

Slowing my stride without actually stopping my forward movement allowed me the split second I needed to assess the situation fully. The man was no longer simply a stranger. He was there to harm Dr. Witmer. Which meant he was now an adversary; he just did not know it yet. He would soon. He would not be allowed to reach Dr. Witmer.

The adversary finally spotted me, his eyes growing big as I approached, running and stopping within a few feet.

The adversary drew back and raised his gun towards me. "Back up! Who the hell are you?"

"I work here. I need you to let the girl go and put down your weapon."

"The hell you say."

His gaze remained fixated on me, yet the gun no longer remained aimed at anyone in particular. He was holding the gun out in front, unable to decide if he should aim it at the girl or the large man in front of him. His other hand remained locked on the girl's arm while she twisted her body away from the man. Her scared, pleading eyes locked onto me.

I recognized the gun, an inexpensive semiautomatic 9 mm pistol based on an M1911 design. I didn't like the gun, it had a tendency to jam during rapid fire drills, and it didn't fit my large hands well. I had never shot that model myself, but I knew its features and workings. It was a single action pistol, requiring that the hammer is cocked by hand or by operating the slide mechanism before the first round could be fired. The hammer was not cocked, and the safety was still on.

Thank God, I am dealing with an amateur.

Realizing the gun was not currently a viable threat, I reached out and wrapped my left hand around the barrel to redirect its aim to the side. The adversary responded as expected. He turned his head towards the gun as his other hand also moved in that direction. Grasping the opportunity, I stepped in closer, twisted my body to the left, and delivered a crippling blow with my right elbow to the adversary's left temple. It was so fast the girl would later tell the police she never even saw the blow that leveled the man who was now lying in an immobile heap on the floor.

7:01 a.m. I was late for my shift downstairs. The man was no longer an adversary.

CHAPTER 2

I had not spoken more than ten words to my mother in nearly 14 years, yet while standing over the man lying on the floor I could hear her voice inside my head. Something about evil and good men doing nothing. Who was I kidding, I knew the quote word for word. Just another example of the lies parents feed their children. It was one that I had bought into as a child, and now because of my mother's influence in my life, I could not help thinking my current situation was partially her fault and with that realization I felt the familiar resentment creeping into my conscious mind.

The weight of the gun in my left hand snapped me back to the present. I quickly removed the magazine making sure nothing was in the chamber and tucked the cheap firearm into my waistband in the small of my back before focusing, once again, on the unconscious man lying on the floor.

Time to employ the familiar mnemonic, ABCDE - Airway, Breathing, Circulation, Disability, Exposure. My training told me that any person with a decreased level of consciousness has a compromised airway due to the tongue and epiglottis blocking it. This man was completely unconscious. The jaw thrust maneuver was carefully employed to guarantee a patent airway. His breathing was irregular. His pulse rate was slow. Not surprising.

Next was determining his level of disability or consciousness. His eyes remained closed, he was unresponsive to voice commands and pinching his nail bed revealed he was unresponsive to pain stimuli as well. That was surprising. The final step, exposure, is always performed at the end of the assessment to look for clues to explain the person's condition. That was easy. My elbow, his head. The distinct smell of alcohol hit my nostrils while leaning over the man, indicating I needed to watch him until an emergency room doctor arrived to ensure he didn't drown on his own vomit.

The poor man's condition looked dire. A doctor was needed on the scene, ASAP.

The small blonde receptionist was hysterical; she wasn't going to be useful. The other receptionist was still staring, still mentally processing. It appeared she had not caught up with the events yet in her mind.

"Oh my God. What...what happened here?" It was Dr. Witmer. Good, she would save me the trouble of making the emergency call myself.

"Call down to security. Tell them to call 911. Man with a gun. The man is no longer a threat, but he is unconscious with a GCS of three. He needs medical attention, stat, so get an ER doctor up here."

Dr. Witmer was a small, thin woman with a face totally devoid of wrinkles or lines, yet her hair was going slightly gray. It made her age hard to guess, probably her mid-forties. The look suited her, she looked kind and caring, like a grandmother or favorite aunt. She looked at my quizzically and started to speak, second guessed herself, then left to call security without muttering a word.

The man remained unresponsive. Little to do but watch and wait for the cavalry to arrive. I directed the second receptionist to help the small crying woman over to a chair. The mother with the small child was standing, watching with her mouth open. She was obviously still processing as well. The son was still wide-eyed and definitely looked entertained; he was going to have one heck of a story to tell his friends.

Dr. Witmer returned. "I called security. They are on their way, and the ER is sending someone up. Who is he?"

"I don't know. I thought you might know. He was looking for you. He had a gun and was demanding to see you."

"Oh my God. A gun? Me? But why?"

"I have no idea. I disarmed him. Didn't have a chance to ask him why first."

Security was first to arrive, interrupting my conversation with Dr. Witmer. The security officer was a short, lean young man in his earlier twenties, wide-eyed and out of breath. I attempted to get the security officer caught up on the situation, but he had trouble processing as well. Confusion seemed to be contagious. Obviously, he was a civilian security officer and not an off-duty police officer.

Within minutes, Dr. Zimmerman rounded the corner in a huff and walked straight towards us, a warm smile on his lips and a confused look on the rest of his face. Ms. Rhodes, an ER nurse, accompanied him. Dr. Zimmerman said, "I would have been here sooner, but you know I'm really used to the EMTs bringing the patients to me, not me walking through the hospital to the patient. You could have saved me the trouble of running, Dr. McCain, if someone had told me you were already on scene."

I said, "Yeah, about that. See, I'm removing myself as the treating physician due to a possible conflict of interest."

"Oh," said Dr. Zimmerman, "You know the man personally?"

"No, I'm the reason he is unconscious with a GCS of three. I sort of hit him in the left temple. Hard."

"Alright then, that would do it, and it answered what was going to be my next question. I'm looking forward to hearing the story later, mate. Now step back and let me do my thing."

I liked Dr. Zimmerman. We enjoyed working together and had a very comfortable banter. I teased Dr. Zimmerman about getting some exercise before giving him the rest of my brief assessment. I watched as the doctor and Ms. Rhodes performed a more thorough assessment, shaking my head as I noticed that the patient's pupils were fixed and dilated on one side. Not a good sign.

I looked around to see if I was needed elsewhere. There was nothing for me to do, so I waited, preparing myself for the inevitable. Police would arrive soon, and they would want to hear my explanation. Hopefully, they would understand that I had acted in defense of Dr. Witmer and her staff and it would all be over soon. Hopefully. Experience had taught me that it would probably not be that easy.

* * *

Dr. Zimmerman directed the transfer of his unconscious patient, now secured on a spinal board, down to radiology for an emergency CT scan. Obviously, Dr. Zimmerman and I shared a common working diagnosis.

It took only a few minutes for Dr. Zimmerman to assess the patient and get the right personnel present for the transfer to radiology, yet a small crowd of on-lookers had already assembled murmuring and watching in astonishment. Dr. Lowe, the Chief of Medicine of Memphis Memorial, was among the group; he was the only one scowling. My brow furrowed in disgust as I realized a meeting with Dr. Lowe would be inevitable after today's events.

My first order of business was to calm down, though. Still jittery from the adrenaline rush, I could not sit and relax, yet I was trying hard to avoid pacing like a caged animal. Something I didn't want to be doing when the police arrived. It seemed essential that I appeared calm and in control.

Dr. Zimmerman was leaving with his patient as the police arrived. Unlike the security officer, the three male officers looked seasoned and efficient. They knew their roles. The youngest officer cordoned off the area, politely moving the crowd back while another officer attended to the man leaving on a stretcher. As a precautionary method, the officer insisted the man, now identified as Tom Harty according to the ID in his wallet, be cuffed to the stretcher. Dr. Zimmerman gave me a look that said: he won't need it, but what the hell, it isn't hurting anything. I nodded in agreement.

The elder of the group, a sergeant, focused on me. "You appear to be sort of in charge around here, mister…"

"Doctor, Dr. McCain. I hit the man leaving on the stretcher if that's what you mean. Does that put me in charge?"

"Maybe, maybe not, but it definitely means you are the one I want to talk to first. What happened here?"

"Full story or the condensed version?"

"Condensed for now."

When I provided him with my brief explanation of the earlier events, he didn't have trouble processing. Nor was he alarmed when I nonchalantly handed him the gun and magazine. Dr. Lowe stepped in the picture during the conversation, introducing himself as the "man in charge" to the sergeant.

After I had finished the story, the sergeant turned to address Dr. Lowe. "Like I told Dr. McCain, I am Sgt. Walters. I'm sure you heard the story just now, and although I know it's going to be an inconvenience, I would like to question Dr. McCain down at the station. Get the whole story."

Dr. Lowe was nodding in agreement.

"I will leave Officer Ferguson here to get full statements from Dr. Witmer and Miss, um, her receptionist. I'm going to have a female officer come down and question the young lady that was threatened directly by the suspect and any other witnesses. Officer Thatcher will stay with Mr. Harty. Any questions?"

Dr. Lowe replied, "No, no questions, Sgt. Walters. Thank you for your quick response and efficient handling of this difficult and unfortunate incident. The hospital is very appreciative." Turning to me, he continued, "Dr. McCain, feel free to take as much time as needed with Sgt. Walters, and take as much time as you need to emotionally recover from today's traumatic experience. Obviously, do not worry about working today." Dr. Lowe's syrupy sweet tone lacked sincerity and seemed to be more for Sgt. Walters' benefit than for mine.

I replied, "Thank you, Dr. Lowe. This will probably take only an hour or so. I will be back after that to work the rest of today's shift."

"We will get someone to cover for you, so you needn't worry about work. Besides, this morning's events will require a meeting with members of the hospital board to discuss any liability issues. I would obviously like to talk with you later, perhaps tomorrow morning."

I expected a personal meeting with Dr. Lowe; however, a board of directors meeting seemed completely unnecessary. Today was not the first time the police had been called to Memphis Memorial; in fact, in a city the size of Memphis, police visiting an emergency room can seem a little routine. Nor was it even the first time I was involved in a physical altercation with a patient. More than once I had been needed to help restrain a psychotic patient or one under the influence of alcohol or some other type of chemical dependency. I shrugged my shoulders and directed my attention to Sgt. Walters.

"Sergeant, how does thirty minutes sound?"

"Sounds fine, Dr. McCain."

The easy part was over. Tom Harty was no longer a threat and no one else had gotten hurt, so it was a success. Now all the questions would begin along with the endless assessments and others second guessing my handling of the situation. The hard part would soon begin, but this time I was ready.

The fight or flight response. Academically, I knew it was an automatic physiological response to danger initiated by the sympathetic nervous system. I also knew that the process originated in the amygdala of the brain and resulted in the release of numerous hormones to boost energy and prepare the body for whichever muscular action is necessary. I had picked fight. I usually did.

The sympathetic nervous system had performed flawlessly. But now I was wound up like a cheap watch. Thirty minutes to walk to Sgt. Walters' office was probably 15 minutes more than I needed to get there; however, the walk would do me some good. It would give me an opportunity to burn off some of the remaining excess energy from the adrenaline and glucose cocktail served up by my adrenal glands.

The walk also gave me to time to consider the questions that might be leveled towards me once I got to his office. My mind was imagining him questioning my handling of the situation. He would want to know why I didn't let security handle it. He might even want to know if I could have avoided hitting Mr. Harty. But Sgt. Walters wasn't there, I was. It was my call, and I was not going to let someone twist my words around this time. Not like the first time. I was smarter, and older, and wiser. And experienced. I would keep my emotions hidden this time.

I also had time to consider why Mr. Harty remained unresponsive.

* * *

I liked cops. I had experience with cops. Before medical school, I even helped provide martial arts training for a police force while living in Huntsville, Alabama. That did not mean that I always trusted their judgment, which is why I didn't know what to expect from Sgt.

Walters. Hopefully, he was being truthful about simply wanting to get my statement. I did not want the visit to turn into an interrogation.

Sgt. Walters' office was easy enough to find. As I approached his desk exactly 30 minutes after our last meeting, he glanced at the clock on the wall. "Nice timing." He was smiling, which seemed like a good sign. Smiling back, I reminded myself to stay in control if Sgt. Walters started to question my tactics. He heard I had the day off and promised not to take up much of my time. He started by requesting basic information: full name, address, phone number, etc. As I rattled off the information, he arched his brow quizzically when he heard my full name. I had grown used to the look, yet I still didn't like it.

"Thanks, Dr. McCain, how about age, height, weight, eye color."

"I'll be 34 next month on the 16th. Six-four, 235, green eyes, and I'm sure you can tell this crazy mop of hair is brown."

"You do have some crazy hair, Doc. They let you wear it like that?"

"Nobody has ever told me I couldn't."

"Well, you are kind of intimidating looking. I wouldn't want to argue with you about your hair. So what do you do at the hospital?"

"I work in the ER."

"What's with the slacks and sport coat? Where's the scrubs?"

"I walk to work every day and don't like to wear the scrubs outside of the hospital. Personally, I don't like scrubs at all; you said it yourself, I can look pretty intimidating. But they make the most sense in the ER."

"I had you figured for sports medicine. You are built like a professional athlete."

"Chalk one up for lucky genetics; my parents were both world class athletes."

His eyes darted to his left, highly indicative of memory access, but he obviously came up with nothing. Not a surprise. I did not want to appear rude, but I was wondering why he wanted to interview me in his office. He could have got my statement at the hospital.

He replied, "I could have, true."

"But?"

"But it looked like Mr. Harty was hurt pretty bad, and you were the person most intimately involved in the altercation at the hospital, so I wanted a very thorough statement for my records."

"That sounds fair enough, yet I can't help wondering if I should have a lawyer present for this."

"If you want one, although I'm not looking at recommending charges against you if that's what you're wondering."

"No, but a superior might. Or an aggressive district attorney."

Sgt. Walters acknowledged the truth in my statement, yet added that it would be unlikely. I had just stopped a man in the act of a major felony. Waving a gun around no less. "I'm not sure how they do things where you're from, but down here in the South, most people, including lawyers and judges, would probably just congratulate you on a job well done."

I had lived in the South long enough to know that he had a point.

"Pardon me for being cautious, Sergeant. It's just that I've been down this road before many years ago, and it was a mess and a half before it was all done. Plus, you guys always remind people after they have been arrested that anything they say or do can be held against them in a court of law; however, you don't remind them that everything they say or do before getting arrested can be held against them as well."

"You have some familiarity with Miranda rights?"

"I do."

Sgt. Walters stared intently at me for a few seconds looking for something. He was sizing me up. "Like I said, I'm not looking for evidence against you; I'm just trying to figure out what Mr. Harty was doing at the hospital before you stopped him."

Would he still feel that way if my suspicions about Tom Harty's condition were true? I saw the fixed and dilated pupil. If my diagnosis was correct, he had a condition with a 60 to 80 percent mortality rate.

"You mind if I record this?"

"I don't mind."

And I didn't mind. Having a recording of my story with all the voice inflections seemed a much better way to prevent something being taken out of context.

While setting up the recorder, Walters said, "I find it ironic that an emergency room doctor hit a guy so hard that he needed to call an emergency room doctor." I was not sure how to respond to that statement, leaving an awkward silence in the room that the sergeant seemed to acknowledge. "Sorry, sick cop humor. I can see you in emergency care; you seem like one cool customer. You don't look the least bit rattled by the earlier confrontation, and you seem comfortable around firearms as well, and around cops. Were you a military doctor or medic?"

"Good guess. I am ex-military, but not a doctor or medic."

"GI bill, then college and med school?"

"No. I was a Navy officer that worked as an aide for an Admiral involved in intelligence matters. I got out early after an injury."

Sgt. Walters said, "Sounds interesting."

"Not really, I got to see a lot of really boring classified stuff and sat in a lot of meetings."

"Then how did you get injured?" he asked.

"Paper cuts...lots of paper cuts. It was horrible. I cannot lick an envelope to this day."

Sgt. Walters gave me a cynical smile before sitting down and motioning that he was ready to start. I found Sgt. Walters to be a very efficient interviewer. He asked just the right questions, open-ended, not leading questions. I was impressed. It was my opinion that half of the process of getting the diagnosis right on a patient was taking a good history. He could teach a class on getting a good history. He was especially interested in how and why I first suspected Mr. Harty. I described the whole story. How I had first spotted Tom Harty, how I had tracked him through the hospital, and how I had disarmed him. No mention that the gun wasn't cocked and the safety was on. It took effort not to smile when I realized Sgt. Walters was not going to follow up on that detail. I also left out the part about my inner voice. The whole process took about fifteen minutes.

My mind kept drifting back to the first time I was involved in a situation like this. What a mess for my family and me. I wished I could read Sgt. Walter's thoughts. I couldn't.

"Thank you, Dr. McCain. Your description of the events was highly detailed. I felt like I was there watching the whole thing unfold. And thank you for letting me record this; I would have gotten writer's cramp."

"No problem."

"I got to know one thing, though. In the elevator, you started to change your mind about Mr. Harty. Was it really his odor that made you suspicious enough to pause and watch him again?"

"Yeah. It just didn't fit; going to a pediatrician's office smelling like that. Then the bouncing sealed it for me."

"The bouncing?"

"Yeah, I knew right then he was up to no good. I just wish I had listened to my initial gut feeling."

"Doctor, I doubt if 99 percent of most police officers would have been tipped off by Tom Harty's behavior." Sgt. Walters made an obvious point of turning off the tape recorder before continuing. "Only one thing about your story doesn't hold water."

"Yeah, what part?"

"I'd bet a month's pay you are holding back on what you did in the Navy. Oh, I believe you were in intelligence, I just don't believe that part about the meetings and paper cuts. Don't worry; my suspicion will not be in the report. And, Dr. McCain, if you ever get tired of being a doctor, you need to look into being a detective."

"I will keep that in mind."

There was a brief knock on the door. Officer Ferguson entered, back from questioning Dr. Witmer and her receptionist; a female officer was still taking statements from other witnesses. Officer

Ferguson had a working theory in place after talking to Dr. Witmer, and it was obvious he wanted to talk. It was equally obvious that Sgt. Walters wanted to hear the theory.

Ferguson discovered that Dr. Witmer had called Child Protective Services last week for suspected child abuse in the Harty family. She named Tom Harty as her chief suspect after hearing stories from the child's mother. Dr. Witmer had never met Mr. Harty, which is why she did not recognize him. Ferguson guessed that Harty went to the hospital to teach Dr. Witmer a lesson. "I guess we will find out when he comes to, if he comes to. Thatcher told me that Harty is still unconscious. He has some kind of swelling around the brain or something. Man, you say you hit him with your elbow, and only once? What is your darn elbow made of anyway?"

I decided to let Ferguson's questions be rhetorical and countered with my own. "Did you hear anyone mention a subdural hematoma?"

"Yeah, that's what they called it. The doctor made it sound serious."

"It is. High mortality rate, somewhere around 60 to 80 percent."

Walters said, "Sounds like you suspected it, Dr. McCain."

"I did. So, does that change anything with you, Sgt. Walters?"

"Not as far as I can tell. He had a gun, you hit him in the head, he didn't hurt anyone. Sounds like a job well done to me. How about you, Ferguson?"

"Give the man a medal, Sarge. But that's just my opinion."

Walters said, "Once again, Doctor, thanks for your time. I don't expect you will hear from us again unless Ferguson convinces someone to actually give you that medal."

We both stood and shook hands. "By the way," I added, "My friends call me L.T."

"Thanks, Dr. McCain."

CHAPTER 3

I loved Downtown Memphis. I lived walking distance from Beale Street and the Medical District while most of my colleagues lived in Germantown or Collierville, towns with high median incomes, good school districts, and country clubs. However, I preferred to live among some of the best Southern barbecue and blues music the world has to offer. Being walking distance to work was a great bonus. Many of my colleagues thought I was crazy. I could not convince them I had found that Beale Street, and its immediate area, seemed somehow insulated from the racial tensions in the city. Maybe it was the music that transcended racial divides. Where else could Elvis have stolen rock and roll from the black blues artists and they loved him anyway.

After leaving the police station, I enjoyed the liberation of an aimless walk through Downtown Memphis and along the Mississippi River waterfront, thinking while my feet beat out a cathartic rhythm for almost an hour. Despite the randomness of my walk, I found myself outside LeClair's. I suspected my subconscious had guided me there, or maybe it was the gnawing hunger in my gut. Either way, it seemed apropos; if a good walk had been liberating, then talking to an ex-soldier should be equally therapeutic.

I found LeClair's on my first visit to Beale Street shortly after moving to Memphis a little over three years ago. I approached on the east end down near the New Daisy Theatre and by dumb luck, I found LeClair's. A one-story building with a simple slogan: Cold food. Hot Beer. Great Blues. I appreciated the sense of humor.

It didn't take long for LeClair, whom I had known for approximately three years, to show up at my booth. I think he once told me his first name was Martin, although I was not sure. Besides, everyone just called him LeClair. Surely, he was at least ten years older than me; however, he had an ageless quality about him that made it difficult to guess his age. His ebony colored skin was devoid of wrinkles except around the eyes; his head was bald, yet it appeared to by choice and not heredity; and he had a set of impressive, muscular biceps on him that would make most body builders jealous.

What I did know about LeClair was that he was born a Louisiana Creole raised near New Orleans, although he was a genuine Memphian now and owner of the bar sharing his name for almost ten years. While serving in the Marines during the Vietnam War, he discovered the Memphis blues sound, a sound different from the New Orleans jazz and zydeco he had grown up with. He loved it. LeClair once recalled that he told himself that if he made it out of that "shithole," his name for Vietnam, alive, his dream was to own a blues bar in Memphis. I admired him for pursuing his dream. Although some of the other bars and taverns along Beale Street were larger or attracted more popular musical acts, I preferred LeClair's.

LeClair said, "Doc, this is a pleasant surprise. I thought you were workin' today. Playin' hooky?"

"Believe it or not, it seems I have the rest of the day off."

"Time off for good behavior?" asked LeClair.

"Hardly, there was an incident at the hospital, and now the administration thinks I need some time to recover. What I need is a hamburger, just the way I like, and some company if you have time."

"I always have time for my favorite doc. And sounds like you have a story, I can't wait."

LeClair walked the order over to his short-order cook. LeClair gave his usual shrug to the cook when he delivered my hamburger order. Half pounder, cooked medium, pickles, lettuce, onion, tomato, with the bread smothered with pesto. The pesto they kept in the back solely for me. No fries.

LeClair said, "I don't know why he gives me that look every time. He knows you always get the same thing for lunch."

"It's because he wants me to like his barbecue, but, no offense, I eat my barbecue at Charlie Vergos. I have told him that he makes the best darn hamburger around, though. You really should convince him to experiment more with the menu. And get me some vegetables. I would probably eat here more if he had some darn vegetables. A man can only eat so much slaw and green beans, you know."

"I know, I know, more vegetables. So tell me what happened at the hospital."

LeClair sat through the whole story, getting up only once to retrieve my hamburger and turn on the music for the incoming lunch crowd. When I finished, he just grinned. "The sergeant sounded cool, so what are you worried about?"

"Who says I am worried."

LeClair replied, "You do, man. I mean, I know you didn't say it directly, but you said it just the same."

"How so?" I asked.

"It's the way you told the story, Doc. I know, that you know, that you did the right thing. So just tell it that way."

"I guess I'm worried about Tom Harty."

LeClair furrowed his brow at me, and then quickly shifted to a laugh. "Why? He was a dumbass. He shouldn't have been all up in that hospital wavin' a gun around, especially on a day that Lieutenant McCain, bad-ass extraordinaire, happens to be workin'."

"Leave it to an ex-Marine to set me straight, thanks."

"There is no such thing as an ex-Marine, once a Marine, always a Marine."

I had said "ex-Marine" on purpose. I did it to all former Marines. I always enjoyed the little tease, and I always got the same response. Don't let them fool you; they enjoy saying it.

"You did the right thing, Doc. I guess too bad about that brain swellin' thing. You think that could come back and bite you in the ass?"

I replied, "I hope not, but hard to say with civilians. In my experience, all civilians, even cops, analyze dangerous situations differently than soldiers. It makes them inconsistent in matters like this."

"I hear ya, Doc. Some civilian might even think you're going to get post-traumatic stress disorder from somethin' like this."

We both looked at each other and laughed. Both of us had been in real life-and-death situations before and understood the absurdity of thinking hitting someone on the head would trigger a traumatic response.

LeClair said, "So when you gonna talk to the Chief of Medicine guy?"

"I figure I might as well just go over there now and get it over with. I don't see how it will be any less unpleasant tomorrow than today."

"What's he like?"

"Honestly, he is the poster child for self-employment. I imagine many a doctor has considered private practice after spending time with him as their boss."

LeClair said, "A real dick, huh?"

"Your words, not mine, but...yes."

"I was thinkin'. Maybe next time you should not hit the guy with everything you got."

"I didn't hit this one with everything I got, probably less than half. I didn't want to kill him, just incapacitate him. And I hope there will not be a next time...four times now is enough."

LeClair stood up to his full six feet, rubbing his hand over his bald head and smiled a mischievous smile. He then shook his head and laughed.

"Doc, stop foolin' yourself man. I think you're my best white friend, so I can be honest with you. There will be a next time. It's just in your blood, man. You are some kind of darn bloodhound for trouble."

* * *

A blood hound for trouble. It pained me to admit it, but I resembled that statement. I did seem to possess an uncanny ability of finding myself in situations similar to today. Part of the curse that goes along with being my mother's son. It seemed that no matter how much I tried to distance myself from my mother, my upbringing, her teaching, was always one step behind. I could even hear my mother's voice in my head reminding me never to feel wrong about doing the right thing.

Which is the same thing LeClair had said to me. I had done the right thing. Regardless of the outcome, regardless of Tom Harty's fate, stopping him was right. Plain and simple. That did not mean I was looking forward to my visit with Dr. Lowe. I highly doubted Dr. Lowe believed in moral absolutes. Black and white. As the Chief of Medicine of a large hospital, his duties probably revolved more around hospital politics and policies, meaning he was more of a politician now than a practicing doctor. And one thing I knew about politicians, unfortunately from personal experience, is that their moral compass had too many shades of gray for my liking. My expectations for the meeting were low. *At least, I shouldn't be disappointed.*

By force of habit, I entered the hospital through the emergency room entrance and attempted to slip through unnoticed, but the elder triage nurse, Evelyn, spotted me. She was waving, so I reluctantly joined her at her desk. "Dr. McCain, we all heard what happened. Lordy, lordy, are you okay? We didn't expect you back today, and you don't need to be here, we got your shift covered. Dr. Chen is covering it for you. You poor man."

It had begun.

I quickly thanked Evelyn for her concern, then tapped my watch and told her I needed to see Dr. Lowe. She nodded sympathetically. I had escaped, almost unscathed. If only the elevator would hurry up before someone else spotted me.

"Hiya ole chap, wait just a minute." It was Dr. Zimmerman. He had done some post-graduate work in England, and it was there that he picked up his tendency to use common British phrases. I had worked with him for over a year, yet I still found it funny to hear these phrases combined with Dr. Zimmerman's strong Boston accent.

"Hey Zimm, I'm heading up to Lowe's office, what's up?"

The elevator arrived, and Dr. Zimmerman rode up with me. "I just wanted to give you the low down on Harty. Acute subdural hematoma, still unresponsive. I know I don't have to remind you of the mortality rates. Bloody hell."

"I know, I heard, plus I noticed he was fixed and dilated on one side when you were checking him out. Let me guess, he has a midline shift on the CT and elevated ICP?"

"Sure does. You are going to make a fine ER doctor some day. By the way, he is on his way to surgery now."

The gnawing feeling in my stomach was returning, and I knew it was not hunger this time. "Do me a favor, Zimm."

"Sure, name it."

"He had been drinking; please check for alcohol abuse."

Dr. Zimmerman replied, "Way ahead of you. We ran all the normal blood tests: CBC, hemoglobin, coagulation profile, etc. I also screened him for drugs and alcohol. He's a boozer, which we both know puts him at risk for acute subdural hematoma."

"Thanks, I figured as much. I knew I didn't hit him that hard."

He walked me all the way to Dr. Lowe's office providing a few more details on Mr. Harty. He put a reassuring hand on my shoulder before walking off. I wished everyone could treat the incident more like Dr. Zimmerman. No reason to make "much ado about nothing" as Dr. Zimmerman might say.

Dr. Lowe's secretary escorted me into his office, a spacious office more ornately decorated than I expected. More tasteful than I expected. The tan walls with a darker adobe colored accent wall were a nice departure from hospital white. The desk, the bookcases, the credenza, the wooden diploma frames were all made of the same expensive looking wood. The chairs were leather. There was just the right amount of personal effects in the professional office. The overall effect was impressive; someone had decorated his office well.

The wait was longer than expected, nearly fifteen minutes. As always, Dr. Lowe was in a dark suit and tie, tailored perfectly, thus giving the impression that he was thinner than he actually was. Most would argue that he was not fat; however, he easily had 40 pounds extra weight on his 5'9" frame. Albeit, it was fairly evenly distributed. He looked to be in his late fifties, perfectly groomed, every hair in place. Success. That is the word that first came to mind when looking at Dr. Lowe. He was dressed for it and groomed for it.

As usual, he was scowling. After entering, he paused, his squinting, disapproving eyes lingering on me past the point of necessity. I could tell right away this was going to be an unpleasant conversation.

Dr. Lowe sat and motioned for me to do the same. It must have been out of habit; I was already sitting. His eyes locked onto mine. I expected him to talk, but he didn't. Soon, an uncomfortable silence filled the room. Apparently, each of us was waiting to see who was going to talk first. He was the one that called the meeting, so I figured he should start. Dr. Lowe sighed scornfully before starting. "I didn't expect to see you back so soon, Dr. McCain. I suggested tomorrow."

"Is this too early? Honestly, I would have come back sooner, but I remembered you mentioning that you were going to have a meeting with the hospital board."

He was reclining back in his chair, hands together and fingers intertwined with the index fingers resting on his upper lip. He resembled a chess player contemplating his next move. The awkward silence returned.

Another sigh. "Dr. McCain, are you sure you want to do this now? I mean, don't you need some time to recover...psychologically?"

Something about the condescending tone of his voice when he said "psychologically" annoyed me. I think he was trying to make it seem as if he was feeling sympathy for my predicament in some way, but, honestly, he sounded like a condescending prick. My inner voice was telling me to behave. Keep my anger in check. A wise old doctor once told me that the person asking the questions in a conversation was in charge. It was time for me to be the one asking the questions.

"Time is relative, Dr. Lowe, don't you think?"

The disdainful look on his face morphed into a puzzled expression. He chose not to answer me, resorting back to using silence. I decided to proceed this time, making sure I was still the one asking the questions.

"Dr. Lowe, were you able to have your meeting? If not, I can come back later. Would you like me to come back later?"

"Yes, I mean no...I mean, yes, I was able to have my meeting, and, no, you do not need to come back later." More silence, followed by another resigned sigh. "Dr. McCain, since you insist upon talking now, then I guess it is best we get started. I just came from talking with some of the board members. I have to admit we are taken back somewhat by today's unfortunate incident." He paused. He was either getting up the courage to continue or was trying to choose his words carefully. "Frankly, we have never been faced with this type of situation before."

His derisive tone had returned, and I could feel my blood beginning to boil. "And what type of situation are you referring to?" I managed to ask the question calmly and respectfully.

"How do I say this without giving you the wrong idea? We realize you might have saved Dr. Witmer's life. I know she is grateful and we are grateful none of our patients or staff was injured. But we also realize that you could have made the situation worse. You are a doctor in this hospital, not part of security. We feel you should have conveyed your suspicions to security and let the professionals handle it." He took in a deep breath, rolling his eyes like he was tired of his own monologue, but he continued. "Furthermore, it is evident you made no attempt to persuade Mr. Harty into ceasing his endeavor. Instead, you engaged in a violent struggle for the weapon, a struggle that ended poorly for the gentleman."

Did this guy think I was going to allow it to end favorably for the "gentleman?"

"That gentleman is now in surgery to relieve the pressure from around his brain. His fate is uncertain. You are a doctor in this hospital, and it seems you have violated the Hippocratic Oath. Finally, the media has been out here all morning interviewing witnesses. We could not keep your name from being mentioned. We feel the hospital is now in damage control. Thus we will all need to meet tomorrow with our attorneys to discuss further ramifications that might arise."

It was happening again. I expected a certain amount of second-guessing from the amateurs, the civilians, but Dr. Lowe referred to Tom Harty as a gentleman, implying that Mr. Harty was somehow the victim, not the perpetrator, while also stating I violated my Hippocratic Oath. How did the idiot think I had violated my Hippocratic Oath? The Oath does make reference to treading with care in matters of life and death, but Tom Harty was a man with a gun, not a patient of mine. I did not owe him any particular consideration. I reclined back in my chair, staring back at Dr. Lowe, saying nothing at all while trying to hide my growing anger.

He was fidgeting, unable to handle the awkward silence, a silence he created by his absurd statements. "Dr. McCain, do you have something you would like to say?"

"What do you want to hear?"

"Excuse me," he replied.

I said it again, just the same, no change in voice inflection, or tone, or volume.

"Dr. McCain, I believe I was quite succinct. As Chief of Medicine, I speak for the hospital administration and the hospital board of directors when I tell you that I would like to hear what you have to say for yourself."

"Please do not take this the wrong way, but is the implication of your question purposeful…sir?"

Dr. Lowe said, "I'm sorry, what implication are you referring to?"

"Sir, do you think of me as obtuse?"

"Obtuse?"

"Not particularly observant, perhaps dull-witted," I replied.

"I know what obtuse means."

"Then please stop asking me what I have to say for myself; I find that particular wording denigrating."

Dr. Lowe tried to stare me down, glaring at me through slitted eyes while I returned his stare indifferently. As he paced around his desk twice, he seemed to realize that I was immune to his intimidation. While sitting, his fist came down on the table. "Then please answer the damn question!"

Dr. Lowe had a reputation for being a hothead, but I had never personally witnessed it before today. Unlike most people, I had no intention of sitting through any more of his tirade, which was obvious as I stood up and headed for the door. "Where do you think you are going? I haven't dismissed you, and you still have not responded to my question."

My hand was on the doorknob, but after a contemplative pause I turned and faced Dr. Lowe. "I can think of no adequate way to answer your question, so I am wondering, does 'you're welcome' suffice?" I was still making sure he was answering my questions.

Dr. Lowe leaned forward in his chair taking an offensive posture, but his stammering lessened the effect dramatically. "You're welcome...that is your response?"

"Yes, that is the safest thing I can think to say. I realize that you did not actually say the words thank you, but earlier you did say you were grateful none of your patients or staff were injured. Grateful is, of course, synonymous with thankful; therefore, I think it is befitting to answer with you're welcome." I paused momentarily while I sat down. "I know some people say no problem, but I don't like that one as much. I like you're welcome, it implies that I would do it again for you if asked, which, of course, I would. I would disarm an alcoholic waving a gun in your hospital again in a New York minute. Are you telling me you don't agree with my actions?"

Dr. Lowe's face was red. He seemed to know he had lost control of the conversation, and he didn't know how to get it back. We went back to the silence game. I could be silent longer than he could; I was going to win again. The redness was spreading down into his neck. The silence was having my desired effect. "But we did not ask. You took it all upon yourself!" His volume was almost deafening.

As the last echo of his words subsided, I realized I had won this altercation. Because that is what the conversation had become. He lost the moral high ground during his earlier monologue and now he was losing his composure. I wanted out of his office before I told Dr. Lowe what I really thought of him.

"This hospital has never once asked me to restrain a psychotic patient or one that is all hyped up on drugs, yet I have done it. Never once have you complained when I prevented injury to your staff in the past. I'm big. I'm strong, and I have an extensive background in martial arts. I'm not trying to brag; it is what it is. Plus, you know I'm ex-military."

Dr. Lowe gave me a bored look, prompting me to get to the point.

"I realize I'm a doctor in your hospital, but I'm also perfectly capable in dangerous situations. More capable than your so-called professionals. The poor security guard that showed up first had no firearm and no training. Trust me; he would have made it worse. You would probably have a dead security guard and a dead doctor right now."

"You don't know that!"

"You're right; I don't know for sure how it might have turned out. But I do know I saved the day. Me. Without being asked. Talk to Sgt. Walters; you can get the full story from him. As for me, ever since I entered your office, I have sensed hostility and contempt in your voice that lends me to believe that you lack objectivity. I realize that for me the conflict upstairs is over and that for you it is just beginning since you have to worry about hospital liability and such. It must be stressful to carry around all that responsibility; I know I wouldn't want it. However, I am choosing not to engage in this conversation any longer." I stood up again during the last sentence indicating my intention to leave. "You really should have started with thank you, or at least, a 'glad to see you are alright' before second guessing me."

"I do not appreciate your tone, doctor. I am Chief of Medicine in this hospital. I will decide when this meeting is over, and you have to listen, like it or not! So sit!"

I remained standing. "No," I said evenly.

"No! No, what?"

"No, I will not sit down. No, I do not have to listen to you. You would like me to, but I do not have to. I will stay momentarily; however, I will not sit, and I am retaining my right to leave if this conversation declines any further. Before you resume, maybe you better ask yourself how you would feel if the life I had saved today had been your own."

The redness in his face and neck was complete. If he got any redder, I was going to need to write him a prescription for high blood pressure medication.

Struggling to regain his composure, he continued through gritted teeth, "Dr. McCain, you are somewhat of an enigma to me. You were a fine resident physician in this hospital. You finished your residency, and you also recently passed all your boards in physical medicine and rehabilitation. We offered you a position in our hospital as a physiatrist; instead, you turned down our offer and applied for emergency care. You said you needed some time to decide some things and would love the flexibility that often accompanies an ER schedule, so we obliged you. Then we discover that you are building your own medical clinic here in Memphis. Yes, we know about your little building, and we realize we were short-sighted in not having a non-compete agreement with you. After all we have done for you, you demonstrate your thanks by embarrassing this institution today, all while potentially involving us in expensive litigation."

"Dr. Lowe, I want to thank you for your candor. I find it refreshing and illuminating. I also find it insulting and misguided; therefore, I'm going to leave before I say something that you might regret. I will show up for work tomorrow as usual unless otherwise instructed. Let me know through formal correspondence; that is, written correspondence, stating if and when I am to meet with the hospital board and/or your attorneys. For now, I'm going to take you up on your offer and take the rest of the day off. Between now and my shift tomorrow, I will try not to save anyone; I would not want to embarrass your hospital. Good day."

I turned and walked out without looking back, careful to not slam the door that I so badly wanted to slam. Dr. Lowe was stammering something as I left, but I had already tuned him out.

* * *

Anger. A normal, usually healthy, human emotion. Unless it gets out of control. Then it turns destructive. For the first time today, I was angry. Incensed was a better word. Not at Tom Harty, but at Dr. Lowe. Dr. Lowe had the distinct honor of being the first person today that I actually wanted to hit; I had hit Tom Harty out of necessity. *I wonder if hitting your boss is considered destructive behavior.*

Hoping to avoid disappointment, I had entered the meeting with low expectations. I should have set my expectations even lower. The "last notch on the limbo bar" low. The impossibly low notch. Even then I might have been surprised. I had expected second guessing. Arm-chair quarterbacking. However, I expected it to come more in the form of how could the hospital have prevented the situation in the first place. Which they could not have prevented. Not without armed guards with metal detectors at the entrances. Hostility, on the other hand, was not expected.

I was half way home, my feet attacking the pavement with each angry step, when anger started to transform into amazement. I was amazed that Dr. Lowe did not realize that we had been lucky today. Lucky I had spotted the man. Lucky my inner voice had alerted me. Lucky Tom Harty was an idiot. Lucky that I had practiced gun disarms probably more than 500 times in my past. Hopefully, the hospital board was not as myopic.

Instead of relishing on the positives that came out of today, Dr. Lowe focused on the negative and tried to browbeat me because I handled it differently than he would have. Of course, I handled it differently than he did. Guys like him run away from those types of situations. That was not a slam on his character. My guess was that most normal people run away from a man with a gun.

And he was wrong about my office building, although I was going to save that explanation for another day. I did not like Dr. Lowe, but I did not want him as an adversary. It appeared I might not have a choice.

The day was simply getting worse. I was going home to disconnect the phone line and turn off my pager. The day might get even worse, but the world would have to wait until tomorrow to tell me about it.

CHAPTER 4

I was not sure who first said something about turning lemons into lemonade, but I was looking forward to a good workout and time to work on a car that I had recently purchased following a bank repossession. The previous owner had purposely blown the motor and vandalized his own car when he realized he could no longer afford the payments. I had been slowly putting the beautiful red Mercedes convertible back together for a couple of months.

My loft apartment was located on the second floor of a commercial office building within walking distance from the hospital. The building had originally been a large department store from the 1930s. On the first floor of the old brick building was John Deland, attorney-at-law. He was a civil lawyer who kept himself busy with real estate, wills, trusts, contracts, and the occasional divorce. There was also a music store, Daddyo's Music, which sold or rented all types of musical instruments and equipment. The owner, Steve West, was a nerdy-looking, tiny white guy who could play the guitar so well that I figured he could give B.B. King or Eddie Van Halen a run for his money. He was also one heck of a business man. I had owned the building for a little over two years, and Steve hinted more than once that he would be willing to take over the attorney's space if the opportunity arose. He would even pay for the build-out.

In between the two businesses was the street access to the second floor. Two large, custom copper doors provided an entrance to the stairway to the second floor. The copper had not acquired a full patina yet, but the doors were still beautiful and looked as if they could withstand a bazooka attack. I climbed the stairs to a small landing at the top. Two doors were located at the top of the landing. I entered the door on the right, but it did not matter since both doors opened into my apartment.

My apartment consisted of the whole second floor of the old building in a completely open floor plan except for two large enclosed bedrooms, each with its own bathroom. The commercial tiled floors looked new, while dozens of black and white photographs of Memphis and the Mississippi River adorned the plain, white walls. The ceilings were over ten feet high and covered with a unique wood grid design. My favorite feature was the numerous windows, each of them slightly more than six feet in height, which allowed ample amounts of ambient light to filter into my apartment from the outside.

Eventually, my goal was to divide the second floor into two large upscale apartments; however, I was in no hurry since the building was turning a profit as it was and I was enjoying all the space. With a little over 5500 square feet upstairs, there was even room for my own gym. I promptly changed into some clothes more appropriate for working on the Mercedes and grabbed a glass of water from the area designated as the kitchen. The message light on my answering machine was blinking. Hesitantly, I hit play hoping the message was not from the hospital. It was worse; the message was from my mother. Without hesitation, I deleted the message. *When is she going to learn, I want nothing to do with her.*

The Mercedes was located downstairs in the old department store's loading dock, which I had converted into my personal garage. I used the freight elevator down to the loading dock and smiled at the progress I had made with the Mercedes. It was in pieces, a genuine work-in-progress, but the new motor and transmission were in place. With any luck, I could get all the different accessories hooked up and have it running within a week. I fired up a Blues compilation CD and went to work. I was able to work on the Mercedes for a couple of hours before heading upstairs to spend the next 40 minutes on the weights followed by 20 minutes on the heavy bag. The time was well spent, in fact, curative as it allowed me to channel my anger towards Dr. Lowe into something more constructive. The infuriation I felt towards Dr. Lowe was gone. In its place, was a state of eagerness as I looked forward to my date tonight.

I took a shower, changed into some casual clothes — jeans and a nice, well-fitting pullover shirt. I had just enough time to walk across town to my girlfriend's place of employment. Upon exiting my front door, the overpowering smell of perfume and hairspray overtook me, forcing me to turn suddenly and spot a TV reporter running up to me with a microphone in hand. Nicole Cassano. A reporter for the local ABC affiliate. A camera man was briskly following her. Dr. Lowe had said that they were unable to keep my name out of the press.

I was a minor the first time that I had been involved in a similar situation, making me off limits to the press; they could not even publish or mention my name. I was 33, not 16 this time. No longer off limits. The press added a new dimension, a new wrinkle to my current situation that I had not considered. My inner voice was cussing me out, telling me that I should have expected the intrusion. It was right, of course, but, honestly, I did not expect anyone to find me so fast; my phone was unlisted, and I used a P.O. Box.

"Dr. McCain!" I turned my back on the pretty blonde-haired reporter. "Dr. McCain, may I have a word with you?" Exasperated, but refusing to show it in front of the camera, I simply unlocked the door and re-entered the building. She was still yelling at me through the heavy door. "Dr. McCain, please, may I have a word with you? I am friends with Ellie. I'm not here to…"

The closure of the heavy door cut her off mid sentence. Apparently, the door could withstand more than a bazooka attack; it could shut up a nosy, pesky reporter. I appreciated the heavy construction of the old brick building. I did not appreciate Nicole Cassano.

I could not blame her though as I imagined the headline: Man lies in coma after attack at Memphis Memorial. She was trying to get her exclusive; however, bringing Ellie into it was too much for me. If I did let anyone interview me, it would not be Ms. Cassano.

Glancing out one of my front windows revealed that Nicole and her cameraman were still milling around my front entrance. They were apparently in for the long haul. I felt violated as I realized that my privacy was going to be more difficult to keep, especially if Ms. Cassano's desire to find me was fueled for any reason. The way I saw it, there was a 60 to 80 percent chance that her interest in me might increase; one directly proportional to Mr. Harty's mortality rate. Plus, if she found me so easily, then maybe other reporters might be motivated as well. Honestly, it just did not seem that big of a story to me, so I could not understand the interest.

I considered giving Ms. Cassano her exclusive interview. Maybe then it would all just go away. But she had brought up Ellie. That was a cheap shot. I was not going to give her an interview. The good news was that I knew she would leave soon. It was shortly after 6:00 and the news broadcast would be over at 6:30. Time to wait her out. To pass the time, I read a journal article discussing facet joints as a major factor in low back pain. The article was a joke. How the authors got it past a review board was beyond me. Their sample size was too small to provide any real evidence, plus saying that facet joints were a potential cause of low back pain was like saying that falling could give you a boo-boo. *Thank you, Captain Obvious.*

At 6:15, I could hear Ms. Cassano from an open window giving her live report from "outside the home of Dr. L.T. McCain."

L.T. McCain. She hadn't even bothered taking the time to figure out my actual name, so how the hell did she find me so fast?

As expected, Ms. Cassano mentioned that I had been contacted "but refused comment." I found it difficult to resist the urge to go back downstairs and open and close the front door repeatedly in a game of peek-a-boo making her think that I was trying to bolt past her. Common sense won the battle over mischievousness. By 6:25, they were packed up in the van and gone.

Tonight's date was planned before I became the unofficial security detail for Memphis Memorial Hospital, and I was not going to break my date with Ellie. Even so, my instincts warned me that dinner with Ellie might get a little weird. I expected to answer a multitude of questions from Ellie. It made sense. Ellie, my girlfriend for the last year, was the chief meteorologist at the local ABC affiliate station, the same news station that employed Ms. Cassano.

Walking was no longer an option if I planned on arriving on time, so I took the elevator down to the loading dock. The Mercedes was not operational, which left a choice between two other vehicles. One was a classic sports car that was a gift from my father, which I never drove. I opted for my 1984 Jeep CJ-7 Laredo, the first vehicle I ever purchased. I bought it new off the lot when I left the Navy and returned to the States from Southeast Asia.

Ten minutes later I was pulling into the TV station parking lot, taking care to park in a discreet location while waiting for Ellie; I did not need Nicole spotting me and trying again for her exclusive. Memphis Minnie was belting out "Hoodoo Lady Blues" on the stereo when I spotted Ellie leaving the employee entrance exactly on time. Backlit by the sun, her silhouette moved gracefully across the parking lot towards her car, the shimmering tresses of her long brown hair trailing behind her as her head moved side to side slowly, scanning the environment. I turned up my stereo just as Minnie sung the words "Boy, you better watch it 'cause she's tricky," hoping it was loud enough to get her attention. It worked. Ellie switched directions, smiling as she headed for my Jeep.

I smiled back, more to myself than for her benefit, as I realized that the beautiful woman heading my way was my girlfriend. She carried her lean, 5'10" frame with a grace usually reserved for dancers; my mother would approve. Ellie was easily the most beautiful woman I had ever met.

"Howdy, sailor, this is a surprise. Were those song lyrics meant for me?" She looked amused.

"No, just a coincidence. Why? You feeling it?"

Her smile turned from amused to mischievous. "Maybe, you never can tell about us Southern girls. So, we are taking your car?"

I think I enjoyed listening to her talk more than watching her walk. Her voice had the perfect Southern accent, with a musical lilt to it that was such a delight that it was nearly infectious. Most of Memphis seemed to agree; Ellie Carmichael was the most popular meteorologist in Memphis.

"If you don't mind some wind in your hair, then sure."

Seemingly from out of nowhere, Ellie produced a scarf that she used to tie her hair back into a ponytail before climbing into the Jeep. I was in the mood for Thai food, and I knew just the place, Thai Garden, on the edge of downtown.

We were greeted at the restaurant by a young Thai woman whose name tag said Sarah; however, I knew her real name was Sirikit. She was always friendly and seemed genuinely happy to see me. I was a regular; in fact, it was my favorite place in all of Memphis to eat, although I would not admit that to my Southern friends. They would only argue that it was un-American to eat so much Thai food in a town famous for its barbecue. *What can I say: I love the spicy food and stupid Americans need to learn to eat more vegetables anyway.*

"Mŏr McCain. Good to see you. We have booth for you, just way you like. Khun Ellie, so good to see you."

I caused Sirikit to commit a cultural faux pas as it is customary to use the first name preceded by the Thai equivalent of Mr., Mrs., Dr., etc., but then I don't give out my first name willingly.

I replied, "Khun Sirikit, thank you. Khuṇ dū s̄wy māk nı wạn nī̂."

She blushed slightly, and then seated us.

"L.T., what did you say to her to make her blush like that?"

"I told her she looked pretty today. At least I hope I did. I only learned a little Thai, and it has been a few years. Hopefully, I did not just ask her to marry me or something."

"And you learned Thai where?"

"Uh, Thailand."

"I thought you were in the Philippines while in the Navy."

"I was stationed in the Philippines. I visited Thailand a few times."

"A few times is all, yet you learned to tell Thai girls they look pretty. Figures. So you were a player while in Southeast Asia. Girl in every port, huh?"

"Khuṇ dū s̄wy māk nı wạn nī̂, Khun Ellie."

"Did you just say you I look pretty today, or did you just ask me to marry you?"

"I am pretty sure it is the first one. If not, we got a problem. Polygamy is frowned upon in most cultures, and, well, I did ask Sirikit first."

Ellie laughed. I admired her. Dating me had to be frustrating at times. All the loss, all the disappointment and turmoil in my life, had made me guarded, causing me to put up emotional barriers. True intimacy seemed foreign to me. I could only imagine most women would find me an impossible nut to crack.

Ellie was asking me about the Philippines when the food arrived. As usual, the meal was delicious; my Red Curry with Roasted Duck was perfect. Thai hot, just the way I liked it. Ellie did not share my love of spicy food, but she had grown to appreciate several of the milder Thai dishes. She had a playful smirk on her face as she pushed her plate away.

"Penny for your thoughts, Ellie."

"Sure."

"What's with the smile, good day at work?"

"Just an average day at work. Actually, I was thinking how much this felt like a real date for a change, with you picking me up…in a car, you driving, the whole nine yards. You even went home and changed, no jacket and tie. And you look great in jeans, I might add. If I had not left my car at work, you could even walk me to my door and try to weasel your way in for a nightcap. You might even get lucky."

I said, "Well, until now the day has seemed relatively unfortuitous. Is unfortuitous a word? Maybe my luck is changing."

"I don't think it is a word, but I catch your drift. So why has your day been unfortuitous?"

All through dinner, I kept expecting her to bring up what happened at the hospital, yet she was looking at me like she was surprised that I had a bad day. She did the weather on the same evening news program as Nicole Cassano. I kept thinking that she must have been waiting for me to bring it up.

"You honestly don't know, do you?"

"Know what?"

"You didn't listen to Nicole's report?"

"No. I caught something about a man with a gun threatening a pediatrician, and that security had taken care of it. Why?"

"Well, apparently you are looking at the new security officer at Memphis Memorial Hospital."

"I'm not following. Wait a minute; are you saying you were involved in that somehow? Oh my god, tell me what happened."

Ellie listened closely, attentively, not interrupting once as I told her how I spotted the man and disarmed him. She remained expressionless as I recalled my visit to the police station and my visit with Dr. Lowe. Only while I was retelling the events involving Nicole did she show any emotion. I was not sure if I was interpreting her expression correctly, but she looked angry during that part of the story. After I had finished, Ellie continued to stare at me, saying nothing. It seemed like an eternity before she finally spoke.

"I'm sorry," she said. "Earlier, Nicole was making some small talk, wondering where you were from, where you lived, etc. I mentioned a loft apartment over a music store downtown. I had no idea she was trying to figure out how to find you. I'm more than a little miffed that she used me that way."

"She was just doing her job, but, yeah, I felt the same way when I found out she was using our relationship to try and get me to make a comment. That's as close as she is going to get with any kind of interview with me."

"My boyfriend, the hero. You must have been scared."

"No."

Ellie looked at me with pure bewilderment. Oh crap, I thought. I knew that look. Another civilian that could not understand my lack of fear. I knew I had better tread a little more lightly or she was going to start wondering what was wrong with me.

"Well, I mean I wasn't scared for my safety. I was focused only on the safety of all those kids and Dr. Witmer and her staff. You know, like a fireman going into a burning building. If he stops to think about it, then it's time to quit and find a different profession."

She was nodding, seemingly in agreement. Maybe I had pulled it off. Besides, it was true. I was not afraid for myself. It never entered my mind, especially after seeing the cheap handgun and Harty's mistakes. If that had been a Navy SEAL with a SIG or a Beretta, then I would have been afraid.

"You are a strange man, L.T. Can I ask you a question?"

Something about her tone made me uneasy. My inner voice agreed. "Okay…shoot."

"What did you do in the Navy?"

"What did I do in the Navy? That's your question?"

"Yes, what did you do in the Navy?"

"I don't understand the question."

"I know you understand the question. Maybe you don't understand why I am asking the question, but you do understand the question. So please, again, what did you do in the Navy?"

"I was attached to Admiral Buie, who was a military attaché in Southeast Asia. I was—"

"Stationed in the Philippines at Subic Bay. You traveled a lot being an aid to a military attaché. Yada, yada. You have already given me that same line several times."

"Right, I've told you what I did. A bunch of classified boring stuff, although I admit the travel was nice. And I love Thai food." She smiled at that, but it was a weak smile. "Why the sudden interest again?"

She was quiet for several seconds before answering. "How has the last year been for you?"

I said, "You mean since I met you?"

"Yes."

"It's been great. You're the best girlfriend a guy could ask for. Better than I deserve."

"I feel the same way. You are the best boyfriend I've ever had."

"Ok." My response was hesitant. I was confused over her change in direction in the conversation.

"L.T., what's my job, my profession?"

"Best darn meteorologist in Memphis."

"There it is," she said.

"There what is? I have no idea what you are talking about."

"L.T., I think I am falling in love with you. There are times, like now, when that scares me, but I can't help it. You treat me like no other man has ever treated me before. I know most people think I am pretty, God knows I have been told it enough times, so maybe it's true. However, you are the only man I have ever dated that didn't treat me like some kind of trophy girlfriend. You respect me. For example, not once have I ever heard you call me a weather girl; you always say meteorologist. And I have never felt safer with anyone than when I'm with you. Period."

I interrupted, "Okay, I am confused."

"I know, but bear with me." I nodded my compliance. She resumed. "I have always felt there was a slight dangerous side to you. I mean, look at how you are built, the muscles and everything. Then there is the punching bag, the martial arts, the sparring at that gym you like. And you walk around with the most confident swagger I have ever seen. Let's face it; everyone sees it about you. Before I dated you, men would stare at me when I went out, even if I was on a date with someone else. But when we go out, when a man spots me with you, they look away lest you catch them looking. I imagine if I was a guy, I might find you a little unsettling. Like, I said, I have never felt safer with anyone than when I'm with you."

"So you've found out you have a thing for bad boys and you never saw yourself as the type of girl that falls for bad boys. Hooray for me, this night just keeps getting better."

Her frown and piercing glare said it all; she was not amused by my attempt at humor. She did not even comment on my attempt. "But now I suspect your dangerous side is not so *slight*, if you catch my drift. It seems unlikely that anyone with a desk job in the military who later becomes a medical doctor could describe such a potentially traumatic experience so, what's the word I am looking for here, so flatly. You act like today was just a normal day. I know you work in an emergency room. I know you have seen people die. But you hit a man in the head today, who might die, and you act like, well, you act like that's normal. I don't get it. You have had one of the most abnormal days I have ever heard of!"

I did not want to have this conversation right then. I did not feel up to it. I would rather a mugger attack me in the parking lot. I was not scared of a mugger. This was serious. It would require opening myself up, and I didn't want to do that. I was happy with the protective cocoon I had built around myself. It had been working for years. I could not escape her scrutinizing gaze, and I knew that if I kept silent any longer, the silence could have disastrous consequences. "Ellie, I am sorry I did not call you." She looked unfazed by my apology. "I described the confrontation with Mr. Harty that way because it is the way I have been taught to describe an incident like that."

"In the Navy?"

"No."

"Then you lost me somewhere. Who would teach you to talk like that?"

Ellie was leaning forward in the booth expecting an answer.

"I can't plead the fifth?"

"No."

"Alright, but let me start by saying I would rather avoid this conversation."

Ellie said, "Look, sailor boy, you can't weasel out of a conversation just because it is uncomfortable."

Damn it, Tom Harty. Of all the hospitals, in all the towns, in all the world, you had to walk into mine.

With a resigned sigh, I began my story. "It's my mother's fault. My whole life I have been big and strong. And fast. A freaky genetic cocktail of speed and strength."

"I get it; you're big, and you're fast. What's that have to do with our conversation."

"Well, you see, I abhor bullies, all types of bullies. I'm not sure when my intolerance for them began, only that I have despised them for as long as I can remember."

Ellie said, "That's not unusual, most people don't like bullies."

"Yeah, but most people aren't the toughest guy in their whole school. I was. Which meant I could actually do something about it, and I did, pretty much each and every time. My mother made sure of it. Her and that damn quote. Heard it my whole life."

"What quote."

"You know, the Edmund Burke quote. 'The only thing necessary for the triumph of evil is that good men do nothing.'"

"It's a great quote," replied Ellie.

"Try living it. It frigging sucks. It makes you hit guys in the head in a hospital putting them in a coma. You know there's going to be a backlash from all that. Besides, it's all a lie."

"What's a lie?"

"The stupid quote. Edmund Burke never even said it. The most popular quote in modern times, and the man they attribute it to never actually said it. Trust me, I know. I researched the crap out of that quote! That quote has haunted me in my sleep. All because of my mother!"

Ellie was looking around the restaurant to see if anyone was staring in our direction, drawn by my increasing agitation and volume. I looked around also. One couple was looking warily at us. I decided to temper my response.

"I know she grew up in Nazi-occupied Norway during World War II. She has told me of the atrocities of the war, atrocities she experienced first-hand. And I know that the war might have been avoided if the rest of the world had not sat idly by while Hitler rebuilt the German war machine. But I grew up in Springfield, Illinois. In the Sixties, too young to give Vietnam any real thought. It was quiet and peaceful, and normal. I like normal. I'm a big fan of normal."

Ellie was still staring at me. She knew this conversation had struck a nerve. The poor girl just did not know why. And I had no intention of clearing that up for her right then. For the time being, my relationship with my mother was off limits.

"Ellie, sorry. You asked a question that deserves an answer. Like I said, I hate bullies, and today was not my first rodeo. Once, in the Navy, I helped someone who was getting bullied."

Ellie interrupted, "So you learned that in the Navy then?"

"No. That ended well, in fact, I got a commendation. It was the military. You are supposed to bonk guys on the head when they cause trouble. It's in your contract."

"So not the Navy then. Keep going; I'm all ears."

"Once at LeClair's, I had to help his bouncers with a problem. I broke one guy's arm, and another one might walk funny for the rest of his life, but I saved one of the bouncers, so that also ended well and LeClair and I have been friendly ever since."

"You never told me about that. Why not?"

"It was before we were dating, and I never saw a reason to work it into a conversation. Hey, Ellie, did I ever tell you about the time I put these two guys in the hospital. Not exactly typical date conversation."

"I see your point. I'm getting the feeling there's more to the story, though. Am I right?"

"You're really not going to let this go?" She shook her head no. "There was this one time, the first time, when I was still a teenager. I might have saved a woman's life, like today. Unfortunately, I hurt the guy then as well, and the whole thing caused a lot of trouble for my family."

"Oh."

One word, but she said it in such a manner that I realized a condensed version of the story was not going to satisfy her. I hated rehashing the past and particularly hated telling this story; however, I was not going to talk to her about what else happened in the Navy, so I guess I had little choice.

"I was sixteen the first time. I was at a place in Springfield, Illinois, where I grew up, a place that was part bowling alley, part roller rink, part arcade with pool tables, even a small bar for the adults. I guess it was supposed to be a one-stop shopping approach to family entertainment. I went out to my car to get something when I heard a man yelling at a woman, calling her some vile words and threatening her. Getting closer, I heard him hit her, not a slap, but a thud, the type of hollow, meaty thud coming from a fist on another person's head. I ran towards the noise and saw the woman just standing there, staggering, when he hit her again. She fell to the ground, conscious, but obviously out of commission. Right after she fell, he spotted me. He was a big guy, about my size, and even in the dark, I could tell he had been drinking. He told me to get lost, but I didn't budge. There was no way I was going to leave him alone with the woman after what I just witnessed. So I yelled back at him, calling him names, trying to get him mad at me and get his focus off the woman, especially since it seemed he wasn't finished hurting her yet."

Ellie unfolded her arms and reclined back in her booth with her mouth slightly agape in a subdued expression of awe. "You were sixteen? Was he your size now, or your size then?"

"This happened in December of '73, so, yes, I was sixteen. Well, it worked; I got the man angrier with me at that moment than at her. Although I was a couple of inches taller than him, he was a little thicker than me, plus he could tell I was a teenager I'm sure, so he wasn't afraid of me. Everything would have worked just fine, just the way I planned if not for one thing. As he was walking over to deal with me, he paused and kicked the woman in the stomach." Even after all those years, I could feel my nostrils flaring as I told this part of the story. "It seemed to please him, so he reared back to kick her again, this time it looked like he was aiming for her head. Luckily for the woman, he was drunk and off-balance, so when he stood on one leg, he staggered backward to regain his footing. That's when I hit the guy, tackled him is more like it."

She was staring at me again, wide-eyed, mouth agape again. "Oh my god, you tackled him? Weren't you scared?"

"Not really. You've heard me mention that I wrestled in high school. Well, I was good. I won the state championship my freshman and sophomore years. Although he was in his late thirties and probably weighed about two-fifty, I wrestled him to the ground and got him to submit. I told him I was going to take him inside and call the cops; however, when I let him up he changed his mind and pulled out a knife."

Ellie said, "Your story just keeps getting worse."

"It's not as bad as it sounds. It was a pocket knife, one a farmer might use, not a switchblade or a big hunting knife. He couldn't get the blade out since he was drunk and his fingers were cold; however, there was no way I wanted to fight a big drunk guy with a knife, so I had no choice but to take him down again. I was yelling the whole time hoping someone would come over and help, but it was cold, and the parking lot was empty. He kept screaming at me telling me he was going to kill me when he got loose, so I maneuvered behind him and put him in a choke hold. I was planning on holding him like that while I dragged him to the front door, but he became unconscious, which was fine with me. I ran into the building real quick and screamed for help and ran back out to see how the lady was doing."

"Was she alright?"

"She was bruised and had a concussion, but, luckily, nothing was broken. Her name was Farah Shriver; it is Farah Schultz now; she remarried. She has two kids and a great husband. I know this because she sends me a Christmas card every year. The guy I beat up was Gary Shriver, an alcoholic jerk. I cannot remember all the charges the police filed against him; however, he had an uncle that was a lawyer who persuaded the D.A. in Springfield to consider charges against me as well. It made my family extremely nervous. I did the right thing. I did what my mother expected of me, but it still cost my parents quite a bit of money hiring an attorney, which, thankfully, later they didn't need. There was even talk of a civil suit, but that never materialized."

Ellie stared a little longer before softly speaking. "You did do the right thing, L.T."

"Just like this time."

"So you choked a guy until he passed out. I don't understand why the D.A. investigated you, especially since you were sixteen."

"Because I almost killed the guy. When I choked him, I crushed his hyoid bone. The sharp ends lacerated his larynx. When the ambulance got there, he was barely breathing, and they had to do a tracheotomy on him to allow him to breathe. He probably would have died if the EMTs had not arrived when they did."

Ellie said, "But it wouldn't have been your fault. You were only sixteen, and he was a big man."

"Everybody involved seemed to agree with you. Even the law was on my side. Plus what jury would convict a sixteen-year-old who defended a woman against a drunken psychopath with a knife. My lawyer's words not mine. He is the one that trained me to tell that story with little emotion. I was sixteen and naïve and very passionate about what I had done. Hell, who are we kidding; I was glad I had kicked his ass. Talking about it makes me want to go and do it again for old times' sake. Well, my attorney didn't want me to appear overzealous in 'attacking' the guy. And he was right; I needed to be matter-of-fact, even morose if I could. I could not handle faking being morose since I was glad I stopped him; however, I could be 'flat' as you called it."

"Holy cow, that is one heck of a story. L.T., I can tell you don't like talking about your past, or your family; I'm not sure why. I guess you will tell me when the time is right, like today. Regardless, I'm glad you told me this story; it partially explains why you were so unemotional when you described what happened earlier today. But why did you seem so reluctant to tell me?"

"Honestly?"

"Yes, honestly."

"Because I thought you might see the true me and not like what you saw."

Ellie said, "What is the true you that you don't want me to see?"

"Ellie, I know I did the right thing today, and I would do it again the same way."

"I can see that about you, L.T."

"Yes, but do you realize what that *really* says about me?"

Ellie fixed her gaze on me, studying me intently. However, she remained quiet. Soon her studying gaze transformed into a questioning look.

"I'm saying that I'm not a nice, kindly, benign sort of guy. I am saying I would do it again the same way even if I knew in advance that Tom Harty would end up in a coma. It's my way."

CHAPTER 5

Conversation was minimal as I drove Ellie back to her car. She did not appear mad, merely pensive, thus crushing any chance of the nightcap she had alluded to earlier. And who could blame her? She just learned that her boyfriend of the last year was not what he seemed. My *niceness* was an illusion.

A gnawing pit was growing in my stomach as I contemplated how she might ultimately react to the realization. It was an unfamiliar feeling. I found it unsettling. It was not until I pulled into the television station parking lot that I discovered the cause of the feeling. Fear.

No wonder I didn't recognize the feeling. The last time I had felt fear was ten years ago in a jungle in Cambodia, and I didn't have time to reflect then, so there had been no gnawing pit in my stomach.

So this is what nerves feel like. I don't like it.

Adding to the problem was the realization that eventually Ellie was going to ask more questions, which was probably going to cause the unsettling feeling to return. I found myself getting angry at Tom Harty for putting me in this situation; however, anger was an improvement. It was an emotion that I was completely familiar with, one that I knew how to manage, how to manipulate to my advantage.

The gnawing pit was subsiding.

The familiar calm of anger had returned by the time we stopped in the parking lot. I joyfully walked her to her car. Then the unexpected happened. Ellie gave me the most tender, most sentimental kiss I had ever received, said good night, and left. If I lived to be a thousand, I would never forget that kiss.

The gnawing pit was returning; however, this time I had no idea why.

Insomnia was an unwelcome visitor that night as I contemplated my discussion with Ellie. She asked a valid question about my time spent in the Navy, and I purposefully avoided it. I was not lying when I told her that most of my naval career was classified; however, I was avoiding her questions for personal reasons, not professional reasons, which felt like lying. I wondered how long, or how much, I could avoid telling her.

I knew some Vets who simply told people they did not want to talk about it, plain and simple. I was not sure that approach would be sufficient with Ellie. Besides, if we continued to date, if I wanted a future with her, then it seemed that I would need to tell her sooner or later. I shuddered at that prospect, especially when I contemplated where the conversation would ultimately lead. I was not sure I was ready for that.

Regardless, the story I told her instead was truthful. It even seemed more applicable to her question. Like today, I had encountered someone intent on harming someone else, and I had been forced to intervene. No way around it either time. I was there. It was my responsibility. To run away would have been wrong. And running away to get help would have been foolish. In both instances, timing was everything. I had to take care of it myself then and there.

There it was, plain and simple. At sixteen, I had almost killed someone. With my bare hands. It made me sound barbaric if you said it that way: I almost killed someone with my bare hands. And here I was 17 years later, and I had done it again.

However, I felt no remorse in either situation. People say that bad things sometimes happen to good people. Well, sometimes bad things happen to bad people as well.

Telling Ellie about the altercation with the man in the parking lot got me to thinking about my parents. They had been wonderful back when I was sixteen. My father kept telling me not to worry. He would take care of everything. My mother had been even more supportive, continuously telling me how proud she was of me. She had been my real rock, always assuring me that I had done the right thing.

I only heard my parents argue once while growing up, and it was during that time. Their voices floated into my room from their bedroom. Dad was worried. He loved me, no doubt. However, he wished I had never got involved. My father, my enormous, powerful father, a man who had 70 pounds on me, said he would have gone for help. It was safer that way he argued. The woman was a stranger he argued. My mother passionately voiced her disagreement with my father. She eventually yelled at my father, "What if the woman had not been a stranger? What if it had been your mom, or your sister?" and stormed out of the room. She slept on the couch that night.

At times like that, I missed her.

The next day, on less than three hours of sleep, I reported to work at 7:00 a.m. exactly as I told Dr. Lowe I would. Several doctors and nurses stopped by to give me support or tell me what a great thing I had done, but otherwise, it was a normal day. Doctors and nurses in a hospital witness death and injury more often than most, so the overall response was more muted than it would have been in a normal setting.

The next couple of days were business as usual. Dr. Lowe did not visit, and I received no memos advising me to report for meetings with hospital administrators or lawyers. No visit from Sgt. Walters either. Or Nicole Cassano. She did call the hospital a couple of times but was unable to get through to me. I thanked the hospital staff for that.

I didn't even see Ellie. A major thunderstorm came through on Wednesday evening. She was at the station nearly around the clock reporting on the weather and a tornado that touched down 30 miles outside of Memphis.

I did get a visit from Dr. Witmer. She was thankful and apologetic. She too had been visited by Dr. Lowe and presumed he was causing trouble for me. In the end, I was impressed with her understated awareness of her situation. I concluded that Dr. Witmer was made of some pretty sturdy stock.

Tom Harty remained unresponsive.

* * *

Friday morning the unmistakable sound of glass breaking emanated from my open bedroom window waking me from a peaceful slumber. The source of the sound was not obvious. It sounded like a large plate of glass. Perhaps store front glass. Wiping the sleep from my eyes, I walked over to the window. None of the store fronts on the other side of the street had any obvious broken glass. I took a quick look around the apartment. All my windows were intact. Daddyo's music had large store front windows with thousands of dollars worth of music equipment small enough to carry away. However, I heard nothing from downstairs, and there were not any individuals running from the store with loot in hand.

Donning some pants, I found myself hoping it was someone else's problem. It had been only three days since the problem at the hospital, and I did not want another source of irritation. I exited my front door and looked to my left. Daddyo's was locked up safe and sound, no broken glass to be found. The lawyer's office was a different story. Mr.

Deland's large plate glass window, the one with the name of his firm stenciled on it, was broken. Shards of glass were everywhere. A brick sat in the middle of the office floor.

Well, damn.

I did not want to be late for work again, although once again I had a good reason, so I quickly went back upstairs and made three calls. One to John Deland, who was in the shower. I left a message with his wife for him to hurry over. Another to Dan James, my favorite building contractor, telling him I needed my window fixed as soon as possible. The third call was to the police station; I wanted them to send over Sgt. Walters.

I was dressed for work by the time the sergeant arrived. He was alone. "I received an unexpected delivery this morning, Sergeant," I said pointing to the brick through the broken window. "Looks like it came via air mail."

"Nice to see you have a sense of humor about things, Dr. McCain, although that was a little lame."

"Yeah, but it was just sitting there, waiting to be said, and remembering your penchant for bad jokes, I didn't want you to beat me to it."

"Okay, you got me on that one. Is this your office?"

"No, an attorney rents it."

"Shouldn't he be calling it in then?

"I own the building."

"Okay, ER doc dabbling in real estate. You just out checking on your investment at six in the morning?"

"No, I live upstairs. I heard the glass break a little after 5:30 and came down to find this?"

"Alright, I'm caught up. You need a report for your insurance. Makes sense, but why ask for me personally? Do you think this is related to the situation at the hospital in any way?"

"I'm not sure, Sergeant. Although the attorney doesn't handle any criminal law, he's still an attorney. He's bound to have upset somebody. Remember what Shakespeare said, 'The first thing we do, let's kill all the lawyers.' Maybe it was aimed at him."

The lawyer joke got a chuckle from Sgt. Walters, but, let's face it; even bad lawyer jokes get a chuckle.

"Plus, I have an unlisted number, and I use a P.O Box. In fact, Dr. L.T. McCain doesn't have an official address. I own a corporation that owns the building, and I'm squatting upstairs while I decide how I might develop it."

"Meaning you should be extremely hard for the average person to find."

"Exactly."

Sgt. Walters said, "Yet, I'm hearing a 'but' at the end of that sentence."

"But three days ago Nicole Cassano did a live report standing almost right where you're standing. I was upstairs and could hear her mention my name in the report. I didn't see the report on the TV; however, I am assuming that someone could have recognized this building from the TV. Maybe Daddyo's sign was in the shot."

"Except why throw the brick through the attorney's window then? You said yourself that the average person wouldn't know this was your building."

"Good point. Unless the person throwing the brick is totally weak and can't throw it that high, which angered him so much he felt he had to break something, and he had a perfectly good brick, so he settled on the attorney's window instead. A lawyer would make a good consolation prize."

He was studying me hard. "I can't tell if you are serious or not."

"You don't like my theory. It sounded good to me. I guess you are leaning more towards this being aimed at the attorney then?"

Sgt. Walters smiled at my facetiousness. "Actually, I'm leaning more towards this being simple random vandalism, but let me play devil's advocate for a second. Maybe you were the target. Maybe you are not as hard to find as you think. It took a reporter only a few hours to find where you live."

"That's because she works with my girlfriend and Cassano tricked her into mentioning where I live."

"Okay, I'm leaning more towards it being random again. So, your girlfriend works at the station with Miss Cassano?"

"Yeah, I'm seeing Ellie Carmichael."

"Now I'm leaning towards you being the target again. You are dating Ellie Carmichael. That alone would garner you a few thousand men in the city that don't like you. I think envy is one of the seven deadly sins."

I said, "And you scoffed at my idea of a complete weakling that just couldn't throw a brick that high."

After some small talk about my relationship with Ellie, I turned the conversation to Tom Harty. I discovered that Walters was aware that Tom Harty was still in a coma, even after the surgery to relieve the pressure on his brain. The police had not left a guard, but he was currently handcuffed to his bed in case he did awaken. In addition to the charges related to the situation at the hospital, he was also facing domestic violence charges at home and child abuse allegations.

Sgt. Walters smiled at me, a knowing type of smile, and told me to go ahead and ask him what was on my mind. I feigned confusion at his response, but he did not believe me, telling me it was obvious that I was wondering if anyone had changed their mind on charging me.

"Well…are they?" I asked.

"No, Doc. Ferguson hasn't got you approved for that medal yet, but truth be told, you are seen as kind of a hero down at the station. You needn't worry."

"Thanks, Sgt. Walters. I don't worry about working officers; I had some experience with law enforcement while in the military. I worry more about politically influenced people, like an ambitious district attorney, or some stupid desk lieutenant."

"You're good. Even our lieutenants aren't that stupid. Trust me."

Our conversation was cut short as John Deland arrived. It took only a minute to explain the brick. He asked if we had any theories.

Sgt. Walters replied, "We were hoping you had some. Anyone come to mind?"

John's eyes darted up and to the right, "No," he replied.

I asked, "So no ideas, no disgruntled clients, or anyone whose butt you kicked in divorce court?"

His eyes darted right again, "No, I cannot think of anyone."

Sgt. Walters got some basic contact information before asking John to check if he saw anything missing. John looked relieved to no longer be talking to Sgt. Walters and walked into his office, his feet crunching on the broken glass. The police response went as I expected. No investigation. They would file a report. It's what I would have done for an isolated incident of vandalism.

John was still searching through his office when Sgt. Walters stepped through the broken window to seemingly ask him one last question. I thanked Sgt. Walters and started to head back upstairs to finish getting ready for work. My hand was on my front door when I heard a loud proclamation coming from inside John's office.

"Well, I'll be damned." Sgt. Walters was standing in the middle of the room surrounded by broken glass holding the brick. "I hate to admit it, Doc, but your theory on the weakling is sounding a little better. The thrower left you a note."

You WILL Pay.

Those three words were hand-written in large, bold letters on a piece of notebook paper that was attached to the brick Sgt. Walters was holding carefully by the corners. The author used a black marker pen in a simple blocky font.

The cryptic message removed any doubt that the brick was intentional, yet it did not definitively identify the intended recipient.

Either way, Sgt. Walters decided he was going to investigate a little further, taking the note and the brick downtown as evidence.

The rest of the day was uneventful. The only highlights were diagnosing a small boy with appendicitis, sewing up a man's hand, and packing a bloody nose that would not stop. After several attempts to stop the bleeding, I decided that the man needed to see an ear, nose, and throat doctor. After placing topical anesthesia in the nose, silver nitrate would be applied to the source of the bleeding with a Q-tip like applicator. The resulting chemical burn would trigger a scar tissue formation to help prevent future bleeding from that site. Altogether, a simple procedure.

The man looked a little worried when I volunteered to personally escort him to Dr. Trueblood's office, the ENT that shared a waiting room with Dr. Witmer. I assured him I was heading that way anyway.

It was my first return to that part of the hospital since the altercation with Tom Harty. The young, blonde receptionist was at the front desk helping someone. Nonetheless, she spotted me. She smiled awkwardly, hesitantly, and then waved. It was all the thanks I wanted; I enjoyed the affirmation that everything was normal again. I liked normal.

When I got home, I noticed the window had been repaired. It looked great. Dan left an invoice, and John left a note telling me to have a good time on my date with Ellie that night.

* * *

If Shakespeare was right and "brevity is the soul of wit," then the kiss that Ellie gave me on our last dinner date had spoken volumes. It was not the fleeting kiss of passionate infatuation; those are too easy to come by and are easily forgotten. Instead, the kiss was a powerful reminder that although neither of us had mentioned the L-word before, the feeling was there, palpable at times; it seemed to have become the elephant in the room.

To say I was a novice at expressing my feelings would have been an understatement of nearly epic proportions. Truthfully, I actually had no idea what the hell I was doing. It made sense that Ellie would want to hear me express my feelings; God knows she deserved it. The words even existed in my brain. I could see them. I just could not make my mouth form the words. Secretly, I wished, I hoped, I prayed, she would say them first.

To make up for my shortcomings in self-expression, I opted to be a man of action. Several days of planning went into the date with Ellie that night. Arrangements were made at LeClair's. Flowers were ordered. I even spent all my time off trying to finish the Mercedes so that I could pick her up with an automobile that actually had a top. In the end, I had the new engine installed, and the car was running like a fine-oiled machine, yet the damage to the interior could not be finished in time. The best I could do was put the top and doors on the Jeep.

After a quick workout, I showered and changed into some jeans with a fitted shirt and sports jacket; she liked me in jeans. I wanted the night to be special, the whole chivalry thing. Walking her out to the car, opening doors, pulling out her chair, the whole nine yards.

The weather was cooperating, and the setting sun was casting a warm glow all about the city of Memphis as I arrived at her apartment on Mud Island. When I moved to Memphis, most of Mud Island was a scrubby sandbar, but a local developer had a vision for the tiny peninsula, and the result was a truly fascinating community that emphasized a social front porch mentality over the privacy fence, back patio reality seen in most suburbs. Ellie had been quick to move into the developing area.

Her front door was open, so I let myself in through the screen door. Soon after, she entered the living room looking absolutely radiant in a white, sleeveless summer dress cut above the knee. She gave me a peck and asked me what I had planned for the evening.

I said, "Dinner, but first I want to walk along the river while this sun finishes setting."

Few words were exchanged as we walked arm in arm along the river enjoying the radiant colors of the setting sun. My timing was impeccable. We arrived at the Hernando de Soto Bridge just as the sky exploded into a virtual kaleidoscope of yellows, reds, violets and purples. The classic double arches of the bridge affectionately labeled the "New Bridge" cut a picturesque silhouette against nature's majestic show.

We stopped to take it all in, watching as the hues darkened until the slightest twinges of red-orange were visible on the highest, wispiest clouds. I had witnessed a few prettier sunsets over the ocean while stationed in the Philippines, but not many.

Ellie was beaming. "How did you plan that one, sailor boy?"

"I figured the world owed me a favor once in a while, although I didn't realize it was going to pay it forward like that. I only wish I knew how to take a decent picture; that was breathtaking."

After finishing our stroll along the river, we visited a popular local Italian restaurant. Over appetizers at the bar, she briefly described her day, and I told her about the broken window.

Ellie said, "The note was a little cryptic. What's up with that?"

"I don't know. Let's face it; the note could have been intended for either one of us. It went through his window, but after your colleague did that bit outside my building she kind of let people know where I live."

"I think you are wrong about that."

"How so?"

"I saw the replay of her piece outside your place. The cameraman was so zoomed in on her that very little of your building was visible. I definitely didn't see anything that would tell anybody where you live unless they recognized your front door."

"Those are custom doors, but it still seems like it would be dumb luck that someone recognized them. Maybe it was meant for John. I could have sworn he was lying about something when we questioned him."

"How do you know he was lying?"

"I may only have a few talents, but human lie detector is among them."

"Human lie detector, huh? Was that a good skill for an Admiral's aide involved in intelligence matters?"

Was the question rhetorical? I could not tell.

"You know how a bunch of intelligence guys can be?"

"Actually, no, I don't. How can they be?"

"Bunch of spooks and spies all gathered together. Telling which ones are lying comes in handy."

She smiled. Thank God.

"By the way, I hope Beale Street is okay with you tonight. LeClair tells me there is a really good blues band at his place tonight. Muddy White Boy. He says it might be the best cover band he's ever had in there. I hope you're interested."

"I'm game. Muddy White Boy, what's with the name?"

"I asked LeClair the same question; he just said 'You'll see.'"

After dinner, we drove over to LeClair's. As we walked up, we saw that the line outside LeClair's was crazy. The doorman was stopping people from going in, telling them that the place was full and they would have to wait until someone left to get in. Something about fire codes and capacity issues. Ellie murmured something about us being too late, but I simply smiled and continued walking. Her arm was interlocked with mine, so she continued as well. After directing her around the line, I nodded at the doorman, who moved to one side to let us in. A few people balked, but I didn't care. I did not even stop to pay the cover charge.

The place was packed. Every table was taken, the bar had people lined up three deep, and people were jammed on the dance floor, dancing to a revved up version of B.B. King's "Whole Lotta' Love." The guitarist was in the zone. I glanced at the band, six seasoned black musicians on guitar, drums, bass, keyboard, and horns. The lead singer was white and looked to be in his early twenties with long hair worn in a Seventies rock star style. He was wearing all black. Black boots, black jeans, and a black Foreigner tee shirt.

The Foreigner shirt was the giveaway. "I get it. Muddy White Boy, it's a play on words." Ellie smiled and nodded, but I don't think she got the reference. She was not the blues aficionado that I was.

"We're never going to find a table." Ellie strained to be heard over the music.

I kept walking, maneuvering us through the crowd to my destination, a small table near the front with a white tablecloth and a RESERVED sign along with a dozen red roses in the center. Pulling out her chair for her, I noticed her mouth was parted slightly, blissfully, with the tiniest of smiles, but her eyes were beaming. She looked impressed. I had hardly pushed in her chair for her when a waitress brought by a Long Island Iced Tea for her and water for me. I did not even have to order.

Ellie motioned towards the band. "They are really good."

"I disagree...they are spectacular. I can understand why LeClair was so excited to book them for five straight nights. He must be making a mint. We will be lucky if he comes by the table at all."

It was the band's third night at LeClair's, and I could tell that word had gotten around. Calling them a cover band was a disgrace; they made each song their own. Their version of "Hoochie Coochie Man" was the best I had heard since the original by Muddy Waters himself, and I equally liked their Blues interpretation of "Urgent" and "Juke Box Hero" by Foreigner. But my favorite was their performance of "Evil" by Howlin' Wolf. The band was impeccable, the singer had soul, and the crowd was eating it up.

During the intermission, Ellie asked, "What is all this?"

"All what?"

"You know what. The VIP treatment at the door, the reserved table, the flowers. You are pulling out all the stops tonight, L.T."

"You deserve a real date once in a while. And what good is it to be friends with the owner if you don't take advantage of the privileges. I only wish I had the Mercedes finished."

"If you picked me up looking the way you do in those jeans in a brand new red Mercedes convertible, I would not be able to control myself. As is, you have earned a *whole* lot of brownie points tonight, sailor."

I was glad she was pleased.

During the second set, the band only seemed to get better. Halfway through the set, the band changed tempo; they slowed it down and played a version of "Built for Comfort" by Howlin' Wolf followed by "Something to Talk About" by Bonnie Raitt that was perfect for slow dancing. There was not a luckier man in the place as she melded her body against mine. We were both breathing heavily as we left the dance floor.

LeClair never did come by the table, yet he spotted my appreciative nod after the second set, and he responded with a nod and a thumbs-up.

We left LeClair's the same way we arrived. Walking with our arms interlocked. Only this time, I was carrying a vase with a dozen roses. The bucket seats prevented too much intimacy on the ride back to her apartment, although she did place her hand on mine while I was shifting gears in the Jeep. After I had walked her to her front door, Ellie took the flowers from me and gently placed them on the ground. She leaned in and gave me a hungry, passionate kiss. I loved every minute of it, and there was more than one minute to the kiss. When she broke the kiss, she pushed me away, bent over and grabbed her flowers. "Thank you for making me feel like a lady all evening. Now go home before I change my mind about remaining so lady-like."

CHAPTER 6

By mid-week, the Mercedes I wanted to finish so badly was ready to be taken to an upholstery shop to repair the slashed bucket seats and convertible top. Just in time for me to fly to Miami for a medical seminar needed to help fulfill some continuing education requirements. Instead of flying back to Memphis, I stopped over in Huntsville, Alabama to visit my best friend, Virgil Johnson. We had been friends since junior high, roommates in college, and even joined the Navy together. He was the only bridge between my past and my present.

Big Clint Eastwood fans, we watched the movie *Unforgiven* on Friday night at the theater and then went to bed early. We were going hiking with friends the next morning and the three and a half hour drive to Memphis meant we needed to get an early start. We were about an hour into the trip when I finished telling him about my date with Ellie the previous weekend.

"Sounds like you guys had a good time."

"The band was amazing. Best darn cover band I ever saw."

"And you got a great kiss and were sent home. Alone."

"Yeah, what's your point, Virgil?"

"Oh, nothing. Just surprised you are having so much trouble closing with this girl."

"I'm not having trouble closing. I'm not trying to close. I really like this girl."

A quick glance revealed Virgil was smirking. "I know that. I just like giving you a hard time. Ellie is a keeper; that's for sure. But us men are always trying to close. You are just thinking long term, not short term. I get that. Mrs. Ellie McCain does have a nice ring to it."

"Whatever man."

Virgil changed the subject. Earlier in the week, we had talked about the incident with Tom Harty on the phone, but I had not finished telling him about my conversation with Dr. Lowe. Virgil was as surprised as I was concerning Dr. Lowe's response. He could not fathom me being chastised for possibly saving lives.

Virgil said, "Did you let him know you have experience in these types of situations?"

"I think nearly everyone in that hospital that knows me is aware that I do martial arts, and Dr. Lowe knows I was in the military."

"Maybe you should have explained yourself better. Told him you used to arrest people while in the Navy."

"You might be right, but I was too irritated to talk to him any longer, and I don't think it would have mattered anyway."

"Why not?"

"I think the real problem is that he thinks I'm building my own medical clinic."

Virgil said, "Let me guess. He found out about the office building you are remodeling and thinks it is for a medical clinic."

"Give that man a star; that's exactly what he thinks. And now he is mad at himself since he realizes the hospital doesn't have a non-compete agreement with me."

"I guess you didn't bother telling him that you are merely remodeling the building as an investment?"

"No. He thinks he is so smart, like he figured something out, so I will just let him revel in his own cleverness for a while. I don't like the man, enough said."

"You are a hard man sometimes, L.T. You could easily clear this up by just telling him your intentions with the building."

"Virgil, I love you, man. You are so practical and honest and a truly decent human being, but you are not a strategist when it comes to human nature. If I clear up the confusion on the building for him, then he will only look for something else to use against me. For some reason, this is personal for him. I don't know why. But if I let him think he already has something over me, then when he finally makes his play against me, it will be very easy to trump him. Strategy, my boy, strategy. Besides, this is more fun."

"And maybe you are not as smart as you think you are. Maybe the only reason this is personal is because of the confusion with the building. Maybe you are allowing your animosity towards him cloud your judgment. Why don't you clear it up for him and see if things get better? Not everything in life is tactical, L.T. Not everyone has a hidden agenda, even if they are an asshole."

I told Virgil I would give his suggestions some thought. He shook his head at me; he seemed to doubt that I would try to clear up the problem with Dr. Lowe. He was probably right about that.

"So how is Harty?" asked Virgil.

"The same. At least he was the last time I checked on him."

"When did you check last?"

"Sunday. So six days ago."

"You don't seem too concerned."

"You know me, Virgil. I can't change the past. I don't deliberate the past. I made a decision, and it was the right decision in my opinion."

"Do you ever listen to the words that come out of your mouth sometimes? You don't deliberate the past. That's bull. Your past is why you are 33 and in your first serious relationship with a woman and I'm still your only friend. You've allowed your past to dictate your future for too long now. What happened with your parents is done. You're right; you can't change the past, but it sure has changed you."

"It's made me cautious is all. Besides, I went to med school and have a great job, and things are looking up for me."

"You copped out, L.T. You should be a Pro Bowl tight-end in the NFL right now, a future Hall of Famer. Or you should have won an Olympic gold medal in wrestling and started coaching at some Big 10 school inspiring young men to follow in your footsteps. You might have been the next Dan Gable. Or if you had stayed in the Navy, you would have been a captain by now with a long list of medals and accommodations; you were on the fast track, my friend."

"No, I should be running my dad's business right now."

"I'm sorry, L.T. I'm sorry that didn't work out for you. It would have been great, although your dad would have wanted you to achieve greatness on your own first before taking over the family business."

"Maybe so, but what's wrong with being a doctor? I help people."

Virgil said, "Nothing, nothing at all. It's an admirable profession. You worked hard at it, and that hard work has paid off. And I don't mean this like the profession is beneath you somehow, but it still feels like you found the best plan B you could find and jumped on it. In your desire to be normal, you have forgotten that your mom was right; you were never meant to be normal."

"Leave my mother out of this!"

"No. She was right about you. You were meant to be exceptional, or inspirational, a leader. You are not a live-in-the-shadows kind of guy, and the sooner you accept that, the sooner you will be happy, truly happy. Stop wallowing in normalcy, L.T., because that is beneath you."

"You're a dick, Virgil." But I was not really angry with Virgil. I couldn't be. He was my best friend. He knew me better than I knew myself sometimes.

Virgil replied, "Sure I am. Wussy."

We were both smiling; knowing smiles that only best friends can still have when one of them has just called the other one out on something. And right then I was sure that I wanted to punch him in the nose and say thank you all at the same time.

We pulled up to my apartment with 20 minutes to spare, long enough to grab the necessities for an easy day-hike. We had just finished packing when the rest of the group started to arrive. Ellie arrived first, followed by her friend and co-worker, Lisa. Paul Deland arrived last. He had brought two friends, Kate and Steve. Introductions were quickly made and we decided we would need two vehicles. Virgil volunteered to follow Paul in his car.

Virgil and I were in the front of his brand new Maxima while Lisa and Ellie were in the back. Virgil was playing a Van Morrison CD. He didn't share my love of the Blues, but he still had great taste in music. After a few songs, I turned in the seat so I could see everyone and asked if anyone had been to Holly Springs before. I got a unanimous "no." I did not know what to expect during our hike. More than once, I had driven between Huntsville and Memphis on Highway 72, which goes through Holly Springs National Forest, and I did not find that part of the trip particularly scenic.

Ellie said, "Why are we going there then?"

I replied, "Paul's sister is a photographer and was supposed to be on this trip. She was there when Paul proposed the idea. She said it was pretty and was up for getting a few more photos of the area."

Ellie asked, "Paul's dad is John Deland, the attorney that rents from you, right?"

I nodded.

"And you dated his sister Beth, right?"

"We went on one dinner date, nothing more."

"Except you bought a lot of pictures from her and hung them in your apartment."

I was pretty sure Ellie was teasing me, yet I could not be sure. She usually could not keep a straight face this long when she was joking around.

"Well, Beth's business was much newer then, and she didn't have a lot of money, so how else was she going to pay for the sex."

Ellie said, "Damn it, L.T., would it kill you to pretend that I am successfully teasing you sometimes. You always have to one-up me." Lisa and Virgil were both laughing.

I said, "I'm sorry, sweetie. I'll try harder next time. I do wish Beth was coming, though."

Lisa said, "Why?"

"Because I don't know Paul that well. I've eaten dinner at their parents' house several times, which is where I first met him. Paul doesn't seem like a bad guy, but we've just never hit it off."

I had always thought Paul was a little too charming, a little too spoiled. Paul was 28, just one year younger than Ellie, yet they seemed worlds apart in levels of maturity. Ellie had her master's degree in atmospheric science and had worked for the National Weather Service before starting as a broadcast meteorologist. Management at the television station had approached her after seeing her speak at a NWS seminar. They were so impressed they offered her the chief meteorologist position that had just been vacated. In contrast, Paul had dropped out of college after two years, bounced from job to job, and seemed stuck in a state of arrested adolescence.

Lisa said, "Not to change the subject, but I'm curious. How do you two know each other? Ellie tells me you have been friends since junior high."

Virgil replied, "I got this one. Picture a short, skinny black kid in a predominately white private school in Springfield, Illinois. It was my first time since second grade in a school in the U.S."

"Were you home schooled?"

"No, I'm a military brat. My dad was in the Marines, and we were stationed overseas a lot. Like, I said, a short, skinny black kid on his second day of school, and during lunch, I was sitting with some kid whose name I don't even remember when suddenly this huge white kid invites us to sit at his table. It seemed suspicious, but we went and sat with the jocks. None of them had much to say, but the big guy, who seemed kind of like their leader, starts asking me a bunch of questions about where I was from and such. Next thing you know, we are friends, just like that. I didn't find out until much later that L.T. had invited us over because someone in his group had made a disparaging remark that ticked him off."

Lisa said, "No shit, you two meet and become best friends because L.T. was trying to make a point with his friends? Amazing. So, you have always been a maverick? That is why you hit Tom Harty isn't it?"

I replied, "Lisa, are you asking as a friend, or are you asking as the producer of the six o'clock evening news?"

"Would your answer be any different? Think about it big guy, would it really?" She was meeting my gaze with a curious intensity, head cocked ever so slightly to one side, an almost imperceptible smirk on her face, but also in her eyes. Ellie had told me she was a great news producer, with an amazing talent for making people feel important and at ease. I had to admit it was working with me as well.

I replied, "Probably not, but I didn't hit him because I'm a maverick, unless you have a different interpretation of maverick than me. I hit him because he needed to be stopped, and I knew how to stop him."

"Yep, the same reason you invited Virgil to sit at your table. You knew it needed to be stopped, and you knew how to stop it, so you just did it. On your own. You are a maverick, L.T., an individualist, a nonconformist." She let out a happy, warm laugh. "I love guys like you. You are the rebels with a cause; you just don't have a clue why."

Ellie and I had double-dated with Lisa and her fiancé, Todd, three or four times. I had always enjoyed her sense of humor. I had never seen this side of her before, but I liked it.

"Thanks, Lisa. Maybe I finally understand why I always feel in opposition to the masses," I replied with a friendly mocking tone. "I'm a maverick."

Lisa said, "Maverick McCain, it has a ring to it. By the way, what is your real name? It's not L.T."

I seldom give out my full name willingly, but I gave it to Lisa on her first inquiry. Man, that head tilt, half smirk thing she did was effective.

Lisa said, "That is an awesome name. It's better than Maverick McCain. It fits you, perfectly. Why don't you use it?"

"My mother named me. I didn't like it when I was growing up, so I had kids call me L.T. Later my mother and I had a major falling out and I saw no reason to ever use it. I am L.T. now."

Lisa said, "Well, L.T. McCain, you are one-in-a-million. You're always going to feel like the odd one out, but keep on being you. The world needs more of you. It needs less sheeple."

"Sheeple?"

"Sheep-people, people who follow the herd. Ellie, if you ever get tired of this one, let me know, I will take him off your hands."

Ellie smiled. "What about your fiancé, Todd?"

"What about Todd. You want to trade, Todd for L.T.? Besides, Todd is in Chattanooga for another three weeks, and you two haven't consummated your relationship yet, so maybe L.T. needs some good Southern girl to show him the ropes."

Ellie turned several shades of red. "Lisa, you're horrible sometimes."

I felt a little flushed as well. "Apparently you two talk about everything."

Lisa grinned mischievously at me. "And that, Ellie, is how you tease someone. I got both of you on that one."

Ellie saw me blankly staring at her. Hesitantly, she responded, "I told you she was good. She got more information out of you in less than an hour than I did in the first month. She does the same damn thing to me, and, yes, we do talk about everything. Maybe the next time I ask you what you did in the Navy, I will bring her along."

The next time she asks. Did that mean she did not buy my earlier pat answer? I smiled at her and shrugged it off. I used to be an intelligence officer in the U.S. Navy. It would take more than Lisa to get me to open up about all I did during my stint.

During the rest of the trip, Lisa found out more about Virgil's life story. Born in Germany, the son of a Marine with three younger siblings, he grew up in Europe and South Korea before moving to Springfield when he was thirteen. Lisa tried to turn the conversation towards his thoughts on civil rights and growing up black during the Sixties, but Virgil quickly informed her that he missed growing up in America during the Sixties. In fact, he informed her that growing up a military brat and then joining the service himself sort of insulated him from many of the civil rights issues prevalent in the States.

She also discovered that Virgil did two years of college at the University of Illinois in Champaign-Urbana before serving four years in the Navy. After the Navy, he moved to Huntsville and finished his Bachelor of Science in Civil Engineering before getting his master's as well. He was dating a nice Korean girl, Jewel Kim, a graduate student at the University of Alabama in Huntsville. Lisa was trying to figure out how serious the relationship was when we arrived at Holly Springs.

Despite my apprehension, Paul ended up being a terrific guide during the hike. He knew the hiking trails well, he picked some beautiful, picturesque places to visit within the National Forest, and he knew a lot of the history of the region. Paul seemed intent on making sure everyone had a great time, and it appeared he was successful.

The last part of the day had been agreed upon in advance: a late dinner in Emmettsville, a small town in Tennessee north of Holly Springs not too far from the Mississippi state line. It also had the distinction of being Ellie's hometown. Paul suggested Falco's Bar and Grill; he had been there before and stated he liked the food.

Falco's did not look like much from the outside, yet the inside had been remodeled to resemble the sports bars often seen in larger towns, just on a smaller scale, and a smaller budget. Lots of televisions, albeit the screens were smaller. Plenty of booths. Modern décor. The smaller size made Falco's feel quaint. Probably not exactly the feeling the owner intended.

The food selection had the typical sports bar offerings: wings, burgers, ribs, and plenty of beer. Those were also limited. Only three choices of wings: mild, mixed, or hot. And the beer selection was in the dozens instead of the hundreds, much to Virgil's dismay, a self-described beer connoisseur. Shortly after the waitress took our order, I thanked Paul for being a wonderful guide.

Paul said, "Thanks, L.T. You should have recognized a couple of today's spots from some of Beth's photographs. She told me that you have bought nearly a couple dozen pictures from her."

"Maybe they should have, but they didn't. Besides, everything I bought from her has had something to do with Memphis or the Mississippi River. I guess now I'll have to go buy some from Holly Springs."

Kate spoke up, "Paul, you mentioned your sister took pictures of the forest, but you didn't mention she was a professional photographer."

"I'm sorry, Kate. I thought I made that clear. She loves landscapes, but she does portrait photography to pay the bills. So if Steve here ever pops the question like he should, then I can help you with the photographer."

Steve swallowed a couple of times, trying to avoid blushing. During the hike, I wondered if Kate and Steve were together. They were quite comfortable with each other, but Paul flirted with Kate frequently during the day. I realized then that it was just playful teasing. Kate and Steve also seemed to be a physical mismatch; she was at least two inches taller than him, and she had an athletic build while he was rather thin. It must have been his confidence. Earlier he mentioned he was the top copier salesman where he worked, and I had been around enough pharmaceutical sales reps to know the confident, almost cocky ones were usually the most successful.

Paul was looking at me quizzically. He looked like he wanted to ask me something, but was having difficulty broaching the subject.

"Paul, if you have a question, go ahead and ask."

"How did you know I had a question?"

Ellie interjected. "He has a sixth sense when it comes to reading people. He does the same thing to me. It's freaky sometimes. I bet he already knows what you want to ask him, but he is just being nice and giving you a chance to ask him yourself."

Paul said, "Okay, I'm game. How about you, L.T?"

I nodded that I was in the game. I was pretty sure I knew the question that Paul wanted to ask. "You have just observed I am the only one not drinking any alcohol and you are puzzled by it. You want to ask me why."

"Dude, do you have ESP or something? How did you know what I was thinking?"

"It's a gift. I just know things."

Paul said, “Whatever dude.” He turned to Ellie and smiled, “Is he like this all the time?”

Ellie replied, “Which part, him being vague with his responses, or are you referring to his mental telepathy skills? Either way, yes, he is like this all the time.”

Paul said, “So what’s the answer? You’ve eaten over at my parent’s house, and I noticed you just drink water or tea, always. But you don’t seem to have a moral objection to it, so I was just wondering.”

“I just don’t. However, you are right; I do not morally object.”

Ellie said, “See what I mean, he likes being vague.”

Paul looked hard at me, studying me, and then smiled. “That’s cool. I think there’s more to the story, but it’s not a big deal. I was just wondering.”

The conversation turned back to small talk as the food arrived. Paul was telling us how much he was enjoying working at a Ford dealership in Memphis. He had not been there long, yet he had already made several sales and was looking forward to his next commission check. I could see him in sales. This was the most time I had ever spent with Paul at any one time, and it was obvious he had an infectious charm about him. Maybe I had misjudged him in the past.

As the meal came to an end, the discussion turned towards continuing the day down on Beale Street. Although it had been a long, hot, sweaty day hiking in the woods, the consensus was that hearing a good band would provide the proverbial “icing on the cake.”

Paul abruptly pushed himself away from the table. He had a sly grin plastered across his face. “Before we go, I have to do something. I will hate myself in the morning if I don’t talk to that pretty blonde sitting all alone over there.”

Steve slapped Paul on the back and said, “Go for it maestro, we’re still waiting on the check anyway. You shouldn’t need too much more time than that.”

Kate punched Steve in the arm telling him not to egg Paul on. I observed the woman in question. She was pretty. Blonde. Petite.

Athletic. The kind of woman that was used to getting hit on in bars. She also looked like she was waiting for someone. My guess was the "maestro" was going to get shot down.

After three years in college, seven if you count med school, and another three years in the Navy, I had watched a countless number of men approach women. The number of different techniques was staggering. I guessed less than half were successful. Physically, Paul was quite average, a lean 5'10", probably 170 pounds, yet he had charm and youthful good looks. His blond hair looked like it belonged in a shampoo commercial. I was interested to see his approach technique.

Paul walked straight towards the woman with a determined, yet tentative approach. He was waiting for something, an opening. Apparently, all he needed was for her to look up because once he established eye contact, Paul smiled and she smiled back. She had a pretty, welcoming smile. Paul changed his pace, closing the gap quickly. I could not hear what Paul said, though I could tell from the woman's facial expression she was intrigued, maybe even impressed. Paul leaned forward. He was saying something. It was do or die time. Would she lean towards Paul or away?

She leaned forward. I was impressed. Paul made it look easy.

Steve turned to Kate, "I told you he was the maestro."

"And I told you not to spur him on. I don't want all six of us sharing Virgil's Maxima unless you are volunteering to go back in the trunk."

Kate and Steve were still teasing each other when I observed a large man in his mid-thirties at the bar staring intently at Paul and the pretty blonde woman. My inner voice instantly warned me.

Paul and the woman were seated on bar stools sharing a tall table in the bar area. The conversation looked quite light-hearted, and the distance between them didn't imply any sort of intimacy. Although she had accepted Paul at her table, she did not look interested in him beyond simply enjoying his company.

The large man continued his icy stare, clenched his fists twice, and then began to slowly, methodically, approach the table.

Seriously, this cannot be happening again. The little pumps in my adrenal glands started pumping.

Glancing back at the table, I observed the lingering remnants of laughter on the woman's face; however, the smile quickly evaporated as she noticed the approaching man. She immediately gestured towards the man, and then towards Paul, making introductions. The stranger's wide eyes and flared nostrils were proof of his anger, yet Paul was still smiling. He did not look even the least bit worried. I found myself wondering how Paul could look so nonchalant. He appeared very adept at reading people today. He had to know he was in potential trouble.

Paul reached out his hand to greet the stranger, who slapped Paul's hand away and moved in closer. The stranger was easily 6'5" and 250 pounds. He was thick. He looked strong. Capable. If he became an adversary, I was sure he would be more trouble than Tom Harty had been. Time to act.

I stood up, purposefully knocking my chair over in the process. I made a spectacle out of it. Sort of kicked it backward into the wall behind me for extra effect. It worked. Most of the eyes in the bar turned in my direction, but I did not see those eyes. Mine focused on Paul's new friend. The big man turned his head toward the sound. Saw me looking at him. Glaring to be exact. My most intense scowl, eyes narrowed, lip almost twitching. The big stranger remained focused on me a moment longer before turning back towards Paul.

Paul kept on smiling and reached out his hand again before doing something quite unexpected; he leaned forward, making himself an easier target for the stranger. *How the hell does Paul not see the stranger as a potential adversary?*

Paul whispered something to the man. I could not hear what Paul said, but this time the stranger took Paul's hand and shook it. It appeared the large man was going to avoid becoming an adversary. Maybe I had underestimated Paul's charm.

One of the bartenders had been watching the entire episode unfold since it started, yet never attempted to intervene. He finally spoke up. "Eric, if there's going to be trouble, you take it outside, you hear."

Eric said, "Mason, there ain't going to be any trouble. I was just joshing around with Paul here. He was keeping Jackie company, and she said he was a perfect gentleman."

"Alright, but you know I don't allow no trouble in here, so don't forget what I said."

Eric turned from Mason and directed his attention towards Paul once again. He glanced for a second at me. I was still standing and still scowling. He patted Paul on the back and laughed. The laugh did not sound genuine, it was a little too loud, a little too forced. His body language was still tense. Either way, I was happy the situation was averted. I sat back down.

CHAPTER 7

Adrenaline. I had a love/hate relationship with the hormone. When needed in times of trouble, it never let me down, delivering the surge of energy necessary to overcome the situation at hand. Thankfully, I had not needed the powerful hormone this time. A common side effect of adrenaline was nausea. This was one of those times. And Paul was still standing at the table talking with Eric and Jackie, forcing me to keep a vigilant eye on the situation. This meant I could not entirely relax. Which meant I was still releasing adrenaline.

It appeared that Eric was giving Paul a chance for both of them to save face; however, he did not look like the patient type. I was beginning to doubt Paul's judgment. My worry was cut short when Paul suddenly returned to our table smiling. He looked amused by the whole thing. He was not frightened in the least.

Steve was grinning widely. "Well, you still got it, maestro. You schmoozed the girl; then you managed to weasel your way out of another jam. How do you do it? Do you ever get tired of being you?"

Kate was not as amused. She stared at Steve. "Damn it, Steve. I told you not to egg him on. If L.T. had not been here, things might have gone very poorly. We are kind of in the sticks, in case you haven't noticed. They might not appreciate a city slicker coming in here and hitting on their women. Sorry, Ellie, I know you grew up here."

"No problem, Kate. Besides, you are kind of right; they can be almost clannish around here at times."

Paul was grinning almost as wide as Steve. "Girls, just calm down. I had it all under control. I haven't been in a fight with a jealous boyfriend since the eighth grade. No one can resist my irresistible charm." He sat down like he hadn't a care in the world. "The darn guy was as big as a house, though, wasn't he? Oh, and L.T., what were you getting ready to do there?"

"Intervene, if necessary. I don't know what you said, but thanks for saving me the trouble. What did you say to him?"

"Nothing much. I just told him that I was waiting to meet the man that she turned me down for."

Ellie asked, "And that worked?"

"It is all in the delivery."

Virgil and Ellie spoke simultaneously, "That sounds like something L.T. would say."

I smiled. It was something I would say, and it was true. I had to admit it; Paul was smooth. I knew that Paul's father, John Deland, was disappointed with Paul for dropping out of college and being too loose with his lifestyle, too carefree. John compared him to Beth, who had her own successful business, and I realized I had allowed John's comments to taint my image of Paul; however, I was willing to admit I might have misjudged him. From what I had learned about him today, he was a good guy. He was funny, charming, witty, clever, resourceful, and had an ability to read people. Paul knew that I was withholding information on why I did not drink, yet he also could read me well enough to know he should not push the situation. And maybe he did not need my help with Eric, the jealous boyfriend. He was going to make one hell of a car salesman.

I said, "Well, Paul's a smart guy. Anyone can see that."

The group was discussing visiting Beale Street again when Paul looked at his watch and quickly stood up. He looked deep in thought, worried perhaps, yet he managed a smile as he excused himself from the table telling us he needed to make a call and he would be right back. As Paul walked off, I stole a glance at Eric and his girlfriend, Jackie. All was not well in paradise. Jackie's body language was becoming increasingly more animated. It was very clear she was not happy with Eric. In turn, he looked like he was taking his lumps without argument. I turned my attention back to the group just in time to hear Virgil asking about Bill Clinton, the presidential candidate who was the current governor of Arkansas. I could not understand how the conversation turned from Beale Street to politics, and I was looking for a chance to interrupt when Eric approached the table. He looked completely demoralized.

"Excuse me," he said, "I don't see that Paul guy. When he comes back will you tell him I'm sorry? I'm the jealous type, and I let it get the better of me tonight. No hard feelings, I hope."

I looked hard at Eric. He seemed sincere. I spoke for the entire group. "None here. We will tell him you stopped by."

"Thanks. Well, I gotta be going. G'night, y'all."

He abruptly turned and left. Alone. Jackie remained seated at the table, absently watching one of the televisions turned to ESPN. It was showing tennis highlights, but they could have announced World War III on the TV, and she probably would not have noticed. She appeared to have won the argument, yet she did not look happy about it.

The conversation turned back to Bill Clinton and the current presidential race. The discussion was lively but uninteresting to me.

Who wanted to talk about a bunch of dumb politicians when Beale Street was calling?

I noticed Jackie leaving the bar a few minutes after Eric. Her gaze was set low, and she looked dispirited. She avoided eye contact with anyone in the bar. Less than thirty seconds later, Paul was off the phone. He held up his car keys and mouthed the words "I will be right back" to me and walked out the front door.

The bill had been paid and we were waiting for Paul, who had been gone for nearly five minutes, to return. The others were still talking politics while I successfully avoided the conversation. Eventually, Kate wondered what was taking Paul so long. I explained what I had seen and the words he had mouthed. Steve volunteered to go out and see what was taking him so long.

As Steve headed for the door, Virgil resumed talking, this time asking me directly. "L.T., what do you think of this Bill Clinton guy?"

"You know I don't follow politics much, but in this case, since he's our neighboring governor, I do know more about him than I would normally. He seems like a smooth character. The pundits say he has a good chance of winning, which just seems so weird to me."

Virgil said, "Why is that weird?"

"Didn't Bush have over a 90 percent approval rating after Desert Storm? How do you lose an election after something like that?"

Lisa said, "Actually it was 89 percent, the highest ever recorded by Gallup, but he might lose because of Perot. I don't think Clinton would have a chance if Perot dropped out, but Perot seems in for the long haul."

I said, "There you go, ask the news producer. I am a political neophyte. Why do you ask? We never talk politics."

"Just curious. I read he dodged the draft to get out of Vietnam. Don't you think that will cost him too many votes?"

I replied, "Vietnam was a stupid war. It's been nearly twenty years since it ended and a lot of people still hate that war, and who can blame them. So, no, I do not think it will hurt him that much, except with people that aren't going to vote for him regardless."

Lisa asked, "But you're a veteran, doesn't that bother you?"

"No, and yes," I said. They were looking at me to explain my strange answer. "No, it doesn't completely bother me if he dodged the draft. Like I said, it was a stupid war, and if he thought so too, and didn't want to go, then so be it. Be a conscientious objector if you like. A lot of people saw it that way; it's why President Carter gave them all amnesty. But also, yes, because there is no way that a man that dodged the draft should ever be our Commander-in-Chief. You can't have it both ways. In my opinion, anyway."

Lisa said, "How could you call what he did being a conscientious objector?"

"Hey, why must someone have to be Amish, or Mennonite, or some other religious sect to conscientiously object? I can't tell you guys a lot of the stuff I did in the Navy other than I was in Military Intelligence. By default, that means I got inside access to some of the plans and strategies of Southeast Asia in the early Eighties. Let me just say that I was not always in agreement with how our government did things. I wanted to object to some of their decisions, but I took an oath, so my personal feelings had to take a back seat. Remember, Carter did not grant amnesty to deserters."

Lisa said, "If you agree with amnesty for draft dodgers, then I guess your power of forgiveness is better than mine. Can you elaborate at all on some of the plans you didn't like?"

"Not really, but look at what you do know from public history. We bombed the crap out of Cambodia during the Vietnam War. Then we sent troops into Cambodia, only to pull them back after public outrage, specifically after the Kent State Massacre. Many experts speculate our involvement helped cause the formation of the Khmer Rouge in Cambodia, leading to massive genocide. Whether it did or not, I cannot say. But later, when Vietnam invaded Cambodia, we propped up the Khmer Rouge because we hated the Vietnamese.

Think about that for a second. We backed a known evil, a regime responsible for the genocide of millions because we were ticked off that we didn't stop the spread of communism in Vietnam. I love our military, but the *politics* of the Vietnam War and the ten-plus years following that war have soured many Americans, honestly, myself included. My point, I don't think a lot of people care if he dodged the draft; if he even did."

Lisa smiled and called me a maverick again. Virgil said, "And you say you don't follow politics."

"I don't. I just lived it for a few years. All in all, I sometimes wish I had just stayed enlisted with you Virgil; ignorance really can be bliss sometimes."

Suddenly Steve came running into the bar. He was out of breath. He looked frantic.

"The son of a bitch is gone!"

* * *

Steve was frantic. His eyes looked like they were glued wide open and he was out of breath. He ran up to the table repeating his previous statement, verbatim. Kate was the first to respond, asking him what he meant by his statement.

"I mean he is gone. His car is gone. Didn't say goodbye. Didn't leave a note. Gone."

Kate said, "He can't just up and disappear. He had to go somewhere."

"Yeah, probably over at that blonde chick's place."

Kate said, "Come on, Steve. I know Paul is not always the most responsible guy in the world, but he wouldn't chase a girl and leave his friends in the lurch. He would more likely throw us the keys and tell us to take his car, and then hitch a ride with the girl in the morning. Maybe he just went to get some gas or something."

"At first, I thought the same thing, until I found this near where his car was parked." Steve was holding a wallet. "It's Paul's. If he was getting gas, he would have come back already."

Kate and Steve were on the verge of arguing about the wallet when Virgil interrupted. "You are overlooking a strong possibility. Maybe he already filled up with gas before he discovered his wallet is missing and now he is stuck at the gas station trying to explain to the attendant what happened, and it is not like he can just call us."

I had been quiet up until that point, contemplating the different options, wondering about the coincidences in front of me. One thing was for sure; I was not buying Steve's explanation. "Jackie. That was the woman's name…"

"Who gives a shit about her name," interrupted Steve.

"Let me finish, Steve. I was going to say that I was watching her before she left and it seemed pretty obvious to me that she was upset with her boyfriend and didn't seem to be in the mood for heating things up with Paul. Plus, Paul seems astute enough to know he had no chance with her. I feel really confident about that fact."

They were all looking at me. Lisa was nodding in agreement.

"Virgil, since you had the gas station idea, why don't you head down to the nearest gas station and look for Paul. Get the number of that pay phone over there so you can call us if you need to. Take Ellie with you since she grew up here and she'll know all the closest gas stations. Kate, I want you by the phone."

Steve asked, "What about me?"

"I need you to show me where you found that wallet."

Virgil left with Ellie and Lisa while Steve walked outside with me and showed me exactly where he found the wallet. I quickly scanned the area surrounding the missing car. Nothing appeared abnormal. I did find a smashed Marlboro cigarette near Paul's parking space that had been recently smoked a little past the half-way point. Hardly abnormal outside a bar. Apparently, the wallet was my only clue.

I asked to see the wallet. Steve handed it over after telling me he had already checked it and found nothing missing. I examined the wallet in the dim light and then moved under a street light to examine it closer. It contained the usual items. A driver's license, a VISA card, some of Paul's business cards from the auto dealership, and $22 in cash. The wallet and items inside were creased in the middle like someone had tried to fold the wallet in half, and there were strange imprints on the outside of the wallet. Things were getting interesting.

"Steve," I said, "I'm going to need John Deland's home phone number. Can you get it for me? I know his office number, but his home number is unlisted, and I don't remember it."

"I can get it. Why?"

"We need to call Paul's family, don't you think?"

"Why? He's a grown man who left to try and close the deal with that blonde chick. I want to kick his butt, figuratively, but I don't think his daddy needs to be called."

"I highly doubt he left to try and close any deal with her. Furthermore, the circumstances of the scene here provide reasonable suspicion that his disappearance needs further investigation. Therefore, his father needs to be called. Now go get that number!"

Steve's eyes widened when I ordered him to get the number. He stood still for a second. Maybe it should not have bothered me so much, but the way he said "chick" was like fingers down a chalkboard. I wanted John's home phone number, but I also wanted Steve to go away. While increasing the scrutiny of my stare, I motioned with my head towards Falco's, indicating my impatience and my desire for him to start moving. He turned and sulked back towards the bar.

I made a few more circles around Paul's parking space looking for anything out of the ordinary. Nothing. The only clue I had was the wallet. Nothing appeared to be missing, so burglary did not appear to be a motive. However, its presence spoke volumes, and that is what worried me.

* * *

Virgil and Ellie returned without Lisa while I was still standing in the parking lot. Virgil's body language was not encouraging. Ellie informed me that Lisa was at the local hospital looking to see if Paul was there. She knew it was a stretch, but thought maybe he had hurt himself somehow and had to leave real fast, driving himself over for treatment.

I said, "Good thinking, it will save me a trip there later either way. If he cut himself, he didn't do it in this parking lot. I checked the area around his car, and there is no blood. We need to go inside and call Paul's parents and then I need to visit the local police station and make a report."

Ellie said, "The police. Why the police?"

"I will explain inside the bar after I have called his parents."

Steve had John's phone number as I requested; however, he wanted to make the call, an option that I did not allow, although I was not looking forward to making the call. Paul's mother answered on the second ring. I did not want to worry his wife. Thankfully she handed the phone over without question. I only needed a couple of minutes to explain the situation to John.

John said, "Let me see if I understand this correctly. My son and his automobile went missing in Emmettsville, Tennessee less than an hour ago. His friend Steve thinks he ditched you guys for a girl, but you think Steve is wrong. You suspect there might even be foul play somehow, but you would rather elaborate when I get there. So, what do I tell Leota in the meantime?"

"I don't know. Maybe you can just go with Steve's theory, and leave my suspicion of foul play out for now. Besides, he could show up anytime with a reasonable explanation. Either way, I am sending the rest of the hiking group back to Memphis, so you need to get here because you are my ride home."

I gave John the name of the bar and its location, hung up, and then returned to the group. I had to tell them something; however, I was unsure if I should share my thoughts completely since I did not want to alarm or frighten anyone. The tension in the group was overt. Everyone was sitting forward in their chair, except Steve, who was pacing near the table. Kate tried to hold his hand and get him to sit, but he brushed her hand away.

Ellie immediately asked, "Steve says you were out there looking around and now you have reasonable suspicion of a problem simply based on Paul's wallet. What is going on here, L.T.?"

"Look, I am not a forensics expert or anything, although I do have some experience with crime scenes, and this looks like a crime scene to me."

Ellie said, "What do you mean you have experience with crime scenes? You are a medical doctor. What does that have to do with crime scenes?"

"I was a Navy cop, well sort of, I was..."

Ellie interrupted, "You said you were a military intelligence analyst, or aide, or something like that. What do you mean you were sort of a Navy cop? How are you sort of a cop?" Her brow was knitted up. She was not smiling.

I sighed, taking in a deep breath before starting. "Please be patient and understand that I have to be somewhat vague with some of my answers since much of my time in the Office of Naval Intelligence is classified. For the first couple of years or so of my commission, I was attached to the Naval Investigative Service, or NIS." Ellie had her arms crossed defensively in front of her. She was clenching her jaw. "During that time, I was undercover as an enlisted Navy Master-at-Arms, which is basically a Navy cop, similar to an Army MP, or Military Policeman. I went through the Master-at-Arms A school and everything before the Navy sent me to Subic Bay in the Philippines, where I performed as an actual Navy Master-at-Arms, even though I was technically undercover for NIS on a special mission that I cannot discuss. So, you see, I was a Navy cop. Sort of."

Kate said, "How does that give you experience with crime scenes?"

"Subic Bay was the largest overseas U.S. Navy installation in the world at that time. It was big. Real big. Tens of thousands of people, and young enlisted military men can be a rambunctious bunch. Master-at-Arms personnel are the police force in a place like that, so I had to respond to many situations involving out-of-control sailors and Marines."

Steve said quickly, "Get to the point."

"My problem is that I cannot come up with a reasonable explanation for the location of the wallet."

While explaining the location of the wallet relative to Paul's car, I watched their faces for their reactions. Surprisingly, Ellie was nodding affirmatively. Steve did stop pacing, only to replace it with an impatient bouncing.

I said, "I find it peculiar that the wallet was found on the passenger side of Paul's car; in fact, it appears to have been located under the front tire of the car parked next to his. There are even tire imprints on the outside of the wallet. That makes no sense to me. Why would he have been on the passenger side at all since he would have approached his car from the driver side?"

Steve answered in a huff, "How the hell would we know?" I ignored him.

Virgil was the first to come out and ask me directly. "L.T., it sounds like you suspect foul play here. What kind do you suspect?"

"I don't know, but here is the way I see it. First, what are the chances of the wallet falling out his pocket, bouncing across the parking lot, and landing up under the car next to him some ten feet away? It seems safe to say that chance is slim. So maybe he had the wallet in his hand for some unknown reason as he approached the car. Maybe he fumbled it, and then accidentally kicked it, and it ended up under the other car's tire, and he could not find it. Once again, unlikely. If he did that, then why not simply come in and ask for help finding it. Or maybe, just maybe, he was knocked down, or assaulted, or threatened, and the wallet went flying and landed over there."

Virgil said, "But who would do that and why?"

"Maybe a certain big guy with a temper who left a few minutes before Paul." I noticed most of the heads in the group were nodding in agreement. "Of course, that still does not answer the question as to where Paul is now. If he had been assaulted, he would have come back into the bar for help, but he didn't. He's gone, and his car is gone. Furthermore, I find no sign of a str—."

Steve interrupted, "Look here, L.T., I only met you today, and you seem like a reasonable fella, but even if you were a Navy cop, you are not a cop now, and you weren't really one then, now were you? I am telling you he left shortly after the blonde chick left and she made him a one-time offer that he could not refuse. A take-it-or-leave-it proposition. He is over there right now getting lucky, and when he comes up for air, he will call this place, or call us at home, and apologize for ditching us. I think you are full of shit, and your theories and suspicions are full of shit! I think we should all pile into Virgil's car and go home. That is what I think." He plopped down into his chair on the last sentence. Leaning back in the chair, he crossed his arms defensively while glaring at me.

"Steve, I realize you might be right, which is why I want all of you to ride back with Virgil and go home. I'm going to wait for Paul's father, which gives me a chance to wait here for Paul's return. Virgil has a cellular phone, so I can call him if I hear from Paul. If I don't hear from him, then I can go over to the police station with John and file a report. Plus, Virgil's car only seats five comfortably so all of you will have a more pleasant trip home if I stay here."

"He's my friend, not yours, so I will stay. Why do you want to stay?"

"I'm staying because I want to do a little more investigating. You can stay if you like, I won't stop you. Just stay out of my way while I'm asking around."

"But you are not a cop!"

"Steve, I've been patient with you and your attitude because your fear is what's driving your anger. You keep reiterating your idea that Paul is hooking up with Jackie, but you don't truthfully believe that, do you? Is your theory that he was checking his wallet for a condom and he got so excited the wallet went flying? I'm telling you nicely this time, lay off man. You are a copier salesman. For three years I was involved in Navy Intelligence. I even got to play cops and robbers for real, so who has the better resume? And don't bother answering that last question, it is rhetorical."

His defiant stare only lasted a few seconds before he yielded to my intense glare. At least he was smart enough to realize when to stop.

I felt bad for the condom comment and decided to try and make it up to Steve a little bit. "Look, Steve, I'm sure I could find Jackie with little trouble, so if you are right, then that would enable me to clear up things pretty quickly, don't you think? In case I can't find her, I think you should go back to your place and see if he calls."

Virgil helped me out by standing up and twirling his keys around his finger while motioning towards the door. I expected an argument from Steve, or maybe from Ellie, but I did not get one from either. I gave Ellie a key to my place and sent them all back to Memphis. Ellie gave me a kiss before leaving. She had a bemused look on her face. Thankfully, she did not look angry.

I asked, "Are we okay? You are not mad?"

"Oh, I am mad, but I'll get over it. L.T., I just want you to stop hiding things from me. You can keep all that classified stuff to yourself, but you need to tell me what you can. We will talk later, whether you like it or not. And good luck."

I wanted another look at the parking lot to look for any clues I might have missed on my first attempt. It felt good to be unencumbered by the others as I walked the whole parking lot. In the end, I found nothing suspicious.

Steve's voice popped into my head a couple of times while I was looking. I could hear him arguing that Paul had gone home with Jackie, yet I was convinced that Steve was wrong. Jackie had appeared intrigued by Paul's charm, nothing more. She had also looked very disappointed with her boyfriend, Eric. I told Steve I could find Jackie and clear up the whole mess; however, in my opinion, that seemed like a dead end.

Instead, I was examining coincidences. Eighteen months undercover in the Navy taught me to be wary of coincidences. The coincidence that was bothering me now was one of timing. It was too coincidental that Paul was missing shortly after a quarrel with a man that was as big as a house and had a temper and an inclination towards violent behavior to boot. The parking lot yielded no new information. Time to talk to the bartender; he, at least, knew Eric's first name.

CHAPTER 8

Falco's had two bartenders on duty. One was a very average looking man in his twenties. The other was a pasty white man in his mid-forties. There was a permanent scowl on his face like he smelled something awful but could not find the source. He was the one Eric called Mason. He seemed to be the proprietor. Mason was probably his first name, but I did not want to start with that kind of implied familiarity. "Are you Falco?"

He was stocking Bud Light into a cooler, not bothering to look up. "Nope," he replied.

"It's just that the name of the bar is Falco's, and it's obvious that you are the boss around here, so I surmised you were Falco."

Mason was still avoiding eye contact. "Falco's dead."

"I'm sorry to hear that."

"I'm not, that's how I got the bar." He finally looked up at me, obviously annoyed by the conversation. "Mister, what is it that you want?"

His attitude matched his scowl. I got the feeling that getting information from him was going to be like pulling teeth. No use trying to butter this guy up.

"No small talk, huh, I like that in a person. I'm guessing you saw me sitting in that group over there, and now maybe you are wondering why they all left and I stayed behind..."

"Yeah, I saw you. You're the one that knocked over my chair. And, no, I wasn't wondering whatcha still doing here."

This was going nowhere fast. He was throwing up all kinds of roadblocks in the conversation, and he had resumed stocking the beer cooler and avoiding eye contact again.

"Mr. Mason, I think I got off on a wrong foot somehow. I am merely trying to get a little information concerning some of your earlier customers."

"First name's Mason, Thompson is my family name. And you are referring to the two sitting at the table your friend caused the ruckus with, aren't ya? Mister, if you're going to ask me something, would you just hurry up and do it."

"I'm sorry for wasting your time, Mr. Thompson. Yes, I was referring to Eric and Jackie from earlier. I was hoping you could give me their last names, or tell me how I could find either one of them."

"You can knock off the 'mister' stuff with me; I don't know you from Adam. All I know is you ain't from around here, and you're a Yankee, probably a damn Yankee. So, even if I could give you their last names, or get a hold of them, I wouldn't. You're barking up the wrong tree here, mister."

I could not help mentally registering the differences in cultures and use of the word mister. When I called him Mr. Thompson, Mason felt it implied too much familiarity. When Mason used mister by itself, it was in a patronizing manner. Maybe I was too much a Yankee to understand. Either way, I was getting annoyed with him.

"Okay, Mason, have it your way. I will just ask some of your other patrons, I guess."

"Mister, I d—."

"Doctor. My name is Dr. McCain. My friends call me L.T. You can call me either; that is up to you. But if you call me mister in a condescending tone again, I am likely to stop being friendly."

Mason looked up from the beer cooler. He was crouched and acted like he was going to stand up, then thought better of it. "Whatever your name is, I don't want you harassing my customers. So I am asking you to leave. If you don't leave, I will call the police." Mason stood and walked over to a phone on the wall. He was avoiding direct eye contact again. "Your call, it's up to you."

"Mason, I'm not trying to cause trouble, truthfully I'm not. All I'm trying to do is find a missing friend. He is the same guy that was involved in the ruckus you mentioned."

"Not my problem."

"No, I guess it isn't. Look, he went out to his car shortly after Jackie and Eric left. One of his friends thinks he left with the girl. I think the big guy, Eric, might have something to tell me. You could help me; however, it looks like you don't want to. Fine, I accept that. But I need more information, or I'm not going."

Mason reached for the phone. He was looking at me, giving me one last chance.

I said, "Go ahead and call. If I can't find Paul, then I will have to file a missing person's report. You will be saving me a trip."

Mason moved his hand away from the phone. I got the impression that calling the police had been a bluff, and I had called him on it. He slowly looked up, making direct eye contact this time, eyes darting up and left as he spoke. "I only know his name is Eric. He comes in here once in a while. He is not a nice guy, so I do not think anyone left in here is likely to know him. I do not know the girl either. She don't come in here much, and when she does, it's always with Eric. Never alone or with other girls. Now please, leave my bar, doctor."

Finally an answer from Mason. Too bad he was lying. I wanted to punch this guy. Instead, I ignored him. The bar was uncomfortably quiet. Everyone was waiting to see what the big stranger was going to do next. Some of the customers were obviously on dates, and my presence was disrupting their good time. Part of me did not give a damn; Paul's well-being was more important than their dates. I did not want to cause any trouble, but I wanted to be able to give the police a better description than a big guy named Eric.

I scanned the bar. There were 20 people left in the bar. Six playing pool at the three pool tables, eight still eating, four sitting at the bar, Mason, and his other bartender. Most were trying very hard to avoid any type of eye contact. A few made a point of turning their backs on me. All except for two men playing pool. Those two were blatantly staring right at me. Mason was still staring at me as well, expecting me to leave. I continued to ignore him.

Stalemate. It was obvious no one was going to give me Eric's last name.

My inner voice was telling me to work the clues. Big guy, no, a huge guy named Eric in a small town. One that had a temper and appeared to have a propensity for violence. There could not be an abundance of men that fit that description. It should be enough for the police to go on. Maybe he already had a run-in with the police. Either way, Mason would not be able to lie to the police like he lied to me.

It made no sense to stay in the bar. I headed for the door. The two men playing pool had not stopped staring. They both looked to be in the mid-forties and had the look of guys who worked outside for a living, probably farmers. I could not be sure, but one of them seemed to be trying to draw my attention, albeit, inconspicuously. Neither man looked dangerous; in fact, the only word I could think of to describe them was *earnest*. I was almost out the front door when I stopped and turned in their direction; the temptation to talk to them was too great. Neither man moved as I approached closer, yet neither did they make their intentions obvious.

I was two feet from the man on the right when he said two words. "Eric Parker." He abruptly turned his back on me and resumed playing pool. The discussion was over. I had a name.

* * *

Eric Parker. The name meant nothing to me. But it meant something to the people in that bar. The man discreetly whispered it to me and then turned his back on me. Only his friend knew what he said to me, and if anyone asked he would be able to deny he had provided me with a name. The man wanted it that way. No doubt. Now, I just wondered who the hell was Eric Parker.

I left Falco's immediately after learning Eric's last name and found myself in the parking lot again. A few customers left, and a few more arrived. Falco's was not packed, but it was steady. It seemed to be a popular place.

I was pacing around the parking lot near the road waiting for John's arrival when a pickup slowed down as it was passing the entrance to Falco's parking lot. Two passengers were silhouetted inside the truck. They appeared to be staring at me. The truck traveled a couple of hundred yards before turning around to make another pass. This time the truck stopped completely. The faces were not visible, yet once again the occupants appeared to be looking my direction. I pretended not to notice the truck while walking aimlessly around the parking lot.

I could not make out the color of the truck in the dark. I could only tell it was two-toned, probably green, maybe blue. Even if it was not green, it was not a factory paint job. Nor was the truck equipped with a factory motor. Someone had dropped a performance cam in the big block motor. It was also equipped with a lift kit. I wished I could see the truck in the daylight; it was probably gorgeous. I also wished I could see the faces of the occupants of the vehicle. The questions I asked inside of Falco's had obviously irritated Mason, and now I had an audience outside the bar. I did not like coincidences.

The truck was still watching me when John pulled into the parking lot; however, it sped away quickly when John stopped in front of me. After he had stopped, John looked back at the truck as it left and then he looked at me again with a puzzled expression. As I climbed into his front seat, John said, "Was that truck bothering you?"

"No, just watching me."

"Why?"

"I don't know. They seemed to leave the second it was obvious you were here for me."

"What's going on here, L.T.?"

"I don't know, but I can tell you what I do know."

"Okay, let's hear it."

I explained the whole day to him, starting with Paul showing up at my place with Steve and Kate, and ending with the conversation I just had with Mason. He showed exceptional calm during my account.

John was rubbing his head with both hands, obviously concerned and exasperated simultaneously. "So you think the big guy, Eric, had something to do with this whole thing?"

"I don't know, John. All I know for sure is that Paul is missing. And I know he almost got into a fight with an enormous man that the people in that bar seemed frightened of."

John said, "Steve could be right, you know. They have been friends for nearly ten years now. I don't like to think of my son as a womanizer, but if Steve thinks he's at this Jackie's house, he might have a point."

"Sure, it's possible. It just doesn't seem probable to me. Trust me on this one; she was not interested."

"You're probably right."

"Either way, John, we aren't going to get anywhere here tonight. Mason is lying. He knows Eric Parker, but he isn't going to tell me anything because he's scared of Eric. He probably had trouble with him in the past; Eric has a heck of a temper. The rest of the people were hoping I wouldn't ask them anything, except for the two guys playing pool that gave me Eric's last name.

John said, "So what's next?"

"Let's go the police station and make a report."

A young couple entering Falco's gave us directions to the police station. They told us it was "downtown, near the fire station, y'all can't miss it." The couple had been right about the fire station; it was huge and nearly impossible to miss. It must have been the only fire station for the whole county. However, we almost missed the police station since the fire station blocked our view. Outwardly, the station looked like a city police station, only smaller.

John rang a bell near the front door, and we waited to be buzzed in. If I guessed right, there would be an officer inside acting as both the dispatcher and night front desk officer. I was right. The officer had a warm expression, very welcoming, in his early thirties. He looked physically soft like he was well-suited to a desk job.

"How can I help you, gentlemen?" His accent sounded more like it was more from the Carolinas than from Tennessee.

"We need to report a disappearance. My son, Paul, went missing a few hours ago from Falco's Bar and Grill."

"Y'all sit over here and tell me what's going on. Name's Officer Willis." The officer used a foot to kick one chair out, and without getting up, he reached over and grabbed another chair from the desk next to his.

Officer Willis looked me over and then asked, "And who might you be, sir?"

"Dr. McCain. I was with his son, Paul, all day up until the time he went missing."

"Then maybe we need to hear from you first, don't y'all think?"

I proceeded to tell Officer Willis the same story I had told John earlier, stopping before retelling the discussion with Mason.

"Alright, let me get this all straight. Paul Deland, your friend, and Mr. Deland's son, has been missing a couple of hours now, along with his car. And he dropped his wallet in the parking lot."

"I didn't say he dropped his wallet. I said we found it. There is a difference."

Officer Willis said, "You're right. You found his wallet. What do you need from us?"

John said, "Help finding him."

"Well, you know we have to wait 24 hours to file a missing person's report for a missing adult, especially one where there's no evidence of foul play."

I said, "Officer Willis, I don't mean to be rude, but I think you've been watching too much television; there is no waiting period on filing a missing person's report. We need you to file the report tonight, and we need you to track down Eric Parker and question him."

Officer Willis slowly looked from his notepad. His eyes were slitted. His easy-going demeanor was gone. With a degree of caution, he asked, "Why Eric Parker?"

"He's the man that had the altercation with Paul in the bar."

"You said Eric; you didn't say Eric Parker. How did you find that out?"

"I can't volunteer that information at this time."

"Why not?"

"Because I don't know who in the world is Eric Parker and I saw the look you gave me when I mentioned his name. Are you as scared of him as the bartender?"

"No, I'm not scared of anyone named Eric Parker. I was just wondering if you were sure about the name."

"I'm sure. It came from a reliable source. Like I said before, Paul left shortly after Eric, who could have been waiting for Paul. This Eric Parker guy had a heck of a temper. Either way, he might know something about Paul's disappearance, especially given the evidence of foul play at the scene."

John was staring at the exchange between Officer Willis and myself. His furrowed brow evident of his confusion.

Officer Willis said, "Look, I don't agree that a dropped wallet is evidence of foul pl—"

I said, "And I keep telling you that the wallet was not necessarily dropped. Why do you keep referring to it as dropped? And who is Eric Parker in this town?"

"Sir, I don't appreciate your tone."

"I don't appreciate the run-around I have been getting ever since I started trying to get information on a man that I feel might be responsible for Paul's disappearance."

I could feel my nostrils starting to flare while I glared at the officer. John obviously sensed my growing frustration because he put a hand on my shoulder and then said, "Officer Willis, what's your plan tonight for my son?"

"Mr. Deland, I'll file the report. I have his name, so give me a physical description, and the make, model and color of his car, his license plate if you have it. I'll radio the other officers on night duty to keep an eye out for him, but that's as far as I'll take it tonight. Y'all will have to come by here tomorrow morning and talk to the chief about Eric Parker or Jackie. I'll page the chief and tell him to come in around noon. Y'all can tell your suspicions to him then."

I excused myself from the desk while John provided the necessary information for the missing person's report. Officer Willis was polite, but he also seemed unimaginative and lazy. Arguing with him over my suspicion of foul play seemed futile. He also knew something about Eric Parker, more than he was letting on. At least he was going to file the missing person's report. I did all I could short of busting some heads at the bar to get more information, and there was no guarantee that would help regardless.

* * *

After leaving the police station, John insisted we drive the streets of Emmettsville. It was a small town, with a population around 14,000. One of those towns with a Main Street that led to a square built around the local county courthouse. Small local business surrounded the square. They were all closed. Some high school kids were seen cruising the square. There was nothing there.

John knew it was a long shot. He said he just could not go home without looking. I couldn't blame him, but his method of looking was aimless. I finally asked him to stop at two 24-hour gas stations in the area. No one had seen any sign of Paul or his car. I did ask about Eric Parker at one of the stations. The attendant replied, "Whatcha want with him fer anyway?" I told the man that he had left something at Falco's. He replied, "That's as good as any place to look fer him; I reckon he's kind of a regular there."

During that time, I had to repeat the events of the entire day several times to John. Unlike Officer Willis or Steve, John was able to understand my suspicions concerning the location of the wallet. He also felt the same about Eric Parker.

John remained surprisingly calm while driving around. If I had a son that was missing, I am not sure I would have handled it as well. Only when John dropped me off around two in the morning did his fear and concern become fully apparent; the dome light of his vehicle was bright enough to reveal his drawn, worried face and bloodshot eyes. I wished him my best and told him to get some sleep, although I doubted he would get much.

Wearily, I shuffled up to my apartment and headed straight for bed. My tired, droopy eyes appeared to be playing tricks on me as I entered my bedroom; Ellie was asleep in my bed wearing one of my dress shirts as a nightgown. It looked fabulous on her. Stripping down to my underclothes, I climbed into bed and snuggled next to her.

She leaned over and gave me a peck on the lips. 'Welcome home, sailor," she said before she turned her back towards me, allowing me to spoon in behind her. It was a fine way to end an otherwise lousy night. I set the alarm clock inside my head for eight o'clock and went to sleep.

CHAPTER 9

My internal alarm clock must have been upset by the presence of Ellie curled up next to me all night because it did not wake me up at eight o'clock. Instead, I awoke to the smell of breakfast. Eggs, ham, coffee, and biscuits, definitely biscuits. It was shortly after 8:45 in the morning.

Donning some pants, I plodded out of the bedroom. I did not have a kitchen, not in the traditional sense. The open floor plan meant I had more of a kitchen area: stove, refrigerator, sink, appliances, and a table along the side wall nearest my bedroom. Virgil and Ellie were sitting at my kitchen table. They had already eaten and were talking about Virgil's relationship with Jewel, his girlfriend, as I approached.

Ellie spotted me and said, "Good morning, sleepy head. Breakfast is on the table, let me heat it up and cook you some more eggs. You want six, right?"

I saw the hefty slice of ham and replied, "No, four would be fine. Thanks."

Ellie said, "I hope you don't mind, but we helped ourselves to your food. Virgil and I both thank you for keeping coffee in the house especially since we know you don't like it."

"Mi casa es su casa, I always say."

When she got up to cook my eggs, I noticed she was still wearing my dress shirt and what looked like a pair of my gym shorts. She looked wonderful. I could get used to mornings like this. In fact, I wanted mornings like this, the warm feeling associated with family. I had no living grandparents, no siblings. I did have an aunt and two cousins in Norway, but I had only met them a couple of times. Apparently, my mother was still trying to stay in touch with me. Too much water under the bridge there. Virgil was the closest thing I had to family. The brother I never had. He would always be there.

Ellie was a different matter. That relationship needed cultivating. We had never had a fight, not even an argument, which meant we had also never been tested. Smooth sailing does not adequately test the seaworthiness of a vessel. Then there was the fact that I had withheld information about my past from her, much like I did with everyone. I was pretty sure I was in love with her, but it did not seem to make it any easier to let her in, let her see the real me with the polished veneer pulled back. I kept thinking she might not like what she sees.

The conversation stayed light and trivial while I was eating my breakfast, but I had a feeling they were both waiting patiently to hear what happened after they left. Ellie waited until I put my dish in the sink. "So, spit it out. What happened?"

"Nothing. He didn't show up, obviously, or I would have already told you. I questioned the bar owner, a real jerk, but got nowhere. We filed a report at the police station and then John drove around for several hours looking for him. Nothing, nada, zip."

"So now what?"

"I go with John to talk to the Chief of Police around noon. Tell him my theory that the big guy might know something, or had something to do with it. Eric Parker was his name. I got it from some guys playing pool at Falco's."

Ellie cocked her head quizzically while her eyes slightly widened, "Eric...Parker?"

"Yeah, you know him."

"Not personally, which is why I didn't recognize him last night. He was six or seven years ahead of me in school, but the whole town knows him in one way or another. He's a local hero. He was a high school football hero who got a full ride to Auburn. My dad told me that he even made it to the NFL. I don't think he played long, but he made it."

"There is more isn't there? I can tell by your cute wrinkled forehead you are worried about something."

She continued, "My dad also told me he has a history of violence."

"I guessed as much."

"However, he never seems to get into too much trouble."

I asked, "Because of his small-town celebrity status?"

"Maybe, somewhat. More likely because of who his dad is?" She paused, the wrinkled brow returned. She was reluctant to continue.

"Who is his dad?" I asked.

Her chest heaved, then she sighed, seeming to resign herself to the fact that she needed to answer me. "Sam Parker, the Chief of Police in Emmettsville."

"Oh, boy. Now that is a horse of a different color, isn't it? But why were you reluctant to tell me?"

"Because if Chief Parker dismisses you and won't follow up on anything, then what are you planning on doing?"

"Ask around a little bit. Maybe go to the sheriff and tell him the problem. I won't let the chief just sit on it and do nothing."

"There is no sheriff. Basically, Chief Parker is the sheriff. It's an elected position, not an appointed one. He's the chief for the whole darn county. They have always called it the police department, instead of the sheriff's office. I don't know why."

"Ellie, thanks for telling me. It's better I find it out now instead of finding it out later. Now I know what I am up against beforehand."

"It seems my concerns are already coming true. You said 'what I am up against,' which means you already see yourself as involved somehow. That dangerous side we talked about is worse than I imagined."

"I'm just helping a friend with a report."

"Why am I not convinced?"

"I don't know; why are you not convinced?"

"Maybe because I saw something in you last night. A certain set to your jaw. A small change in your attitude, your body language. The way you glared at poor Steve. It was like Dr. McCain had been replaced by Lieutenant McCain, ex-Navy officer, and you seemed totally okay with that."

"Steve was a jerk. But since you seem a little worried, I'll tell you what I'm going to do. Today is Sunday, so Virgil has to go back to Huntsville. I'll ride over with him since it's not too much out of his way and meet John at the police station. I will give the Chief my side of the story, and then press him to follow up on my suspicions. If he doesn't, then I'll convince John to take the problem to the State Police. He's an attorney so he must know someone who can help. I will be L.T., boyfriend of the prettiest and sweetest woman I know. Besides, I cannot argue with anyone who looks that sexy in one of my shirts."

She did not look entirely convinced, but her brow was no longer wrinkled. "I will hold you to that, L.T."

* * *

A bleary-eyed John was waiting for us outside the Emmettsville Police Station. I had slept like a baby. He looked as if he had not slept a wink. While introducing Virgil, I spotted someone waving to us from the front door of the station. The man was average height, athletically lean, much like a distance runner. He looked about 60 years old with a full head of sandy brown hair that was slightly receding in the front. There was an intelligent gleam in his eyes, and he possessed a large friendly smile. The smile was something else; he appeared to have more teeth than any human I had ever seen, resulting in a megawatt smile on an otherwise ordinary looking man. Chief Parker did not look like I had expected.

He hollered, "Welcome gentleman. Come on in; I've been expecting y'all." We followed the man inside. "My office is right over there. I was expecting only two of you so let me grab an extra chair."

John said, "Thanks."

"I take it Paul did not show up last night, or else I would have probably just gotten a call."

Last night Officer Willis looked suited to desk work and acted like a man that was putting a lot of effort into conserving energy, but Chief Parker moved and bounced around like he had energy to spare. Virgil and I cast a glance at each other, measuring the surprise in the other one's face. His smile was surreal. I wondered why he even bothered turning on the light in his office; his teeth could light the room.

He started speaking again while he was still carrying in the extra chair. "I'm the Chief, but then you probably guessed that. And from Officer Willis' report, I garner you are Mr. Deland and Dr. McCain, but who might you be?"

"Virgil Johnson, L.T.'s friend. I was there last night as well, although I probably have little to offer that L.T. did not already report."

Chief Parker said, "Who is L.T.?"

"I am. Dr. L.T. McCain."

"You are the guy who saw everything last night, then. The one mentioned in Willis' report. What does the L.T. stand for?"

I told him.

He said, "That's an interesting name."

"Yeah, my mother is an interesting person."

"Now tell me, Doctor, do you have anything else to tell me that you didn't tell Officer Willis, something you might have remembered since then?"

"Nope, nothing new," I said. I noticed he called himself "The Chief" earlier. Was omitting his last name intentional, or habitual? "And what do you like to be called?"

"Chief is fine."

It was intentional. I was going to allow him to play his game a little longer and see what happens.

I said, "Well, Chief, for the purpose of clarity, would you like to tell us what Officer Willis put in his report?"

"I will do you one better than that. You can read it for yourself; it's pretty short. Let me know if we need to edit anything."

I was right about Willis; he was well-suited for a desk job. The report was typed, well-written, brief, to the point and mostly accurate. Mostly. There was one mistake, and I was sure it was intentional as well. I handed the report to Virgil hoping he would catch it and point it out.

Chief Parker said, "Before we continue, do y'all see any reason for me to get a statement from any of the other people mentioned in the report? And have you heard from any of them since last night to make sure Paul has not been in contact with them?"

I replied, "That's up to you, Chief. But I am dating Ellie Carmichael. I think you know her family; I am told."

The Chief said, "Why, yes I do. Wonderful family and she is a beautiful girl. Congratulations." He did not even flinch when he found out I knew Ellie and her family, leaving me wondering how long he planned on keeping up his charade.

"Thank you. As I was saying, I know she didn't hear from him. And Lisa didn't know Paul before yesterday, so I highly doubt he called her. Virgil is from Huntsville and crashed at my place, so I know he didn't hear anything either."

John said, "And I already called his friend Steve, who told me that neither he nor Kate heard from him."

Virgil had finished reading the report. He was squinting his eyes at me, looking perplexed and questioning at the same time. I gave him the slightest nod hoping he would pick up my cue, which he did.

Virgil said, "There is one problem with this report. Eric's last name was Parker, not Harker."

Thank you, Virgil. I did not want to be the one that pointed out the mistake. If Chief Parker could play his cards close to the chest, then so could I.

I took the report and faked surprise as I discovered the error. "Virgil is right; the last name is Parker. This report needs to be amended." The Chief's expression remained unfazed. "Do you know if anyone tried to contact Mr. Parker last night? Or Jackie for that matter?"

"Officer Willis must have heard you wrong. He told me he could not find any Eric Harker listed in any database, and he did not have Jackie's last name, so no one has questioned anyone so far. I'll have Officer Willis correct the report to reflect the proper name, and then I will personally talk to Eric Parker. I will even find the young woman and talk to her." His mega-watt smile was in full force after finishing his last sentence.

John said, "I appreciate that very much, Chief. Should I call your office for updates, or are you going to call me?"

"How about we call you. But before y'all go, can y'all tell me if Paul had any known enemies or people that might want to do him harm for any reason. And does he have any previous history of disappearing like this?"

John's eyes darted up and to the right before answering. "I cannot think of anyone who might be after Paul for any reason at all. He is just an average guy, a car salesman. And he definitely never mentioned anything to me, that is for sure. Or his mother either." John stopped to clear his throat. "I mean what kind of trouble could an average guy get in? Oh, and he does not do drugs or anything like that, so that is out of the question. I am not sure why you are asking me these types of questions." I wondered if John noticed he was shuffling his feet the whole time he was talking. Or that he had not uttered one contracted word in his denial.

"I'm not trying to upset you, Mr. Deland; these are just standard questions. But I wouldn't want to involve Mr. Parker or Miss Ge—, Jackie, in any type of investigation unnecessarily."

John said, "That makes sense. So now what, Chief?"

"Well, I got everything I need from y'all, so now I get to go do my job, which is find Mr. Parker and his girlfriend and see if either of them know anything. I wouldn't get my hopes up, Mr. Deland. I can appreciate Dr. McCain's concern, but to suspect foul play simply based on a lost wallet is pretty far-fetched in my opinion." At least he did not say dropped wallet. "Before I let y'all go, is there anything else you can think of, anything at all?"

I said, "No, Chief. Thanks for your time. By the way, I hope you don't mind, but I will be doing a little poking around today on my own. I was an investigator in the Navy years ago so I might have some luck. I will let you know if I find out anything new."

For the first time since we met Chief Parker, his smile diminished in intensity. "Well, doesn't that beat all, a Navy investigator, you don't say. Of course, I don't mind at all, but I can't speak for the entire local population. You just be careful, I don't want to have to stop looking for Paul because I have to respond to some kind of trouble."

I could not be sure, but that sounded eerily like a thinly veiled threat. *Maybe I am just reading him wrong.*

"But I do appreciate you keeping me in the loop. Now can y'all see yourself out; it appears I have some work to do on the Lord's Day."

CHAPTER 10

The town of Emmettsville, Tennessee was starting to irritate me: rude bartenders, lying cops, and a missing friend. My promise to Ellie was still intact, yet I was wondering how long I could keep it that way if John and I did not get some cooperation from the police. My time investigating in the Navy had taught me patience, but I had my limits.

I had planned on telling John before our meeting with the Chief about the relationship between Eric and the Chief; however, Chief Parker had invited us in before I had a chance to tell him. He did not realize that Chief Parker was lying by omission when he failed to mention his last name, nor did he know the mistake in the report was intentional. It did not make any sense; Chief Parker had to know I would figure it out since I was dating Ellie.

However, my inner voice was telling me that John was not being truthful either. Many people claim that eyes darting up and to the right are a sign that the person is visually constructing the image in their mind; that is, they are lying. It is a myth, with a little truth mixed in. During my time undercover, I had been trained to look for a multitude of visual cues to determine if a person was lying, and John had been guilty of more than one: eyes darting, shuffling feet, and providing too much information to name a few. Not one of the clues by itself could tell a person anything, but cluster enough of them together and an experienced person could get pretty good at spotting lies in a person, especially in the amateur liars.

Once outside, I offered to buy them both lunch. John insisted that he buy and I realized it would be an insult to argue; however, I wanted to pick the place. I wanted a country diner, the type with the lunch counter up near the cook station. Being Sunday, one like that was easy enough to find in the downtown area. We just looked for the cars. We quickly found two about a block apart and chose the busier one.

As we entered the restaurant, several people openly stared in our direction. Chief Parker's advice to be careful was playing in the back of my mind. Maybe it had not been a threat. Maybe he had been warning us that some of the locals might not be too welcoming to outsiders. Everyone we had encountered in the town so far had been white. Maybe they were surprised to see a black man. The three of us walked straight to the lunch counter and sat down. As a child during the Sixties, I remembered a time less than 30 years ago when Virgil would not have been allowed to sit at the counter. I hoped there was not going to be a problem today.

"What can I get for you boys?" The man asking the question appeared to be in his late fifties, which meant he would have been a young man during the civil rights movement. His smile was honest and friendly, and he was showing no sign of prejudice towards Virgil or us.

Virgil said, "Any specials?"

"Meatloaf, my momma's recipe, with mashed potatoes and vegetables, or a steak sandwich with fries."

Virgil said, "Which do you recommend?"

"My momma's meatloaf, of course."

We all agreed to the meatloaf. I took a long look around the restaurant. No one was paying any particular attention to us. I must have been wrong about earlier; the people staring were probably watching us because we were newcomers, not because Virgil was black. It was nice to know.

John said, "Ok, if no one else is going to say it, then I will. Wow, did you catch those teeth?"

I said, "Are you kidding me; the image is still burned into my retinas. I can't get it out."

Virgil said, "I didn't know teeth even came in that shade of white."

I said, "Teach that man to fly, and Rudolph would be out of business on Christmas Eve."

"Sounds like y'all met our Chief." It was the man who took our order. "It has the same effect on everyone the first time they meet him. Never heard the Rudolph reference before though. That's a good one."

"Sorry, we weren't trying to offend," I said.

"No worry. He catches some teasing from the locals as well. Y'all want to know somethin'? Those are his real teeth. He whitens them, I hear, but they are his. We went to school together, and he had them back then, but he was a heavy kid back then, so no one paid him much mind. Good lookin' fella now, and one heck of a Chief."

I hoped to tell John about the Chief's last name before this man beat me to it. "Sir, could I trouble you for another ice tea, half unsweetened, half sweet." I love tea, and I usually drink it sweetened, but after nearly ten years in the South, I still thought Southerners added too much sugar, plus I needed to get the man to leave for a few seconds.

I quickly turned to John, "I have to tell you something. The Chief's last name is Parker. He is Eric Parker's dad. Ellie told us last night. Sorry, I was going to tell you that before we went in there, but he met us at the door and then for various reasons once we went in I didn't want to let on that I knew who he was. Once again, I'm sorry."

"Oh, man." John's wide-eyed look said it all. He opened his mouth to speak, twice, yet no words came out either time.

I said, "I wanted you to know before I start hitting this guy up for some information. He is friendly and talkative and could be a gold mine of information. Both of you just follow my lead. Okay?"

They both agreed. John said, "Thanks for telling me. It clears up some of his behavior now. Like he started to say Miss something that began with a 'g' before catching himself."

I mouthed "we will talk later" as the man returned with my tea. He was smiling and looking at me funny at the same time. "You're from above the Mason-Dixon line; that's for sure. Down here, we either drink our tea plain or syrupy. I might have to try the half and half sometime; I go in for plain myself."

"Born in Missouri, raised in Illinois, but then my accent gave me away I am sure. By the way, is this your diner?"

"Yep. Sorry for my manners. Raymond Briar, at your service, but everyone just calls me Ray." I heard the short order cook say something about an order up and Ray left us, returning shortly with our three plates of meatloaf. His pride left him lingering until we had tried our first bite. "I can tell by the smiles on yer faces that you love momma's recipe."

It was delicious and very different than most meatloaf I had in the past. There did not seem to be any breadcrumb filler, and I could taste the smallest tinge of bacon and sausage along with sun-dried tomatoes.

Virgil said, "Ray, I thought my mother's meatloaf was the best until now. I stand corrected." John nodded in the affirmative.

I said, "Ray, tell your momma I want the recipe."

"Son, she ain't even give me the recipe yet. She is 82 years old, and she still works two Sundays a month, and the special is always meatloaf on those days. She tells me the recipe is in her last will and testament. But I will tell her you liked it."

"Thanks, Ray. You don't know me, but I am dating Lloyd Carmichael's daughter, Ellie. You know her?"

"You bet I know her and her whole family, for that matter. I see her on the news doin' the weather. Boy, you got yerself a real sweet girl. How did a big lumberjack lookin' fella like you score a girl like that?"

"Believe it or not, she came into the emergency room where I work with a cut foot that needed stitches. I liked her immediately, so I got one of the other doctors to sew up her foot while I asked her out."

"Why didn't you sew it up yerself?"

"Conflict of interest, we are not supposed to date patients. She said no at first, but I told her that if she said yes I would keep quiet about her name. I was just teasing her, and she knew it, but it worked, and we've been dating ever since."

"So you know her given name then?"

I replied, "Sure do. Marigold Eleanor Carmichael. Pretty name, but she doesn't like it very much."

"Well, she went by Marigold till about junior high. Then she started insistin' on Ellie."

I had buttered the man up enough, and I felt I had earned enough trust that if I started to ask questions, it would not make him suspicious. "Ellie tells me that you guys had a local boy play professional football. Is that true?"

"We sure did. Chief Parker's boy, Eric, got drafted by Chicago, although he never made it off the practice squad."

I said, "What's his story?"

"In high school, he was a wide receiver. I remember watchin' him play. He could catch anything you threw at him. The concentration on that kid, and the intensity. It was a sight to see. He had a major growth spurt while at Auburn and they made him a tight end, which made sense. He's a big boy. He ended up startin' his junior and senior year at Auburn. He even caught a touchdown against Alabama, and you know how much all us SEC teams want to beat Bama."

"Don't I know it. You guys must have thrown him a parade for that one. He get injured?" I asked.

"No, it just never worked out for him. In the end, I guess he just wasn't fast enough for the pros."

I knew enough about the NFL to know that speed is what often separates the men from the boys when it comes to a career in professional football.

"He live around here now?"

"Sure does. Drives a beer truck for a distributor out of Memphis. Gurston, or Grayston, or somethin' like that. He has approached me a few times to let him deliver to us, but I never bothered with a liquor license."

It was going even better than expected. Ray only served people who sat at the counter, and he worked the cash register when needed, which left him available for talking, and he liked to talk. I was not sure how to ask him about the girlfriend, but then an idea came to me.

"Virgil and I were in Falco's last night, and I think I sort of met him. Is he a little bigger than me, looks like he works out a lot, with close-cut brown hair?"

"Sure sounds like him?"

"Actually, Virgil met him and his girlfriend. What did you say his girlfriend's name was, Virgil?"

Virgil said, "Jackie…I forget the last name; it began with a 'g' though."

Ray said, "Well, I'll be darn, so he is still datin' Jackie Geddes. Good for him. He kinda got loose with the women after his first wife left him and moved away. I heard Jackie had been good for him, calmin' him down some, so I hope it works out for him."

It only took a few minutes, and I had Jackie's name. Now John had two names to give to the State Police when he left here. "Ray, not to change the subject, but I would like some apple pie with ice cream just like on your menu. And I know Virgil would like some too. And give the bill to John here, he owes me a lunch." I figured he could afford to buy me some pie after that performance.

While eating the pie we engaged in a little more small talk with Ray, but he got stuck on the cash register for several minutes and left us alone after that. I told John to leave Ray a big tip; he had earned it even if he did not know why he had earned it.

* * *

Having done what I came to do, I was looking forward to getting home. Earlier, Ellie had asked if she could keep my apartment key. She said something about a surprise awaiting me when I returned. I was more than a little intrigued.

I was giving Virgil a brotherly hug good-bye near his car when someone yelled from the street. "Well, idden dat sweet. Y'all see that boys, the biggun give his little friend a hug."

I turned to discover a group of six men of various shapes and sizes in the street walking our direction; their conspicuous Cheshire cat smiles doing a poor job of disguising their aggressive body language. The smell of too much Old Spice hit my offended nostrils as they formed a half circle around us. Already my heart rate was quickening as my adrenal glands started their all too familiar function.

I said, "Hello gentlemen. Nice day today, huh?"

The one that spoke earlier spoke again. "Nice day fer us. Maybe not so nice fer y'all though."

The guy was huge, 6'2" and easily 300 pounds. His immaculately clean bib overalls were straining at the front to control his girth. The dark blue overalls appeared ironed. I wondered if this was his idea of dressing up for church. His gait was plodding, and his movements were slow, but his size alone meant I should consider him a primary threat.

However, I was more concerned with the short, stocky guy that made a point of lining up slightly behind me on my left side. He was about 5'8" with a thick torso and arms; in fact, he reminded me of a fire hydrant. His nose had been broken before, and there was a long scar along the left side of his chin. His confident swagger caught my eye initially, but his stance told me he was the one I better keep my eye on. He was standing alert and ready with an almost imperceptible smirk on his face.

John said, "Now gentlemen, we don't want any trouble. We just want to be on our way." John's voice gave away his nervousness.

Virgil remained quiet. I discreetly backed Virgil up until his back was against the building behind us, thus preventing them from forming a full circle around us. Sure, Virgil was 6'1", but he was very lean and topped the scales at 175 pounds on his heaviest day, and I needed him out of the way if I was going to have to attack these men. There was no way I was going to let them strike first.

The big one was standing with his arms crossed and resting on his protruding abdomen. Whether by selection or by self-appointment, he appeared to be the leader and was still doing all the talking. "Hear that boys; he don't want no trouble. Maybe we're tryin' to keep y'all out of trouble. See, lotsa folks in this town would be mighty offended to see homos goin' around huggin' each other in public around here."

"I appreciate your concern, but we're not homosexual. This here is my brother," I said while motioning towards Virgil. "Can't you see the family resemblance?"

A tall skinny guy with a scruffy beard pointed his bony finger at me and said, "We know y'all ain't brothers. So what do you and Mr. Tibbs here think y'all are doing in our town anyway?"

Another tall skinny guy who was obviously related to the one with the scruffy beard started laughing. "Ha, ha, that's a good one, Aaron. Mr. Tibbs. That's just damn funny. So is that what they call you, nigger boy? Do they call you Mr. Tibbs?"

The rest of the group started laughing out loud, even the fireplug, who slapped the second skinny on the back while whispering something to him. I heard the fireplug call him Hank. I was surprised any of them got the reference from *In the Heat of the Night*; the movie seemed to be above their comprehension level and ironically was a movie about overcoming racism. If they had seen it, then it appeared that lesson was lost on them. *Change of plans, I am going to hit Hank first out of spite.*

I could not afford to look behind me to see how Virgil was reacting since I needed my focus on the six men, although I did feel him put a reassuring hand on my back, seemingly reminding me to maintain my composure. Nevertheless, my blood was beginning to boil, and my muscles began to tense. How did this turn into a racial attack on Virgil? I could not resist the opportunity. I looked at Hank and asked, "Are you two brothers?"

"What of it?"

"I was just wondering if you guys ever noticed that your parents named you after Hank Aaron, the home run leader, who, by the way, is black. They must be disappointed to have named their kids after 'The Hammer,' only to watch them grow up into skinny little runts like you."

That wiped the smile off their racist faces.

The monster in overalls took his arms off his belly and stood with balled up fists down at his sides. "You better watch yer tongue, mister. We ain't gonna let some damn Yankee talk to us like that!" He was leaning forward into my space, trying to use his size to intimidate me. The only thing I could think was what an idiot he was to stand there and make himself an easier target.

Now I was smiling. "You better get used to it. I have only begun to insult you and your skinny racist friends. Besides, there are only six of you, so it is hardly fair. You might want to get some more friends and come back and try again when you actually have a chance."

With my expertise and experience with wrestling and martial arts, I had not lost a one-on-one fight since I was ten, and that guy had been fourteen. However, this was not going to be a one-on-one fight. No room for one-on-one tactics in a non-sporting situation. This was combat. If I could not avoid a fight, which was still the preferred approach, then I would finish the fight as quickly as possible. Hit early, hit hard. Attack the most vulnerable parts of the body. If it caused serious bodily injury, so be it. Not my problem. For now, I was still hoping to avoid a confrontation by keeping the idiots talking long enough that someone called the police.

Aaron was smiling. "You think y'all are going to walk out of here, ain't that special. Hey, y'all know what's left when you beat the shit out of a lawyer, a Yankee, and a nigger?"

Overalls and Hank said no.

"Nothing," said Aaron.

Now I don't know who to hit first, Hank or Aaron.

I said, "It isn't going to work boys."

Overalls cocked his head to one side. "What ain't gonna work?"

"Getting us all riled up hoping we will do something so your Chief Parker can come in here and arrest us. I know he sent you. If he didn't, then he told you who we are, and he hoped you would come on your own."

Ever since the conversation with these men had started, by appearing to retreat, I had unassumingly moved the nine of us to the right so that all of us were visible to the customers inside Ray's diner. The glass window of the diner was now directly behind me. Having that much glass behind us increased the risk of injury caused by the surroundings, but the chance that having an entire diner watching might dissuade them was worth the risk.

"Now take your redneck butts back to him and tell him you failed, or go ahead and attack me. Either way, I am walking out of here unhurt because I am without a doubt the most dangerous SOB you idiots have ever met. If you leave now, you all get to leave here unhurt as well. Use those sixth-grade educations to make the right decision boys. Move along and avoid pain and permanent injury. Let us leave your town right now. You can even say you ran us out if you like." At that point, I reached behind me and started tapping loudly on the front plate glass window of Ray's diner. "Do or die time boys. Make the right decision."

I could feel the sweat forming under my shirt. My heart rate and breathing quickened. Adrenaline surged. Muscles tensed throughout my entire body. The six idiots in front of me did not realize they were playing with a dangerous weapon. One that was loaded and cocked, ready to go off on the first one unfortunate enough to move in our direction.

Currently, it was a stand-off. I hoped I had mixed in the appropriate amount of bravado to deter them and not accidentally provoke them. If not, they were going to find out what happens when you mess with someone that has been to hell and back. Someone that can open the door to hell anytime he needs to because he has the key. One wrong move on their part and Overalls would be on the ground with a crushed windpipe, gasping for air that might or might not come. Fireplug was going to be lying next to him with a knee that would require surgery and months of rehabilitation. Strategically, Hank and Aaron would have to wait until after I removed the two biggest threats.

Fireplug spoke directly to us for the first time, "Don't go thinkin' you're so smart and that you figured anything out, 'cuz you don't know shit. Maybe Eric sent us. Or maybe it was Mason. Or maybe we just speak for the town as a whole. Either way, we'll back off and let y'all leave. But hear this Yankee Doodle dick head, if any of y'all come back, we're gonna beat the shit out of you for fun. And I will lead the parade myself next time."

With that, the six of them all turned and left us standing there alone. I had been wrong about one thing; Overalls was not the leader, Fireplug was.

CHAPTER 11

A fight avoided is a fight won. However, our victory left me feeling hollow. Incomplete. I wanted to hit someone. Hard. I had missed a good opportunity. I knew I had made the right choice, though. I would have won the battle, but lost the war if I clobbered six buttheads only to end up in jail.

"What the hell just happened back there?" asked Virgil.

I was riding with Virgil as he headed east towards Huntsville. My eyes were glued to the road behind us looking for a tail. So far, I had not seen anyone other than John. The heightened vigilance left me nauseous as a result of the adrenaline surging through my body, leaving the disgusting acidic taste of bile burning in my throat.

"Chief Parker was sending us a message. Get out of town."

"I heard you say that to them. You really think he sent those men to run us out of town?"

"It makes sense, doesn't it? Them showing up shortly after I tell the Chief I'm going to poke around a little bit. And how would they have known your name was Virgil?"

"They didn't call me Virgil."

"No, they called you Mr. Tibbs. Do you think that was only a coincidence?"

"Who is Mr. Tibbs?"

"Man, I keep forgetting you completely missed the Sixties in America. It's from a movie, *In the Heat of the Night,* with Sidney Poitier playing a detective named Virgil Tibbs. The second skinny a-hole was referencing a famous line in the movie. It's one of my favorite movies. How have you never seen it?"

"Just haven't I guess."

"But you see why I know the guy knew your first name?"

"Sure, I guess so. Could be a coincidence, though. Maybe he just saw the resemblance between me and Sidney Poitier. Besides, I thought white folk thought we all looked the same anyway."

"Only the stupid ones."

Virgil said, "Well, they looked plenty stupid."

"Okay, can't argue with that logic. Seriously, though, Virgil. Do you really think it was a coincidence?"

"I guess not. If the Chief sent them after us, now what?"

"How about we turn around so I can beat the hell out of all of them? I like that idea."

"We didn't need to leave for you to do that."

"Sure we did, Virgil. I said so I can beat the hell out of them, not you. I wanted you out of there."

Virgil said, "Afraid I can't handle myself?"

"You and John would have just got in my way."

Virgil said, "Then it would have been six on one."

"Yeah. Just the way I wanted it."

"Just like that time in the Navy, huh?"

I replied, "Yeah, just like that time."

"Well, I'm not turning around, so, what now?"

"I can't answer that right now; I'm too mad. Mad enough that I am sick to my stomach. A big part of me wants to go back there and fu—, mess those guys up. How dare the Chief send men to do his dirty work like that and how dare they sling racial insults at my best friend."

"Holy crap, L.T., you are mad; you almost dropped an 'f' bomb."

"Aren't you mad?"

"Sure, I'm pissed too, but somehow I've managed to go 34 years without anyone ever using the 'n' word around me. It caught me off guard. At first, I wasn't even sure I heard him correctly. You know, I've often wondered how I would handle it if it ever happened. Part of me wants to go back and help you clobber those guys; the rest of me knows it would just get us into more trouble than it is worth."

"Says you maybe. I still think it might be worth it."

Virgil said, "They were ignorant rednecks. Busting them up wouldn't ever change their mind. If you could pound common sense or common decency into someone, then I would agree. I would 'lead the parade' as that one dude said. But you and I both know it doesn't work that way. You have to let this one go, man."

"Okay, but let the record state that I still want to knock their teeth out, the ones they have left."

"Record noted. Nice to see you are getting more agreeable in your old age."

"Don't bet on it, Virgil. You know I can't let the Chief get away with what he just did, and if his son hurt Paul in any way, then I'm going to help hold them both accountable."

"How are you planning on doing that? You crazy enough to take on a chief of police?"

"Maybe. It makes more sense to go after Eric, though, don't you think. His dad is just protecting his kid. He's a roadblock, not a suspect. Best to try and stay out of his way."

"So you are going after Eric? You're going to hunt him down. And when you find him? It's not like you can beat it out of him."

"Oh, I am sure I could take him."

Virgil said, "I didn't mean it that way. I mean you just can't go around kicking butt to get your way."

"Oh, I thought you actually meant I couldn't take him."

Virgil said, "No. I would *never* bet against you in a fight. Not after what I saw what you did in the Navy."

"Good to know," I said.

"L.T., this isn't your fight. It isn't your responsibility. Taking this on is going to cause trouble. Not to mention you promised Ellie."

"You worried about me?"

Virgil said, "Yeah, but not in the way you think. My fear is that you're going to sink your teeth into this and then like a damn pit bull, you won't let go no matter what. Look at what's happening already. Some guys insult us and now you want to take them all on. Let the authorities handle it."

I spent the next couple of minutes contemplating Virgil's advice. It was good advice. There was only one problem; I was too mad. Also, although my nausea had finally abated, the taste of bile still lingered ruining my memory of the world's best meatloaf. Not to mention that my inner voice would not shut the hell up.

"Virgil?"

"Yes."

"I have a bad feeling about this whole thing."

"Me too," said Virgil.

There was another pause while the ramifications of my statement lingered in the air, casting doubt that neither one of us wanted to be the first to say out loud.

After a few minutes, Virgil said, "L.T., thanks."

"Thanks for what."

"Getting us out of there in one piece. I noticed you were moving the whole group of us over to the window, although I didn't know why until you started banging on the glass. How the heck do you think of that kind of stuff in the heat of the moment like that?"

"It is all about situational awareness, and experience and training, and remembering what your goals are."

Virgil asked, "And what were your goals?"

"Avoid the fight, plain and simple. I was also thinking exit strategy."

"All I was thinking was I hope I don't piss myself when the punches start flying." I had to wait for him to stop laughing at his own joke. "One thing, though. You were calling them names and seemed to be baiting them into a fight. That strategy just seems weird to me."

"Sure, because you've never been in a fight in your life, other than the one you told me about in third grade in Korea. It's hard to explain, but just trust me that there is a dynamic to most fights, often starting with psychological warfare. I could tell that if I had demonstrated any weakness, it would have empowered them. My cockiness was an act designed to keep them wondering more about why I appear so sure of myself than on what they wanted to do to us."

Virgil said, "I'll be damned, you have multiple black belts and know how to kill people with your bare hands, but deep down inside, you are a pacifist."

"Not even close, Virgil. I'm someone who never wants to be on the losing side. If it had escalated, I would have pushed you out of the way and told you to get out of town while I started inflicting major damage. Some of them would not have walked away. That is not pacifism."

Virgil and I drove for a few more minutes before pulling over so I could ride back to Memphis with John. Virgil wished me luck and then was on his way. John wanted to go around Emmettsville on the way back. I assured him that the danger was over. I'm not sure he believed me; his knuckles were white while driving through the town and he hardly spoke a word. Subconsciously, I think I wanted someone to try and stop us. I still had a lot of pent-up aggression, and the lingering taste of bile reminded me of my desire for retribution. Once we were clear of Emmettsville, he felt safe enough to talk freely again. "Do you think Chief Parker sent those guys after us?"

"Don't you?"

"I guess it makes the most sense."

I said, "Virgil asked me the same question. I guess he didn't want to think a police chief might resort to nefarious means either. Fortunately, I am more cynical than you two."

"Nefarious…who uses words like that?"

"Are you making fun of my word vocabulary? I pay good money to be in the word of the month club; now I have to listen to your persiflage?"

"Persiflage? Really? Now you are just showing off. I don't even know what the hell that means."

"Teasing. You can thank my mother for that; she was quite the wordsmith, and I guess it rubbed off on me. My vocabulary aside, I think I barely avoided incarceration for assault and battery."

"But they instigated the whole situation."

I said, "Do you think that would have mattered to the guy who sent them in the first place?"

"No, I guess not. But don't you mean us? Virgil and I would have helped the best we could."

"You must think I'm crazy if I was going to let Virgil hit any white people in that stupid town. So I was going to have to take them all out myself and quickly, especially the big one in overalls and the short, thick guy that looked like a fireplug. Once I incapacitated them, the other four would have backed off anyway."

"Christ, L.T.! Incapacitate them how?"

"Unless those guys were *much* better than they looked, the guy in overalls was going to get hit hard in the throat and then I was going to kick Fireplug's knee backward. I would have punched Hank and Aaron in the face out of spite. The other two would have run off by that point."

He was looking at me with an incredulous open-mouthed, wide-eyed stare. "Are you that good? Seriously, would it have worked?"

"It was going to have to work. No choice, so I would have made it work. I've been in worse situations than that one and come out on top. Besides, these guys were not committed, and I was, if for no other reason than to keep Virgil out of trouble in an all-white town in the South. He is the best friend I have, and it will be a cold day in you know where before I let anyone hurt him. And I am *very* good."

"Remind me never to make you mad."

"Everyone always says that, but anger has nothing to do with it. If it did, I would have decided to hit Hank and Aaron first."

John was quiet for several minutes, during which time I concentrated on refocusing my rage, which seemed to be growing in intensity instead of diminishing with time. More than once I fantasized about punching Hank and Aaron in the face, retribution for their racist remarks. While driving, John was biting his lower lip and nervously gripping and re-gripping the steering wheel. The poor guy had to be a nervous wreck.

"L.T." There was a slight stammer in his voice. "I don't know what to do now. I am scared for Paul. Hell, he is still missing. In a town where the Chief of Police possibly just sent people to run us out of town. Now, what?"

"We investigate."

"How do we do that?"

"I'm still figuring that out, but the first thing I'm going to do is find Eric Parker tomorrow and have some face-to-face time. We know he drives a beer truck, so I will track him down and confront him outside of Emmettsville so as to avoid Chief Parker and his goons. I am going to ask him some questions, and he is going to answer them."

"What if he doesn't cooperate?"

"He is going to answer my questions."

"How can you be so sure?"

"Because I'm not going to leave him a choice. I can see by your face you are worried, well, don't be. I'm not going to beat it out of him."

John said, "I wasn't thinking that. I was just thinking how serious this is all getting. Besides, I don't care if you break every bone in his body if he did something to my son."

"Good, you are getting mad. Now I need you to channel that anger and do something important."

He replied, "Sure, just name it."

"You went to law school in the South, and I understand the good old boy network runs pretty deep down here, so make some calls to your attorney friends that do criminal law and ask their opinion on whom to talk to. If any of them do prosecution work, that is even better. Eventually, we will need help from someone that can make everything official. Don't hold back anything. Tell them what is going on, the name of the town, the name of the Chief, everything." I knew John was withholding information from me, and maybe it was none of my business, but he would need to give someone all the necessary information. I decided to drive home my point. "And I mean tell them *everything*, John."

"You seem to be implying something, L.T."

"I am. I know you haven't been honest with the Chief earlier or with me. You are an inexperienced liar, which is a good quality in a man by the way."

"Shit! Do you think the Chief noticed?" The sheer intensity of his anxiety startled me.

"Maybe, but he was pretty busy worrying about his own butt, and his son's, to pay too much attention, so maybe he didn't notice. If he had, I think he would have pressed you on it since it would have given him a good reason not to suspect his son."

"Damn. Damn. DAMN!" He was banging the steering wheel with his hands. "I have to tell you something." John resumed biting his lower lip and fidgeting in his car seat. He did not speak right away.

He was going to tell me something bad. I could feel it. Something that was going to make it even harder for me to walk away from helping him. *Shit, I am already more involved than I want to be.*

I did not want to push him for answers; ignorance can be bliss. And it's not like it was my fault that Paul was missing. Another part of me, a deeper part of me that I could not ignore, a part of me that I could not turn off no matter how hard I tried, felt obligated to help in any way I could. Years of conditioning had gone into the making of that undeniable, unyielding component of my character. Years of hating bullies. Years of sticking up for anyone in trouble. Years of watching my mother give her time and energy to worthwhile social causes. Years of watching my father offer assistance to his employees if they were struggling. Not to mention years of living with my damn name and its implied legacy. Then again, even the years of conditioning could not adequately account for the feeling of obligation that was as integral to me as my inner voice. The feeling was more elemental, more innate. The years of conditioning only honed to a fine edge a facet that already existed inside me and was as much an intrinsic component of my consciousness as my DNA was to my very existence.

"I lied to you about the store window," he said.

I already knew he lied about the store window. Was that it? I thought he was going to tell me something bad. John was studying me trying to gauge my reaction. He resumed biting his lower lip again.

"I know who broke your window."

"Who?"

"Okay, I don't know exactly who. More like I know why." He paused again. His pauses were beginning to irritate me.

"Is this important now? It was just a window."

"I think it might be." More lip biting.

"It relates to Paul somehow, doesn't it?

"Yes. And I'm afraid it might be related to last night as well."

"My window is related to Paul's disappearance. Is that what you are trying to say?"

"I think so. I don't know. Maybe."

"John, please just spit it out. I made a promise to Ellie that I was not going to get involved any further than today. Please don't make me angry with you by having to drag everything you know out of you one piece at a time, because my help might be more fragile than I care to admit."

"I'm sorry. I do appreciate your help. I guess I'm just scared."

"Don't get scared, get angry. Then channel that anger. Trust me; few people know more about anger than me. I have been mad for 17 years. I am an expert on anger. Now tell me what you know...please."

John resumed talking, this time without any pauses. "I've been getting calls for a couple of weeks from some guy demanding payment to cover gambling debts that my son owes to someone down in Mississippi. He has called four times, and I have refused to pay each time. You found that brick in my office the morning after the second time I told the man no."

"That explains the note and your strange behavior that morning," I said. He threw me a quick questioning glance. "I thought you were holding back information that day too. I figured you would tell me sooner or later. I wasn't expecting this."

"I'm sorry."

"Don't worry about that right now, just finish your story."

"Sorry. Paul doesn't know that anybody called me. If he did know, then he never let on, and neither did I. My wife doesn't know either. It seems the guy in Mississippi was not happy with the rate of repayment that Paul offered him, so he commissioned the fellow on the phone to collect it for him. He wanted me to cover Paul's debt instead. He said that quick repayment would guarantee Paul's continued good health. I refused to pay, but now I wondered if I made the wrong decision. Maybe this Eric guy was the one calling me demanding the payment. Maybe he took him hostage or something, or worse."

Despite my current indifference to my mother, I had loved and admired her once, and she had taught me that cursing demonstrated an inability to articulate your thoughts to others fully. It was very difficult to avoid cursing after hearing John's confession.

"Holy crap, John, you have a big problem."

"I know."

"A really big problem!"

"I know. I know!"

"You do realize Paul is caught up in organized crime, don't you?" John was speechless, his mouth open but unable to form words. "You must realize that illegal gambling normally implies organized crime. Plus, this fellow down in Mississippi has enough clout that he commissions others to do his collecting. Sounds organized to me!"

"Shit!"

"You think. And if that meeting last night was planned ahead of time and Eric Parker is involved somehow, then it's also possible his father is a dirty cop."

John jerked his head towards me while letting his foot off the gas. "Don't you think that's a pretty big stretch?"

"Sure, but then so is thinking the meeting with Eric was preplanned. It seemed pretty spontaneous to me last night. But here we are a day after Paul goes missing and the Chief of Police has lied to us and sent men to run us out of town."

John was quiet, very quiet for a couple of minutes. He was soaking it all in, weighing the evidence, considering the ramifications. It was a lot to consider, especially for a parent. When he finally looked my direction, he was still quiet with a concerned, questioning look on his face.

"I know, John. I'm sorry. I will still talk to Eric. It needs to be done. He will tell me something I promise. We have to find out if that meeting was prearranged. Either way, it's even more obvious that we need some official police help."

"The man on the phone warned me against involving the police."

I said, "Sure he did. He wants his money, not trouble. In my opinion, you are going to have to call someone. ASAP. We both know Chief Parker isn't going to be any help."

Talking my way out of the fight earlier was easier than convincing John that we needed police involvement. He kept making excuses. I did not want excuses; I wanted results. Investigating was one thing. That required asking questions, looking for clues, watching. If I did discover who was responsible for making threats against Paul, then we would need the police to administer the proper justice. I was not willing to be a vigilante, especially against the Chief of Police in a small town in Tennessee.

CHAPTER 12

I left John with a plan. A plan that I was going to make him deliver on, or I would not help him. We would need official help at some point. Maybe they would even be willing to take over the investigation if John and I were able to give them enough incriminating information. If we were lucky, someone was already investigating organized crime in that area. I just hoped Paul was okay. I prayed that this was still a missing person's investigation and not worse.

John begged me to allow him to pay for the broken window. I told him not to worry about it. Insurance covered it. He insisted. Realizing he was trying to thank me for my help, I finally allowed him to reimburse me the deductible.

The intoxicating smell of rosemary, basil, and what smelled like cumin hit me as I opened the front door of my apartment. Maybe I was wrong about the cumin, but it smelled divine regardless; my mouth was slightly watering proving that the primitive Pavlovian response is not limited to just dogs. I quickly found the source of the smell. A slow cooking roast and vegetables. Near the roast was a note telling me that Ellie had gone for a run and that I should not eat without her. I hoped it tasted as good as it smelled.

The whole incident at Emmettsville seemed to leave a dirty film on me. I knew it was psychological, but a good, hot shower could not hurt. While enjoying the shower, I contemplated my next move. John had a plan. I had a plan too, one that was in direct conflict with the promise I had made to Ellie earlier today. I hoped she would understand. I needed her to understand. Besides, I only anticipated talking to Eric and then letting the authorities taking over after that.

I closed my eyes as I basked in the heat from the comforting spray. I could feel the tension washing from my body into the awaiting drain. Tension that had been building since last Tuesday; the day I stopped Tom Harty. Each day I expected news concerning Mr. Harty. Each day there was no news. He remained in a room hooked to a ventilator. His nutrients entered his body through a tube in his esophagus. A liquid formula complete with all the nutrients and energy he needed. A catheter was inserted into the urethra to collect his urine, and a large diaper to collect his number two. Various other wires and leads were applied to monitor his vitals. Finally, he still had that handcuff on his right wrist. His own personal purgatory.

I came close to putting two more men into the hospital today. Better than the morgue.

I was rinsing the shampoo from my hair when a cold draft hit my unsuspecting body. Something, or someone, had opened the shower door. I reacted in alarm. Instinctively, my muscles prepared themselves for a fight as my eyes fought to focus through the heavy steam. I could make out the silhouette of a person in the steam.

It was Ellie. She was standing outside my shower with one towel wrapped loosely around her body, another towel on her head. She must have used the shower in the other bedroom.

Ellie said, “Holy cow, did I scare you?”

"Momentarily startled is all."

"You going to stay in there all day? Food's ready. I just need to get dressed, and we can eat."

I was peeking around the door to cover my nakedness from Ellie, who was still standing there like this was an everyday occurrence. It wasn't, and I felt a little awkward.

"Yeah, well, are you going to stand there all day gawking?"

"Maybe. Lisa teased me about our level of intimacy. Could be I was just checking out what I've been missing."

I was not sure where the whole incident was going, but I did open the door a little more to give her a better look.

"Ms. Marigold, it's not much to look at; however, I want you to remember that I'm built more for performance than for aesthetics."

She blushed and turned away before the door was completely open. She cast a quick glance over her shoulder and started to leave the bathroom. I cleared my throat with a loud "Ahem" as she reached the doorway.

She paused. Without turning around, she said, "I guess it's only fair you get a small sample of what you've been missing as well." With that, she dropped the towel giving me a wonderful view of her naked backside before leaving the room.

Man, does she ever know how to make an exit.

* * *

Ellie thought the day I ended Tom Harty's rampage was a strange day. It paled in comparison to the one I was experiencing. Ellie slept over last night. That had never happened before. She cooked me dinner. Also a first. Then, the shower conversation and dropped towel. Definitely a first. Surprisingly, it had all seemed normal.

That was the strange part.

I could not help wondering where this was headed.

Ellie was already dressed in a T-shirt and shorts as I entered my bedroom. No bra. The towel was still wrapped around her head. I dressed in a similar casual manner and walked out into my kitchen. Ellie followed and began serving the roast. My nose had been right; there was cumin in the roast. And plenty of vegetables. My kind of meal.

I started to clear the table, but she protested. She insisted that I relax. I walked over to the living room area and sat in my favorite chair, reclining back while watching her move around in my kitchen. The T-shirt looked good on her. Real good. She was continuing the tease that she started in the bathroom, and she knew it. Once Ellie cleared the dishes and started the dishwasher, she walked over and sat on my lap giving me a big kiss.

"Okay, sweetie, tell me how your day has gone."

"Oh, you know," I said, "Weird, and getting weirder."

Ellie pushed herself off my lap and walked over to the couch. She plopped down. She looked happy. I hoped what I was going to tell her did not ruin that. I started with our visit with Chief Parker and ended by telling her about the six men. She was scowling by the end of my story.

"I can't believe the Chief sent them. My dad would be disappointed to hear this. The way he talks, the two of them are friends."

"Sorry, Ellie. I'm just telling you how I see it is all."

"I'm going to call my father tomorrow and tell him all this."

"Don't do that just yet. No use causing trouble between friends if I am wrong."

She was still frowning. "I know I don't live there anymore, but I hope you don't have a bad image of my hometown in your head just because of the last 24 hours or so."

"How could I? It produced you and your wonderful family. Even the Garden of Eden had a snake in it."

"Thanks."

"Think nothing of it."

Ellie asked, "So what's John going to do?"

"I told him to call his attorney friends and figure out who to talk to that might be able to help him. A D.A. or a state's attorney, someone. Obviously, we can't count on Chief Parker."

"We? You said 'we.' Was that purposeful?"

"About that..."

"Yes, about that. You promised me no further involvement after today." She was giving me a disapproving look.

"Sorry, Ellie, but I'm going to see this through a little longer. John needs me. His son needs me. And I haven't been this mad in a long time. This is something I have to do."

"You have to! I'm not buying that for a second. You don't have to get involved any further. You want to! Just give him advice or counsel, but stay out of the dangerous stuff."

"Who said anything about dangerous stuff?"

Ellie said, "I suppose those six men outside the diner were not dangerous?"

"That was not an ideal situation, but it was not all that dangerous."

"There were six of them!" She flared her nostrils as she yelled that last statement.

"Ellie, I can tell you are getting mad at me, and I'm not trying to make things worse by telling you this, but you and I have different ideas on what is dangerous or not."

"You said yourself you were trying to avoid a fight with them."

"Ellie, I was trying my best to avoid a fight with them not because I was scared. I would have won the fight, no doubt. But I didn't want to get arrested, and I was not going to let Virgil get arrested in a town that throws the 'n' word around so cavalierly. Besides, now I know what I am up against. I didn't foresee Chief Parker as a threat. I won't make that mistake again. I have to do this, Ellie."

"Who the hell are you?"

"Whoa, what's going on here? You seem angry. What do you mean by that question?"

"L.T., look at this from my point of view. You never talk about your past, except in little bits and pieces. In the last week and a half, I have found out you have broken up all kinds of fights; you were a Navy cop, sort of, and you don't even feel the least bit threatened by six grown men threatening you. In fact, you are convinced you would have won that fight. Oh, and when you see a man waving a gun in a hospital, you run towards the guy and bash him on the head and take his gun away. Now you tell me that you feel like you have to? I just don't get it."

There was genuine anguish on her face. It hurt me to witness it. Furthermore, I didn't know how to fix it. How do you explain something that seems like it should not require an explanation? I was at a loss for words. Maybe I was over-analyzing the situation.

"Ellie, I don't know how to explain it, but I will try. Evil should not win, at least, not on my watch."

Damn it, Mom. See what your influence is doing to me.

"That's it? That is your big explanation?"

"I feel like I'm involved in an argument that I cannot win. Or maybe, I should say that I feel that I could win, but it would come at too high a cost. I am not trying to be glib, but honestly, I wouldn't even know where, or when, to start."

Ellie apologized for making the conversation sound like an argument. She asked if she could start over. I tentatively agreed. I could hear Virgil's voice warning me that this would happen, warning me to let go of the situation and listen to my girlfriend. It was like his voice had become my conscience. I preferred my usual inner voice.

Ellie stared hard at me for almost a minute before speaking again. "I have had a wonderful life. A beautiful family and now a wonderful job, but it has also been pretty privileged and sheltered. So I'm willing to admit maybe I'm the one being unreasonable. Now I have this great boyfriend whose secrecy is a mystery to me, and I'm not sure how much more of it I can take. Please convince me that I need to be more understanding."

"Okay, Ellie, I will try."

I went to the fridge and refreshed my iced tea. I was stalling, plus I figured my mouth might dry out if I was going to have to tell her my life story.

"I have avoided talking about this long enough, and now seems like as good a time as any, so come sit on the couch." She perched herself on the edge of the seat directly across from me and gestured her readiness with slightly lifted eyebrows.

"You don't know my parents. My dad is Marcus William McCain. He played 16 years as an offensive lineman in the NFL. Most people have never heard of him since the offensive line gets very little recognition; however, he was good, a pro bowl player. You know a little about football, so you know how big those linemen are."

She nodded.

"Now you know where I got my size and strength. My mother was Ingrid Karlsen, a prima ballerina out of New York before she met and married my dad. She was also very good. According to Dad, she was even better at her craft than he was at his. So when I told you that I am a genetic freak, I meant it, because although I got size and strength from Dad, my mother gave me speed, agility, balance, and, actually, more explosive power. Not to mention no stinking body fat."

"So that explains why you look like a moppy-haired Thor. By the way, where did you get that mop of hair?"

She was joking around. I hoped that was a good sign.

"From my mother as well. She had a heck of a time pulling it back into a ballet bun. Mom was awesome. She quit the ballet when they got married, and believe it not, she taught my dad ballet, which helped his football career; in fact, he never made the pro bowl once until Mom helped him with his footwork and balance. They were a great couple and absolutely wonderful parents. You see, I grew up very privileged and loved, just like you did."

Ellie's mouth was open in mild amazement. She was going to say something and then thought better of it.

"Their impact in my life was more than just the obvious physical attributes. Do you remember how Lisa called me a maverick?"

"Yes."

"Well, I pale in comparison to my parents. I was a young kid when Dad quit football and started his own trucking company, Borders Trucking. You have probably seen some of his trucks on the roads before. He built his business into a multimillion dollar trucking company by doing something the other companies didn't do. He not only cared about his employees, but he also cared for them. He was an industry leader in providing employee benefits like health insurance and retirement benefits for his drivers during a time when truckers were not treated that well at other companies. He always felt it was his responsibility to treat them like people, not commodities, and they loved him for it. When his partner didn't agree with him, my dad leveraged everything he had, borrowed a lot of money, and bought the guy out. He took one hell of a risk, and it paid off."

"So that's where you get your entrepreneurial spirit."

"Sure, I guess. Plus, I got an undergraduate degree in business. Working for Dad was not easy, though. He was not soft on his workers. He demanded hard work, and he got it from them. In return, his drivers made the best money in the trucking business. Sure, it cut into his bottom line, but he didn't care, and while other companies often suffered from driver shortages, Borders Trucking always had a surplus of applicants. His drivers knew they had it good. For example, some labor union people showed up a few times and my dad's workers ran them off themselves."

"You love your dad, I can tell."

A lump was forming in my throat, making me uncomfortable. I could feel my eyes starting to water. Man, I hated talking about the past.

"As for my mother, well, she was involved in so many social causes that I lost track of them all. She never did it for appearances, like it was expected for her to do something with her time since she was an executive's wife. No, instead, she became involved to institute real change. She would become part of the board of directors of some local charity and then re-organize it until it was operating at peak efficiency. If you were dead weight, then she gave you a chance to 'start performing, or start packing,' as she put it. She was caring and ruthless at the same time, kind but not nice, loving but not soft."

"Sounds like someone I know." Ellie was looking at me, inspecting me.

I smiled at her and kept on talking. "Ellie, my parents actively, even proactively, used their talent and influence to help hundreds, if not thousands of people, while I just react and help one at a time. And neither of them would back down from a fight, ever. So I inherited not only their physical characteristics, but I also inherited their innate sense of right and wrong and the compulsion to act when we witness wrongdoing."

"They sound like truly special people."

"They made me who I am today. In the nature versus nurture debate, I'm not sure which had a bigger impact on me; however, I don't think it matters. I cannot, and will not, turn a blind eye to any situation where I think I can help. 'Silence is consent' my mother used to say. And I am not really the silent type. I'm so much like my mother sometimes it scares me."

"So why have you never mentioned them before now? It seems like they had a truly positive impact on your life."

There it was. The big question, the one I was trying to avoid, but knew I couldn't. The answer to that question changed the whole rest of my life. I had to answer it, but suppressed feelings percolated to my conscious mind. Eyes watered. Vision blurred. I tried to choke back the ever growing lump in my throat. I was speechless, powerless to continue.

The feeling of helplessness led to frustration. Frustration gave way to pure anger. Finally, an emotion I could control. My watery eyes were drying up as the anger swelled inside me instead. The lump in my throat was gone. Ellie would get her answer.

"Because my dad is dead. He stopped to help someone with car trouble on the side of the road, and a drunk driver ran him over and killed him." There, I said it. The rest would be easy. The story was not hard to tell; the admission that dad was gone was always the seemingly impossible hurdle to get over. "The jerk-off was driving on a suspended license after his third DUI. He never even saw my father. He was so drunk he didn't even remember doing it later."

"Oh my God." Ellie had her hand over her mouth as if she were embarrassed she had ever asked the question.

"Yeah, oh my God. Dad, he was killed instantly. Major brain injury. Mom, she saw the whole thing. I wasn't there. I was on a bus. See, it happened the night I won sectionals in wrestling my junior year. They were driving back from watching me qualify for state again while I rode the bus back." That darn lump was returning to my throat. I had to pause to regain my composure. Ellie was quiet, allowing me to continue at my desired pace. "Needless to say, I didn't win state that year. In fact, I never wrestled again. My mother wanted me to go. She said Dad would have wanted me to continue my dream. Truth be told, my dream died that night. Wasn't anything left to continue, so I quit. Hell, I quit everything. Barely finished my junior year. Didn't go out for football my senior year. That dream died too."

"L.T., I had no idea. I'm re—."

"You want to hear my stupid dream?"

"Sure," she answered hesitantly.

"I had two going at that time. I was good, Ellie. Some were already saying I had the potential to go all the way to the Olympics in wrestling. I was on my way to being a four-time state champion in wrestling. No doubt about it. I would have had a full ride at the school of my choosing. I would have chosen Iowa. Dan Gable started coaching at Iowa in 1976. I would have been part of his rookie year as the head coach."

"You said you had two dreams."

"The other one was pursuing a life in football instead. I had the rare combination of speed and power that had NCAA coaches scouting me. I wanted to play tight end. I say 'wanted to' because in high school they had me playing outside linebacker as well. In college, I would have insisted on being a tight end, if I had played. My passion was for wrestling. I liked football, but I loved wrestling. No money in wrestling, though, and I can be quite pragmatic at times.

"So you could have been one of those guys we watch on TV scoring a touchdown."

"I believe I could have. Never know now. When I quit everything in high school, nearly all my friends eventually gave up on me since most of them were friends because of sports. All of them except Virgil. When I was ready to play sports again, I didn't want to play with any of the jerks, nor for any of the coaches that gave up on me either. I was no longer a team player kind of guy so I went out for tennis to be with Virgil and we got second in state in doubles our senior year. I started with the martial arts my senior year, which was therapeutic for me. It taught me to channel my anger, and I had a lot of anger."

"I am sorry about your dad. You obviously loved him very much. We can stop talking about this if you want." Small tears had formed in the corners of Ellie's eyes. I hoped she did not start crying. If she did, then I doubted I could hold it together myself.

"We started this conversation; we might as well finish it. It's about time you figured out what makes your boyfriend tick."

"Only if you want to."

I didn't want to. But I did need to.

"My mother suffered even worse than I did. She felt responsible since they had been arguing about the Gary Shriver situation. She quoted that stupid Edmund Burke quote at him. We had both heard it hundreds of time from her, but that time dad wasn't buying into it. He spotted the car on the side of the road and decided he should help. When he got out of the car, he made an off-handed comment about doing something for the lady in the car so that evil did not succeed. She felt that by making him mad, she had made him careless. She saw him get hit in her mirror. Saw him hurled through the air. No one should have to see that."

"So that's why you don't drink? Because of what happened to your father?"

"No. I don't drink because I need to be in control at all times. It's essential that I always keep my anger in check."

"It's been 17 years, L.T. You are still angry? That seems unhealthy."

"It is. I've learned to live with it."

"Have you?"

"I think so. I can't seem to make it go away, so I channel it."

"I don't mean to sound cold, but you're not the first one to lose a parent. You have to move on. You need to forgive the drunk driver."

"Ellie, I already forgave the man. Edward Pitt was his name. My beef is with a man call Scott Beyers."

"Who is Scott Beyers?"

"Scott Oswald Beyers, more appropriately known as SOB, is the man who took my mother from me. And my last remaining dream."

* * *

I teared up after mentioning Scott Beyers. I also clammed up. My walk down memory lane was over. Ellie sensed the conversation was over and did not press me anymore. I needed out of the apartment. Despite the enormous size and the general lack of walls, it felt small. Confining. Unnerving.

Ellie agreed to a stroll around Downtown Memphis. Walking hand in hand, I recalled happier memories of my parents as we relished in the fresh, clean smell that can only come after a good rain. I told her of my father's time in the NFL. He had played in St. Louis his entire career and even though offensive linemen seldom reach notoriety, he was well-known and respected in the community. I described how he met my mother in Scotland while he was visiting the Scottish Borders. She was in Edinburgh performing, and they met at a cafe. He called his trucking company Borders Trucking in honor of their meeting.

It started to sprinkle again as we stopped at LeClair's. An old blues artist was playing some classic covers. Although his voice and the guitar play were good, his tempo was too slow for my taste. We stayed long enough for me to get the name of the beer distributor, Cornerstone. LeClair assured me that none in the area began with a "g" and it was the only one the sounded like Grayston or Gurston.

Ellie admitted she was still worried about me and didn't truly understand my compulsion. However, when I told her the last time I had been this angry I dropped out of college and joined the Navy, and that I needed to redirect my anger into something positive, she finally relented and reminded me to be careful. After the walk, Ellie went home leaving me with a twinge of disappointment. I think she had planned more than a dinner for me that evening.

The evening had not been a total loss, though. I had opened myself up making myself vulnerable, and it had felt slightly liberating. For Ellie, it seemed to have a dissimilar result; she had appeared pensive during the rest of the evening. Unlike Virgil, Ellie seemed to need to understand me while Virgil was content with simply appreciating me. Maybe it was a woman thing; I didn't know.

CHAPTER 13

Monday marked the beginning of a four consecutive 12-hour days in the emergency room. Seven a.m. to seven p.m. However, I was not going to work just yet. First, I had an unscheduled appointment with Eric Parker.

LeClair informed me that the drivers got an earlier start so they could make some of their restaurant deliveries before the lunch rush. My goal was to catch Eric while he was still in Memphis to avoid the need to track him down on his route. It seemed reasonable that getting to Cornerstone at six in the morning should be early enough; however, I had no idea how long I might have to wait. Thankfully, Dr. Chen agreed to cover for me until 9:00 a.m.

Cornerstone was located in South Memphis in an industrialized area, sandwiched between a large supermarket distribution center and a business that made computer components. As expected, the facility was surrounded by a six-foot high chain link fence with barb wire.

There were two chain link rolling gates, one for the incoming and outgoing delivery trucks and another for the employee/visitor entrance. Neither gate was guarded. I parked in the employee section arranging my Jeep for a good view of the entrance and waited.

A good classic rock station was keeping me entertained until some inane morning deejays started their nationally syndicated morning show, interrupting what had been a good music set. I was contemplating how anyone could listen to these idiots with their crass, immature humor when Eric drove through the front gate in a new, bright red Camaro Z28. I almost missed him while I was searching for a new station. As I pulled in behind his vehicle, I realized I had no idea what I was going to say to Eric.

Eric did not immediately exit his car. His head was bobbing rhythmically to music, at least he was not stupid enough to be listening to the mindless morning show.

Showing up at an unsuspecting person's car window can startle someone, so I allowed him to get fully out of his car before approaching. He spotted me and briefly looked my way without the slightest look of recognition on his face. I paused for a second, unsure if I wanted to do this here in his employer's parking lot. If he decided to get violent, I did not want it to reflect poorly on him and cost him his job. On the other hand, if he hurt Paul in some way, then what did I care about his job.

"Eric," I said loudly, "Eric Parker."

He turned focusing on me with a friendly smile. "Yeah. How can I help you, sir?"

I was younger than him by a couple of years, so the "sir" surprised me momentarily until I remembered I was dressed for work: slacks, dress shirt, and sport coat.

I said, "I have a couple of questions for you if you have time."

"It'll have to be quick. I'm on my way into work."

"Do I look familiar to you?"

"A little."

I said, "We met briefly at Falco's on Saturday."

His eyes darted up and left while he nodded affirmatively. "Phil's friend, the guy who knocked over the chair. I didn't recognize you all dressed up."A brief look of concern set upon his face, yet there was no perceptible change in his body language.

"His name is Paul, and, yes, I am the guy who knocked over the chair. Paul is who I wanted to ask you about…"

"Why would you want to talk to me about Paul?" Nothing menacing in his voice, yet the tone was abrupt and defensive.

"Because no one has seen him since Saturday night."

"Excuse me."

"I said no one has seen him since he followed you out of the bar on Saturday night."

Eric stared at me blankly while he contemplated my statement. "Wait a minute, your friend is missing, and you think since I gave the guy a little shove earlier that I had something to do with it?"

"I'm not sure what to think, Eric. All I know is that Paul went out to the parking lot a few minutes after you and your girlfriend. I was hoping you might shed some light on things for me. When we went outside to check on him, he was gone, you were gone, Jackie was gone. All we found was his wallet."

"So."

I said, "Let's face it, it's not like he was on your favorite person's list."

"Listen, if I had wanted to hit him, I would have hit him in the bar, and it would have been over."

I said, "Well not completely over, but I follow you."

"What do you mean 'not completely over'?"

"You would have had to deal with me."

"I'm not scared of you!" he yelled while taking an aggressive stance, his nostrils flaring, his eyes wide and locked on mine. His fists were balled up.

"I never said you were scared of me. You look like you got 20 pounds on me, so why be scared of little ole me. I just want to know what happened in that parking lot after Paul went outside."

It wasn't Eric's eyes darting to his left that put me on guard; it was the momentary freeze of movement following his eye movement that screamed the fact Eric was getting ready to lie.

"I have no idea what you are talking about!"

"I think you do, Eric. I'm pretty sure you are not being completely truthful with me."

"Eat me, bitch."

"No thanks. The offer is not even the least bit appealing to me."

"Mister, you can go fuck yourself."

"I love how all you southern gents use 'mister' in such a condescending manner. It's like it is an inherited trait to start your insults with a polite prefix. For some reason, I find it charming."

Eric was standing there staring at me, chest heaving, face red, jaw clenched, while he repeatedly balled up his fists. It was an act, though; he had no intention of fighting me. I could see it in his eyes. One thing was for sure; he was a liar and a coward. I avoided looking smug. I did not want to rub it in his face.

"Let me repeat myself. Go fuck yourself, mister. There you go; I used it at the end of the sentence. Is that any better, asshole? I am done talking with you." He turned and started walking towards the front entrance.

I said, "No Mister A-hole. I'm disappointed. I'm also disappointed you weren't able to help me. I guess I will have to talk to your girlfriend, Jackie Geddes, instead."

He abruptly turned to stare at me again. He put together a half-hearted attempt to be intimidating, but we both knew it just was not in him. "How do you know her name? Who told you?"

"Didn't your dad, Chief Parker, tell you? I used to be an intelligence officer with the United States Navy. I have been poking around. It's something I'm good at."

"You talked to my dad about this? When? What the hell is going on here?"

"Yeah, I talked with your dad. So did Paul's dad, John Deland, an attorney here in Memphis who is making calls so we can make your life a living hell if you and your dad don't start playing ball."

"So my dad knows all about this?"

"Darn straight, Skippy, and it sounds like you need to talk to him yourself. Plus, you need to get your story straight, because you are hiding something, Eric. I have this pesky inner voice that tells me you are lying, and it's seldom wrong."

"What the hell…" He started the sentence with a look of genuine confusion on his face, but he trailed off. I saw fear behind his eyes; at least, it looked like fear. Either way, he looked like he was done talking.

"And you can tell him that the next time he sends six goons to run me out of town he needs to send some *real* men. I would have hardly broken a sweat taking them out. Wait, don't bother telling him, I am tired of you and your family, and I will tell him myself. Congratulations, you guys have managed to tick me off."

Eric was still standing there slack jawed as I left. It was time to meet with Chief Parker again.

* * *

It was true. I was mad.

Trained lied spotters can detect lying 90 percent of the time, and I had been trained by an intelligence agency. Eric was lying. No doubt about it.

But Eric's lying was only the tip of the iceberg. Recalling my interaction with the Chief and the untimely visit from the Emmettsville Goon Squad created an avalanche of anger that was enveloping me. Now my wrath was obscuring my focus. I was feeling out of control, which just caused me to declare a personal war on the Chief of Police of Emmettsville.

Maybe not my smartest move. Yet, transforming my anger into action always worked for me in the past and I did not feel like changing now. No, for better or worse, I was going to press forward. My search for answers was becoming a quest. It would take more than some insults or threats to turn me back now. In fact, if they continued down that path, I was likely to turn my quest into a crusade.

* * *

I was still contemplating my next step when I arrived at work. Only 15 minutes late for my seven o'clock start. A glance at the emergency room control board revealed that the morning activity was very light. Dr. Zimmerman was involved with a worker's comp patient removing a foreign object from the patient's hand. The nurses were busy, but the rest of the doctors were on standby. As I grabbed my scrubs, Evelyn wished me a good morning and said she would let Dr. Chen know he could leave.

"Good morning to you too, but let me find Dr. Chen. I bought him a treat," I said showing her a bag from The Mill Bakery.

She smiled as she spotted the bag. "Lemon poppy seed muffins? No wonder he always says yes when you ask him to cover for you."

I nodded and walked away smiling; Dr. Chen's love of lemon poppy seed muffins was nearly legendary at Memphis Memorial. The nurses even had a lemon poppy seed muffin cake made for his birthday one year.

I found Dr. Chen relaxing in an office with his feet up on the desk dictating some notes. I tossed the bag over the back of his head into his lap. He waited to finish dictating his last sentence before turning towards me. He took a loud appreciative whiff of the bag and then started speaking before I could thank him. "You're welcome, McCain, but I think you're going to wish you had taken the whole day off." Whatever he had to say must be bad since even the presence of his favorite treat failed to make a dent in the solemn look on his face.

"Should I even ask?"

"I guess that depends."

I said, "Depends on what?"

"Whether you want to hear the news from a friendly face or if you want to wait to be blindsided by Dr. Lowe, who, by the way, has been down here twice already this morning looking for you."

Dr. Lowe had avoided me since the encounter in his office following the incident with Tom Harty. If Dr. Lowe was looking for me, then I had a pretty good idea why, and although doctors get used to delivering bad news, I still thought I might make the situation easier for Dr. Chen. "Tom Harty, huh?"

"Yeah, a couple of hours ago. Pulmonary embolism is suspected."

"Thanks for telling me. And you are right; it is better hearing it from a friendly face than hearing it from Dr. Lowe. He is not exactly my favorite person."

Dr. Chen said, "Sorry. Zimmerman and I both agreed that we should forewarn you before Dr. Lowe got a hold of you." He gave a long pause before resuming. "Honestly, I was surprised Harty hung on as long as he did."

"Me too, but I never stopped pulling for him."

"You might have been the only one. I heard no one other than his mother came to see him, not even his wife."

Even though I knew he was an alcoholic and a potential child abuser, I still found Dr. Chen's last statement particularly disheartening and saddening that almost no one cared about the man during his final days. I asked Dr. Chen about Dr. Lowe, how did he look. Dr. Chen said he look harried. I advised Dr. Chen to leave before he got roped into working for me. He was smart enough to take my advice. He looked into the bag, smiled, wished me luck, and made a hasty exit.

I walked over to the ER control board. My name had not been added to the list of available doctors yet. A couple of nurses were milling around the counter attempting to look busy while the head nurse, Mrs. Bachman was shuffling some papers around. She looked up and discovered me studying the board.

I said, "I have relieved Dr. Chen, and I'm available when needed."

She replied, "I'm sure you are, but I have been advised to leave you out of the rotation this morning." She was very matter-of-fact.

"Dr. Lowe's orders?"

"Yes, Dr. McCain. He wants to talk to you."

"Thanks, I'll head up to his office then."

She said, "I don't think he's there, but you can try." Once again, her tone was as flat and sterile as the white on the walls.

"I realize it is a slow morning, but I already told Dr. Chen to go."

"That's not a problem, Dr. McCain. I have been advised to call in another doctor for today."

"Mrs. Bachman, which is it, morning or the whole day?"

"I'm sorry, I don't follow." She was maintaining the same aseptic tone.

Maintaining a similar flat tone, I said, "Mrs. Bachman, I am aware that Tom Harty passed away earlier this morning and Dr. Lowe wants to talk to me about that. What I am wondering is, could you please tell me if you have been advised to keep me off the schedule for the morning or the entire day?"

"The entire day." She remained monotone and flat, but my pesky inner voice told me that she had enjoyed the exchange.

"Well, thanks for telling me before I changed into my scrubs. Have a nice day, Mrs. Bachman."

I left without giving her any chance to respond and headed up to Dr. Lowe's office. His secretary informed me he was in a meeting elsewhere and I was to wait for his return. She had no idea when he was going to return. She could not even narrow it down to the morning or the afternoon. She was very polite and apologetic that she could not be more helpful.

"Ma'am, how Dr. Lowe found a gem like you to work for him is beyond me. I know I should probably sit here and wait while hoping some of your precious attitude would rub off on me, but I'm going to go home instead. When Dr. Lowe arrives, he can page me. Oh, and don't worry, I will tell him that you asked me to stay. I wouldn't want any trouble to fall on you for my indiscretion." I gave her a wink on the last word, which resulted in a smile.

* * *

Tom Harty's death hit me pretty hard once I got clear of the hospital. After remaining comatose following the surgery to relieve the pressure from around his brain, his prognosis was poor at best; bleak was probably a better word, but doctors don't use the word bleak in their medical charts. When he stabilized, deep down in my gut, I knew his chances were probably less than 5 or 10 percent that he would ever wake up from the coma and the odds were even less that he would ever function fully like before; however, I never wrote him off. Sure, part of my concern was selfish. I mean who wants to hear that they caused someone's death. Ultimately, an avoidable early death just seemed wasteful.

Feeling the need to blow off some steam physically, I walked back to my apartment for a workout. I ignored the blinking light on the answering machine until after my workout; however, it was good news, my Mercedes was finished and ready for delivery. My pager went off while I was waiting for them to deliver the car. I did not respond. It was the hospital, and I was not going to let it interrupt my happiness as I waited. Besides, I was enjoying the feeling of insubordination.

When the car arrived, I was tempted to let Dr. Lowe wait even longer since the car looked great and the new motor I had installed purred like a kitten, a 322 horsepower kitten. A lonely, winding road across the river in Arkansas was calling my name, begging me to conquer its curves with my new toy; however, I had made Dr. Lowe wait long enough.

* * *

Dr. Lowe's secretary gave me a quick double-take as she noticed my casual attire, jeans and a tee shirt, and then waved me into his office as soon as I arrived. Dr. Lowe was sitting at his desk waiting for me with an indignant look on his face. He motioned for me to sit using a small dismissive backhanded gesture that immediately irritated me.

"No thanks, Dr. Lowe, I think I will stand."

"I would prefer that you sit."

"Pardon me, sir, but after our last meeting, I'm not overly concerned with your preferences."

"Nor are you particularly concerned with your attire, Dr. McCain. You're starting off this meeting on a bad foot."

"I've already been informed by Mrs. Bachman that I have the day off. I came as I was when you paged me. I keep an extra sport coat in my locker downstairs, would you like me to get it?"

He dismissed my question with a slight shrug of his shoulders and a nearly imperceptible flippant nod of his head. "Mrs. Jones asked you to wait for my return. Were my orders not clear enough?"

"Sir, we both know I got your message and that I chose to leave. Surely, you didn't think I was going to wait around with nothing to do for an indefinite amount of time. You paged me, and I am here. That's good enough."

"I don't like your tone this morning."

"Dr. Lowe, what do you say we just get to the brass tacks here? Tom Harty has died, and you want to talk about it. Good, let's do that, but I will start. In the process of saving lives, I hit a man who died. While I don't feel responsible or guilty, I do find the whole thing unsettling. It feels kind of like losing a patient; it's not your fault, but you still don't feel good about it. You know that feeling, right? So, please keep the condescension level to a bare minimum today. Better yet, try not to go there at all."

"Dr. McCain, I'm not sure how to proceed. Sit, please."

He said please, but he did not mean it. He was still jockeying for control. Well, he could stick it where the sun doesn't shine. I remained standing.

"Sir, since you seem more interested in a power struggle than with the discussion at hand, let me help you out here. You're the boss. I'm the guy who has to do what you say, but I'm also the guy that will not be talked down to. I don't need this job that much. You took me off the schedule today. Why?"

Up until that moment, Dr. Lowe had been sitting behind his desk trying to look imposing. The aggressive body language was replaced by a scowl while he leaned back in his chair, arms crossed in front of him. Unhappy and defensive was better than aggressive from my point of view.

Dr. Lowe said, "I didn't want you on the schedule until I had talked with our attorneys to discuss liability issues."

"You guys have had two weeks to discuss potential liability. Personally, I don't understand why there would be liability issues, but then I don't have to think about things like that in my position. So what did you find out?"

"There are currently no criminal charges against you or this hospital, and all three attorneys doubt that any criminal charges will be brought. Civil charges seem to be a possibility. With the right attorney, the Harty family might be inclined to try their chances in that arena. The attorneys all agree that the opposing side would lose, although it might be cheaper to settle if that were to happen. They are more worried about image issues and wanted to know if we would have your cooperation if we needed to launch an aggressive anti-smear campaign."

"Your problem is my problem, Dr. Lowe, so sure."

"I'm happy to hear that."

"I'm happy to help. Since we are both happy, may I ask if the hospital board feels the same as the attorneys?"

"I should find out this afternoon, but I expect them to agree with the attorneys."

"So, am I in the rotation tomorrow?"

"Let's assume yes, Dr. McCain, unless you hear from me otherwise."

"Good. Before I go, is everyone still worried about my office building?"

Dr. Lowe said, "We will be talking about that this afternoon, I'm sure. I will let you know."

"FYI, my plans for the office building that I'm restoring are the same as for the other one I own. You were aware that I own two buildings, weren't you?"

"No, I wasn't aware of a second building."

"Do you know where Daddyo's Music is located?"

Dr. Lowe replied, "Sure."

"That's my building. I live upstairs and rent out the bottom. My plans for the new building are to do the same: office space on the bottom and up-scale apartments for rent on the top. Hopefully, that will resolve any issues you and the board have about me opening up my own clinic."

"Thank you very much, Dr. McCain. I'm sure the board will appreciate the new information."

Now that the meeting was over, I decided to sit, reclining back in the chair with my hands interlocked behind my head. "So, I have a day off then?"

"Yes, I guess you do."

Quickly standing, I said, "I won't take up any more of your time, Dr. Lowe. All in all, I'm going to turn lemons into lemonade. I have someone I would like to visit today anyway, and I have a beautiful red Mercedes convertible outside that is just begging me to take it for a spin."

"Oh, I didn't know you drove. The word around the hospital is that no one has ever seen you drive a car."

"There is more to me than meets the eye, Dr. Lowe. I own three cars; the newest addition is a 1992 Mercedes 500SL convertible parked outside."

"You're making me think we pay our doctors too much," he said with a smirk.

"Why, Dr. Lowe, I think you are teasing me. Don't worry; I got it for a steal since it was a bank repo with a blown motor and a slashed up interior. I know a guy that can keep an eye out for great deals like that if you are interested."

Dr. Lowe said, "Thanks for the offer, but I'm taken care of in the car department."

Keeping Dr. Lowe on a short leash seemed to be the best way to get through a discussion with him; it worked today. Maybe a visit with Chief Parker would go better the second time as well with the same approach.

One could hope.

CHAPTER 14

Maybe it was the prospect of driving the Mercedes with the top down on a beautiful August afternoon, or maybe I was looking forward to my unscheduled appointment with Chief Parker, either way, I could feel myself smiling during the drive to Emmettsville. Chief Parker had got a pass on our first meeting; he was not going to be given the same consideration the second time around. My plan was simple. I was going to tell him to start investigating or else. I was still unclear myself on what the "or else" entailed. I figured it would come to me.

My heart was racing slightly as I pulled up to the police station. Facing off with Dr. Lowe was one thing, but facing off with the Chief of Police in a small rural town in Tennessee was more than a little nerve racking. Furthermore, if he was involved with organized crime, then that complicated matters even more. Fortunately, my undercover work in the Navy had led to the arrest of several high-ranking officers, men who seemed infinitely more dangerous than a small town chief with a radiant smile. They were able to send trained military personnel after me, not six idiot civilians. This gave me a small boost of confidence; however, in the end, as I envisioned those six rednecks insulting my best friend, it was my rage that impelled me to walk into that police station.

Two uniformed officers were talking to each other near the front desk as I entered. Both turned towards me as I approached; however, one retreated to his desk after telling the other officer he would talk to him later. I was greeted warmly and informed that Chief Parker was not in the office.

I said, "When do you expect him back?"

"Not sure exactly. I think he's taking a late lunch."

"Officer Dunbar," I said while pointing to his name tag, "We reported a man named Paul Deland missing Saturday night. Can you tell me if the officers were asked to continue looking for Paul yesterday or today?"

His face turned a little white as I asked the question. "You'll have to talk to the Chief on that one."

Just as I had expected, Chief Parker called off the search. What a bastard.

"Late lunch, huh? I'll tell you what. I'll be back in an hour if I don't find him before that."

In the end, it took approximately 15 minutes of driving to find Chief Parker. Officer Dunbar had been honest; the Chief was having a late lunch. He was at Ray's Diner with another officer. I hoped it was merely a coincidence that I found him at Ray's. I did not want to think that Ray had a hand in what happened outside his diner yesterday. The diner looked relatively empty. Chief Parker was sitting at the lunch counter with the other officer while Ray was behind the counter wiping things down. I had never worked in a restaurant, but I had eaten in one four to five times a week for the last four years, and one thing you can count on: there is always someone wiping something down somewhere.

Ray spotted me immediately, his face lighting up as he recognized me. "Doctor, how are you? I know you liked the meatloaf, but I didn't expect to see you again so soon."

"Hello, Ray. I didn't expect to be back so soon either. Could I trouble you for a steak sandwich, medium, no fries? Vegetables, or slaw instead, please. And an iced tea the way I like it."

"Sure, coming right up."

The other officer had seen me come in but did not recognize me, and the Chief, whose back was to the front door, had not turned around yet.

I said, "By the way, I will be eating with Chief Parker."

The Chief turned after hearing his name, his toothy grin in full force. The grin quickly diminished as he realized who was addressing him. "Dr. McCain, you're here to see me?"

"Yes, I am. And it's not exactly a social call. So, Chief Parker, would you like to talk now, or would you like to talk in your office?"

He turned to the other officer and asked him to excuse himself. Without waiting for him to start asking questions, I said, "I told you I used to be a Navy investigator. Well, I've been investigating. Didn't take much, yet I know you are my suspect's father, I know your town is full of liars, and I know it's full of racists that are not particularly bright. Oh, and Jackie's last name is Geddes. How am I doing so far?"

The smile was completely gone, a blank stare looking back at me, a bona fide deer in headlights look on his face. Ray brought me a half sweet, half unsweetened tea. The Chief waited until Ray returned to the kitchen before speaking. "Your suspect?"

"Please don't do this, Chief, it's beneath my intelligence, and it should be beneath yours as well. You know that I'm looking at Eric *Parker*, not Harker, as a person of interest. We both know you purposefully withheld your name on our last meeting. You wanted to play your cards close to the chest, I got that, but that ship done sailed. You're busted. Now, I want to know what you've done so far in looking for Paul Deland."

"My officers have been given details of his appearance and the make and model of his car along with his plate number. They've been advised to keep an eye out for him."

"In other words, no change in the status quo since Saturday night. Keep your eyes open is your whole strategy. No investigation, no conversation with your son, or Ms. Geddes, or anyone else in the bar that night."

The deer in head lights look was replaced with a scornful look on his face. "I don't answer to you, Dr. McCain. You said yourself there is no evidence of any foul play. Just a lost wallet, and the fact that my son Eric gave Mr. Deland a little push in the bar earlier. Well, I don't know how they do things where you come from, but a little push in the bar for flirting with your girl is not unlawful."

"Are your law books missing a few pages?"

"What are you talking about, Dr. McCain?"

"Officer Willis didn't know how to handle a missing person's report, and you don't know the technical definition of assault or battery. Because your son is technically guilty of both."

"Not the way you described it to Officer Willis."

"Exactly the way I described it. Assault requires an overt or direct act that would put a reasonable person in fear for their safety, and physical contact is not necessary. Come on; you know this. Oh, and Eric slapped Paul's hand so the requirements for battery could also be established, but I did not come here to argue legal technicalities with you, Chief."

"Then please enlighten me as to why you did come here, Dr. McCain."

"To inform you that I'm coming after you and your son, plain and simple."

"What exactly do you mean by that? Is that meant as a threat?"

"I know this sounds horribly cliché, but it's no threat; it's a promise. Your son lied to me when I talked to him this morning. Something happened in that parking lot that night that he doesn't want to talk about. I'm going to find out what, and if he has harmed Paul in any way, then his father and I will make sure he goes down. You're not going to investigate, so I will."

"You talked to him…where? When?"

"This morning outside Cornerstone. So, I know you two haven't talked yet. And he made the same mistake you made yesterday."

"What's that, Dr. McCain?"

"He made me mad!"

He paused to ponder my proclamation, a puzzled expression on his face. "Pardon me, Dr. McCain. I thought our conversation yesterday was cordial."

"The conversation was cordial, I guess. However, you weren't truthful. Then you sent six men to run us out of town yesterday. Outside of this very restaurant. So now our relationship is no longer cordial. It is adversarial."

"What the hell are you talking about?"

"Chief Parker, are you trying to insult my intelligence again? Word of warning, the next time you send some guys to harass me, send the ambulance to clean up the mess."

Chief Parker's mouth was open in a classic look of disbelief, his head shaking side to side slowly. "Doctor, I have no idea what you are talking about."

"You are good; I will give you that. You should give your son some lessons on lying; he stinks at it. But then you are an elected official, which makes you a politician, so you've had more experience."

The transformation from disbelief to shock on his face was effortless and instantaneous. He looked surprised and was at a temporary loss for words. "Doctor, not only do I *not* know what you are talking about, I don't appreciate you slandering my honor."

"You're good, but the Chief doth protest too much, methinks. I don't see any honor about you, just a title, and some great acting on your part. I could almost believe you if I didn't already know you are full of crap."

Chief Parker's squinted eyes and furrowed brow were having no effect on me as I stood to face him with my best "I'm not impressed" look on my face. The image of the six men was still burnt in my mind, and I knew I was talking to the man who sent them. His attempt at intimidating me had no effect.

"Seriously, Chief, a stare down. Not going to work on me. I'm too mad."

Chief Parker said, "That makes two of us."

He abruptly stopped as Ray brought me my food and another tea. The tension in the room was thick, which seemed obvious to Ray who quickly walked away. The other officer must have sensed it as well since he had not taken his attention off us since the Chief excused him.

Chief Parker resumed, "You seem to be forgetting your place, Doctor. I'm the Chief of Police here. You are nothing, a nobody in this town. A civilian."

"To be accurate, I'm a veteran, but that's another argument. For now, you are the inept police chief who will not do his job, and I'm the guy who is going to see that it gets done anyway. Just think of me as Emmettsville Internal Affairs, and I have my eyes on you. My advice for you: get busy working the case, or stay out of my way."

"I'm not going to sit through any more of this. You watch yourself. My officers will be advised to watch for you. Step out of line, and we will arrest you. Good day, Doctor."

"If they show the same ineptness watching for me as they have looking for Paul, I shouldn't have too much to worry about. But, thanks for the warning, and good day to you too, Chief Parker." I placed extra emphasis on the "P."

* * *

One particular style of martial arts that I studied when I was younger focused on using your opponent's energy against him by redirecting their energy into a different direction, thus leaving them vulnerable to counter-attack. I did not actively practice the art any longer due to its heavy emphasis on defense. I preferred to focus on offensive styles and ones that duplicated real-life situations. However, the lead instructor received both a Christmas card and a birthday card from me every year because he taught me something more valuable; he was the man who taught me to redirect my anger, to channel my anger into something positive. That man, Brent Johnson, might have indirectly saved my life more than once. He surely changed my life.

Right then, while finishing my coleslaw, I realized that my anger over what had transpired yesterday had clouded my judgment, leading me to wage a private war with the chief of police and his son before I had done my research. All I knew about Chief Parker was what Ellie had told me, which was second-hand information since she did not live here anymore. I was not approaching this with the same methodical, logical manner that I had employed when I worked for NIS.

I needed to slow down and gather more information, to get my anger under control, yet the fact that Paul was still missing was driving me forward. My instincts, my inner voice, kept pushing me to move faster, telling me that time was of the essence. It was a feeling that I could not shake.

I needed more information on Chief Parker, preferably from someone who knew him well. Someone came to mind, someone who I was sure would help; however, it involved crossing a line that might cause problems with Ellie. She was already concerned, and when she found out that I had threatened Chief Parker matters were only going to get worse. Despite my apprehension, my inner voice kept reminding me of the potential time element, pushing me to move forward.

* * *

Lloyd Carmichael, Ellie's father, was an interesting man. Much like my father, he had built a company from the ground up. Lloyd's specialty was building aluminum bass boats. His was not a high volume business; he made his profits by making arguably the highest quality aluminum boats on the market. He no longer owned the company, which he sold for a tidy profit a few years ago when he realized neither of his girls was interested in taking over the family business. The company was smart enough to keep him on as a technical consultant. He once told me he did not need the money, but 53 was too early to retire completely.

Ellie's parents still lived in her childhood home located on the edge of town, a spacious two-story brick farmhouse that was probably built at the turn of the century, yet it looked extremely well kept. If I had been even half a minute later, I would have missed Lloyd altogether. Instead, I saw his truck pulling out of the driveway towing an aluminum bass boat, probably on his way to go fishing. My attempt at waving him down failed so I pulled in behind him, hoping the lake he planned to fish was not too far away.

Twenty minutes later he turned at a sign indicating a boat ramp up ahead. I could not see the lake yet, but already I could smell the water, hidden somewhere in the thickly forested area. I followed him all the way to the boat ramp, getting out of my vehicle when he stopped to prepare his boat for the water.

He did a double-take as he realized I was the one who had been following him, a huge smile spreading across his already friendly looking face. "L.T., I had no idea that was you behind me all that time. Why didn't you flag me down or something?"

"There weren't any good passing zones on that winding road, Mr. Carmichael. And I figured a bunch of honking and high beam flashing would have just made me look like a madman."

"L.T., if I don't have to call you doctor, then you don't have to call me mister. I told you before; you can call me Lloyd." He was unhooking all kinds of clamp and straps that were holding the boat to the trailer. "So what brings you all the way out here?"

"I need to ask you something."

A mischievous grin spread across his face. "You drove out here to ask me something, huh? I was hoping you might be the one doing that someday."

A nervous lump formed in my throat as I realized what he was hinting at. "Mr. Carmichael, Lloyd. I wish I were driving out here to ask you that, but not today I'm afraid. Actually, I need to ask you some stuff about Chief Parker."

"Oh."

"Did Ellie tell you a friend of mine has a son that went missing in Emmettsville on Saturday night?"

"She did."

"Did she also tell you I suspect that Eric Parker might be involved?"

"She did."

"So can you help me?"

"You feel like going for a boat ride, L.T.?"

"Sure."

"Tell me what you know and what you think, and I will see if I can answer your questions. I'm not making any promises, but I'll do what I can to help."

"Fair enough, sir."

I helped him with the boat the best I could, which meant I pulled his truck away from the boat ramp and parked it after he backed the boat trailer up to the water. I knew very little about boats. Which also meant I was surprised how fast they could go, and how unstable they felt at full throttle and full trim, as he called it. After about five minutes, he slowed down, pulled over into a quiet, secluded cove, and got out his fishing pole. "Alright, tell me what you know."

Which I did. Lloyd kept casting and re-casting out some fishing lure while I talked; I knew even less about fishing than I did about boats. Once I finished telling him everything that happened on Saturday and Sunday, including the six men that tried to run us out of town, he asked me to tell him what I speculated. I started at the beginning, which meant I told him about John receiving demands to pay Paul's gambling debts and I concluded with my assumption that Chief Parker sent his goons over to scare us out of town. During that time, Lloyd stopped fishing and stared at me while sitting on his fishing chair, or stool, or whatever they call it.

He was sitting forward, leaning on his elbows shaking his head slowly left and right in disbelief. "Wow. I don't know what to say."

"I understand Chief Parker is a friend, but I'm telling you the truth. No one else knew Virgil's name except the Chief."

"Didn't you give Officer Willis a list of names?"

"Okay, so Officer Willis knew everyone's name as well. But he wasn't even there on Sunday when we met the Chief, so he wouldn't have known to tell any of those local yokels about him."

Lloyd was scratching his chin, obviously thinking how to proceed. He did not look like he was preparing to lie; he looked as if he were trying to be cautious. "Chief Parker is what I would call a friendly acquaintance, not a close friend. Being on the City Council in the past, I have worked with him, and the relationship has always been friendly. But we've never been fishing together, if you know what I mean."

"I do. It must be like golf for doctors."

"Exactly. That being said, I still don't like to think of him being corrupt. It just doesn't fit, although as much as I hate to admit it, your take on the story does make the most sense. So what do you think I can do to help?"

Somehow being in that boat, asking my girlfriend's father questions about a friend, even if just an acquaintance seemed wrong. I went for the easy solution to a problem, not thinking how Ellie might feel about me being there. I decided to temper my questions to information that anyone in the town might know.

"Just tell me what you know about him and Eric. Family history, hobbies, friends, anything suspicious, such as living beyond their means. I don't know what I'm looking for other than information."

Lloyd half-heartedly cast his fishing lure back into the water and started reeling it in. Suddenly, he jerked the pole back and started reeling faster while the pole bowed. I was intrigued by all the action. There was a brief, frenzied struggle followed by a net and a fish. Lloyd twisted the hooks out the fish's mouth and promptly released it back into the water. We were in a bass boat, so I assumed it must have been a bass.

Lloyd said, "Sorry for the interruption. I had a pole in my hand; it was a force of habit."

"Don't apologize. I'm the one intruding; besides I've never been fishing in my life, and that looked like fun."

"A doctor that doesn't play golf. A man who has never been fishing. You probably don't hunt either. What do you do for fun? No, wait, don't answer that; you are dating my daughter."

I felt myself blush slightly at his inference, especially given my encounter with Ellie in the shower yesterday.

Lloyd started talking after that, telling me first what he knew about Eric. Other than providing some examples of violent behavior in the past, he did not tell me anything I had not already heard before. I did notice a pattern in the stories, though. In each of the three episodes Lloyd described, Eric never thrashed any of his victims excessively; the fights were over after a few hits, thus showing Eric demonstrated restraint.

Lloyd was able to fill in more detail on Chief Sam Parker, the chief of police for over 16 years. He was well liked in the community. He even ran unopposed in the last two elections. He married young and raised three kids, two daughters who married and moved up towards Nashville, and Eric. Money had never been an issue for the family since his wife took over her father's small local Ford dealership. There was nothing extravagant about his lifestyle; in fact, most guessed they lived below their means. Sam's one luxury was a nice hunting cabin a few miles out of town with a beautiful view of the lake behind him and about 100 acres of timbered hunting land.

"Sound's expensive," I said.

"Nothing fishy there. He inherited the land from his father, and the cabin is a log cabin that he and some friends built by hand. I'm telling you; he is a good, clean Southern Baptist man with a good work ethic and a reputation for fairness. His son is his only black eye, and most of the town is willing to overlook Eric's indiscretions."

"It doesn't make sense, Lloyd. If he is a good, honest, ethical chief, then why would he send those guys after us before he had even bothered talking to Eric unless he was hiding something personal himself? That's the part I keep getting stuck at it."

You are sure he hadn't talked to Eric yet."

"I'm sure. When I confronted Eric earlier today, he had no idea that his dad knew anything about Saturday night. Are you thinking that Eric sent them?"

"It would make more sense to me if he did. They are more his age, plus the big guy in the overalls sounds like the Carson boy, who also played high school football around here. Maybe he knows Eric."

"Maybe. But what about the organized crime element? You guys got any of that around here?"

"I wouldn't even know what that looks like."

"Drugs, gambling, prostitution, illegal liquor distribution, pill mills."

"L.T., if we have that kind of stuff around here, then I guess I'm either too old or too naive to know about it. I wouldn't know what a prostitute looks like if one bit me on the butt, and I have no idea what a pill mill is. If there was anything like that in this town, I'm sure it would get discussed at city council meetings, but it never comes up."

"So, small-scale infrastructure at best, nothing pervasive into the community. Good."

He was rubbing the bridge of his nose with both hands, digesting everything I had told him. The thought of rubbing fishy hands on my face disgusted me, but then I didn't make my living selling fishing boats, so I imagined fish just smelled like money to him. Although it was probably only a minute, it seemed longer before he spoke again. "Was anything I told you helpful at all?"

"Information is always helpful. Now I just need time to process it all, and maybe go back to town and poke around a little more. Maybe someone else will say something that when combined with what I learned here will give me that light bulb moment."

* * *

Lloyd finished our afternoon by allowing me to drive his boat and showing me all the different types of gadgetry on board: depth finders, trolling motors, live fish wells. I could hear the pride in his voice as he explained what everything did and how he helped design what he felt was the best overall bass boat on the market. After the boating experience, I had dinner with Lloyd and his wonderful wife, Virginia, which was nice even though I spent much of my time answering questions about my past. I think they were unintentionally vetting me. Lloyd was impressed to discover my father was Marcus McCain, partially because of his time in the NFL, but mostly because of Borders Trucking. They were sad for my loss, and both gave me a scrutinizing look when I revealed that my relationship with my mother was so dysfunctional. Lloyd avoided any mention of problems with Eric and Sam Parker in front of Virginia, so I just followed his lead.

After dinner, I took Lloyd for a ride in the Mercedes. He questioned my choice of driving an $80,000 sports car until I told him about the bank repossession and blown motor. I also reminded him that he made his living building expensive bass boats. He feigned surprise on that observation. Nearly 30 minutes later, we pulled into his driveway again.

"L.T., can I ask you a question now?"

"Sure."

"Why are you doing all this? I mean most guys would just tell the police what they know and see if the system figures it out."

"You are my girlfriend's father; that's for sure."

"How so?"

"She asked me a similar question. To answer your question, it's kind of like it happened on my watch. Plus, the system in this county seems broken, so who else is going to do it?"

"So you feel obligated?"

"Yeah, I guess so. I mean I know Paul's disappearance is not my fault. It's just that I have experience from the Navy at handling corrupt officials and officers and such, so it just feels like I have to."

"Sounds like there is a story there."

"One heck of a story, all classified, but one heck of a story."

Lloyd said, "So where to now?"

"I don't know. Town. I will figure it out."

"Good luck."

CHAPTER 15

Falco's was my first destination. It made no sense to start there since Mason was not exactly cooperative; however, I did not know the town well enough yet to come up with any other ideas. I quickly discovered nothing much had changed at Falco's. Before I made it halfway to the bar, Mason started shooing me away.

"You are not welcome here. Get out now!" Nearly every head in the bar turned to stare at me.

"I didn't come here to cause trouble, Mason."

"I don't care why you came here, just get out. You caused enough trouble here already."

"I caused trouble. I caused trouble! I asked you some questions while looking for a missing friend; that's all I did, you friggin' nitwit. Oh, and I prevented a fight in your bar. Don't tell me I caused you any trouble. I'm not in the mood for you today, Mason, so lay off me before you make me angry."

"Shit man, you just don't know when to stop, do you?"

"I know exactly when to stop."

"Then leave, man. No one wants you here."

"Therein lies our problem, Mason. You think I should stop just because you want me to. I'm not about to stop just because a bunch of a-holes in this town are making things difficult for me. The proper time to stop is when I find my friend. Capiche?"

"You calling me an asshole?"

"Only if the shoe fits, Mason. You could change all that. You could hear me out."

"Damn it, man, just tell me why you are here and be on your way. But make it quick."

Mason was less of a coward than I had previously imagined, which made me realize how much he must fear Eric Parker. Maybe the two of them had actually in the past.

"I'm thirsty. Can I have an ice tea, please?" It was all I could think of at the time. My whole investigative experience consisted of one case, a year and a half undercover. Sure, the outcome had been successful, but it relied on subterfuge, and now I had no idea how to ask direct questions, cop questions.

"You came in here for tea. Sure, I'll get you some tea. I'll even give it to you if you leave immediately after you're finished."

"Thanks, but I will pay for it."

Mason said, "So you're planning on staying." He did not look pleased with that realization as he served me my tea.

"You want an honest answer, Mason?"

"You don't know me well enough to feel the need to be honest with me, so do whatever you want mist..."

At least he was careful with the "mister" thing this time. Maybe he was softening up a little.

"Mason, despite your animosity towards me, I'm going to be honest with you; I'm not entirely sure what I am planning on doing. My friend is still missing. Your local small town hero, Eric Parker, had something to do with it or knows something about it. And your chief is doing nothing. Did he even come out here and ask any questions?"

"Not that I owe you an answer, but he was out here about an hour ago."

"Really?"

"Yep."

I said, "Do you care to elaborate?"

"If it will get you out of here, then sure."

"You got a deal, Mason."

"It was a simple meeting. He was asking me questions about that night. It seems someone called the police station earlier today and told him that they saw Eric hitting someone in the parking lot Saturday night. I guess he hit the guy hard enough that he went down holding his stomach."

"Really?"

"No shit. Seems the fella who made the call drove off when he saw Eric looking at him. He was too scared to call until today. Chief Parker wanted to know if I saw or heard anything about what happened in the parking lot. He already knew what happened in the bar that night from you and your friends."

"Did you see or hear anything?"

"Nope."

I said, "Well, a deal is a deal. You kept up your side of the bargain, so I will keep up mine and get out of here. Good luck with everything, Mason, and thanks for the tea."

"I don't want your luck; I just want your departure. Since you kept your word, let me give you a word of advice, Yankee. Let the Chief handle things. You're only going to get yourself in hot water if you keep poking around."

"Thanks. The Chief sort of gave me the same advice," I said while moving away from the bar. "By the way, do you know what time Ray's diner closes?"

Mason said, "Nine, I think. Why?"

"Thanks." I did not feel like answering him.

My plan was to apologize to Ray for meeting with the Chief in his diner earlier, and then look for another bar and see if any ideas came to me. I made it to the diner a few minutes before he closed. Ray was a friendly, good-spirited man with a genuine affection for people. If my presence was unwelcome, he did an excellent job hiding it from me while assuring me that the apology was not necessary. I stayed long enough to finish another ice tea; he remembered the way I liked it.

As I drove around town looking for another bar, a police cruiser moving in the opposite direction slowed down as it passed, but did not turn around. Maybe he was just admiring the red convertible. A few minutes later I found a small local bar with some cars and Harleys parked out front. Not the kind of place that would serve me tea, yet it looked like the right kind of place to start asking questions. Now I just needed a plan. Nothing came to mind, so I settled on simply walking in and feeling the place out.

I was careless. My instincts were rusty, and my inner voice was spending more time complaining than reminding me that I still needed to be cautious, which is why the hard shove from behind as I walked towards the bar caught me completely off guard. Only my innate sense of balance kept me from falling as my feet tripped over the curb in front of me. Whoever pushed me had timed the push perfectly. Someone was going to wish he had not done that.

Despite my best efforts, I collided with the brick wall in front of me, my wrist feeling a twinge of pain as my outstretched arm prevented me from hitting my head and shoulders on the wall. Immediately, I turned to see Eric, Fireplug, and a tall, lanky man I had not seen before staring at me. The tall man was not skinny; he was wiry with dirty hands and heavily muscled, sinewy forearms. Fireplug had a satisfied smirk on his face, one that was going to disappear soon when I smashed his face with my elbow.

"Seriously, not you again," I said looking directly at Fireplug.

Fireplug said, "Yankee, I told you not to come back here."

Smiling smugly, I said, "And I told you to bring more guys, not less. So it appears neither of us was paying too much attention to what the other one said."

He replied, "The three of us will have no problem takin' care of you."

"You're an optimist. I admire that in a person."

The tall, lanky guy said, "So where's your nigger friend? I was really hoping we'd have a whack at him."

My blood pressure must have immediately shot up as the adrenaline began its familiar course through my body. The fight or flight nervous system was in full force, and their racist comments were causing me to lean more towards fight than flight. I could hear Virgil's voice reminding me that beating such mindless idiots would not solve anything. I disagreed.

I said, "So this is your idea of a parade, huh, Fireplug?"

He replied, "What did you call me?"

"Fireplug."

"What the hell is that supposed to mean?"

"You remind me of a fire hydrant. I don't know your name, so I gave you a nickname."

"Well, we know your name, but we're gonna call you a nigger-lovin' Yankee just the same."

"Always with the racial slurs. Why not just stay focused on me. Let's face it; your beef is with me, not Virgil."

"But I so enjoy gettin' your goat, Yankee. You should see your face every time someone says 'nigger.' It looks like someone just slapped your momma."

Fireplug was smarter than I thought. He had observed that racial slurs were a trigger and he was using that trigger to instigate a fight. I was not going to give him the satisfaction.

Fireplug continued, "You should know your little window trick isn't gonna work this time. That was pretty clever what you did yesterday, but there ain't anybody in the bar behind you that would give a shit if we beat up a damn Yankee."

"Good to know," I said.

Fireplug said, "Last warning. Go home!"

All three of them moved in closer after Fireplug yelled at me. Virgil was right about fighting them; it would not do any good. However, my mind was made up. Virgil and John were not going to get in my way this time. No worries or inhibitions to get in my way either. I was not going to leave.

"No."

"Did you just tell us no?"

"Yes, I told you no."

The tall, lanky guy said, "We aren't dicking around here. You need to leave!"

"No," I replied as calmly as I could muster, which was not an easy task as I was still infuriated with him for his earlier racial insults towards my best friend.

Fireplug said, "What the hell do you mean by no?"

"I am declining to acquiesce to your demands. You should be familiar with the word. Ugly bugger like you probably hears it every time you ask out a pretty girl."

"You tryin' to piss me off?"

"Yes."

"What?"

"You seem to be having trouble keeping up, which is a shame since I am using *really* short sentences. Yes, I am trying to tick you off. No, I will not leave town."

I could not help myself. I was trying to make them mad. I was still not sure if they were planning on actually attacking me, but I wanted them mad if they did. Three mad amateurs. It hardly seemed fair.

And it was obvious these guys were total amateurs. They were making mistake after mistake. They should have attacked immediately after I tripped over the curb. They should have fanned out to flank me and force me to defend myself from multiple angles, yet they were standing next to each other. Finally, none of them were in a fighting stance. Eric was standing with his hands on his hips sticking his chest out in an attempt to intimidate me with his size and the lanky guy was doing some lame scare tactic of pounding his fist into the palm of his other hand repeatedly.

Fireplug said, “Are you tryin’ to be funny?”

“No, I’m not trying to be funny; it just comes naturally. I can’t help it. I am a funny guy. Everyone says so.”

“We’re fixin’ to kick the shit out of you, Yankee!”

I starting laughing, a big haughty, condescending laugh. “Now you are being funny. I’m glad to see you getting into the spirit of things, but we still haven’t heard from Eric or Dwayne here.”

The lanky guy stopped pounding his fist and said, “Who you calling Dwayne?”

“I apologize if I got your name wrong. You just look like a Dwayne to me. Weird, huh?”

Eric said, “You talk too much, asshole!”

“You talk too little, Skippy.”

Eric said, “Keep calling us names, this is not going to end well for you.”

“I only reminded Fireplug that he is, in fact, ugly. I guess I did call you Skippy. Sorry about that, but it seems to fit. I didn’t call him anything yet, except Dwayne. Of course, maybe that is an insult in itself. I’m not sure since I never met anybody named Dwayne before, until now.”

Dwayne said, “Dwayne is a nigger name, you asshole.”

“I’m pretty sure it’s Irish in origin.”

“Well, my name is not Dwayne, dumbass.”

"Hey, I only said your name was Dwayne. You're the one that called yourself a brainless buttock."

As fun as it was, all the posturing was getting stale, and they seemed no closer to letting me leave or attacking me. Leaving was my first choice, yet beating the hell out of them was sounding better and better all the time.

I said, "Gentleman, what are we doing here?"

Fireplug answered, "Eric wants you to leave town and not come back, and you already know how I feel about you."

"I gathered that, but what is happening right now?"

The one I called Dwayne said, "He told you what's happening!"

"No, he talked about wants and feelings." All three were staring at me questioningly. "You know, Eric wants me to leave and apparently my presence has offended you on a deep emotional level. Since we are talking about wants and feelings, I have a few of my own. First, I want to know what the hell Eric did to Paul on Saturday night and why no one has seen or heard from him since. Second, I want to avoid a fight with you guys."

Dwayne said, "You scared?"

"No, not really. Just that if four guys our size get into a fight, someone is going to get hurt. There is no way around it. So, I feel it is my responsibility to tell you guys that I have a lot of experience, and I mean a lot. It was my job to arrest unruly Marines and sailors, even a few Navy SEALS when I was in the Navy, so I know how to handle myself, and I really don't want to hurt any of you. Or get hurt, in case I underestimated you guys. Guess it's all up to you gentlemen on how this turns out."

Three on one. Acceptable odds. Thinking about wants and feelings, I could not help thinking that I wanted to feel my fist in their faces; yet, my pragmatic side insisted that a strategic retreat still made the most sense. I was looking towards my car. Eric moved slightly to one side apparently signifying he was letting me leave. Fireplug made no change in his position.

Looking directly at Eric, I said, “Thank you.”

I stepped off the curb and headed towards my car. The one I called Dwayne moved towards me. “Where do you think you’re going?”

He reached out to grab me. I intercepted his outstretched arm, grabbed his wrist, and twisted it into a wrist lock that forced him to his knees. Grimacing in pain, he refused to ask or beg me to let go. Impressive, but stupid. I could have easily done major permanent damage to his wrist. Maybe he knew his friends would come to his aid. They did. Fireplug pushed Eric towards me, egging him forward while he hung back.

I yelled, “Stop. This is going to end...”

I was going to say “end poorly,” but my sentence was cut short. I let go of Dwayne’s wrist to deal with the 250-plus pound onrush known as Eric. Talking was over. Eric was taking the direct approach, semi-running at me with his head down preparing to tackle me. I let him get close before side stepping his advance. I pushed him over into Dwayne. The two of them got tangled up as Eric fell over him. I quickly turned to find Fireplug. He had moved his position until he was directly behind me, obviously planning on attacking me from behind while I was engaged with Eric.

I glared at him. Gestured with my fingers for him to come at me. He stayed put. “Pussy,” I said while walking back three steps until I could see everyone in my field of vision. Fireplug was a patient son-of-gun. He did not look angry. He looked amused. Satisfied even. This made me think I had been underestimating him.

Dwayne and Eric extricated themselves from each other. Dwayne was rubbing his sore wrist. Eric was dusting himself off. The idiots finally started to circle me, trying to flank me. I continued to back up into the middle of the road as I tried to keep all three men in sight simultaneously. I was cussing myself for not incapacitating Eric when I had the chance.

“You guys had enough yet?”

Fireplug said, “Wishin’ you had left town?”

"Not really, just trying to keep this friendly."

"Past that point, bitch."

At least he did not prefix it with "mister."

"So be it."

No turning back now I thought. Good. Now if only Hank and Aaron would show up, my day would be complete. With them now circling me, I needed a change of tactics. I needed to bait one of them to advance so I could take them out one at a time. Eric seemed like the easiest target; he demonstrated little self-control over his emotions.

"Eric," I said, "I found Jackie earlier this evening. She told me how disappointed she was that you interrupted her good time with Paul."

"You fucker!"

"No, I didn't, but I got the impression she was hoping Paul might."

It worked. Eric was mad. This made him stupid. Anger overruled caution as he advanced towards me. As soon as Eric was within striking distance, I lashed out with a quick left jab to the face followed by a hard right strike to his temple with my heel of my right hand, staggering him backward. He tripped over the same curb I had tripped over earlier. He was stunned. One down.

Dwayne lunged at me again, this time grabbing my wrist. I underestimated his grip strength. Simply pulling my wrist loose was not a quick enough option. I spun my forearm until his wrist became vulnerable for another wrist lock. He was a fast learner. He immediately dropped to one knee while twisting to minimize the pain of the tremendous two-handed wrist lock I had on him; however, he was right where I needed him. Letting go with one hand, I used the other to maintain his position while I viciously slammed my elbow into the side of his head. I swore I could hear the thud echo in the street. Dwayne fell to the street with another thud. Two down.

I took too much time setting Dwayne up with the wrist lock. I knew it. I felt it too as I received a hard hit to the back of my head. Spinning, I discovered Fireplug with his arm cocked back ready for a big swinging punch. He took too long. I was able to dodge the punch easily. Fireplug had not expected me to be so quick. His momentum spun him nearly completely around when he missed. I gave him a shove into the curb expecting him to trip, but he recovered remarkably well and got into a fighting stance. Fireplug had seen what I did to Eric and focused his efforts on preventing a strike to his head. I kicked him hard in the thigh. I could see in his eyes that he had not expected a kick.

Fireplug was forced to back up giving me a chance to quickly examine my surroundings. Dwayne appeared unconscious, and Eric was still on his butt looking stunned, leaving a one-on-one with Fireplug. Virgil had been wrong. He said it would not be worth it. So far it was worth it and then some.

Smiling ear to ear, I said, "You're screwed, douchebag. If you come over and let me knock you out, then it's over. Otherwise, I'm going to throw you through that window."

"Fuck off, Yankee."

"Have it your way."

He took a fighting stance as I advanced, this time watching my feet. Using that to my advantage, I shot a hard kick to his forward leg. It would sting, although that was not its purpose. Its true purpose was distraction. I faked another kick, which he easily averted, although his head was now unprotected. Quickly I stepped forward, closing the gap and then jabbed with my left hand causing him to stumble back and trip over the ever popular curb. An uppercut would have been awkward before given our considerable height difference, but not now.

My right hand connected with the bottom of his jaw in a brutal uppercut. The sound of his teeth slamming together brought a smile to my face. He might have gone down regardless; however, I allowed my forward momentum to shoulder check him into the wall behind him. His head slammed into the plate glass window, the same window I told him I was going to throw him through. *Oh well, not today, I guess.*

The one I called Dwayne was still lying right where I left him. Eric was back up and charging towards me for another try. Admirable, yet stupid, especially since he was using the same tackling approach that had already failed him once before. This time I allowed him to make contact with me. I braced for the contact and shifted my weight allowing me to stay on my feet as he wrapped his arms around my torso. His head was off to the right of my torso, up under my armpit.

I could not believe it was going to be so easy. I immediately circled my right arm around his head and under his neck. My left hand grabbed my right, and together I applied upward pressure. Eric was in a front naked choke, otherwise known as a guillotine choke hold. I could not afford the time it would take for tracheal compression to cut off flow to his lungs, so I shifted my grip slightly to provide a blood choke. Both carotid arteries were compressed, cutting off blood flow to the brain.

Panic immediately followed as Eric realized his predicament. He started clawing at my hands, a typical mistake, as it allowed me to move in closer to help provide the leverage necessary to complete the choke. Eric was strong, maybe stronger than me, but he had no training for these types of situations. He did not even think to simply turn his chin towards my ribs to prevent compression of the arteries on both sides.

He was the Chief's son, so I was trying hard not to put any obvious cuts or bruises on him, hence the reason I utilized the choke. However, it was a three-on-one fight. I would have to let go if one of the other two men attacked before Eric was unconscious. The one I called Dwayne was still not moving, and Fireplug was sitting on his ass in front of the window.

I continued the choke. Within 20 seconds, Eric became limp in my arms.

I had won.

* * *

As Eric went limp in my arms, an Emmettsville squad car screeched to a halt in the middle of the street. The officer immediately exited and went for his gun, removing it from his holster and pointing it at me in a squared off Isosceles shooting stance.

"On the ground, now!"

I yelled back, "Let me put Eric down first!"

"I said on the ground. NOW!"

"This is the Chief's son. If I drop him, then he is going to land on his face. Just wait, please."

One of the most common ways street fights end in death is from a person hitting his head when he is falling after being knocked out or choked out. I stood a good chance at facing battery charges; I did not want to face manslaughter charges.

"Make it quick!"

Eric was barely conscious as I lowered him to the ground while turning him face up.

"I said make it quick, asshole!"

"He's a big guy. I lowered him as fast as I could."

"Now, join him on the ground. Face down, arms up behind your head!"

Emmettsville had pissed me off for the last time. There was no way I was going face down in the street. I sat down on the curb and glared at the cop pointing his gun at my body.

"Are you hard of hearing, mother fucker? I said face down. Now! Now! NOW!"

Stupid civilian cop. We never used vulgar language like that while making an arrest in the Navy. It was like the entire Emmettsville police force got its procedures from watching too much television or movies.

"No. I won't budge from this spot without your permission, but I'm not going on my face for you."

"Don't argue with me."

"I'm not. I'm just refusing your request."

"That's not an option!"

"Officer, whatever your name is," I could not read the badge from that distance, "Three men attacked me, so I defended myself. I tried to do as little harm as possible. Either way, you have two unconscious men on your hands. I'm not a threat to you so why don't you spend your time calling an ambulance. Better yet, let me make sure they are breathing okay while you call an ambulance. You can keep the gun pointed at me if you like. And I would prefer you call in some backup."

The officer was one of those guys who would look like a cop even if he was out of uniform: the blocky, muscular frame, the short hair, the mustache, and that young cop cockiness. He ignored my request for an ambulance and remained where he was with his gun still fixed on me. "Don't tell me how to do my job! I don't need any backup to handle you."

"The backup is for me. I don't trust you."

Admiral Buie once told me that my instincts were so spot on most of the time it was scary, and right now I did not trust this police officer. My inner voice was telling me that his timing was too coincidental, pulling up at the exact moment that I had won the fight. I desperately wanted someone else to witness the unavoidable arrest. Another officer. An EMT. Anyone. The whole town could not be dirty. I got my wish; however, it came from the bar as several people came out to watch the spectacle outside. Curious onlookers, thank God.

"Officer, my name is Dr. L.T. McCain, and I'm an emergency room physician. Can I check on the guy in the street just to make sure he is okay until the ambulance gets here?"

"Mister, you are pushing your luck with me."

"Doctor," I corrected. "I can assure you it is not purposeful. Not that it changes anything, but I used to do what you are doing while I was in Navy. Just keep the gun on me while I check on him. You have an audience now, with lots of witnesses, and you know my name. I promise you; I'm not trying to pull any funny stuff."

The officer remained exactly as he had started, gun pointed at me in an aggressive stance.

"Scott, let him check on Tyler," said one of the male onlookers.

"Don't tell me how to do my job. And its Officer Crane, not Scott."

The same voice said, "Sorry, Officer Crane, it's just that I remember you from diaper days. Let him check Tyler, Officer Crane. And you should probably get the Chief over here. His idiot son finally started a fight he couldn't win."

Officer Crane motioned with his gun towards Tyler, the one I called Dwayne earlier. As I checked his vitals, Officer Crane leaned into his car and told the dispatcher to send over an ambulance and to get the Chief. Tyler regained consciousness as I was checking him. Breathing and pulse were normal for his condition, and his pupils were equal and reactive to light as I blocked light coming from the streetlight above. *Thank God.* I left the rest of the assessment for the EMT. I turned to attend to Eric, but he was sitting up with his back against the brick wall of the bar.

Officer Crane said, "If he's okay, then you need to lie face down and put your hands on the back of your head."

"Seriously?"

"Do I look serious?"

I knew the question was rhetorical, but I almost answered him regardless, telling him what I thought he looked like. Sometimes it is best to keep some thoughts to yourself.

The same male voice as before said, "Scott, I mean, Officer Crane, let him be. I saw the whole thing go down. He was defending himself. These three assholes attacked him. If you're going to cuff him, then you better get three more sets ready, Scott."

"Damn it, Charles, just because you're my dad's cousin don't mean you can tell me what to do! You," he said while pointing at me, "Sit over there on the curb while I sort this all out. Damn it." He was mumbling away, obviously annoyed.

I sat and waited. Officer Crane holstered his gun. In my opinion, that was a mistake given that none of the four men in the fight were cuffed and he still did not have backup; however, I was relieved.

Officer Crane walked over to Eric talking quietly. Fireplug was up and pacing in front of the bar window looking mad as hell, yet remarkably unhurt. I hoped he at least had a headache. Officer Willis pulled up after a few minutes, just shortly ahead of the ambulance. Charles gave me a thumbs up during all the commotion.

Eventually, Chief Parker arrived in a new Lincoln wearing civilian clothes. At first, I thought how could he afford a car like that, then I saw the dealer's tags and remembered his wife owned a car dealership. Neither Officer Willis nor Officer Crane had come over to talk to me once since I sat down, and Chief Parker was in no hurry to talk to me either. He never even looked my direction. However, he gave his son Eric the same silent treatment.

My butt was going numb sitting on the curb, so I leisurely reclined until I was resting my back on the sidewalk. My heart rate was returning to a normal rhythm as the adrenaline rush dissipated. Charles was talking to the Chief. Although I could not make out all the words, he was obviously giving the Chief a version of the story the Chief did not want to hear. The only sentence I heard in its entirety was, "I don't give a shit if he is your son, Sam. He finally got his ass kicked, and it's about time." I smiled at that one.

After several minutes of reclining on the sidewalk, someone kicked the bottom of my shoe jolting me out of my repose. Chief Parker was standing over me. "Get up; I'm taking you in."

"As in arresting me? Is this some kind of joke?"

"No joke. But let's think of this more as detaining you and taking you down to the station while we ask you some more questions."

"You detaining the three guys who started the fight, too?"

"No, just one. The other two are being taken to the hospital. You must be some kind of deadly weapon, Dr. McCain. If you really are a doctor. You sure don't look like any doctor I ever saw."

"I suppose you are cuffing me too?"

"Out front, please, as a formality."

"Can I put the top up on my car?"

"No."

"Is my car under arrest?"

"No."

"Then give me a second, please." He raised his eyebrows questioningly. "Charles," I said, "Can you do me a favor?"

"Sure, son. Name it."

"Watch my car for me. Put the top up if it starts to rain, please," I said while throwing the keys over to him.

"You got it. I'll have these at the bar when you finish."

"Thanks. If I don't get them tonight, Lloyd or Ellie Carmichael will come get them. Thanks again."

The Chief gave Charles a disapproving look, which Charles returned in spades. Chief Parker nodded at Officer Willis who came over holding a pair of handcuffs. I was being arrested. *Could this day get any worse?*

While working undercover as a Navy Master-at-arms, I made nearly 100 arrests. Being arrested was virgin territory for me. Riding in the back of a squad car, instead of the front, was new as well; however, what did I expect after busting up the police chief's son. I was surprised to hear that Eric needed to visit the hospital. I did not hit him all that hard, and I went kind of easy on him with the choke hold. My guess was that his dad did not have the heart to arrest him in front of everyone, or maybe he was going for the sympathy vote to help bolster up his case against me while he tried to convince everyone I was a "deadly weapon."

Replaying the events of the fight, I concluded Fireplug and Tyler had been the aggressors in the conflict. I had witnessed Fireplug pushing Eric into action. For a man with a history of violent acts, Eric seemed reluctant to engage in physical conflict with me earlier. I was having a hard time figuring him out.

"You're awful quiet back there," said Officer Willis from the front seat.

Being arrested, even in the semi-polite manner with which they did it, still left me feeling surly. To prevent myself from being combative with the officer, I chose to remain quiet. Officer Willis stared at me in the mirror briefly and then shook his head side to side negatively.

After arriving at the station, the events became fairly routine. I was told to sit while the two officers spoke with Chief Parker. Fireplug was sitting in a chair across the room from me smiling even though he was cuffed with his hands behind him. Surprisingly, they appeared to be treating me better than one of their own townspeople; maybe Fireplug had a history of trouble.

Several minutes later, Chief Parker approached me gesturing for me to stand up. "We're going to lock you up overnight. There will be a bond hearing in the morning. Come with me."

"Am I being charged?"

"I'm going to let the D.A.'s office make that determination."

"Okay, Chief, you're the boss. Show me the way."

There was no use fighting the situation; nothing could be gained by it regardless. After stripping me of my belt and shoe laces and other personal items, Officer Willis led me to my cell. It was a pretty typical older style cell: bars across the front, stainless steel toilet/sink combination unit, and an actual cot. In the Navy, we gave them a concrete bench with a one-inch thick foam pad to sleep on. I also had the entire cell to myself.

Officer Willis said, "Enjoy your stay, boy," as he closed the cell door behind me.

CHAPTER 16

Arrested.

After defending myself. Just thinking about it was enraging me, my blood pressure rising until I could tell the veins in my neck must be showing even more than usual.

The night in jail was the icing on the cake. If I was not mad at the town of Emmettsville before, I sure was now, and if the Chief wanted a war, then he had one. He had pissed off the wrong guy. The adrenaline that was re-entering my bloodstream was a direct result of the anger I was feeling. Good, I thought to myself. I knew how to handle anger. I was a damn expert at anger management. I got shit done when I was angry.

"Time for your phone call, boy," said Officer Willis on his return.

"That's the second time you called me boy, Officer Willis. Should I expect a complete lack of civility from you for the rest of the night?"

Willis cast me a sideway glance, but he did not answer. If I never had another asshole call me boy or mister again, it would suit me just fine. Those words were like fingers down a chalkboard every time I heard them. Add one more person to the list of people in Emmettsville that I wanted to hit.

It was bound to cause some hurt feelings, but I opted to call Virgil over Ellie. He was the one person I knew that would carry out my instructions without the need for big explanations. Not only did I not have to explain, but Virgil also managed to tease me before agreeing to help me in every way imaginable. While on the phone, I looked for Fireplug, but he was not visible, and when they walked me back to my cell, I did not see him in any of the other cells either. In the end, I guessed that only the Yankee was getting arrested today.

Nothing to do but wait, which I did not relish. Not that I was impatient, I just hated being idle with no current objective or purpose. I could sit at a stakeout for hours if needed. There was an objective to a stakeout. However, waiting for the sake of waiting, because it was the only option at hand, that was maddening. Plus, I had based my entire anger management technique for the last 15-plus years upon redirection, and at that moment I had nowhere to redirect my growing anger. A girl I dated briefly in college had told me that my coping mechanism was based on avoidance, not redirection. Maybe she was right; however, I finished a four-year degree in three years and graduated med school magna cum laude, so I did not feel like changing a working plan.

Being fingerprinted and having my mug shot taken broke up the monotony somewhat, although I was still too keyed up to sleep. Three hundred push-ups and sit-ups were not helpful either. Absent-mindedly, I started performing a series of stretches and ballet moves that my mother taught me when I wrestled in junior high and high school. Although it had been 16 years since I performed the routine, it all came back to me like it was yesterday. The extreme concentration required to maintain balance during the exercises allowed me to focus on something other than my current situation. I could feel the anger being redirected, thus preventing a mental meltdown.

"What the heck are you doing, boy," said Officer Willis as he walked by my cell.

"Ballet." I smiled at him while performing a difficult series of deep-knee bends.

"Whoever heard of a big guy like you doing ballet; are you *funny* or something?"

"I'm funny and something."

"I meant are you some kind of queer."

"I know what you meant, Pillsbury."

"What's that supposed to mean?"

"Forgot your name. It was the first thing to come to mind."

Willis looked at me with disgust. He warned me to mind my manners and then made another comment about ballet and homosexuals.

"You know, my dad had 70 pounds on me, and he did ballet."

"Why would he do a thing like that?"

"He played in the NFL for 16 years. Go to the library and look up Marcus McCain; you might learn something."

"I ain't never heard of such a thing. How would he even learn something like that?"

"My mother taught it to him. Now if you don't mind…"

"Sure thing. Besides, you look too damn funny for me to stick around. How in the hell did a fairy looking guy like you beat up three guys?"

"You know, Pillsbury, if you are going to ask me pointed questions like that, then you better Mirandize me first. You guys really need to brush up on your police technique around here."

He issued some passive-aggressive mumbling under his breath as he walked away, but I didn't care, at least he was gone. Finishing the ballet routine my mother had taught me had a calming effect on me allowing me to get some much-needed sleep despite the lumpy, smelly cot. Some people have yoga. Some have meditation. I guess I had ballet.

It was three in the morning when I woke up with a crick in my neck from sleeping on the horrific cot without a pillow. The sharp pain prevented me from turning my neck to the right. I fought three men and did not get a scratch, yet I was miserable due to a lumpy cot. Irony. There was one osteopath at the hospital, Dr. Hutchens, who still did manipulation and might be able to help me. If not, then I was going to have to find a chiropractor tomorrow.

Two nights ago at 3:00 a.m., I was asleep in my bed curled up next to Ellie. Now, I was in jail. What a turn of events. I was also no closer to finding Paul. And if John Deland did not come through with any real help soon, then I was done investigating Paul's disappearance. I hated quitting, yet it truly seemed like I had done all I could do.

Sleep was slow to return, and when I awoke the crick in my neck seemed a little worse, but today was today, and yesterday was yesterday. Time for court and bail and trying to figure out my next step. I was surprised that no one had tried to wake me since my internal clock told me it was around eight in the morning. People were milling around in the office area outside. I could feel the energy somehow. Something seemed amiss. The background noise indicated a large number of people were present. I heard occasional yelling. The office seemed chaotic.

The morning was all kind of a blur. I was walked out a back door and taken to the courthouse for a bail hearing by Officer Willis, who should have been off work. That is where the first surprise of the day occurred. I suspected the judge to set bail and levy order of protection against me. Instead, after the bailiff called out the docket number, the judge dismissed the case with the prosecuting attorney in agreement, and I was told I was free to go. My jaw dropped in surprise, which was duly noted by the judge who told me that I could thank Chief Parker before he literally shooed me out of his courtroom.

My second surprise occurred outside the courtroom. One of Emmettsville's finest was waiting for me outside. I recognized him as the officer sitting with Chief Parker at Ray's diner yesterday. He was standing next to my car with a big friendly smile on his face holding my keys.

"Good morning, Dr. McCain. I'm Lieutenant Patrick. The Chief apologizes for not being here himself this morning, but something very important has come up. He asked me to retrieve your car for you."

"What's going on?" I asked.

"The Chief wanted you to know that he talked to the prosecutor this morning and had all the charges dropped. You acted in self-defense. Charles Mann, you met him at the bar last night, saw the whole thing, and then Eric Parker gave an identical account of the story. Eric also wanted me to pass on his apologies. I can tell by the look on your face that you are confused, Doctor, but I'm telling you the truth. You are free to go. No charges will be made against you; scout's honor. The Chief would like you to contact him tomorrow since it is possible he may need your statement when he brings charges against Eric and his friends. Unfortunately, he will be too busy to talk to you today."

With that last sentence, I noticed a drastic change in his body language from easy-going and affable to one that was tense and worried.

"So, that's it. Free to go. Apologies. Curbside service. This is a strange town, Lieutenant, a really strange town."

"Please call the Chief tomorrow at your convenience. Now, if you don't mind, I am needed elsewhere."

That was my second surprise.

The third surprise was that no one else was there to meet me leaving the courthouse. I had asked Virgil to call Ellie and John and the hospital for me, yet neither Ellie nor John was there. Even Lloyd failed to show up.

On the way out of town, I got a glimpse of the police station. There were a dozen squad cars parked outside the station along with a black SUV with the words Tennessee Bureau of Investigation emblazoned on the side. From what I could see from the outside, the scene looked hectic. No wonder Chief Parker wanted me to wait until tomorrow to call; something bigger than dropping charges on me was going on.

I stopped at the first pay phone I could find and called Ellie at home and the office; however, she was not at either location. Virgil was not home either, and I could not reach John at the office or his home.

For the first time that morning, I thought about the hospital. How was it going to look when they found out that the reason I was not there was that I had just escaped assault and battery charges, especially on the heels of Tom Harty's death yesterday.

Instead of driving by my apartment, I drove to the hospital and walked straight to Dr. Lowe's office. I was still wearing the same clothes from yesterday; however, I doubted that it would make any difference in Dr. Lowe's decision. His secretary looked at me with sympathy as I approached her desk.

"That bad, huh?" I asked.

"Dr. McCain, Dr. Lowe is not in at the moment."

"Let me guess; he is in a meeting concerning my future in this hospital." She tried not to frown. "It's okay. I expected it. If it is not too much to ask, do you know whether I am fired or not?"

"Doctor, you know I cannot answer those types of questions." Her words were saying one thing, but her eyes were saying another. She glanced at a piece of paper on her desk, then back at me, then again at the paper before saying, "I'm not sure if you know this or not, but I used to work for Dr. Witmer. I think the world of that lady. What you did for her was heroic. I just wanted you to know that. Now, if you will excuse me, I need to use the ladies room." She stood up and tapped the same piece of paper she had glanced at earlier before excusing herself. She was heading the wrong way for the ladies room.

The paper was face down on her desk. I quickly picked it up and read it. It was a draft of an official letter addressed to me. The hospital was putting me on unpaid leave after careful consideration of my most recent activities. The time span was currently undetermined, but not to exceed two weeks.

I wish I could say that was my fourth surprise; however, I had to admit I had somewhat expected it. Two weeks ago I hit a man in self-defense of another doctor. Yesterday that man died. Something everyone thought would have happened sooner. Regardless, the Board of Directors had held a meeting to discuss my future with the hospital. The Board decided favorably. No probationary period. No words of warning. Just report to work tomorrow as scheduled. Only, I did not report to work as scheduled. Instead, I was late for work because I was sitting in jail facing battery charges. If I had wondered how far I could push my luck with the hospital, I guessed I had found it: don't beat up three guys and get thrown in jail on the same day that someone else you beat up dies.

Well, shit. Hard to argue with that logic.

My fourth surprise came later. As I pulled up to my apartment, I saw Virgil's black Maxima parked outside my building. Virgil had taken a day off from work to drive over and help me through my unusual day. That was my next surprise; no one was waiting for me in my apartment. No Virgil, no Ellie, no John. I did have another message on my answering machine from my mother, which I promptly deleted.

I realized that Virgil and Ellie were probably on their way back from Emmettsville since I was unable to reach them to save them the trip. In the meantime, a shower and change of clothes sounded appealing. I swore I could still smell that stinky cot on me. I was fresh out of the shower drying myself off when I heard loud pounding on my front door. Virgil and Ellie both had a key, so it surely was not them.

The last surprise was the worst. It was the one that changed my day from a series of pleasant or unexpected events to one that put Tuesday, August 11, 1992, on my growing list of truly bad days. In fact, the day marked a turning point in my very future in Memphis, but I did not know that then. At that time, at the exact moment I opened my front door, I knew that Paul Deland was dead.

John Deland was standing at my front door, eyes red and bloodshot, unshaven, wearing jeans without a belt, and a polo shirt that was only partially tucked in. He looked like hell. "They found him this morning." It was all he needed to say. The morning was making sense. The squad cars, the Tennessee Bureau of Investigation vehicle, the commotion inside and outside the police station. Chief Parker could not see me because he was knee-deep in a homicide investigation.

Leota was sitting in the front seat of John's car. Eyes forward. A nearly catatonic stare. I ushered John into my foyer. Told him I was sorry. I did not know what else to say. John barely heard me. He had come to see me for a reason, and hearing I'm sorry was not that reason. He pushed past me and walked up the stairs to my apartment. Finally, he focused on me. "L.T. Whatever it takes, whatever it cost, I want you to help me nail Chief Parker and his son, and whoever else had a role in his murder."

I did not know what to say. Just a few hours ago, I had decided to cease all activity related to Paul's disappearance. Now I was stammering in front of John in shock. "We don't even know if they had anything to do with anything, John."

"What's going on here? You were all gung-ho before. What gives now?"

"Maybe this seems callous to mention at this time, but I was never gung-ho. I have helped you because you are my friend and it was the right thing to do. But now you are asking me to help you take on a police chief. I'm not ready to commit to something that big."

"So you won't help!"

"I am not a private investigator; I'm a doctor. This is nowhere near my level of expertise. Murder. I don't know anything at all about investigating a murder."

John started flailing his arms around in total exasperation. He wanted to strike someone or something. I knew that feeling. "But you were helping me before, and you had to be thinking it might turn out that way given my son's gambling debts and all."

I hated to admit it, but he had a good point. From the minute I first heard of the gambling debts, I had thought the worst. My inner voice had been warning me even before that. Then, I met with Eric, and I had threatened a police chief. What had changed?

The stakes had changed. That's what the hell had changed. I was placed on unpaid leave at the hospital. Even worse, someone had killed another human being over debt. I realized I had not even asked John how much Paul owed. It might seem a trivial question to some. I mean how do you put a price on someone's life. However, someone had put a price on Paul's life. Knowing the price would give me some insight into the type of people I might face. Was he killed because he owed a seemingly insurmountable amount of debt? Or was the killer just crazy, or trying to make an example?

What the hell am I doing? Just tell John you're sorry and that you can't help him anymore.

"John, you are mad right now, and you want revenge, I got that, but I wouldn't even know who I need to seek revenge on."

"Then why did you beat up Eric Parker and some of his friends last night?"

"I see Virgil did get a hold of you. I didn't beat up on anybody last night. Eric and two of his friends attacked me, and I acted in self-defense. The judge dropped the charges this morning; in fact, Chief Parker himself told the prosecutor to drop the charges."

"You are supposed to be my friend! You must have some idea how to help."

"I am your friend, but you have to realize this is not the usual friend request. This is not like asking someone for a ride to the airport. Besides, homicides are investigated by a team of people, you know, forensic specialists and detectives working together. I don't know anything about forensics, nor would I have access to that type of information. I would be in over my head. I'm sorry, John."

"I don't want your pity!"

"John, I lost my father to a drunk driver when I was sixteen so I can empathize with your loss. This is not pity. I'm just trying to tell you that I don't know how I could help."

John went into a rant yelling about the whole thing being his fault. I did not even try to calm him down. I let him yell. I let him curse. I knew he would need to appear strong in front of his wife and daughter, but at that moment it would feel good to vent some of that anger.

"I'm sorry, L.T. Sorry for yelling and trying to coerce you into helping. It wasn't fair of me to ask. It just that when I told Leota about the gambling debts and that it was only $15,000, she blamed me for Paul's death. She didn't say it, but I saw it in her eyes. My son has been shot in the head and killed over $15,000, and it is all my fault."

Fifteen thousand. Not an insurmountable amount of debt. One that could have been repaid. So why kill Paul? Why ask the father for money and then kill him anyway? It made little sense; organized crime is all about the Benjamins, the mighty dollar. The shot to the head had been at close range. John said they found powder burns on Paul. Somehow, that sounded personal to me.

That still did not mean I wanted to get involved. It was not my fight. It was not my responsibility. Mom and her stupid falsified Edmund Burke quote were not going to influence me this time. I found myself getting angry at John for even asking. I was his landlord for God's sake. Some guy he played tennis with and invited over for the occasional dinner. The nerve of him to ask.

A slight dangerous side to you.

Let's face it; everyone sees it about you.

Ellie had said those words to me in the Thai restaurant the night I killed Tom Harty. I didn't care how people saw me. Not this time.

I consoled John for a few minutes before reminding him of his obligations to his wife and family. Leota was waiting for him in the car. He needed to be there for her and Beth, not up here seeking revenge. Before leaving, John looked at me as if he had just added me to the list of people that had hurt Paul.

CHAPTER 17

The Beatles wrote a song about Mother Mary comforting them in times of trouble; the best I could come up with at the moment was LeClair's. Other than some nasty bread and disgusting, sulfur-smelling water served in the jail last night, I had not eaten, and I did not feel like cooking. After leaving a note for Virgil, I drove over to LeClair's, arriving about 20 minutes before he opened for lunch. The front door was still locked, so I walked around to the service entrance in the back.

LeClair noticed me shortly after entering. "Doc, you look like crap."

My neck was still hurting, and my head was leaning to one side to alleviate the pain. Furthermore, I had not shaved. I probably did look like crap.

"Thanks for noticing. It's all his fault," I said pointing to Jimmy, his short-order cook, "I'm having withdrawals from his awesome burgers."

Jimmy smiled and flipped me the bird at the same time, while LeClair motioned me in. "I'll be with you in a second, Doc. Go on in." Turning to his cook, he said, "You heard the man, make him a burger."

LeClair was preparing his bar for the lunch crowd; therefore, I grabbed a tea on my way to a table. I didn't see him until he showed up with the burger.

"Thanks," I said.

"I figure since we've become the type of friends that use the back door now, then you would know to just take care of yourself, which you did," he said pointing at my glass of tea. "But now it's going to complicate things come tip time."

Returning his wry smile with my own, I said, "Not really, I just won't tip you. Get one of your waitresses to take care of me and I will buy you lunch at your own place and tip her for both of us."

While smiling, he said, "You really that hungry, or am I fixin' to hear another legendary story from Dr. McCain?"

"Both, my good man, both."

"Oh good, maybe I will have lunch with you this time." Attracting the attention of one of the waitresses that had just shown up, he ordered a burger just like mine, but he went in for the fries. "I figure it's time I tried what Jimmy's been servin' you for the last couple of years."

"You sure you got a few minutes, LeClair?

"All the time in the world for a friend."

That is when it hit me, LeClair and I had made the transition from friendly acquaintances to friends. It had happened so gradually that I had missed it, yet it was true, we were friends. We had not engaged in even one conversation outside his bar, but that was because to be friends with LeClair meant you had to interact with him in his world, and his world revolved around his bar.

"It feels good to hear you call me that."

"Damn, Doc. You're gettin' all mushy on me, how much crap you get into this time?"

He sat through the whole conversation detailing the events of the last couple of days without saying a word. He managed to nod several times, and he moaned appreciatively once when he tasted the burger, but otherwise he just listened.

"That's one heck of a story, Doc. So, what's your take on it?"

"Some type of organized crime tie in, although I don't know how that works in the rural South."

LeClair said, "Same as anywhere else I presume. Got some chiefs and got some Indians. There's always someone on top telling others what to do. But I'm like you; I don't know how a bunch of rednecks in the sticks do it."

"But do you think I'm right, LeClair?"

"I think you are thinkin' in the right direction. I would bet the gamblin' has somethin' to do with the whole damn thing. And no one other than someone like the Mafia would let a man get in for 15 grand before he started collectin'."

My undercover work in the Navy was something I did not discuss. Not because it was traumatic or something I wanted to avoid. No, it was more basic than that; my time in the Navy was highly classified. Even if I gave the ultra-condensed version of the story, I risked giving out too much information; however, now seemed like a good time to bring it up.

"I never told you this, LeClair, but I have some experience with organized crime, albeit, indirectly."

"Really, how so, Doc?"

"You were in the Marines, so you can appreciate what I'm saying when I tell you the details are HIGHLY classified..."

"I know, don't ask about the details."

I said, "Thanks. When I was in Naval Intelligence, I worked undercover for over a year investigating a smuggling operation out of Southeast Asia. The product was being smuggled to gangs in Southern California. The whole thing was very hush, hush. So, I sort of know how this kind of thing works. On the flip side, that was more than ten years ago, and I'm a doctor now, not an investigator."

"I heard that, Doc. So what you gonna do about this Paul fella then?"

"I don't know. It's not like I can claim that I don't have a dog in this fight. Because I do. Someone killed my friend's son; they made racial slurs towards my best friend, and I just don't like them. But at the same time, it's not my job, so why should I be expected to do anything at all."

LeClair said, "You want my advice, leave it alone. Get out. Let the cops handle it. Even if that chief is dirty, now that the State Police is involved, he won't be able to keep his son out of trouble. You hearin' me, Doc? Get things right at the hospital, be a doctor, get married, make big, tall, pretty babies with Ellie." He was not smiling when he talked to me; he looked as serious as a heart attack, to borrow a phrase I heard him use often.

"I'm starting to agree with you. I hate quitting, but a man also needs to know his limitations, and I feel like there's nothing more I can do." LeClair's advice was sound and rang true. Get out of this now and let the professionals handle it. He had been a comfort to me after my encounter with Tom Harty, and today he was giving sound advice again. "I will let John know as soon as possible that I can't help him anymore."

"Now you talkin' straight, Doc."

"Pisses me off a little bit, though...well, I'll be a son of a..." My conversation was cut short by the presence of a man I immediately recognized coming in the front door of LeClair's. I had expected Virgil to show up; however, the presence of an old friend from my Navy days stunned me to the point of speechlessness. "I'm sorry LeClair; I have to go say hi to someone."

* * *

Boyd Dallas spotted me immediately, donning his big infectious smile ear to ear as I approached. He had been looking for me. "Lieutenant, how the heck are you?" Bypassing my outstretched arm, he gave me a big hug, slapping me on the back as men will do, especially a former Marine like Boyd. "Damn, Lieutenant, where do you find time for all these muscles?"

I replied, "I haven't worked out since I carried your butt all over the whole Cambodian jungle, Sergeant, but my girlfriend thanks you for the effect it had on my physique."

"You carried who? No way some Navy officer was going to carry a highly-trained Marine out of any jungle, especially since you were carrying out Admiral Buie instead."

"Figuratively carried your butt, not literally. Oh, wait I did carry it literally as well if my memory serves me right. Or course, I did swear to secrecy on that one, much like I promised not to tell anyone that when you put direct pressure on my inner thigh to ebb the flow of my precious blood you accidentally touched my Johnson."

"No, sir, I promised not to tell anybody that you enjoyed it," he said while throwing a playful jab at my midsection, which I intercepted easily then wrapped into an equally innocent wrist lock. "L.T., looks like you still got it. What am I saying, how many guys did you beat up last night?" His huge grin returned. Obviously, he had already talked to Virgil.

"Only three. I could have taken four or five, but they weren't Marines, so they at least put up a little fight. Get over here; I want you to meet someone. But first, where's Virgil?"

"Parking the car. He dumped me as close as he could get me. One of the advantages of a bad ankle."

Returning to LeClair, I said, "I would like to you to meet Sgt. Boyd Dallas, USMC MP. Boyd, meet Lance Corporal LeClair, USMC, Vietnam, and owner of this fine establishment. You two get to know each other while I go look for Virgil."

As I started towards the front door, I heard Boyd make some sort of squid reference, which got a hearty chuckle out of LeClair. I was not sure why Virgil had brought Boyd, although I was dying to see what was on their mind. Maybe Virgil thought I would still be in jail and having a former Marine Military Policemen might come in handy in getting me released. Before making it to the front door, I spotted Virgil striding across the street. He entered the bar shaking his head at me in mock disbelief while smiling.

"So when you told me you were going back to trumpet the black cause in the South, I guess you weren't kidding."

"They started it," I said returning his smile.

"So how did you get out so fast?"

"Let me buy you guys lunch, and I will tell both of you what happened. How's that sound?"

"Sounds great. By the way, Ellie rode over to Emmettsville with Boyd and me, but you weren't there. When we got back to your place, she saw the note and told us to go on over without her. She needed to go to work and thought we might need some guy time."

"Thanks. How is she? Mad? Upset?"

"Quiet and contemplative, although I can tell she doesn't know what to think of you right now. I think you are going to have some 'splainin' to do," Virgil said in a spot-on Ricky Ricardo imitation.

"Thanks for the warning."

I walked Virgil over to the table and offered to buy both of them lunch. They agreed. Boyd told LeClair that he did not want any L.T. tofu burger. He wanted a big, juicy American burger. Boyd called me Lieutenant Tofu a few times in response to my healthy eating habits while we served together in the Philippines; I believe everyone should eat at least five servings of vegetables a day. Although I did not eat tofu, he enjoyed getting his digs in where he could.

"You got it, one big juicy Marine burger coming up. You want Jimmy to cook it or just slice it off the cow and serve it warm?" LeClair asked with a rhetorical flip of his wrist over his shoulder as he walked away.

Unsure how much Virgil had told Boyd, I started my story a couple of weeks earlier to when I stopped Tom Harty. Like a true Marine, he smiled and congratulated me on stopping Harty and felt no sympathy for him when I told him he died a couple of days ago. In fact, he sounded almost exactly like LeClair when he stated that the idiot shouldn't have been waving a gun around and expect to walk away when Lieutenant Tofu was around. He also congratulated me on "kicking the shit" out of those rednecks yesterday. I finished by telling them about the visit I had with John earlier that morning. LeClair rejoined the table near the end and when I finished all eyes were upon me, each seeming to cast the same question.

Boyd said, "Well, you going to tell us or not?"

"Tell you what?"

"What's next?"

"Honestly, I don't know. I want to help. I even feel like I should, but I'm not sure I could help."

Boyd said, "Keep talking, why not?"

"Boyd, you were an MP. You know investigating a crime of this magnitude is not a one-man operation. I can't do it on my own, although, to be honest, I have one hell of an idea. Too bad it's too late."

LeClair said, "What's your idea, Doc."

I said, " I believe Paul's gambling debts got him killed. Not too many people will kill someone for flirting with their girlfriend in a bar. Punch him in the face, sure, but shoot him dead, up close, execution style, I doubt it. Money, on the other hand, well, let's just say I've seen guys shoot someone for a lot less than $15,000."

Virgil asked, "Does that mean you no longer suspect Eric or his father?"

"I'm unsure of the level of involvement of Chief Parker or his son Eric. That guy I called Fireplug was the leader of the group when the Chief sent those guys after us, and he was there again last night with

Eric. So, the father and the son have some mutual acquaintances. Let's just say that, for now, their behavior is suspect."

Virgil said, "Makes sense so far." Boyd and LeClair were both nodding in agreement, although Boyd was smirking slightly.

"The problem I have is that without support from a team of officers or prosecutors, we can't investigate the Chief properly, and I'm not sure if he is involved anyway. Furthermore, we have no way of getting the forensic details since I'm sure the State Police isn't going to share with us. That means I would have to start my investigation from scratch."

Boyd interrupted, "I don't see an idea here."

This time I smiled. "I'm getting to it. Be patient, Jarhead." I got a friendly "bite me" from Boyd before continuing. "I would like to do the same thing in this case that I did in my investigation in the Navy."

Virgil said, "But none of us know what you did in the Navy. It was so classified you never even told me."

"I'm still not going to tell you who I busted; it really is too classified. However, I don't see anything wrong with telling you how I did it. ONI, the Office of Naval Intelligence, knew something was being smuggled out of Southeast Asia by servicemen, yet all their investigations came up with nothing."

Boyd said, "Something, as in drugs."

"I will neither confirm nor deny that statement, Sergeant," I responded with a knowing wink. "The problem wasn't just that they couldn't infiltrate the group, they didn't even have any leads on who to infiltrate. I came up with the idea of setting me up undercover as a dirty Navy Master-at-Arms who was also smuggling 'stuff' out."

Boyd said, "How did that help? Wouldn't they just try to bump you off if they saw you as competition?"

"That's just it. My fake operation was kept small, so I wasn't competition. Instead, I was seen as an opportunity. ONI set me up with a fail-safe way of getting my merchandise out, but I had a problem. I couldn't get my hands on enough stuff. Word got around that a dirty Navy cop could move anything he wanted; however, he had a supply problem. So eventually they found me."

Boyd said, "Damn, Lieutenant, that's pretty smart. Whose idea was that?"

"Yours truly."

Virgil said, "So that's how you got the Navy Commendation Medal."

Boyd said, "You got the Navy Commendation medal? I thought that only went to O-4 and above."

"Admiral Buie made an exception for me. Since I had come up with the idea, then went to Master-at-Arms school, then stayed undercover for over a year and a half usually operating naked, then helped bust a lot of servicemen, and I mean a lot, well, he thought I deserved it. And no one argued with him. That's how a lowly little lieutenant JG got the award."

"Maybe I missed somethin', but did you say naked?"

"Sorry, just means having no backup."

LeClair said, "Shit, Doc, you did a lot of shit in a short time. And I had no idea you were decorated."

Boyd said, "That's nothing, he got the Navy and Marine Corps Medal, the highest non-combat medal you can get as well." Boyd was enjoying bragging on me, and he was there when I earned that medal so I could not be mad at him; however, I still cast him a dirty look. "But that is another story for another time. L.T. doesn't like it when we tell him how awesome he is."

A few moments of awkward silence followed Boyd's announcement that I was a decorated officer; however, Boyd was quick to kill the awkward moment. "So your idea, if you could do it, would be to pose as someone moving into Emmettsville in competition with whatever organization is there and let them come to you. However, everyone already knows you, so it is too late. Does that about sum it up?"

"Perfectly," I answered.

Boyd smiled as big as I had ever seen him smile and said, "I'll be your huckleberry."

"Say what?"

"I'll do it."

"Do what?"

"Catch up, L.T. I'll go undercover. You can't do it, and neither can either Virgil or LeClair. You need a Southern white boy with law enforcement experience who can take care of himself in a pinch, right? So, I'm your man."

"I can't let you do that."

"Let me, just try and stop me."

I said, "Why, though? Why would you do that for someone you don't even know?"

"Because it would be fun."

"Because it would be fun? That's it?"

"You want more. Okay, how about because the only reason I am not a Marine MP or a Huntsville cop is because I trashed my ankle in that damn helicopter crash and no one will hire me. I miss the action. And it will be fun. Let's not forget the fun."

LeClair said, "Oorah, Marine."

Boyd said, "If the Chief is dirty, then he needs to go down. If he isn't dirty, he might need our help. If you want one more reason, even though I was born and raised in Alabama, I don't particularly like rednecks, especially Tennessee rednecks. And didn't you tell me Eric played football for Auburn? That's a strike against him. Roll Tide all the way."

LeClair said, "Doc, I think you have a volunteer. I agree with the sergeant; it does sound like fun. Makes me almost wish I was white so I could take his place. I would like to help, though. Count me in if you find a need for me."

I said, "LeClair, you told me to stay out of it."

LeClair replied, "I changed my mind."

Turning to Boyd, I said, “You do realize what you are getting into, right?”

Boyd said, “Damn straight. I thought we already covered the fact that it sounds like fun.”

Virgil said, “I think L.T. is trying to say it might be dangerous.”

Boyd said, “Exactly, I thought we already covered the fact that it might be fun.”

Virgil said with a laugh, “No use trying to argue with that logic. L.T., you got yourself a volunteer.”

“So when do I get started!” said Boyd with a degree of enthusiasm that made me realize I had my man if I wanted to pursue this further.

The three of them were staring at me expectantly, two of them wanting to help me in some way, in any way. Boyd looked like a hunting dog eager to get to work, bubbling over with energy and excitement.

I had not been looking for volunteers when I explained my idea earlier; however, I was beginning to think Boyd had manipulated me into telling him my idea so he could volunteer. A helicopter crash in Cambodia had left him with a limp after the surgeons pinned and fused his ankle bones, drastically affecting his ability to run. Months of physical therapy had helped his walking gait; in fact, he had managed to turn his limp into a unique swagger that worked for him. Regardless, the permanently impaired ankle resulted in a medical discharge while also making him unfit for civilian police duty. Now here he was riveted on me, waiting to see if he could get back in the game.

I smiled.

Boyd exclaimed loudly, “Awesome. Is this the time when we synchronize our watches?”

* * *

After the lunch crowd had thinned out, LeClair did something that surprised me: he locked the front door. He then motioned us over to a booth that was the furthest from the kitchen and told the staff that we were not to be disturbed.

"If any of y'all need something to drink, just get it yourself; I don't want anyone overhearin' our strategy session. You do have a strategy, don't ya, Doc?"

"First thing we need is a legend for Boyd."

"Legend?"

"Sorry guys, I guess I'm reverting to old vocabulary. We need a credible backstory for Boyd. Luckily, he is Southern, so we don't need to teach him an accent or how to act Southern. He knows the language, the geography, the idioms, etc. Off the top of my head, the best thing I can think of is illegal alcohol distribution."

"I always wanted to be a bootlegger. Seriously, why alcohol though?"

"I can buy that legally and then you can sell it to whatever bars in Emmettsville want to buy it at a reduced cost. Sure, I lose a little money, but it just seems the easiest."

Everyone agreed that alcohol was the easiest and least risking service to provide. I would provide the money to buy the liquor. Thus I would absorb the loss. I also agreed to pay Boyd's expenses, which he would not accept. In the end, he agreed to let me pay for any lodging costs; however, food and drinks he would have had to buy regardless so he would not hear of me footing the bill.

"What about fake name and identity? What do you think about that?" asked Boyd.

"Pick a name you want to use. It doesn't matter what; I don't think anyone is going to ask for ID. Pick a city you are familiar with to use as your base of operations. When at all possible, tell real stories to whomever, just change the names. In other words, try to talk in as many half-truths as possible so that it is easier to remember what bull crap that has been coming out of your mouth."

Boyd decided on Graham Anderson from Florence, Alabama as his alias. Dry counties still existed in that part of the state, and we felt it might give him credibility as a bootlegger who is now trying to spread out. Virgil was even going to get him a fake Alabama driver's license; he had a friend who was a graphic artist who once told him how easy it was to duplicate Alabama licenses.

"If the fake ID is not hard, then sure, make one up. The more window dressing we have, the better," I said. "As for the limp, if any asks, tell them the truth; helicopter crash in the Marines. My guess is that a lot of enforcers for organized crime are ex-military, so being a Marine should not work against you; hell, it might even work for you. Besides, you look the part."

We spent about an hour helping Boyd fill in some backstory for Graham Anderson until he seemed real enough. Then we took turns firing off different questions to see how he held up under pressure. I was impressed. Instinctively, he seemed to understand the importance and safety of half-truths. We all felt he would do fine. Boyd looked as happy as a kid in a candy store and wanted to get started immediately. I wanted him to wait at least until after I had talked to Chief Parker. Maybe I could get some information from him before starting.

"Leave it to an officer to want to delay. I think you guys invented the concept of 'hurry up and wait.' I might have one problem, though. My vehicle is pretty vanilla. All I have is a Ford F-150. Nice vehicle, new, clean, respectable. Not exactly good ole boy material."

"Too bad I drove the Mercedes into Emmettsville yesterday; otherwise I could let you drive that."

"A Mercedes, you are joking right?"

"Yes, I'm joking, Boyd. I know no self-respecting good ole boy would show up in a bright red German sports car. Any ideas, guys?"

"I got one, but you might not like it," said Boyd. I motioned for him to continue. "There's a guy in Huntsville selling a '68 Mustang fastback. Not the prettiest car since he ran out of money restoring it, but the engine, drive train, and front end are completely done. He is dumping it for almost nothing since his wife wants him to get rid of it."

"Is it worth what he is asking?"

Boyd said, "I'm not the car nut you are, L.T., but it runs like a top, seems fast enough, and looks like something a redneck might drive. All for under two thousand."

"Car is mine when we're done, but until then enjoy the hell out of it, Boyd. I'll give you the money. You take care of it. You know what boys, for what it's worth, we have a plan. I can't believe a soldier was silly enough to volunteer, but he did." Boyd simply smiled. "Let's get what we need to get started and get the show on the road by this weekend. Can anyone think of anything we forgot?"

Virgil answered, "Not to rain on your parade, L.T., but what are you going to tell Ellie? She begged me to drive over here and try to talk you into ceasing all your activity in Emmettsville. I even brought Boyd with me to try and help me talk you into stopping. Instead, he talks us all into getting involved."

"Yeah, she ain't going to like me too much when she finds out I'm responsible for your change of heart," said Boyd.

"First, it's not like you had to twist my arm. In fact, I thank you for reminding me of who I am, I mean really am. I want to do this. I just started to wimp out when I thought I couldn't do anything. Second, we won't tell Ellie that you talked me into anything, so she won't be mad at you. In fact, no one outside of this circle is ever to know that Boyd did anything other than going back to Huntsville after doing what he came here to do. If I handle myself right, no one will even know I am investigating anything since I will just be your handler, Boyd."

"Ah, secrets," said Virgil. "Sounds like the beginning of a slippery slope."

"I know, but my girlfriend, therefore, my call. Besides, it gives her plausible deniability, thus protecting her if things don't go well."

That got nods all around.

Lying to my girlfriend was not a way to build trust. I knew that; however, it had to be done. Even if our mission to find Paul's killers failed, Boyd's physical safety must be ensured. Ellie would never purposefully cause danger to Boyd, but keeping her out of the loop also prevented her from accidentally endangering him.

Boyd said it would be fun. Well, the fun was going to begin.

CHAPTER 18

Boyd had his legend in place before he and Virgil traveled back to Huntsville. They followed me to the bank so I could give Boyd the money for the Mustang. I also took out a couple of thousand for LeClair so that he could buy the alcohol. I was glad he was taking care of that for me; I would not have known the best things to buy to look like a legitimate distributor of illegal alcohol.

After dropping off the money at LeClair's, I went back to my apartment where I discovered three messages on my answering machine. One was from Ellie telling me she was sorry she was not there, but she would see me later, and she hoped my talk with Virgil and Boyd went well. She was going to be disappointed if she found out I was not done with my investigation. Another one was from my mother. Two in one day. Virgil must have called her because she hinted at the fact that "things are not going well" in Memphis and that she worried about me. Good old Virgil, keeping my mother in the loop. I did not want to talk to her, but I was going to tell Virgil to let her know I was fine.

The last message was from Dr. Lowe. In his syrupy, condescending tone, he was calling to inform me that due to my "recent activity," the board was in session with the lawyers to discuss any potential complications. Obviously, they did not know that the charges had been dropped. However, I did have the day off again, along with the next day. Clever, I thought. Two days off would give them time to send me the letter I knew was coming.

Boyd was planning on returning tomorrow with the Mustang and some gear. He had smiled very mischievously when he said "gear." Even Virgil was smiling, but neither would tell me what was so funny. Boyd called his employer, and they granted him vacation time for the rest of the week. Since I did not want even one second of Boyd's time wasted, I decided to see if Chief Parker could see me today. Although the Chief could not talk when I called, he relayed a message telling me he could meet at the station at six that night.

I had a few hours to kill. The first thing I did was see Dr. Hutchens, the osteopath, for some cervical manipulation for the crick in my neck. Next, I stopped by Dr. Lowe's office, but he was not there. I asked his secretary to inform him that all charges had been dropped. I told her that Dr. Lowe would understand. Finally, before leaving town, I bought Ellie some flowers. Two dozen red roses with a card telling that I was sorry for inconveniencing her earlier. I delivered them myself. She was on the set when she spotted me holding them. The flowers were an obvious happy surprise; however, I was equally as surprised when she ran off set quickly and kissed me. Lisa took the flowers and shooed me out of there.

* * *

Delivering the flowers myself made me 10 minutes late meeting with Chief Parker, who met me at the door of the police station. There was still a strange buzz in the station, a feeling that things were not normal; however, everyone, including the Chief looked more physically spent than hectic. The Chief did not even speak when he greeted me. He merely turned and walked back to his office where he promptly plopped down into his chair.

"Long day?"

"You have no idea. Well, maybe you do. You did tell me you used to be a Naval Intelligence Officer. Can I ask you something?"

"Sure."

"Were you any good?"

"I don't know. I have a medal that says I was. But I also have a medal for being a hero, although I never felt like a hero. I was just trying to stay alive." He looked at me tiredly. "Sorry, Chief, I guess I was good in my own way. I only had one case, a long undercover case that ended very well for me. So, maybe I was good, or I just got lucky. Why do you ask?"

Chief Parker asked me to sit. He had a few questions he wanted to ask. Specifically, he wanted to know what made me think Eric had something to do with Paul's disappearance. I explained the confrontation in the bar again, as well as the discovered wallet and the conversation I had with Eric at the beer distributor. He listened to my description of where I found the wallet. The fact that nothing looked to be missing. The Chief said he would have suspected Eric too.

Chief Parker said, "Another thing, Lloyd Carmichael called my home around midnight last night and told me about the six guys that threatened you on Sunday. He also told me that you suspected that I sent them. I'm here to tell you face-to-face that I didn't send them. Do you believe me?"

"I'm not sure, Chief. If you didn't send them, then you must have tipped them off somehow. They knew Virgil's name and Mr. Deland's occupation."

Chief Parker said, "I didn't talk to anyone about our conversation. When you left, I drove around trying to get the courage to face the fact that my son might have done something awful. Not just a little push, or a fight this time, but something I couldn't help him with this time. It must have been someone in my office, though, which is why we are having this conversation alone."

I was not sure if I believed him, although I could tell Chief Parker needed to hear the words. I told him I believed him.

"Good, then you are ready to hear the rest of what I have to say. Yesterday I got a call from someone who told me they saw Eric punch Paul outside of Falco's on Saturday night. Apparently, he hit Paul in the stomach, knocking him down. The caller said that Eric saw him watching the whole thing, which is why he didn't call sooner; he is scared of Eric. I talked to Eric, and he admitted to punching Paul; however, he went back and helped him up and apologized and then went over to Jackie's house to mend things up with her. That's the last time he saw Paul. When you showed up yesterday morning saying that no one had seen Paul, it really freaked him out."

"I heard about the anonymous caller."

"You did? Where?"

"Does it matter?"

"No, I guess not."

The Chief withheld information from me on our first meeting and had proven himself to be very adept at lying. I wanted him to feel as if I would discover any attempts at lying, so I did not tell him that Mason mentioned the anonymous caller. I asked him if he believed Eric. He did. He also talked to Jackie and got a similar story. I was not sure I believed Eric, but it did appear that the Chief believed him.

"What about last night?" I asked.

"What about it?" he replied in a curt tone. "Sorry, I didn't mean for that to sound defensive. What would you like to know about last night?"

"Whose idea was it to attack me? How did they find me? And how is he doing now?"

"Eric told me that Junior and Tyler came by his place and told him you were in town telling everyone that Eric had something to do with

Paul's disappearance. Junior told him that he had run you out of town once and with Eric's help he would run you out again. Eric didn't think it would go down like it did."

"No offense, but I'm sure three big, strong guys like that probably never thought a doctor could kick the crap out of them, so I'm not surprised it didn't go down as expected."

"Dr. McCain, I didn't mean it that way. Eric didn't expect it to get violent, and when it did, he didn't want to make it worse. He says he really tried to stay out of it."

I had witnessed Eric's reluctance last night first hand. Not once did he throw a punch at me, and I did witness Junior pushing him into battle. I believed he was telling his father the truth.

"I saw a cop car slow down when I passed it last night, Chief. Maybe that same person told Fireplug, I mean Junior, about us on Sunday and was the same guy who told him how to find me last night."

Parker rested his elbows on his desk and rubbed both hands along his temples. He was troubled, yet tip-toeing around why I was in his office; I could just feel it. "You're studying me, wondering why I am volunteering all this information; I can see it on your face."

"Sure."

"I probably have no right to ask you this after the way my office and this town has treated you." He paused, apparently afraid to finish the rest of the sentence. I leaned forward invitingly, letting him know he had my undivided attention. "I think I need your help. Someone is trying to frame my son for Paul Deland's murder."

* * *

A day of surprises and bombshells. It is what that Tuesday in August had been since I first found out that I would not face assault and battery charges. I did not expect yet another bombshell. It was far from being the worst day in my life, but I could not remember one with more twists and turns.

For the first time, I noticed that the Chief did not look tired, or worried, he looked downright frightened. His world was being turned upside-down. It appeared someone was framing his son, and he could feel his control slipping away. Now he was reaching out to a complete stranger asking him for help. The poor man was desperate. My inner voice was whispering for me to be careful, urging me to approach this new revelation with a degree of caution.

"What happened," I asked.

"How much do you want to know?"

"You are asking me for help, right? So, tell me everything."

Chief Parker told me everything he could. Early that morning, the station received a call about a man sitting motionless in his car in a wooded area. One of the deputies went out to take a look and found Paul in his car tied to the steering wheel. Dead. When the Chief arrived on the scene, he knew it was Paul immediately. The man in the car matched the description. When he saw that the license plate numbers matched, his heart sank. Once he saw the bullet hole in the back of Paul's head, the Chief knew he needed help and called the Tennessee Bureau of Investigation.

The forensic experts were immediately suspicious. Paul was shot in the back of the head on the right side just above the ear. Powder burns above the ear as well. It appeared the shooter was standing over Paul instead of sitting behind him. Plus, no blood spatter in the car anywhere.

"Execution style shooting," I said. It was more a statement than a question.

"Looks that way."

"So why tie him to the steering wheel, I wonder."

"The forensic guys were talkative enough during the process. Telling me what they saw. Also, talking into one of those little recorders and taking lots of pictures. Unofficially, he wasn't killed in the car. The whole scene was staged. I'm going to have to wait for the official report."

"Okay, but you said something about Eric being framed."

"I told you Paul was tied to the steering wheel. When the techs cut Paul loose, we could tell he had been tied with a tee shirt that had been cut into strips. I recognized the shirt; it belonged to my son."

I watched the color drain completely out of Chief Parker's face before he put his head down on the desk. He used his hands to massage his temples. Poor man probably had the headache of a lifetime.

"Are you sure."

"Yes." His head was still on the desk. His fingers still running through his hair. It almost looked as if he was pulling his hair.

"Did you say anything?"

The Chief looked up and stared at me. "No, but I know I should have."

"Well, you didn't, so you are just going to have to play dumb and let them figure it out on their own, which they will. Forensic science is freaky good now and only getting better. They will probably find DNA on the sweat or something." Chief Parker was absently nodding his head in agreement; his eyes fixed on some spot on the wall behind me while biting his bottom lip. "Chief." I waited until I had his attention. "Chief, your son didn't kill Paul." I locked eyes with the Chief, staring intently at him to study his reaction.

"How do you know? You were sure he had something to do with his disappearance, why the change of heart?"

For the first time since Paul had gone missing, I really started to doubt Eric had anything to do with what Paul's disappearance or murder. Paul had died in an execution-style shooting. No way Eric could have pulled that off; he lacked a killer instinct.

"Honestly, because your son can't fight. I think my mother could kick his butt."

"Excuse me. You changed your mind because my son can't fight?"

"Yep."

"But he attacked you. Maybe you were just the better man."

"The three of them bit off more than they could chew, no doubt, but he lacked conviction in the fight, not just technique." I was telling the Chief the truth, at least as I saw it. "In my opinion, anyone who would lack conviction in a fist fight could hardly be seen as a calculated killer. I would bet the house on it. And this was a calculated killing."

Chief Parker looked slightly relieved. "So now you understand why I need your help. The forensic guys are going to realize that's Eric's shirt sooner or later. And when they do, they are going to make Eric a suspect. With his history, plus with the encounter on Saturday night, then the shirt, I know I would think he did it."

"Chief, I understand why you need my help, but you need to know something; I have no idea how to investigate a murder."

"I thought you were a hot shot Navy investigator."

"Like I told you. One case. A long undercover case that was an entirely different type of investigation than what you need. Chief, you are just going to have to work the clues." I did not feel the need to tell him I was already planning on investigating. "Find out who saw Eric hit Paul and see if he saw anything else. Plus, you need to figure out who has ties to organized crime in this town."

"Organized crime, why?"

I explained to the Chief what John told me about Paul's gambling problem and the threatening calls that John had received. I told him how John had thought Eric might have been the one making the calls. Chief Parker was quick to point out what a strange coincidence it was that Paul just happened to flirt with Eric's girlfriend.

"I agree, Chief. But to tell the truth, before John told me about the gambling problem, I thought maybe Eric had beaten him to death in the parking lot and then drove Paul off in his own car to cover things up."

"Holy shit, you actually thought my son was capable of something like that?"

"Chief, your son has a heck of a temper. I'm still not sure how it would have gone down if I had not knocked over that chair. Besides, that was before. Now I just think he is a bully."

"Who can't fight worth a shit."

"Exactly."

"You don't think much of him, do you?"

"Honestly, I've lost interest in him for now; I got other fish to fry. For starters, do you have organized crime in your town, Chief?"

"Since we are being honest, not that I'm aware of, and it seems something like that would stand out like a sore thumb in a small town like this."

"Chief, I'm not saying they are running around in suits dressed like Mafioso."

"I know. Look, we got our fair share of pot heads, meth heads, alcoholics, brawlers, like any other town. I've never noticed anything too organized about the whole thing. If that kind of thing exists in my county, then we've had no trouble with them. Apparently, until now, if your suspicions are correct."

I had driven over to see how I could use the Chief in my investigation. I never considered that Chief Parker would want my help with his. Just a day ago, I had considered him a potential suspect. Now I had doubt, and my inner voice was annoyingly quiet on the matter. Even if I did help him, I would need to provide him limited information until I could fully trust him, and he must be completely in the dark about Boyd.

He said, "I can tell you are thinking about something, Dr. McCain. Maybe you don't want to help. Maybe you don't trust me. Maybe you got your own thing going on. I don't know. Just let me say, I'm sorry about your friend. I'm sorry I arrested you last night. I'm sorry for my son and his friends, including the six guys the other day. I didn't know about them until Lloyd Carmichael called me. I assure you that I had nothing to do with sending them after you. You do believe me, don't you?"

"I do now." His imploring eyes were having an effect. I realized we had a mutual interest in getting to the truth. Sure, his interest might lie only in saving his son, yet I could not help but think this might be the ally in law enforcement I needed. "Chief?"

"Yes."

"In my own way, in my own time, I am going to help you. I will be giving you information that will help you prove Eric's innocence. Don't ask me how; just trust me to do it. I only ask three things in return."

"Name them."

"First, you will tell no one in your department that I am feeding you information. And I do mean no one. Someone in your department told those six men all about us. They knew Virgil's name; they knew John Deland was an attorney, and they knew I was poking around. I'm not saying you have a dirty cop, but you do, at least, have a loose-lipped cop. Maybe he thought he was trying to help; I don't know. Either way, you get the picture, this conversation never happened. Second, you will tell me what you know, when you know it. Those forensic boys are going to give you a report. I will want to see it. You following me?"

"Sure, and the third thing?"

Standing up to my full height, I placed my hands on his desk and leaned forward into his space. "No matter who it is, even if he used to carry the collection plate at your church when he wasn't helping little old widows, when I find the guy responsible, you promise to arrest him and charge him with murder. Deal?"

"Deal."

CHAPTER 19

Chief Parker and I had talked for another 30 minutes before I left. He apologized several more times for the way his town had treated my friends and me, and we exchanged phone numbers. Before leaving town, I had one errand to run. As I pulled up to the bar, I chuckled as I saw someone trip over the same curb that nearly everyone in the fight last night had tripped over. Inside was a standard small town tavern. There was plenty of seating at the bar with a few tables away from the bar, one pool table, and a dart board. Inside, I eyeballed around twenty people, a few looking familiar from last night. I was there to see one man in particular.

Charles Mann, the bar owner, had stood up for me last night. I heard him tell Chief Parker off, and Lt. Patrick informed that his account of the fight helped convince Chief Parker I had acted in self-defense. Charles spotted me immediately upon entering and invited me up to bar where he offered me a beer and introduced me as the man who whooped Eric and Junior last night. Several more people offered to buy me a beer after that introduction.

After all the introductions and congratulations, Charles asked, “They really drop the charges this morning like Lt. Patrick said when he picked up your car?”

“Sure did.”

“Well, I’ll be damned, didn’t see that one coming. Course never saw Eric lose before, either. A time of firsts I guess. So what brings you by?”

“I wanted to thank you for taking care of my car.”

“You come by just to thank me?”

“Yes and no.”

“You got something on your mind: I can see it. Let’s hear it.”

“You’re a townie, I take it?”

“All my life.”

“And I noticed you have what I might call an adversarial relationship with Chief Parker.”

“Adversarial relationship, I like that, but it’s more like I tell him like it is when his son is out of line.”

“So maybe you can tell me what the heck is the deal with Eric Parker. Everyone makes him out to be a real tough guy and sort of a trouble maker, but he can’t fight worth a hoot, and he seemed reluctant to fight anyway last night. Junior was pushing him into starting.”

“That’s because Junior Estes is a dick. His old man was a dick. Someone once told me the grandfather was king of the dicks, but that is before my time.”

“So, runs in the family.”

“You know what they say about the sins of the father being handed down?”

“Yeah, but I did my own reading on that saying myself. Look it up in Ezekiel. ‘The son shall not suffer for the iniquity of the father, nor the father suffer for the iniquity of the son. The righteousness of the righteous shall be upon himself, and the wickedness of the wicked shall be upon himself.'"

"Hmmm. So you are saying each one is a dick because he chooses to be a dick."

"I guess so." I chuckled at his interpretation.

"Well, that does make sense. Besides, it would explain why Junior's older brother, Jackson, is not a dick. The two boys took over their dad's junkyard when he died off. Jackson runs it much better than his old man ever did, and everyone seems to like him okay. I even heard talk Jackson is opening up a pawn shop; he already bought the building. It's over on Baltimore near the laundromat. He'll probably do well; people seem to trust him alright; his brother, not so much."

I described my earlier encounter with Junior, including a description of the other men. Charles knew some of the other boys, informing me they were all talk, no action, except, of course, Junior. He laughed when I told him about my interaction with Hank and Aaron.

"You have any trouble with them in here," I asked.

"This here is a bar full of working stiffs, farmers, and veterans. We ain't going to allow some punk kids to cause trouble in here if you know what I mean. Eric tried that once in here. Started a fight over the outcome of an Auburn-Tennessee game. Took three or four of us, but he went out on his ass, literally. The peckerwood broke my damn TV. Chief came down and tried to cause some trouble after we threw Eric out. When the whole bar volunteered to testify against him, he dropped it pretty quickly. Even paid me for the TV."

I smiled as I visualized Eric being thrown out. "You see much of him anymore."

"Every damn week; I have to buy beer from him."

Charles went on to tell me a couple more stories concerning Eric. A few I had already heard from Ellie's father. There was a consistent theme: his trouble was usually related to women. Eric had even admitted to me on Saturday night he was the jealous type. Junior, on the other hand, was the kind of guy who went looking for trouble. Numerous fights. Petty theft as a juvenile. Some accusations of theft as an adult, but nothing that ever stuck.

"I'm telling you, young man, a cloud of trouble seems to follow him around."

I replied, "I know the type. So, what's Tyler's story?"

"Not much. Name's Tyler Shriver. Owns a tire shop not too far from the Estes' junkyard. Deals mostly in used tires, but can get new ones if you want to order them. Never heard of anyone having much trouble with him even though he follows Junior around like a little lost puppy. Don't know much about him otherwise." The dirty hands and strong forearms were making sense. Lugging tires all day would do that. "If you don't mind me asking, what's their beef with you?"

"Charles, did you hear about the person they found dead out in the woods early this morning?"

"Just a little; hearsay mostly."

"His name was Paul Deland, and he is the son of a close friend. I was at Falco's Saturday night with Paul and some other friends when Paul went out to his car and never came back. Initially, when Paul was just missing, I thought Eric was involved somehow."

Charles said, "So you don't think Eric had anything to with your friend's death now?"

"Not really. He doesn't seem the killing type. I can see him pushing someone around or even getting into a fight, but I just can't picture him shooting someone in the back of the head."

"Yet here you are asking me questions about Eric, young man."

"Friends call me L.T. And you're right; here I am asking questions."

"L.T., as in Lieutenant?"

"No, my initials."

He accepted my cryptic answer without further questions. "L.T., I think you're right about one thing; Eric's no killer. Funny thing, though, never heard of him hanging around with Junior before last night. Never knew Eric to hang around anyone other than some of the meatheads down at the gym, you know, ex-jocks like himself. After his divorce, Eric and a couple of his gym friends would hit the town and sit around pretending to be God's gift to women. Must have worked, I think all of them have steady girlfriends now."

"Well, they all seemed buddy-buddy last night."

Charles said, "Nothing like a good beating to bond them together." He laughed at himself. "So, whatcha doing now? Trying to figure out what happened to your friend? Got any leads or ideas?"

"I am trying to figure out what happened to Paul. His dad is a friend of mine, and I have experience in this sort of thing from my Navy days." I lied. "I have no idea where to start." I lied again. "But I won't stop until I've caught them." That was not a lie. "Well, actually I have one obscure lead."

I was not sure if I wanted to share my concern with Charles. What if Charles knew members of the same criminal group I hoped to find? Then it donned on me. If anyone involved discovered I was actively looking for them, then it should divert attention away from Boyd. It might even force them to come after me much like Eric did.

"I know Paul owed somebody some money and I think the guys I'm looking for were trying to collect that money. And one thing I know about money is that it always leaves a trail. I will find them; you can count on it."

"Don't doubt that one bit, L.T., but you should know one thing, if money is involved, then you better start being more careful. Not all Southern boys are as harmless as the three you faced last night. This ain't the Dukes of Hazzard, you know. A lot of good ole boys like a good fight over girls and other shenanigans, but most of them same boys would shoot ya for a hundred dollars. Catch my drift?"

"Money is the root of all evil. Gotcha. I want to thank you for your time, Charles."

"Actually, the love of money is the root of all kinds of evil. 1 Timothy 6:10."

"Touché." I smiled at his correction of my mistake; it was a personal pet peeve of mine to hear people misquote popular sayings and he had caught me in one. "One last question?" He nodded. "For reasons I can't explain, have you heard of anyone around here running booze?"

"You mean moonshine? Hell, I know of a half dozen men that make their own spirits."

"No, I mean selling stolen liquor to the bars at a discount. Anyone ever approach you in that way?"

"Told you before, this here is a bar full of folks that make an honest wage doing an honest living. No government freeloaders ever water down here. You know what that means?" I looked at him egging him to continue. "That means I run an honest bar. Pay my taxes even when I know that asshole Uncle Sam don't know what the hell he is doing with my money."

"Which means no thief in his right mind would ever consider approaching you in that way."

"You're damn right."

"Figured as much. I was hoping someone might have been stupid enough to try, so I had to ask."

He smiled hard at my comment. "Wish I could've been more helpful. Going to pray for your success. Going to pray for them responsible too, 'cause I don't think they realize they done grabbed a tiger by the tail."

I had plenty of time to think during the drive home. I thought about Charles' advice to be wary of people when it comes to money. It was good advice. Money is a powerful motivator. Of course, I already knew that; in fact, I was counting on it. Once Boyd stepped on a few toes, I figured it was only a matter of time before someone approached him. It might not lead anywhere, but it was the only idea I had at the moment.

I also thought about last night's surprise attack. I was not careful enough. If Eric had approached the fight last night with more conviction, the fight might have gone a different way. I could have lost. Or I might have had to cause some real injury to keep from losing. Thankfully, it was just two racist idiots and one reluctant participant that only wanted me to leave town. Next time, it could be someone with a weapon wanting to stop me from investigating because I was getting too close. I was going to need to be more alert and more prepared.

Despite my late return, Ellie was waiting up for me in my apartment. I expected it. That did mean that I felt ready for the inevitable conversation. She looked as if she was still dressed for work. I hoped she had not been sitting in my apartment for the last three hours.

She was reading a book when I entered. I started to speak, but she held up a finger to shush me, so I sat down and waited. A minute later she closed the book, and then casually reclined back on my couch. She said, "You're really going to have to buy a TV if you continue to date someone who makes her living on TV."

"I suppose you want me to get cable too, or can I just get by with a good set of rabbit ears?"

"I think you can afford to spring for cable. Maybe even get HBO or Showtime."

"But I so enjoy the theater experience. I wouldn't even know how to buy a TV."

"We could go to Circuit City. I could help you. It's not that hard. Thousands do it every day."

I could not get a read on her. She did not appear mad, or glad to see me, or disappointed, or surprised. It was eerie, like the eye of a hurricane. I asked, "What are you reading anyway?"

"*The Hunt for Red October*. I found it over there on the shelf. Not my usual genre, but it's pretty good."

"Good to know, maybe I will read it sometime."

"You haven't read it?" Her tone was somewhat incredulous.

"With med school and residency, I am at least seven years behind on my pleasure reading."

"Excuses, excuses."

She seemed to be teasing me. Or was she testing me? Either way, it was a weird conversation, and there was a strange tension in the room.

"So you like spy thrillers, huh?" If so, she would love my story. Not that I would ever share it with her.

"Damn it, L.T. You going to make me drag this out of you, too? You got arrested!"

"The charges were dropped. Chief Parker dropped them himself."

"I know that, and I'm happy for you."

"Then why do you sound so mad?"

"I'm worried about you, you big idiot. My boyfriend gets arrested after getting into a fight with three men in my hometown. He spends the night in jail. Oh, and he goes on a boat ride with my father and asks him questions about organized crime and prostitution and all kinds of other illegal stuff. Why are you dragging him into your nonsense?"

"Sorry for dragging your father into it. I was just asking him some questions. Nothing that could blow back on him."

"I'm not worried about my father. I doubt anyone would think he was helping you in any way. Besides, he is like a saint in that town. I don't think anyone would ever want to hurt him. Regardless, you were still asking him about organized crime. Why?"

"It's an idea I have. Paul owed some guy some money. Gambling debts."

"So."

"So, it was fifteen thousand. This was not a friendly game of poker between friends. He was betting on something big and lost. First thing I thought of was the Mafia, but this is rural Tennessee, so it has to take on some other form."

She glared at me intensely, started to speak, changed her mind, and then asked a different question. "You were outside a biker bar. What were you doing there? You don't even drink."

"I was getting ready to go in and ask questions when the three stooges jumped me from behind."

"Why can't you just let this go?"

"I thought we discussed this already. I can't. And now Paul is dead, so I'm in no matter what now." I could see the worry on her face increase and her body stiffen up. "Don't worry. Chief Parker is now on my side. He even asked for my help, which also means no more trouble from Eric. The whole thing just got easier."

"And more dangerous. Someone killed Paul. You think it might be organized crime, for God's sake. What if they kill you for trying to find them?"

"Not likely."

"Damn you, L.T. How can you be so cavalier?"

"You think I'm cavalier?"

"Yes."

"Don't mistake my confidence for lack of concern. From here on out, I will be on my A-game. Look both ways before crossing the street, checking my rear view mirror. Trust me; I know I'm looking for someone who is dangerous. Besides, whoever killed Paul hasn't come after me yet, so why should they start now? I can't tell you what the Chief and I talked about in detail, but trust me when I tell you the killer, or killers, are not going to do anything to bring undue attention to themselves like attacking me."

She plopped down on my couch with a big sigh. "I hope you are right."

"Me too."

"Are you irritated with me yet for worrying?"

"No. Are you irritated with me for making you worry?"

"No, just worried. Then, I get mad at myself for worrying. You are a big boy used to a certain degree of danger. I'm just glad I didn't date you when you were in the Navy; I would have been a nervous wreck all the time."

I said, "So we're on the same page now, right? I make you worry. I'm going to help Chief Parker catch some bad guys. You're going to worry. I will be ultra-careful. You will still worry."

"You could still stop the whole darn thing and save me the grief." I looked at her absently. "I know, not going to happen."

I said, "For know, it works for me knowing the prettiest girl in Tennessee is worrying about me. Just realize I might be the toughest man in Tennessee. I know it's not what you expected when you started dating a charming doctor, but it's what I am: tough as nails."

I patted the cushion next to me motioning for her to sit. Her forehead was still wrinkled pensively, yet she accepted my invitation. After a long hug, she pushed me away and said, "Okay. I trust you. But if you are wrong, I'm going to take up kickboxing and beat you myself."

* * *

Boyd arrived around noon the next day driving my new '68 Mustang. He was right; it was perfect. When he finished this job, I was going to enjoy finishing the restoration on the car. It was a dark factory green that had been sun faded over the last 24 years, yet it did not have a stitch of rust anywhere that I could find. It had probably spent its entire life in the South avoiding rust-inducing road salt. The sexy, guttural lope of the engine immediately identified it as an American V-8 with a performance cam and headers. Not stock, which was good because I was never impressed with the speed of the older Mustangs.

Once I saw the interior, I realized why the car was priced on the low side. The headliner was falling down, the seats were ripped, the dash vinyl was cracked from too many Alabama summers, and the factory steering wheel had been replaced by a tiny little steering wheel that only rednecks find attractive. Other than that, I felt Boyd had practically stolen the car for me.

"You know," I said, "I hate that stupid steering wheel, but I think the interior helps with its intended purpose. Gives it street cred."

"That's just what I was thinking."

"So you ready for this?"

"Damn straight, I am."

"Then come on up and let's get you ready to be on your way."

"Sure. So were you able to smooth things over with Ellie?"

"For now, but I don't know how much more she is going to be able to handle. She's worried, plain and simple."

"Yeah, I could tell that during the ride over to Emmettsville yesterday. You can tell our kind of excitement just scares the hell out of her. She must have had it pretty easy growing up because one little fight shouldn't make someone come unglued that bad."

"She did have it easy. Wealthy parents that cared for her. No skeletons in the closet. No drama in her life that she ever talks about."

"You forgot to mention drop-dead gorgeous and smart."

"She feels her looks have been as much a problem for her as they were an asset."

"Only the pretty girls think that. Let me guess, can't trust that men respect her for her mind. Okay, thinking about it, I can see that. Men are pigs. Present company excluded, of course. So what more do I need?"

"Money. I called Paul's dad this morning and told him I would still help him, but I didn't tell him about you. When he asked how he could help, I told him all I needed at this time was money. He told me where to find some in his office. Here, $2000. Use it for lodging and stuff."

"I thought you were going to give me a gun or something."

"Man, I hadn't even thought about that. I got a couple of Glocks, a 9 mm and a .45. You're welcome to either one. I got an extra magazine for the 9 mm and two extra for the .45."

Boyd busted out laughing, holding his gut while bending over in an exaggerated laugh. "It's like you don't know me at all, L.T. Don't worry about me; I came loaded for bear. I got two Sig P226s, a Heckler

& Koch MP5, and a Remington Model 700 .300 Win Mag with a suppressor."

"Holy crap, man. Where did you even find guns like that? Not the Sigs, but the other two. No, wait. Don't tell me. I probably don't want to know."

"Let's just say; I'm resourceful."

"And like a good Boy Scout, you come prepared."

"No, like a good Marine being ready is not what matters. What matters is winning after you get there."

"General Krulak said that, right?"

"Damn straight. You never cease to surprise me sometimes; the things you know. You should have been a Marine."

"No, someone has to carry you guys around from point A to point B. And once again, here is a Navy guy buying a Marine a car so he can get from place to place. See, you Marines need the Navy."

"Whatever, squid," he said with an impish smile. "You always got a comeback for everything, even more so than me, and that's saying something. Before I go, what is Emmettsville like?"

"You saw it. Small," I said.

"I gathered that. How small?"

"Approximately 14,000. The highway turns into Main Street and goes right through the middle of town. Most of the businesses are on Main Street or within a couple of blocks of Main Street. There is a main square with some diners and other shops around the courthouse. The police and fire station are about a block off the square. Only chain restaurants I saw were fast food, a small McDonald's and a Hardee's. No movie theater, just bars and small diners. It is clean and quaint and quiet, with lots of trucks."

Boyd said, "Does it have a Wal-Mart?"

"No, it has a small K-Mart though. And I remember a hardware store and a small farm implement business. Oh, and a small hospital."

"Ok, I know the type of town. Rural, sheltered from the outside world, quite a bit. Probably very white."

"I don't think the town is as sheltered as you think. Two of the three largest aluminum bass boat manufacturers in the country are located in Emmettsville, and there is a company that makes some kind of pistol grip or holster that gets shipped all over the world, so the town is used to outsiders. But, yes, it is very white."

Boyd said, "If they are used to outsiders, then don't you find it odd that your reception in the town has been hostile? Yankees buy bass boats and guns too."

"I never thought about it. At the time, I just figured they were working on the Chief's orders or were friends of Eric."

"Yet, you no longer think the Chief or Eric had anything to do with Paul's death, or that the Chief sent them after you after all. Food for thought, don't you think?"

"I didn't say I no longer think they were involved; I said I had doubts. It does get me thinking. Let me ponder on that one for awhile. In the meantime, I think Falco's is as good a place as any to start. Who knows, we might get lucky right off. I told you about Mason, the owner. Kind of a dick, but I think you can do this. I really do. Just be careful and call me when you get there and give me daily updates and..."

"Yes, mom."

"Okay, you're a big boy, I get it. Now get over to LeClair's and get the liquor. He says he has more than you can carry in one load, so I will bring the rest over to your hotel later tonight after it gets dark."

Boyd said, "I should be settled and able to get a decent room by five o'clock. I'll call you, and we can figure out a time and place to meet up."

The rest of the day was rather monotonous. I was waiting again with nothing to do. I killed some time with a long workout and lunch. I even delivered a note to Ellie thanking her for her understanding. Finally, I cleaned and serviced my .45 caliber Glock 21 along with loading both magazines. I could hear Charles Mann's advice about being careful and I decided it was time to be prepared.

Everything was business as usual until Boyd did not call. Five o'clock came and went, then six, then seven. By eight o'clock, I started to worry. At 8:30, I could take it no more. I grabbed my Glock 21 and began the journey to Emmettsville.

At first, I started out angry, driving the Mercedes hard on the straightaways. However, 20 minutes into the drive I started to feel foolish as my inner voice warned me that I was overreacting. Boyd was a grown man, a former Marine Military Policemen, and the survivor of a horrific helicopter crash and an eleven-day grueling hike through the Cambodian jungle with hostile Vietnamese soldiers chasing him. He never once lost his cool during the ordeal. He never once gave up hope either. He remained equally unflappable during the surgeries to fix his shattered ankle and the months of physical therapy. Boyd had a survivor's instinct. He would be okay. Plus, he had enough firepower to wage war on a small country.

My anger calmed down to frustration as I admitted to myself that I was somewhat jealous of Boyd. He was operating in the trenches, doing the grunt work, while I operated in the background providing money and support. I was yearning for a way to make my involvement more substantial. I wanted a piece of the real action, even more so now that the stakes were potentially higher, which is why I had created a situation in my mind when one did not exist.

By the time I realized I was overreacting, it was too late to turn back towards Memphis, so I finished the drive to Emmettsville hoping I could find Boyd. I was disappointed in myself for allowing my frustration to affect my judgment again so soon. Two nights ago, I had allowed three men to surprise attack me. Frustration, even more than anger, had caused blinders to go up around me. I felt inwardly ashamed that I had allowed that to happen.

Admiral Buie had commented on my situational awareness while I served under him. He deemed it my greatest asset and said it made me perfect for intelligence work. He would have been embarrassed to see my performance two nights ago. Thankfully, my martial arts training and athleticism saved me from getting my butt kicked.

Admiral Buie was almost like a second father to me while I was in the Navy, so he knew me well. I disagreed with him on my greatest asset. I would never admit it to Boyd, but I felt my ability to improvise, adapt, and overcome, an unofficial mantra of the United States Marine Corps, was my greatest asset.

While I was in college studying business at the University of Illinois in Champaign, a unique and forward thinking professor introduced my class to the OODA loop - Observe, Orient, Decide, Act. John Boyd, an Air Force Fighter Pilot, came up with the OODA loop as a strategy for winning head-to-head competitions such as aerial dogfights. The professor demonstrated how both human beings and organizations could use the OODA loop to learn, grow, and not only survive, but thrive in a competitive, rapidly changing environment. John Boyd's contribution to military strategy was, in a nutshell, based on the idea that whoever made it through his 4-step decision-making process the fastest ultimately wins in a conflict or competition.

I immediately embraced the concepts of the OODA loop. John Boyd intended his loop for combat, so I applied the OODA loop strategy to my martial arts. It made me virtually unstoppable. Not even my instructors could keep up with me during sparring; I was always one mental step ahead of my opponents.

It was about that time in my life that I found my inner voice, a seemingly innate part of my conscious and subconscious mind that nearly always led me to see things quicker and fuller than the next guy. I had always surmised that it was my development and utilization of the OODA loop that gave birth to my inner voice. I once tried to explain my inner voice to Virgil. I told him I could actually hear a voice. He thought I was crazy. It was the only time I ever saw him look at me like he had no idea who I was, so I did not mention the inner voice to him again. Instead, I told him it was like intuition, but on crack. He teased me, saying more probably more like on steroids.

My martial arts training, my heightened situational awareness, my ability to quickly observe, orient, decide, and act had made me into a man who excelled during tough, tense situations. I found that I loved action. I lived for action. No, I was made for action. Despite my yearning for normalcy, it was time to start acting like Lieutenant McCain again.

CHAPTER 20

Finding Boyd ended up being easier than I had expected. I had told him to start at Falco's and, sure enough, when I pulled into the parking lot I noticed the dark green 1968 Ford Mustang 390 GT Fastback immediately. I also noticed Eric's Camaro Z28. Boyd and Eric were most likely in Falco's at the same time, which in itself, did not surprise me. It was a small town with a limited number of options for eating out. What did surprise me was seeing Boyd walk out with Eric and Jackie laughing like the three of them were long-time friends.

Slowly and quietly, I backed the Mercedes up until it was hidden by a large pickup. Although I was intrigued by the sight of Boyd with Eric, I was distracted by the truck next to me. It looked vaguely familiar. It was a beautiful two-toned green Ford F-250 Ranger XLT from the late seventies with large mud tires and a lift kit elevating it off the ground more than the factory specifications. I could not be sure without hearing it, but it looked like the truck that had been watching me in the parking lot the night Paul went missing.

Soon Eric and Jackie drove by and exited the parking lot followed shortly by Boyd in the Mustang. I waited several seconds before leaving the parking lot to follow Boyd. After a few minutes, it became apparent that Boyd was headed out of town. He had to know that was me behind him.

He answered my question when he double tapped his brake lights before quickly accelerating. I could hear the powerful motor roar; it was not a stock motor. Obviously, Boyd wanted to play, so I obliged him flooring the accelerator on the Mercedes. The Mercedes kept up with him better than expected, and I am sure my ride was smoother, yet horsepower always wins in the straightaways. He slowed down substantially heading into the first turn and then motioned with his arm out the window for me to follow him. After several minutes, Boyd pulled into a heavily-wooded field and stopped.

"Wow, that was fun," he yelled as he exited the Mustang. "Your Mercedes is faster than I thought."

"I was thinking the same thing. I guess I did a good job on the motor. So what are we doing out here?"

"I scouted out this area earlier so we could have a discreet place to meet and transfer the alcohol. Plus, we might need an agreed-upon place to meet in the future and this place works great."

I said, "Good thinking, Boyd. You are already thinking ahead. I'm impressed."

"Thanks. As an MP, I never got to be sneaky. I wore a uniform and a badge or those armbands. I like this sneaky stuff."

"I should have thought of this kind of stuff, but, to be honest, NIS took care of the smaller details for me so I could focus on the investigating. We made another tactical error that became obvious to me earlier."

"Let me guess. You could not reach me."

"Bingo."

"Were you getting worried about me?" He was teasing me. "Because you needn't be," he said with a big smile while pulling a SIG 9 mm out from behind his back. Now I knew why he was wearing an untucked button down over a tee shirt in August. I shook my head in mock surprise. "So what's the solution? It's not like cell phones are going to work out here."

We had mulled over the idea for a few minutes before I worked out a solution. I felt foolish for not thinking of it sooner. A pager. A recent magazine article I read mentioned that many high schools were banning pagers due to their heavy use among drug traffickers. Even if Boyd wore a pager on him, it would not look suspicious.

Boyd said, "Another logistical problem solved. Now go look at the surprise I have for you in my front seat."

I glanced in the passenger window and saw a set of headphones plugged into a nondescript metal box with a bunch of knobs and buttons on it. "What is it?"

"You know the company I work for is a research company, right?"

"Yeah, something to do with security."

"We invent and build new security devices. Long perimeter intrusion detection devices, microphones, infrared, motion detection. You name it; we've tried it. We even got one engineer who built a fiber optic microphone that's completely undetectable. The CIA couldn't find it when they swept our conference room for bugs. You'd like him. Ex-Navy like you, likes to work out, a comeback for everything, and some of the funniest damn stories."

"So what's the device?"

"Sorry, I get kind of excited about the spy shit sometimes. You're looking at a prototype unit that can receive signals from several different types of bugs that transmit their signal back using a UHF signal. Nothing new really, other than we think we have found a way to do it cheaper and smaller than anyone else out there with crystal clear audio."

"You stealing stuff from work?"

"No, it's a prototype. Under that tarp in the back seat, I even have our version of a laser microphone that lets me listen through windows from a *long* way away. Another prototype. The engineers want me to test the stuff in a real-world situation. And don't worry, they don't know any details."

"I'm impressed."

"Oh, that's not all."

"No?"

Boyd had a wide, self-satisfied smile on his face. "Believe it or not, I already found out where both Chief Parker and his son live, and I already have contact microphones on the windows."

"Holy cow, you've been busy."

He gave me a look of pure satisfaction. "So when do you want to start?'

"Start what?"

"Listening, dork."

"How about now, I got nothing better to do. Now help me with this alcohol," I said while opening my trunk.

"I don't have any room. You said it yourself; I have been busy. So busy that I haven't got a hotel yet, which means I still have the liquor in my car from earlier. We will have to get it later. And I have no room in my car, so we will have to take yours to listen to the Chief. Just put the top up and close the windows so no one can make me out in the car."

"Sure thing. Besides, it's the Navy's job to give Marines a ride."

Personal experience had proved that stakeouts could be long and boring, often with little to no results. Furthermore, it was late in the evening, so we had no guarantee that either of our targets would even be awake. Hoping to increase our success, I called Chief Parker on a pay phone on the way to his house. I knew he would not have a forensic report back yet, but it gave me a chance to call. I also made up a story about Eric, telling the Chief that someone had overheard him bragging about coming into some money recently. My goal was to get him talking with his wife, or better yet, hoping he might contact Eric while we listened to the conversation when we got outside his house.

As I pulled onto the Chief's street, I asked, "So how did you find their houses so fast?"

"After leaving LeClair's, I figured I would just wait at the beer distributor and see if I could spot Eric leaving, which I did. Following him was easy. I got lucky on the parent's house; Eric stopped by there on his way home. That's why I haven't found a hotel yet."

"Way to go, Bird Dog."

"Bird dog, really? You don't even hunt."

"Maybe not, but it fits. Matches your enthusiasm, plus it seems like all I need to do is point you in the right direction, then sit back and wait for you to get it done." He laughed at that one. I think he liked the name. "So after planting the bugs, you decided to follow him to dinner and buddy up with him?"

"No, after putting the microphones on the windows, I went to Falco's and Eric pulled in at the same time I did. He commented on the car; we struck up a conversation, and then he introduced me to Jackie. I sat one table over, but we kept talking, so it was almost like I had dinner with them. That big son-of-a-bitch gave you no trouble the other day? Shit, L.T., seriously how tough are you?" he asked in a rhetorical, teasing tone.

Within minutes, we arrived outside the Chief's house. Boyd spent a few minutes describing how the UHF receiver worked, as well as its range limitations and the fact that his current prototype unit could not record conversations, although future units would have that function. Boyd started fidgeting with some buttons, and soon we could hear voices from inside the Parker house. The sound quality was perfect. The television was on. They were watching Letterman. We caught the tail end of his Top Ten List; it was something about Top 10 Signs You're on a Bad Cruise.

Chief Parker and his wife continued to watch Letterman through the end of the first guest, a popular Italian-born actress. I could not recall anything she had been in, and I did not find her interview particularly stimulating. The musical guest was George Thorogood, so as far as stakeouts go, this was not going to be a bad one. If we were going to be bored, at least, we could listen to some good rock and blues. However, it was not meant to be as Chief Parker turned off the television right before Thorogood's performance and the couple went to bed.

I said, "I knew I didn't like that guy. Makes us sit through a worthless TV show and then shuts it off just when some good music is going to start."

Boyd said, "You know what they say, 'If it's too loud, you're too old.' Well, that was a bust. Getting late, do you want to drive over to Eric's?"

"Probably a waste of time, but I still got nothing better to do."

* * *

I was impressed with Boyd. Professionally, we had served together briefly in the military where I had the chance to see him under fire. In situations of extreme danger and duress, he had shown that he was unflappable and resourceful. Now he was showing an uncanny ability in understanding the complexities of an investigation. He said he liked the "sneaky stuff." He was also proving he was good at it. The toys he brought with him were a bonus and I had a feeling they were going to come in very handy. Hopefully, we would have no use for the firepower he also brought with him.

Within minutes, we parked near Eric's house. Boyd pushed some buttons on his receiver and it became immediately clear that Eric was not alone. He was in a heated argument with a woman. Both were angry and both were yelling.

Boyd said, "That's Jackie's voice." I nodded an acknowledgment.

Jackie's voice boomed over the speaker. "What did your dad say?"

Eric replied, "Just that he heard a rumor that I was bragging about coming into some money recently."

"What did you tell him?"

"The damn truth. I had no idea what the hell he was talking about. He kept yelling at me to tell him the truth or he wasn't going to be able to help me. I don't even know why he thought my coming into some money was important to him, but he said it was and to trust him. I asked him where he was getting his info and he wouldn't tell me."

"Did he believe you in the end?"

"He said he did. But obviously he is still asking around about me, so I'm not so sure."

Once again, the sound quality was excellent; I gave Boyd a big thumbs up. My ruse had worked; obviously the Chief had called his son after we left. I also made myself a mental note to call the Chief tomorrow and tell him the rumor about the money had been a false alarm. The father and son were communicating, and I did not want a lack of trust to ruin that communication. The two inside the house were relatively quiet while someone was obviously flipping channels looking for something to watch at 12:40 a.m.

"I'm fixin' to go, Eric. I got to get up for work."

"Don't go. Sleep over."

"I'm tired."

"Come on. I'll let you sleep."

The conversation went on like that for a few more minutes ending with Eric telling Jackie that he loved her and wanted her to stay.

"I know you love me, Eric. I don't doubt that for a minute, but you also drive me crazy sometimes. I want to go home and you keep trying to pressure me to stay. Ultimately, it's because you are just too damn jealous and insecure about our relationship. It's your jealousy and your temper that got you into this mess in the first place. You know that, right?"

Eric spent the next couple of minutes apologizing for his jealousy and professing his love.

Jackie listened quietly before responding. "Like I told you before, I accept your apology. And I know you have gotten better. You didn't hit Paul in the bar, but you still hit him out in the parking lot, which somebody saw you do according to your dad. Obviously, I told your dad the truth that you were at my house for a couple of hours immediately after we left Falco's and everyone knows you couldn't kill anyone. It just looks bad is all I'm saying."

"It looks worse than you think, Jackie. Can you keep a secret?"

"You know I can."

"Dad says that someone tied the guy to the steering wheel with a tee shirt."

"So?"

"It was my tee shirt. My father recognized it, and when I went to look for it in my laundry, I couldn't find it. I think whoever is trying to frame me took it out of the gym bag in my car, probably that night."

"Oh, sweetie, what are we gonna do?"

"I don't know."

The conversation went on for several minutes with both of them repeating the same sentiment only with different sentences. Eric was scared. His girlfriend was worried for him. There was genuine concern in her voice for Eric. Eventually, the conversation turned to Eric's encounters with me. He accurately described both encounters to Jackie.

Jackie said, "So he really is a doctor from Memphis?"

"Dad says he is, but he is the toughest damn doctor I ever saw. I probably got 20 pounds on him, but he tore through all three of us like we were nothing. I don't think anyone even got a lick in on him. I know I didn't. Whoever heard of a badass doctor?"

"But he didn't start it?"

"No, I told you, Tyler kind of started it." He went on to describe the fight as he saw it, right up to being choked until he felt he could not breathe any longer.

"Sweetie," Jackie said, "Why were you there with Junior and Tyler to begin with? It's not like you guys are friends or anything."

"They just showed up and told me the doctor fella was running around town implying I had something to do with Paul being missing. Junior was saying he tried to run him out once before when he was in town with Paul's dad and some black guy. He kept saying it would be a pleasure to help me run the 'nigger-loving Yankee' out of town. It would be like two birds with one stone. I thought we would just be able to scare him out, you know."

Jackie said, "Well, that didn't work."

"No shit. He wasn't even the least bit scared of us; I could tell that real quickly. I know this sounds weird, but he looked more annoyed than scared. Impatient is a better word, like we were keeping him from something. Next thing you know we were all on the ground and he was just standing there unscratched and not even breathing hard. Actually, I was basically unconscious. My father says he argued with Officer Crane. Apparently, the doctor did not want to drop me on my face when he was told to put his hands in the air or whatever."

Boyd said, "You need to tell your stories with more flare, L.T. It was just so matter-of-fact when you told it, but it is funny as hell to hear this guy's version. Damn, I wish I had been there." He was trying hard to stifle his laughter.

Jackie said, "Is he going to press charges against you guys?"

"My father, or the doctor?"

"Either, I guess."

"My father says it might come to that. He is waiting to see what the doctor says."

After a few minutes of them contemplating his father pressing charges, Jackie said, "It's almost one in the morning. I'm going home to bed."

Eric spent the next several minutes in an unsuccessful attempt to get Jackie to stay. During that time, Boyd and I discussed what we had just heard. Boyd stated that the entire evening had been a colossal waste of time. I disagreed reminding him that all information is useful in one manner or another.

* * *

Boyd tapped my arm and pointed towards Eric's house. Jackie was leaving. She walked to a bluish-gray Pontiac Grand Prix and sped off in a hurry. He asked me to follow her so he could see where she lived. Apparently, he had plenty of microphones. Driving a red German sports car in a small town has its obvious disadvantages: it stands out like a sore thumb. Even so, Jackie did not spot us as I followed a safe distance behind her. However, on Main Street, a police cruiser did an abrupt U-turn and settled in behind us.

I shoved Boyd down into his seat. He looked at me with surprise until I told him the cop was following us. We decided to forget about following Jackie; it was not all that important. Not worth the risk of someone spotting Boyd with me. Boyd was thinking; I could see it on his face. My plan was to simply drive out of town until he stopped following, although I was not sure what to do if the officer signaled us to pull over. Boyd told me to stay on the main road and see if I could time one of the stop lights just right so as to run a yellow. If I could get far enough ahead of the cop, then he was going to bail out without being seen.

"You sure?" I asked.

"Yeah. And don't worry about me. I will walk out to my car."

"That will take you an hour at least."

"So." He gestured towards his left leg. "I know it ain't pretty to look at, but it is functional you know. I can even run on it."

"I know. I wasn't thinking about you; I was thinking of any little kids that might see Quasimodo lumbering through town."

"Well, that makes sense, but it is one in the morning. If they are out this late, then they need to be scared."

The speed limit on Main Street was 20 miles per hour. Boyd's idea was only going to succeed if the traffic lights were on a timer; otherwise, we were going to need someone coming off a side street at one in the morning to trigger a red light for us. As we hit the last light heading out of town, we realized his idea had failed.

Boyd said, "No worries, he will stop following us when we hit the city limits. Outside his jurisdiction."

"His jurisdiction is the whole blasted county, Boyd. The police department in Emmettsville is more of a *sheriff's* department for the county. Chief Parker is elected, not appointed."

"What the hell?"

"Don't ask me; I don't live here. Ellie told me about it."

Boyd asked, "Now what?"

"I was prepared to drive until he stopped. What if I outrun him instead?"

"Can you?"

"Do you doubt my driving ability, Boyd? Because I'm not into guns like you, or hunting, or fishing. I don't even play golf. I can fight, I can drive, and apparently I have a knack with sutures."

"Good to know. Hey, I got this button loose on my shirt, can you fix that for me?"

I punched him playfully in the arm. "You know, I'm pretty sure I have more car than him."

"Then go for it."

"Alright, I will. But I want to go back the other way since we are getting farther away from your car."

I was telling the truth when I told Boyd I could drive. My dad was a 290-pound offensive lineman who had been big his whole life, big, strong, and slow. He told me that he had not moved fast since grade school; that is until he bought his first American muscle car. After that, he got hooked on speed and cars, which was an interest that he passed down to me. I even competed in a go-kart racing circuit for a couple of years as a teenager. I never won a single race, but I was a competitive second or third several times, which meant that unless the officer behind me was a retired race car driver, then I stood a good chance of getting away.

We were traveling at a steady 55 mph a couple of miles out of town while I looked for an opportunity. I needed just the right intersecting road. Unfortunately, on the winding two-lane road the upcoming intersections were poorly marked, and the heavy forest made it difficult to see the intersections until it was too late. Finally, a road sign indicated a 4-way intersection up ahead, one I could see far enough in advance to set up my plan.

The police cruiser was a Ford Crown Victoria, maybe three to four years old, plenty of horsepower, but not the most nimble of cars. I was counting on that. I did not want to get into a high-speed pursuit.

Signally far in advance for a left-hand turn, I slowed far below a necessary safe speed. The police cruiser was also signaling a left-hand turn. Immediately before the turn, I dropped the automatic transmission down into second gear accelerating quickly into the turn. For a split second, the headlights of the Crown Vic could not be seen as the trees blocked my view. Using the small window to my advantage, I turned off my headlights and then spun the car 180 degrees in the middle of the road before the police cruiser came speeding around the corner trying to make up some lost distance.

It took the officer a second to realize he had just passed me in the dark heading the opposite direction; he traveled at least 50 yards before I saw his brake lights light up. I floored the accelerator, turned right and sped down the road back into town. The 0 to 60 mph specifications on the Mercedes were impressive for a luxury sports car, which I used to my advantage.

Heading into the first curve at nearly 90 mph, I soon discovered the car's shortcomings; it was heavy. The steering response was neither crisp nor especially responsive. Flinging the 500 SL into the first corner required a lot of effort, and I badly wanted a manual transmission. The car was obviously designed more toward a luxury roadster than toward making it a sports car.

I had difficulty maneuvering through the first corner efficiently. Boyd must have sensed my problems with the car because he reached out to brace himself against the dashboard as if he expected a crash. I heard him murmur an "oh shit" as the car whipped into the curve, the tires squealing through the turn as they fought to maintain proper contact with the road.

Although I had overestimated the handling of the 500 SL, I did manage to maneuver through the first turn successfully. Boyd's fear was short-lived. He was enthusiastically yelling as we exited the curve. By the second or third curve, he was egging me on to go faster. On the straight away heading into town, I was able to squeeze 130 mph out of the car. Boyd sounded as happy as a kid on his first roller coaster. We never saw the police car even once in the rear view mirror.

At the first intersection in Emmettsville, I turned down a side road to get off Main Street in case another officer was looking for us. "Well, that was exhilarating," I said. "I need to remember this is a luxury sports car, emphasis more on luxury than sports. Scared me a little bit on that first turn."

"Whatever," yelled Boyd, "That was awesome. You know you enjoyed it." I mumbled a weak acknowledgment. "L.T., you need to stop lying to yourself. That was scary, but that's why it was fun, and you know it. Just because you have a cerebral job and do the real estate investing thing doesn't mean you don't like the adrenaline and excitement. Maybe you aren't the junkie I am, but you like it. That's probably why you like the ER and why you still do the martial arts stuff every week. It's also why you are trying to find Paul's killer."

"I'm trying to find Paul's killer because it is the right thing to do, not because I'm an adrenaline junkie."

"Sure, I know it's the right thing to do. I agree. But it was way too easy to talk you into investigating this crime after you had already decided to throw in the towel. Just saying. By the way, how come he didn't chase us?"

"I think he tried, but he would have had to do a three-point turn with that big car unless he was crazy enough to try to whip around in the middle of the road going fast in reverse. Would have been pretty risky in that big car on a narrow two-lane road with no shoulders. By the time he got turned around, we were probably three-quarters of a mile ahead of him."

"Let me out here. I will walk," said Boyd. "Call you tomorrow. I'm going to stay in town and try to find a room tonight."

"Let's hope your undercover work as Graham, the new bootlegger, gives us more information than listening to Eric did. Not to rain on my own parade, but I am now thoroughly convinced Eric had nothing to do with Paul's death, which means we have no suspects."

I hated making Boyd walk that far with a bad ankle, but he insisted especially, since I needed to get back onto Main Street to exit the west side of Emmettsville. Boyd's words were buzzing in my head as I drove home. Over seven years of college and four years of residency, plenty of money left by my dad for whatever I needed it for, a wonderful girlfriend, everything a guy could want, yet I was looking forward to tomorrow and my day off from work to see how I could help Boyd. If he told me I was enjoying myself again, I was planning on punching him in the arm.

The interior discussion I was having with myself was interrupted by my pesky inner voice. I had no suspects, yet Eric's conversation with Jackie held a clue. My inner voice insisted on it, telling me to replay the conversation and focus on what I heard. One of them had asked an important question, one that I told myself to come back to later; however, the car chase had redirected my focus, and now the memory of the conversation was vague. My mind had effectively paraphrased the conversation, but I needed a word-for-word account. When I crawled into bed a little after three in the morning, I still had not solved the puzzle.

CHAPTER 21

Jackie was sitting across from me at Falco's dressed in a blue top that flattered her well-proportioned figure. She was talking to me, asking me a question, yet I could not hear what she was saying despite the proximity. Suddenly, her eyes grew wide with surprise, (or was it fright?), as she looked past my left shoulder. Turning quickly, I spotted Eric walking briskly in my direction.

He was mad. He looked ready for action, yet he stopped a few feet from the table and said, "No hard feelings, I hope," before abruptly turning and walking straight out of the bar. He left me there sitting with his girlfriend. Alone. She was avoiding eye contact as I looked back in her direction. She looked dispirited. I was confused.

My inner voice was warning me, screaming at me to quickly examine my surroundings as the smell of Old Spice permeated the room. I had learned not to ignore my instincts. Whipping my head around revealed Junior and Overalls standing slightly fanned out behind me. Overalls was wearing the same ironed overalls as the other day, and he had his hands crossed and resting on his protruding abdomen. Junior looked ready to pounce.

Junior spoke. "Don't go thinkin' you're so smart and that you figured anything out, 'cuz you don't know shit."

I had no idea what he was talking about. I was beginning to speak when Overalls interrupted me. "Nice day fer us. Maybe not so nice fer y'all though," he said.

I stared at them silently with a confused look on my face. It was like they were suddenly including me in a conversation that they had started without me.

Junior said, "I will lead the parade myself."

As I opened my mouth to respond, someone grabbed my wrist, someone that I had not seen before. Someone I had missed. Instinctively, I twisted my forearm to position myself for a wrist lock. The grip was strong. I turned toward my adversary. It was Tyler. He had already dropped to his knees even though I had not finished the wrist lock. Slightly smarter than the last time; he was learning.

As I went to deliver a crippling blow to the side of his head again, he suddenly got free of my grip then sprung to his feet a safe distance away. Tyler smiled. He looked satisfied with his success in avoiding the wrist lock for a third time. In a smug tone, he said, "Who you calling Dwayne?"

I could not comprehend how Tyler had suddenly seemed to spring out of thin air. Was my situational awareness becoming that rusty? *Remember the sequence: observe, orient, decide, act.*

Observing was the easy part; it was the orienting that was causing the bottleneck in my brain. Jackie was still sitting at the table with her eyes downcast. Overalls and Tyler were standing in front of me while Junior was farther back. He was pushing Eric towards me. *When did Eric return?*

And finally, both Hank and Aaron were standing at the bar talking to Ray, who was holding a glass of tea. *What is Ray doing in Falco's?*

Eric walked closer as Junior pushed him from behind. Eric said, "You talk too much, asshole!"

I had not said a word, and these assholes were beginning to get on my nerves. Anger and frustration were boiling up inside me. I was aware of each heart beat as I felt the blood pulsating through my temples.

Out of the corner of my eye, I also noticed the other two men from Sunday walking in the front door. All six of the original goons were now present, along with Eric and Tyler. Panic was beginning to sit in.

Suddenly, everything in the room became crystal clear. I was able to shoot right through the orienting stage into making a decision: I had my .45 tucked into the holster in the small of my back. As I reached behind me, Officer Crane walked out of the bathroom. He glanced furtively around the room and began to draw his weapon.

I did not want to shoot a cop. It appeared he was leaving me no choice.

Luckily, I never had to draw my weapon.

Junior spotted Officer Crane and started heading for the door brushing his shoulder against me as he walked past. He whispered, "Are you tryin' to be funny?" Then he left.

Everyone else except Jackie and Eric followed Junior out the door. Even Officer Crane left. He was the last one to leave. Before exiting he yelled over his shoulder, "Mister, you are pushing your luck with me."

What the hell just happened?

I was forced to observe and re-orient myself. Jackie had moved to a new table several feet away. She was murmuring something incomprehensible to Eric. Ray was smiling from behind the bar pushing an iced tea in my direction. All I could do was stand in the middle of the room with my mouth open. The two men who had given me Eric's name on the night Paul disappeared were once again staring at me from their pool table.

The room began to spin. Objects and people went out of focus. I did not feel dizzy, yet I had an uncomfortable feeling in my heart, fuzzy thoughts, and a loud ringing in my ears. The sudden stress and onset of anger and frustration seemed to be causing a vasovagal response. Although I had never suffered from a vasovagal episode before, I immediately recognized the symptoms and knew I was going to faint if I did not lie down and elevate my legs to return oxygen to the brain. While looking for a suitable location to lie down, black cloud-like spots appeared in my vision. Falling to the ground, I started to slip into unconsciousness.

No one was coming to my aid; in fact, everyone was simply ignoring me. Through the spots in my vision, I could still see Ray behind the bar holding a glass of iced tea. Eric was mumbling something to Jackie.

Jackie responded, "I know you love me, Eric. Why were you there with Junior and Tyler to begin with?"

It was the last thing I heard before I blacked out.

CHAPTER 22

When I awoke, I was lying comfortably in my bed. My internal clock told me it was 9:45 a.m. Thursday. The bizarre set of events had been a dream, a dream that was already fading into my subconscious leaving me a little unsettled as I contemplated its meaning, if any.

Was the dream trying to imply that my situational awareness was that bad? Did Ray's presence mean that I could not truly trust anyone in the town? Were Junior and his friends finally going to stay out of my way? Why did Junior and Tyler even care? Could their bigotry towards blacks and Yankees make them that hateful?

Maybe it was just a stupid dream. Maybe dream interpretation was a waste of time. I mean, why does a dream have to mean anything? I never put much stock in that kind of pseudo-science when we discussed it in my psychology classes in undergrad. The irony that a man with an inner voice was arguing against dreams being a portal into the subconscious mind was not lost on me.

I wanted to stop wasting time analyzing my dream and try to find the answer to other questions, yet my inner voice kept redirecting my thoughts to the dream, insisting there was an answer to a big question hidden in the dream. I did not deny that the answer was there. It was just that I could not see it.

* * *

All my life, for as long as I could remember, I had been bigger than average, and even faster than I was big. Therefore, growing up I had never been one to sit on the sidelines; in fact, I was a starting varsity football player my freshman year. Sitting in my apartment analyzing a dream while waiting for Boyd to call was nerve-racking. I was on the sidelines, and I hated the feeling.

While waiting for Boyd to call, I ate breakfast, worked out on the weights and heavy bag, and grabbed a shower. Someone had left a message on my answering machine while I was in the shower. My disappointment would have been obvious from a mile away when I realized the message was from my mother leaving an impassioned plea for me to call her. It hurt to hear the genuine concern in her voice; I needed to find out what Virgil told her. There was also a number on my pager that appeared to be from Emmettsville.

When I returned the call, a female voice with a pleasant Southern accent answered on the second ring informing me I had reached the Emmettsville Police Department. I was not sure if the Chief had called me on police business or if it was personal. I decided to play it safe and made up a different reason for calling. I asked for Chief Parker, telling the receptionist that L&M Realty out of Memphis was returning his call concerning the land for sale near his hunting cabin. She put me on hold. The line went completely silent. At first, I thought the call had disconnected, and then I realized the police station merely wasted no money on hold music. The silence was shortly interrupted.

"Chief Parker, how can I help you?"

"It's me, L.T."

"What's with the L&M Realty?"

"I didn't know if I needed a cover."

"That makes sense, but how do you know about my cabin?"

"I thought you were a dirty cop, remember? I looked into you a little. If you were still a suspect, by now I would have known if you preferred boxers or briefs. I might even know how long you watched Letterman last night with the wife."

"I did watch Letterman last night with the wife. How did you know that?"

"Lucky guess." There was an awkward silence as he considered my last statement; it seemed like a good idea to keep him a little unsettled when thinking about me and my presence in his town. "Change of subject, Chief. First, the rumor about your son coming into some money turned out false. My source was unreliable."

Chief Parker said, "Good to know since I questioned him last night and he denied the whole thing."

"Second, did any officers happen to mention following me last night a little after one?"

"Not to me."

"Would they have called it into the night dispatcher?"

"Not necessarily. Why?"

"Because one of them followed me from Main Street several miles out of town, but I gave him the slip."

The Chief said, "Why didn't you just pull over?"

"The officer never actually hit his lights, plus, I had something in the car I didn't want him to see. Don't worry; it was nothing illegal, just something useful in my investigation that I didn't want anyone to know about."

"Including me?"

"Yes."

"I don't understand. Aren't we on the same side?"

"We have a common goal, Chief. Finding Paul's killer. Only time will tell if we are on the same side, although I currently trust that you will do the right thing when I find the person responsible."

"Don't you mean 'if' you find him?"

"No, I mean 'when.'"

Chief Parker said, "I can't tell if you're cocky, or just thoroughly convinced."

"Neither, but failure is not an option, so I will find him. You can bet on it."

The Chief said, "I wouldn't bet against you, that's for sure. So what did you mean when you said that you currently trust me?"

"Don't read too much into that, Chief. I just meant that I trust you now, unlike before. And I believe if I found out the killer was your best friend I could still trust you to do the right thing."

"Yet, you are withholding information from me; you are driving around my town at 1:00 am, and I get the strange impression that you know exactly how long I watched Letterman last night."

I said, "Chief, I am not withholding information, I'm just not telling you how I'm getting my information."

"What's the difference?"

"You would need a warrant to do some of the things I'm doing without a warrant. I'm giving you plausible deniability, so the less you know, the less you might have to lie about later on. It is as much for your protection as it is for mine, I promise."

He was silent for several seconds.

"Chief, I can't tell you how I'm getting my information. You know that. I can't go undercover in your town since I'm too well known now, which means I have to investigate and ask around directly. If I had, say, a local member of your town in the car with me, then I could not risk that person being seen with me. Catch my drift?" It was a little white lie, but he seemed to need the reassurance.

"Okay, that makes sense. So did you find out anything useful last night?"

"I found out you don't like George Thorogood. The rest I'm still working on. See if you can find out who followed me and why. I have to go."

After hanging up with the Chief, I realized I had not asked him why he had called me in the first place. My focus had been on figuring out which officer followed me the night before; however, I was no closer in finding out the answer. Maybe the Chief could figure it out for me. It would provide me a good test of his leadership ability in the office while also letting me know how much I could trust him.

If Chief Parker remembered that George Thorogood was the musical act last night on Letterman, then my parting reference should have left the Chief a little unsettled, which is exactly where I wanted him. It is also why I mentioned my knowledge of his hunting cabin. I did not want him to feel he could hold back any information from me without me finding out. I was telling him the truth when I told him we had a common goal; it did not guarantee mutual trust.

Before heading out to buy Boyd's pager, I left a brief message on Virgil's machine asking him to call me; I wanted to know what he told my mother. Once I purchased the pager, I plotted a different route to Emmettsville involving a winding blacktop that gave me an opportunity to push the Mercedes 500 SL around the tight corners. The automatic transmission was a royal pain, reminding me once again it was a luxury sports car and not a true sports car. Regardless, it was one gorgeous vehicle and had the smoothest ride of any vehicle I had ever ridden in. My biggest complaint: how could an $80,000 vehicle not have a CD player in it even though it had a built-in hands-free cellular phone? All I needed was a phone contract.

With the top down and the stereo up, I did not hear my pager. I returned the call from the first available pay phone. The number belonged to a hotel called the Traveler's Inn in Emmettsville. He added 202 to the message; his room number. I asked for Graham, aka Boyd, but he was not in his room. Apparently, we were going to play phone tag again today. I needed to get the pager to him soon.

* * *

Unlike yesterday, I could not find Boyd anywhere. He was not at Falco's, or outside the Chief's house, or Eric's. I even checked around the police station wondering if he had the nerve to bug it as well. Eventually, I decided to see if he might find me instead by parking my bright red, very obvious, vehicle on Main Street while I grabbed lunch at Ray's once again.

He did not find me. Nor did he page me.

This time I did not panic. Instead, I decided to drive out to Junior's junkyard. I was not sure if seeing Junior again was the best idea in the world, but it was the only idea that I had. During the 10 minute drive to E's Salvage Yard, I changed my mind more than once. In the end, I pictured his head bouncing off the window of Charles' bar and thought that even if the visit did not go well, I might have a chance to hit him again, which seemed like a great consolation prize if I failed to get any worthwhile information.

The junkyard was east of town on a blacktop road in a small valley surrounded by woods on all sides with the closest building a mobile home that was at least a half mile away and looked like it was going to fall over the next time it saw a strong wind. The extreme isolation was unexpected, yet even on a Thursday afternoon, the place looked busy. I saw a flatbed tow truck loaded with a late model Oldsmobile driving through the front gate. There were also almost a dozen vehicles parked in front of the office.

Before getting out of my car, I did a perfunctory check of my surroundings. E's Salvage Yard had the look of a successful business. It was clean. The building was well maintained. The signage was clear and visible. Someone had even planted some hybrid roses of various colors next to the building. I could see customers waiting at a counter through the front window. The last thing I noticed was the security cameras. There were two covering the parking lot and front door and one more aimed at the front gate. Even though Charles had said that the big brother had managed to make the junkyard successful, I had not expected it to look like it did. After stepping through the front door, I nearly changed my mind one last time.

There were three men behind the counter with eight men waiting to be helped. Oddly enough, one of the clerks was discussing the potential sale of an expensive scientific calculator with a customer. It was a peculiar conversation for an automobile junkyard. Then I remembered that Charles had mentioned that Jackson was thinking about opening a pawn shop in town; maybe he was doing some of that business out of the salvage yard for now.

"Not that we would have anything for that beautiful car out there, but how could I help you?"

The man addressing me was a pleasant-looking man approximately my age. His accent was Tennessee. It had a pleasant tone and cadence to it that exhibited a degree of warmth and intelligence. Although he was three inches taller and not as blocky, it was easy to see he was Junior's brother. There was a familiar set about the eyes.

"I'm not here for parts for the car. I was hoping to find Junior Estes."

"Maybe I could help."

"Maybe. I'm Dr. McCain."

He broke out in a warm smile, not forced, but also one that did not reach the eyes. It was a practiced smile.

"So you're the fella my brother tussled with. He's right; you don't look like any doctor I ever saw. How did he word it? Yeah, 'surfer hair on steroids.' I heard tell it you were some kind of Navy SEAL or something, but now that I met you I can see you are too big for a SEAL."

"You have military experience?"

"No, but some of the fellas from around here went in for that sort of thing, and one thing I also noticed is that they were always under

200 lbs, usually closer to 150, and they are always tough as nails. Mean too."

"I heard you were pretty smart, Jackson. I guess I heard right."

He did not look the least bit surprised when I mentioned him by name, not even a flinch. "Now that we are both aware that you did your homework, Dr. McCain, how can I help you?"

"I have a simple request. I would like a truce with your brother. My beef is not with him, nor is it with this town. All I want is to bring the man who killed my friend's son to justice. Nothing more, yet nothing less either."

"Is your last sentence meant as a thinly veiled threat, Dr. McCain?"

"No. I'm just trying to convey my level of conviction."

"Meaning you don't plan on leaving our fine town until you have administered justice?"

"I'm not planning on 'administering' any type of justice, Jackson. I'm only planning on pointing the proper authorities in the right direction. It will be very legal and very proper. Vigilante justice is not my plan if that is what you were implying."

"You seem like a reasonable man, Dr. McCain. And I do admire your level of conviction to your friend. You are causing me to rethink my preconceived notions of Yankees, no offense."

"None taken."

Jackson said, "However, you are exhibiting a level of naiveté that I would not have expected considering your education level."

"How's that, Jackson?"

"You seem to be under the illusion that our fair chief, Sam Parker, is the *proper* authorities. Seems like it's going to be hard to get any cooperation from the very man who would like to see that the truth doesn't get discovered." Jackson lifted one eyebrow very slightly, inviting the question without stating the obvious.

"Jackson, I wish I had met you first instead of your brother. Things might have started out differently between us. As is, neither of us is probably ever going to trust the other completely, yet I thank you for your kind words and your warning about local law enforcement. It is something I have already considered."

"Aha, so you are not all hair and muscles. So what you want to know is whether I can convince my brother to stay out of your way."

"I hadn't planned on having this conversation with you, but yes, I would like to avoid any further trouble with your brother."

"I'm not sure who you talked to, and it doesn't matter, but they were right; I am the one that is easier to get along with. However, I am not my brother's keeper, as the Good Book says. All I can promise is that I will say something to him."

Actually, Cain had responded to a question from God with another question, "Am I my brother's keeper," but I did not feel like correcting Jackson; I was going to have to ignore my pet peeve for the moment. Instead, I replied, "Thanks."

"No need. Now that it looks like Chief Parker's boy might have something to do with your friend's death, it's in Junior's best interest to distance himself from Eric. I will try to appeal to his sensible side."

Jackson's revelation that he was aware of some of the details of the murder came as a surprise. "So, the talk around the water cooler is that Eric had something to do with Paul Deland's death?"

"We don't have a water cooler, but it is a small town. People talk. What was that thing Ben Franklin said about secrets?"

"Three people can keep a secret as long as two of them are dead," I said. "At least that's how I remember it."

Jackson said, "Sounds about right." With a nod towards some of the others in the room, he said, "Not to be rude, but I should help my guys get caught up. Good luck, Dr. McCain. I will try to convince my brother to mind his manners."

Charles Mann had described Jackson Estes as a good businessman that many in the town liked and trusted, and after my meeting with Jackson I had to admit that my first impression was favorable. His used auto parts business was busy, it was clean, and it looked profitable. As I sat in my car, I looked around the salvage yard. The flatbed truck I had spotted earlier was leaving. Someone was driving the Oldsmobile that had been on the flatbed back with the rest of the junk cars. Interestingly enough, the car sounded like it ran just fine and the rear and left side of the vehicle looked undamaged. The gentleman that had bought the electronic calculator was leaving. He was carrying an SLR camera with him as well. Jackson was definitely running the pawn shop out of the junkyard for the time being.

I left thinking that I had visited a few junkyards with my dad and I could not recall one looking as good as E's Salvage Yard. If Jackson had half as much influence with his brother as he had talent in running a business, then maybe I would not have to worry about Junior Estes hampering my investigation any longer.

Not wanting to return to Memphis without giving Boyd his pager, I decided to drive around Emmettsville in my shiny red car with the top down and the radio playing being as obvious as I could to see if any police cruisers decided to follow me during the daylight hours. I cruised Main Street; I drove around the police station a couple of times, and I even drove over to Falco's more than once. No one seemed to pay me any attention.

While stopped at a traffic light, I caught a glimpse of myself in the rearview mirror. At first, I did not recognize myself. The man in the mirror looked too happy, too at ease to be me. It almost looked like I had more color. Maybe it was all the sun I was getting riding around in the convertible, although that did not explain the smirk on my face.

Boyd had been wrong when he said I liked the adrenaline and excitement as much as he did. It was the hunt, not the adrenaline, that I was enjoying. He was right about one thing; it had been easy to talk me into investigating because just like my mother, I could not tolerate injustice. If Boyd was going to be my undercover asset, then I was going to take the more direct approach. Right after I gave him his pager.

In my experience, effective disguises are often simple. Dressing in a different coat, wearing a hoodie, or even donning a ball cap can be very effective if it varies from the norm. My favorite was wearing an oversized sweatshirt to hide my physique combined with a ball cap since my hairstyle was unique; my bushy hair which I wore on the long side required almost no maintenance, but it did make me easy to spot in a crowd, even from a distance. The sweatshirt and ball cap combination was the disguise I used when I decided to break into Boyd's room.

Finding the Travelers' Inn was easy, and it was a relief to see that I could enter the building from a back entrance unseen from the front desk. I quickly made my way to room 202 and pulled out my lock pick set left over from my days in the Navy. On a whim, which seemed foolish at the time, I had packed it along with the Glock this morning. It had been years since I picked a lock, which was evident as I struggled to depress all the internal tumblers to gain access. In the end, I was successful, although I was disappointed with myself for taking longer than I liked. It took only a few minutes to place the pager on the bed with a note on how to use it. I also thought up a rudimentary code using popular numerical references, such as 911 for emergency and 411 for information, and wrote it on the note before leaving the hotel.

Nearly 15 minutes later, I found Boyd. Found his car to be more exact. It was parked near the back entrance of Falco's. Soon after, Boyd exited the back door of the bar, opened his trunk and carried in a couple of boxes.

Well, I'll be. Graham has made contact.

It seemed fitting that Falco's would be involved somehow. I wondered how he had approached Mason. How he had weaseled his way in so quickly. Maybe he had a knack for the undercover work. Of course, not being a Yankee probably helped with Mason. Either way, the legend was working.

CHAPTER 23

Boyd Avery Dallas was enjoying himself. When he told the others that investigating would be fun, he had not been kidding. All his life, he wanted to be a cop. When he played cops and robbers as a kid, he always had to be the cop. And the good guys had to win. He would not play otherwise. All his friends knew that about him — his love of police work, and his love of guns. When he graduated high school, his class had voted him "Most Likely to Shoot Someone...In the Line of Duty." They made him a plaque. His mother was aghast by the award. He loved it.

He joined the Marine Corps directly out of high school in 1978. He made it clear that his MOS had to be Military Police. He would accept nothing else, except maybe Marine Corps Scout Sniper. He kicked butt on his ASVAB, the timed test all enlisted military personnel take before entering the service and then excelled at everything he did in boot camp to ensure he would get his first choice of MOS.

After getting his wish, he started his specialized training, the Military Police Basic Officers Course, in Fort Leonardwood, Missouri. Ten weeks of training in Military Police procedures in Fort "Lost in the Woods." Traveling on Uncle Sam's dime always seemed appealing to him, so upon graduation from MP school, he asked to be stationed anywhere outside the US, preferably in Southeast Asia. He got South Korea. He loved it. Next, the Marines stationed him in the Philippines. He loved it there as well.

The Philippines is where he first met Lieutenant McCain. It was 1982. Lt. McCain was an of aide to Admiral Buie, a real big wig in Southeast Asia. Boyd was a Sergeant by 1982. His love and mastery of firearms assured him a frequent role as protection detail for VIPs. Admiral Buie was one of those VIPs. The Admiral was said to be a military attaché, but everyone knew that was just a fancy way of saying he was involved in intelligence gathering.

Lieutenant McCain was the Admiral's mysterious shadow. Officially, he was a Lieutenant Junior Grade, one grade above an Ensign. Word around the water cooler was that there was no record of him serving anywhere as an Ensign. It was like he simply showed up one day in the Navy as a Lt. JG, which, of course, was not possible. The whole thing freaked out Boyd's boss, a Gunnery Sergeant, who could not dig up any information on Ensign McCain through official channels. Boyd was not worried. The Lieutenant was part of the Office of Naval Intelligence; he was obviously a Navy spy. It was not until after L.T. and Boyd left the service that Boyd found out that L.T. had served nearly his first two years of service undercover as an Enlisted Navy Master-at-Arms.

Normally, a Marine Sergeant and a Navy Lieutenant would not have become close friends while in the service; they operated in different worlds. However, their worlds became infinitely intertwined on a beautiful Sunday evening in March 1982 when the helicopter they were traveling in crashed in the Cambodian jungle.

Two Marines died in the crash. Two more Marines died in a gun battle with Vietnamese troops that converged on the crash. Admiral Buie, Lieutenant McCain, Second Lieutenant John Gehrke — the pilot, and Boyd were the only ones that managed to survive the crash and the eleven-day hike across the Cambodian countryside before finding safety in neighboring Thailand.

The lives of all four survivors remained forever changed. Admiral Buie, who never should have been in the helicopter in the first place, was asked to retire shortly after recovering from his injuries. Lieutenant Gehrke and Boyd were both declared physically unfit for active duty as a result of their injuries. The last Boyd had heard of Gehrke, he was flying a traffic chopper on the west coast somewhere. Boyd was left with a permanent limp, courtesy of fused ankle bones in the left leg.

Lieutenant McCain was the only one that fell into the same pile of shit yet managed to come up smelling like roses. At the behest of Admiral Buie, he was awarded the Navy and Marine Corps Medal, the highest non-combat medal in the Navy as a result of his heroism.

L.T. did not escape completely unscathed, though. He left the jungle with two bullet holes in his left thigh, one entry wound, one exit wound. The result of a clean in-and-out injury that missed every major artery. Boyd always surmised it was the holes in the Lieutenant's thigh that clinched the Navy and Marine Corps Medal for him. Lucky bastard, thought Boyd, even when he gets shot it somehow works out for him. Once healed, the physical scars were hardly noticeable. Just some strange looking tissue that would not grow hair. Not that anyone would ever notice; L.T. liked to wear long shorts to cover them.

Boyd was unsure of the depth of the emotional scars inflicted on L.T. He didn't know L.T. before the crash, so he had no reference; however, during the physical therapy they often did together, Boyd noticed that although L.T. was quite affable and social, he purposefully avoided any conversations that focused on himself. He surmised it was a kind of defense mechanism. Boyd had asked Virgil about it a few times, but Virgil had been vague, just saying "It's complicated." Boyd was convinced there was some dark history in L.T.'s past, but he also knew better than to push.

Then again, maybe those eleven days were what changed him. Other than the two Marines that died during the initial gun battle, Lieutenant McCain was the only member of the party that ended up killing any Vietnamese soldiers. He killed two soldiers with his bare hands; he drowned the one that shot him in a river. That could change a man, even one that seemed as strong as L.T.

What Boyd did know was that he admired the hell out of his friend. It was undeniable; none of them would have left Cambodia alive if not for him. For someone with no combat training, he had proven himself unbelievably resourceful. And tough. He had to be the toughest man Boyd had ever met. When L.T. moved to Huntsville after leaving the Navy and started teaching self-defense techniques to the local police department, Boyd thought maybe he was going to stay. Maybe become a cop himself. Instead, he took some classes at the University of Alabama in Huntsville and left for med school the next year. Boyd missed his friend when he left, but he was happy for him. He knew L.T. would make a great doctor.

The two stayed in touch while he was in medical school, even getting together during the summers. Once L.T. moved to Memphis to begin his residency, his busy schedule took over. Until a couple of days ago, Boyd had not talked to him in over two years. So, when Virgil asked him to travel to Tennessee to help him talk some sense into L.T., he jumped at the chance. His help did not go the way Virgil or Ellie planned, but that was because talking sense into L.T. did not mean talking him out of getting involved. Boyd liked Virgil; they both lived in the same town and even hung out together at times. However, his allegiance was to L.T., and L.T. needed help solving his problem, not running away from it, which was why he was enjoying himself immensely delivering *illegal* alcohol to Mason Thompson.

Getting Mason to buy what Boyd had to offer had been easier than expected. He immediately opined that Mason was not new to buying bootleg liquor. He carried in the last box and sat it down in the store room. Mason was holding the door for him, which he locked after Boyd exited the room.

"Mason, I want to let you know I appreciate your business. Like I was saying before, I've been supplying booze down in Alabama, mostly to dry counties, but one of them recently voted to go wet, so now I got a surplus problem."

"What can I say, always happy to help a friend in need, especially one offering those prices. I'm not going to open them up and find colored water inside am I?"

"If you do, it will be a surprise to me. It looked pretty darn authentic when I stole those bottles."

Mason said, "You able to steal that much alcohol?"

"Na, normally I just buy it in bulk from a state with lower liquor taxes then transport it across state lines. You know, Smoky and the Bandit, only without the Trans AM with the puking chicken on the front. But I have been known to opportunistically liquidate on occasion, especially in the face of competition."

"Makes sense."

"Do I have any of that around here?"

"Any what?"

"Any competition."

Mason invited Boyd into his office and offered him a seat. "There are a couple of local boys I buy from, but you keep offering up those prices, and I will always have some room for your stuff. I can guarantee that, Mister. Hey, can you get me any Corona? I want to have a Mexican night."

Boyd promised to get him plenty of Corona before leaving for the next bar. The next two bars wanted nothing to do with him. One was the bar owned by Charles Mann; Charles was quick to ask him to leave. The next bar, a bona fide dive at the edge of town, was very welcoming. The owner was a small, wiry man in his mid-forties with a strong smoker's rasp to his voice, yet an amazing bounce to his step and a large friendly smile. He bought over half of Boyd's supply and even helped him carry it in from the car.

"Young man, let me offer you a beer." Boyd knew better than to refuse. The two sat down at the counter in the empty bar and sipped ice cold draft beer. "What brings you up here from Alabama?" Boyd went over his cover story with the man, who seemed to have no trouble accepting it. "You planning on making regular deliveries to this area?"

"As long as I have a customer base. So, far only found two of you in town wanting to buy."

"Falco's?" Boyd nodded. "Let me save you some trouble. Me and Mason probably the only ones in this town that will want what you are offering, but I got a couple of friends in the area that'll welcome you with open arms at these prices. I shouldn't tell you this, but you could even raise them a little and we would still buy from you." He jotted down the directions to the other bars on a cocktail napkin.

Boyd said, "Mason mentioned something about some local boys in the same line of business. Anything I need to worry about?"

"I don't rightly know. They never had any competition before that I know of, so I don't know how they're going to react. Guess you have faced this before, though?"

"No, not really. There were a couple of us supplying the dry counties down in Alabama. Each of us knew about the others, and we were all okay with it. In fact, we colluded on the prices and purposefully tried to avoid dealing with the same product."

Boyd found that lying about his legend was quite easy. He was glad he had taken the extra time allowing L.T. and the others to drill him before starting. Boyd listened to Tim, the bar owner, give him a brief life story about being a marathon runner and the local track coach before taking over the bar five years ago. The raspy voice was not from smoking; it was due to nodules on his vocal cords caused by years of yelling as a coach. Tim did not volunteer any information on the competition, and Boyd knew better than to ask, yet it was good to know the competition existed. Now if he could just flush them out.

Boyd drove to the next town and was able to dump the remainder of the alcohol on the first bar that Tim recommended. He had $1800 in cash from his endeavors. He felt bad that L.T. had to absorb nearly a $400 loss on the liquor, even though L.T. had already accepted that fact. Boyd found himself wondering how L.T. could afford to be so indifferent towards money. He had to be in debt up to his eyeballs. L.T. finished his residency only last year and already he was driving a new Mercedes convertible, and Virgil told him that he owned the building where he lived. Maybe the rent from the building was much better than he imagined. It had better be, especially considering his current unpaid leave.

Boyd was considering his next move while he drove back to his hotel. The Traveler's Inn, with its interior corridors met the official definition of a hotel. It had only the most basic of amenities. No bar, no continental breakfast, no mini bar, not even a coffee pot in the room. Just a lumpy bed with some equally lumpy pillows. At least the shower was hot with plenty of water pressure. He had stayed in worse.

Boyd noticed it immediately. The small piece of Scotch tape he placed at the top of the door was broken. The Do Not Disturb sign was still in place, but someone had ignored the sign. Someone had been in his room. Maybe they were still in there. He placed his hand inside his jacket; hand firmly on his pistol in case it was needed. Boyd put the key in the door and then threw the door violently open. The door crashed into the wall. No one was behind the door. No one was in the room either, unless he was in the bathroom. Boyd eyed the bed. He saw the pager and the note from L.T. and then smiled when he realized who had been in his room. He checked out the bathroom anyway, just in case. Better to be safe, than sorry.

He read the instructions on pager usage. He even tested it with the phone in his room. L.T.'s numerical code was laughable. Why didn't he just use Military Police radio codes? He played the list of codes over in his head and then he realized the answer. The codes were too confusing, and many did not apply to their situation. Plus, L.T. was not a Marine and Boyd remembered that the Master-at-Arms personnel used a different coding system than the Marines.

Boyd realized L.T. did not leave him a code for pager received, so he called L.T.'s pager from the hotel and left the hotel number. Boyd waited for ten minutes for a return call, which did not come. The two of them needed to talk to figure out the next step. Boyd was talking time off from work to have his fun, so he wanted to make full use of his time. He decided to drive south into Mississippi and find a state liquor store and buy up all their Corona. He could deliver it to Falco's tomorrow.

He replaced the Scotch tape on his door and headed out after leaving a message at the front desk for L.T. He told the desk to tell any callers "thanks for the package." He decided that after he got back, he could get a bite to eat and then listen in on the Chief or Eric again. Maybe he might hear something useful the second time around.

CHAPTER 24

Seeing Boyd delivering liquor to Falco's made me smile inside. I watched from outside for several minutes before deciding to let Boyd do his thing without me hovering over his shoulder. He had his investigation; I had mine. Except mine was at a standstill. I was waiting to see if my plan for Boyd gave us any leads.

While I was in the Navy, the plan had taken nearly six months in the Philippines before I had any contact with the people I was looking for. It had taken another three months before I met with anyone within the leadership of the organization. That was only after at least one successful transport of drugs out of the Philippines into Southern California. The group was careful. And dangerous. It took another six months to meet the men in charge of the operation. The sting to get any credible evidence on the suppliers and the head honcho required another three months of planning. In the end, I had to pretend to get greedy and ask for a bigger slice of the profits to get the meeting. Their greed ended up being their downfall. They never suspected a thing. The look on their faces when they realized they had been fooled by an E-4 Master-at-Arms was priceless. However, it paled in comparison when they saw me walk into the military court in my Lieutenant J.G. uniform.

It had taken a little over 18 months of investigation. Not to mention the 40 days of A school before beginning the investigation. Boyd was taking a week of vacation, and I had an undetermined amount of unpaid leave facing me; it was promised to be less than two weeks. We did not have 18 months.

I was driving around town trying to think of a plan while my inner voice was talking to me in earnest. Unfortunately, it was talking so fast that I could not decipher what it was saying. After a few minutes, I could make out the noise inside my head. It was no better. My inner voice was coming up with so many ideas that I would have needed a dozen full-time investigators to follow up on everything. I liked it better when it was quiet inside my head. I was circling the block near the police station for the third time when I came up with an idea that should, at least, shut up the voice inside my head. My car came to a stop outside the local library. It was time to find out more about organized crime in the South.

Like everything else in the town, the library was quaint, looking almost exactly as I had expected a small-town library to look. Other than some offices off to the side, all the books and tables and the two computer stations sat in one room with a small photocopier station in one corner and a children's book and reading area in the farthest corner. One unique feature was the set of stairs leading to a small balcony that traversed the back wall and the two side walls providing access to a couple of elevated sitting areas and bookshelves that were built into the walls.

The librarian was not quaint. She was young and very pretty with short blonde hair and an athletic physique. She was wearing a pullover shirt tucked into jeans that fit very well. Not at all what I expected from a small-town librarian.

"Sir," she said, "You look lost. Can I help you?" She was not a local either; the accent, or more accurately, the lack of accent, was classic Midwest.

"I look lost?"

As I approached, I noticed her name tag said Jenny. "A little bit, yes. First time in a library?"

I could not recall having met the woman before, so her sarcastic tone caught me off guard. "No. I spend more time in them than most people, I imagine."

"Really?"

"Yes, really. You just weren't what I expected."

"I see; another person that feels I don't meet the librarian stereotype. Should I grow my hair out and put it up in a bun and buy some of those glasses on a chain to wear around my neck?"

"Miss, I don't think it would make any difference. If you lived to be a hundred, you would not look like the stereotypical librarian."

"Is that meant as personal flattery or as a denigration of librarians?" The woman was obviously annoyed with me. I had no idea why. "I have a master's degree in library science. It is a real degree, you know."

"I'm aware that library science is a real degree. I got my undergrad from the University of Illinois in Champaign-Urbana, which allegedly has the best library science program in the country."

"It does. It's also where I went to school. So did you play football there?"

"Now who is adhering to stereotypes? No, I did not play football there, although they did want me to."

"I'll bet."

"Miss, I'm not sure if you are aware of it or not, but Southerners are known for their hospitality. They often take great pride it in. You are going to have a hard time fitting in down here with that attitude."

She was eyeing me, studying my face. The stern look slowly replaced by a slightly warmer countenance. "You said undergrad. People that say that instead of 'degree' are usually implying they have some amount of higher learning."

"I did graduate medical school from UAB, does that count?"

"Well, I'll be. I didn't see that one coming. You work at the hospital here?"

"No, I work in the emergency department at Memphis Memorial."

"You ever hear of a Mulligan?" I nodded. "Well, I'd like one now." I smiled, allowing her the second chance to make a first impression. "You know, I've been here about 18 months, and during that time I think nearly every guy at the gym where I work out has come in and flirted with me at work, harass me is more like it. I thought you were some new guy I hadn't met yet, so I apologize for my attitude. I swear they must have a pool on me, seeing which one can get lucky with me first."

"Wouldn't surprise me; boys will be boys."

She smiled for the first time and held out her hand. "Name's Jenny, how can I help you today, sir?"

"I'm Dr. McCain; friends call me L.T. I was hoping to dig up some information on organized crime in Tennessee."

"Organized crime? Interesting choice of subjects for a doctor."

"Unrelated to my work. It's of personal interest."

She directed us to a computer and began putting in search strings. Too many matches came back for my taste on the first few attempts, so we decided to focus the search. After a couple more searches that left me less than impressed, I settled on a book she found without the benefit of the computer that provided an overview of organized crime in the United States. The book largely focused on the famous Italian and Sicilian Mafia families in the United States and their rise to power. It also mentioned the changing tide in organized crime as the Mexican and South American drug cartels entered into the American landscape mostly after the Vietnam War.

I was almost ready to give up when the author started discussing organized crime in the South. According to the author, many experts refused to call the criminal elements in the South organized due to their uniqueness; they operated without any apparent structure or hierarchical command. One scholar coined the term "Dixie Mafia" to describe organized crime in the South, although "Southern Mafia" and "Good Ol' Boy Mafia" were also used.

Jenny returned after several minutes to sit across from me. "How's it going?"

"I want to thank you for the book. It's really up-to-date. I have spent the last half hour reading about the Dixie Mafia."

"Never heard of it."

"Me neither. It's a relatively new term."

"Learn anything interesting?"

"A little." I had piqued her interest. "I would have never guessed it, but apparently the Dixie Mafia started in Biloxi back in the Sixties and then radiated out from there. The Biloxi connection got shut down a couple of years ago after the feds got involved following massive political corruption, which drove it more underground. Now it exists in pockets throughout the South. Sort of regional, like the Dixie Mafia down in Muscle Shoals, or the Dixie Mafia over in Purdy."

Jenny said, "Organized crime in the South, go figure.

"Organized crime is everywhere in one degree or another, but this seems like a strange group of guys. They have no set chain of command, they are not connected by family origin or nationality, they even often specialize in different arenas, yet they are still unified enough to be considered organized crime, at least by the experts on the subject."

"So disorganized organized crime. That sounds about right for a bunch of rednecks. What holds them together?"

"Ideology."

"Ideology?"

"Yeah, it seems a common hatred of Yankees, Jews, Blacks, and Commies is enough to band them all together, loosely speaking, of course. Well, that, and a common goal of making money by whatever means possible."

Jenny commented about learning something new every day before throwing another book at me and walking away. The book told the story of a man whose father had been a corrupt sheriff in Alabama. He had insisted that everyone call him "Chief," which rang a little too close to home in my current situation. The author discussed growing up in an environment that thrived on corruption and greed. He admitted to selling stolen goods, illegal booze, and drugs, and helping run prostitutes as a young man. It all seemed so normal at the time. Only when he realized that the Dixie Mafia was heavily involved in contract killings did he realize his life was not normal. The author spent a lot of time discussing how the members of the Dixie Mafia usually created small, seemingly legitimate business to use as fronts to buy and sell stolen items. Many times the items were provided by others within the network that did not want to get involved in the distribution process; they preferred to concentrate on procurement, which was especially true for younger criminals involved in anything from petty theft to grand theft auto. Despite the simple writing style and bad grammar and punctuation throughout the book, you could almost feel the guilt dripping off the pages. The author had found Jesus and the book appeared to be written as an atonement for his sins.

I thanked Jenny for her help and left. Boyd probably would have told me that the visit had been a waste of time, but, as I told Lloyd a few days ago, information is always helpful. The visit also quieted down my inner voice. It had only one thing to say to me, "Work the clues."

* * *

I seldom hated my inner voice. However, this was one of those times. What clues did it want me to work? I had nothing. Ever since Paul had gone missing, I kept coming up with nothing. I was driving around town aimlessly because I did not have any clues. I was hungry, but that was not a clue. I decided against eating in Emmettsville and started the drive back to Memphis. Once again, I pushed the Mercedes through the corners trying to get a good feel for the automobile's capabilities. My mind emptied itself of everything except the road for the next 45 minutes until I heard my pager go off. I recognized the number as the Traveler's Inn; Boyd would have his pager with him from here on out.

Without going home, I drove to the Thai Garden and got a healthy dose of vegetables along with a simple dish of chicken in a red curry sauce. While eating, I tried to work the clues. Nothing came to mind again. I had effectively talked myself out of my only suspect when I realized he could not fight. The rest of my time in Emmettsville I had spent dealing with Junior Estes and getting arrested. My conversations with Lloyd, Charles, and the Chief had not been helpful. None of them had an inkling of organized crime in their county. Charles had mentioned that there were some rough characters in the area, but none he knew of were into gambling. Emmettsville seemed to be a quiet, peaceful town. Only one problem, someone stuck a .22 up to the back of Paul Deland's head so close as to leave powder burns. And someone was trying to collect $15,000 in gambling debt from Paul. They had to be related. When I went to bed hours later, I was still trying to figure out the connection.

CHAPTER 25

Everything was going well with L.T.'s plan. Boyd had sold all the liquor yesterday and was currently making his second delivery to Falco's. The Corona beer that Mason wanted. No one had even questioned the validity of his cover story, or legend as L.T. called it. They bought it hook, line, and sinker. Boyd had to admit that playing Graham was fun. He felt that he had a real knack for investigating. After all, he had easily found and bugged the homes of both Eric and the Chief. He did not have any leads for L.T. yet, but he felt that would surely change soon.

Mason looked surprised to get the Corona so quickly. After Boyd had finished carrying in the boxes, Mason had him wait outside while he got the cash. A two-toned green pickup pulled into the parking lot while Boyd relaxed against the side of the Mustang. It was a good looking truck. One that he felt he had seen somewhere before. His train of thought was interrupted as Mason exited the back door.

Mason did not have the money. There was not enough in the safe, but he assured Boyd that his bartender would show up with it in a few minutes.

Boyd realized later that he should have been more suspicious, but the conversation with Mason distracted him from watching the green pickup. If he had been paying attention, he would have noticed two men exiting the pickup with 12 gauge Remington 870 shotguns. If he had noticed them at 40 yards, the superior effective range of his SIG P226 would have given him the upper hand. He was deadly with his pistol at that range. But he did not see the shotguns until the two men were 15 yards away. At that range, his upper hand was gone. Those two shotguns could have nearly cut him in half.

Even if the shorter man had not introduced himself, Boyd would have recognized him as Junior Estes from L.T.'s description about their fight a few days ago. He really did look like a fireplug. A fireplug with a mullet. He assumed the tall, wiry man was Tyler. Junior thanked Mason for tipping them off, told him he could keep the liquor he had bought, and then ordered him to go inside. Mason wasted no time slipping through his back door and closing it.

"Now, what to do with you," Junior said to Boyd. "You packing?"

Honesty seemed the best policy, even if the two shotguns were not actually trained on him. Both men were carrying the guns loosely, casually in fact. Boyd figured it was best to keep it that way. "I am. Inside the jacket, shoulder holster."

"Well, aren't you fancy? Tyler, get his gun."

For the first time, Boyd realized he was dealing with amateurs. Tyler lowered his shotgun even further and stepped between Junior and Boyd to retrieve Boyd's SIG. He was blocking Junior's ability to cover him effectively, thus providing Boyd the perfect opportunity to gain the upper hand. However, he could not bring himself to do it. Deep down, in a way he could not fully explain, he felt he was not in any real danger. Not if he played along and let them have their way. It was just a turf war. As long as he ceded without a fight, they should have no reason to do anything other than run him out of town.

"Wait," said Boyd, "You're doing this all wrong. Back up." Tyler stopped. "You are standing right in front of your man covering you with the shotgun." Tyler was staring at him, confused, but Junior caught on pretty quickly. He yelled at Tyler to move. When Tyler moved to his right, Junior moved to the left, his shotgun this time leveled on Boyd.

"Why'd you do that?" asked Junior.

"Cause I don't want to shoot anybody and the temptation was getting too great. Your boy here, well, he just about got both y'all killed."

Junior squinted his eyes at Boyd in thought. "So what you're hopin' for is a civilized discussion?"

"Exactly. Between two merchants that just happened to find out that they are in direct competition with each other. Y'all obviously have something you want to say to me. How about I keep my pistol right where it is, and then we can talk about whatever it is that y'all want from me."

Junior said, "I could do that. If I was the one in charge, that is. But I'm not. So, I got a counter offer." Boyd's expression signified he was ready to hear Junior's offer. "How about you hand over your piece…slowly…to Tyler, then we go talk to my brother."

"He can't come to us?"

"Afraid not. He sent me to get you, so I'm gonna get you."

"And if I refuse?"

Boyd heard Junior click the shotgun's safety to fire. "You kinda lost that option, don'tcha think?" The shotgun made for a compelling argument. Boyd removed his SIG P226 from his holster, slowly, and handed it to Tyler.

Junior smiled for the first time and congratulated Boyd on making a good choice. He nearly apologized before ordering Tyler to grab some duct tape from his pickup and then use it to tape one of Boyd's hands to the steering wheel of the Mustang. They wanted to tape both of them, but then he would not have been able to shift gears. Junior informed him that the tape was not personal, just precautionary. Tyler climbed into the passenger seat of the Mustang with his shotgun. He attempted to keep the shotgun trained on Boyd, but its length was presenting a problem.

Boyd said, "You should use a handgun to cover me from that position, or sit in the back seat if you are going to use the shotgun."

"Shut up. You already made me look like a fool once. It won't happen again. Just follow Junior."

Boyd started the Mustang and followed Junior out of the parking lot. Doubts started to enter his mind. Being dragged into the lion's den was one thing, but willingly walking in was different. He wanted a discussion with these men. He just did not want to have that discussion in some dark room tied to a chair or something.

Tyler was a horrible guard. A couple of minutes into the drive he gave up trying to hold the shotgun on Boyd. Instead, he settled on looking menacing whenever Boyd looked his direction. When Boyd saw the sign for E's Salvage Yard, he really started to doubt his decision to give up his pistol. He should never have given up so easily. It was time to figure out how to get Tyler out of his car.

"Hey, Tyler, I ought to let you know, so you don't look like a fool again, that I have another gun in the glove box." Tyler gave him a confused look before deciding to open the box and look inside. There were some papers in the box, but no gun. "It's there, I promise, feel up inside on the top. There's a chamber in the top where I hide it. Just feel for it."

Tyler resumed rummaging through the glove box before feeling the top of the box, yelling again that there was no gun. Boyd assured him the gun was in a special chamber and told him that if he could not feel the opening, he would surely be able to see it if he looked up inside. Tyler gave him another strange look before he tilted his head down and tried to look up inside the glove box.

It was the opportunity he was waiting for. He slammed on the brakes which drove Tyler's head into the dash. Tyler immediately yelled out a "what the fuck" while Boyd reached across Tyler's back to pull the passenger door handle. His trick almost failed. He almost failed to grip the handle before Tyler straightened up. Almost. He was pretty sure he felt the door open slightly. If it didn't, then his idea would not work. He turned to the car hard to the left on the country road, accelerated, and pushed on Tyler's shoulder. The door flung open. Tyler, along with his shotgun, went out the open door. Tyler tried to grab the door but was unable. Boyd saw him tumble out the door onto the pavement, a look of pure dread on his face at the prospect of being flung out of the car.

Boyd stopped in the middle of the road with the car aimed toward the left ditch. Tyler had rolled across the pavement and was probably 10 yards from the Mustang. Boyd had his chance to get away, but there was a problem. The duct tape prevented him from being able to turn the wheel sharp enough to turn the car around completely. Boyd shifted into reverse while turning the wheel the other direction as much as he could. He was trying to complete a three-point turn in the middle of the two-lane road while being limited to only a three-quarter turn of the wheel. "Shit," he yelled out loud. It was taking too long to get the car turned around. The taillights on Junior's truck lit up, and the reverse lights came on. The truck was approaching at a high rate of speed.

The Mustang was only half turned around. Now or never. Boyd turned the wheel as far to the left as his taped arm would allow, revved up the motor and popped the clutch. The rear wheels spun loose as Boyd hoped. That was a good sign. It allowed him to swing the rear end of the car around. However, the car also lurched forward into the ditch. He had hoped to avoid the ditch. The Mustang was leaning heavily to the right as the right front wheel fell into the ditch. If Junior's truck had not been bearing down on him, then Boyd would have had time to back up one more time. In his mirror, Boyd also noticed that Tyler had picked himself up off the pavement and was running toward the Mustang. Boyd floored the accelerator hoping that by keeping up his forward momentum he could maneuver the car back out of the ditch. The right rear wheel was spinning madly. He was still moving forward, but his momentum was slowing. Suddenly, the wheel jerked to the right in his hand, and the car came to a complete stop. Boyd realized his predicament immediately. He was stuck. He turned off the motor and waited for the inevitable.

Hindsight is 20/20, or so they say. Boyd was not so sure. He had given up pretty easily earlier to avoid shooting two people. It seemed like the right thing to do at the time. Then he changed his mind and tried to escape, but failed. Tyler had been pretty angry when he opened the driver door. Boyd guessed being pushed out of a moving car might make a person mad. Plus, Boyd had made him look like a fool again. Boyd could feel the small amount of dried blood caked around his left eye from the cut on his brow caused by Tyler hitting him with the butt of the shotgun. Junior had been more understanding. He simply walked over to Boyd, told him not to move, and then cut the tape loose from the steering wheel.

Now he was sitting in a tool shed duct taped to a metal chair. The tool shed was inside E's Salvage Yard. Junior left the shed immediately after making sure they had used enough tape on his wrists and ankles. With time, if he had been unsupervised, he could have escaped, but Junior left Tyler in the shed to watch over him. And Tyler was sure as hell not going to let Boyd make a fool of him again. For the last 20 minutes or so, Boyd had been trying to decide if giving up easily had been the mistake or if the escape attempt was the mistake. Time would tell he guessed.

Junior returned with another man, taller, less blocky, same eyes. Obviously, the brother. Jackson wasted no time getting to the point. "So what's your deal? My brother tells me that you are cool as a fucking cucumber. Fancy shoulder holster. Expensive SIG." Jackson pulled Boyd's gun from behind his back; it must have been in his waistband. "Nice gun."

"Thanks."

"Shut up. He also told me about how you gave up without a fight when you probably could have dropped both of them back at Mason's. Then you go and push Tyler out of a moving car and try to escape. So, I got a question for ya. You a fucking cop?"

The question caught Boyd off guard. He figured that he was dealing with some small-time bootleggers. Now, he was not so sure. If they were brazen enough to kidnap someone they thought might be a cop, then maybe he had underestimated them. He could hear L.T.'s voice telling him to tell the truth about his Marine background.

"Used to be."

"What do ya mean used to be?" He glared intensely at his brother. "You better not have brought me a cop. Damn it, Junior."

Boyd felt much better about the fact that Jackson was worried they might have grabbed an undercover officer. "I wanted to be a cop my whole damn life. I used to be a Marine MP, but I was injured in a helicopter crash, and they kicked me out. Now, no one will hire me."

"Bullshit. You said yourself you wanted to be a cop your whole life. Why should I believe you?"

"Look at my ankle, the left one."

"What?"

"Cut the tape off my left leg, roll up my pant leg, and look at my ankle."

"Why the hell would I want to do that?"

"So you can look at the scars from the two surgeries I had. They put in pins, fused some bones together. Best doctors the military had worked on me. They did a good job for a bunch of hacks. I can walk, I can run. Running ain't pretty, but I can do it. All that hard work with the rehab. Fuck man, I did everything those therapists asked me to do, and then some. And they kicked me out anyway, and no department around will give me a chance. I can shoot the balls off a flea at 50 yards with a handgun. I can hit targets at 600 yards with a rifle. And the bastards in charge will not even let me teach firearm technique. It's left me more than a little disgruntled."

Tyler pulled a knife out of his pocket and moved toward Boyd. He was prepared to cut the tape loose from his leg. Jackson waved him off. "No need. This boy is telling the truth."

Junior said, "I told you he weren't no cop."

"Shut up, little brother. Talk to me outside."

L.T. had made Junior out to be a real hot head, yet, so far, Boyd was more afraid of Jackson than Junior. Jackson was a schemer. The brains of the bunch. And right now, the brain was outside discussing something with his little brother. The brothers re-entered the shed a few minutes later. Junior almost seemed to cast Boyd an apologetic look before walking up and punching Boyd right in the face. It stung like hell. Made his eyes water.

Junior said, "My brother has a few questions. You better answer him honestly."

"You could have lead with that. I've proven myself to be cooperative so far."

Tyler yelled, "Until you pushed me out of the car, asshole!"

Boyd smiled, "I told you to cover me with a handgun."

"Fuck you."

Jackson interrupted. "Enough, both of you. Listen carefully, if you answer my questions that will be the only punch you receive all day. Don't answer the way I like and Junior will wear himself out on your face. FYI, he don't wear out easily."

Boyd was rethinking his former decision to give up his gun so easily. He nodded in agreement.

"Who ya working for?" Boyd looked at him questioningly. "Don't look at me like that. Who sent ya, dumbass?"

"No one. I'm freelance."

"Bullshit. Did Dunham send ya?"

Boyd said, "Who's Dunham?"

Jackson nodded, and then Junior hit Boyd in the left temple hard enough that he temporarily saw stars.

Jackson said, "Don't answer my questions with questions. If ya don't know Dunham, then just say so, but leave the questions to me." Boyd nodded. "Good, I'll ask again. Who sent ya?"

"No one, and I don't know anyone named Dunham."

"So, I'm to believe you just happened upon our fair town by chance. Is that what you're sayin'?" Jackson stared hard at Boyd as he nodded. Boyd could tell Jackson was not entirely convinced.

"So ya got no boss?" Boyd shook his head. "Let me word this another way then. Is there anyone out there that is going to miss you?"

"Other than my mom?"

Jackson nodded to Junior, who punched Boyd in the face again. It hurt more than the hit Tyler gave him with the shotgun. He knew he was going to have a black eye from that one.

"Yes, other than your mom."

Boyd was trying to figure out how far to push them. Maybe they weren't part of the Dixie Mafia, maybe they were. Either way, they had already given up one name: Dunham. Whoever he was. Tyler ended up helping him make up his mind. He carried over a portable propane blow torch and handed it to Junior, who looked at Boyd in a manner that told Boyd he would do it, for no other reason than Jackson had told him to. Boyd saw no use pushing them any farther.

Boyd said, "I can think of one guy. He's the closest I got to a boss. We will have to page him though, and you will have to type in a message for me. He doesn't ever answer his phone directly."

Jackson walked over and patted Boyd on the shoulder congratulating him for making a good choice. Boyd felt relief that Jackson had left the room, although Tyler looked disappointed. Boyd figured he really wanted to see that blow torch in action.

* * *

Boyd felt like an idiot. He felt like an idiot because he got careless. He got so involved in playing Graham that he forgot that he needed to keep his wits about him. He needed to be on guard. He should have learned by L.T.'s mistake outside Charles' bar. But he didn't. While looking for someone tied to the Dixie Mafia down in Mississippi, he had run into Junior just like L.T. had. It seemed like everywhere L.T. or Boyd turned, Junior was there getting in the way. Junior and his brother were obviously bootleggers as well. And they were also the type of guys who will fiercely protect their interests. How fierce, he did not know.

L.T. had set him up as Graham in to flush out anyone in the area with ties to organized crime. He had flushed out the Estes brothers instead. And in less than 24 hours. He had to admit that he figured it would take days, maybe weeks, for L.T.'s plan to work. Now, Boyd was seriously beginning to question L.T.'s assumption that Junior was just some A-hole that hated blacks and Yankees. What if the Estes boys were the ones they were looking for? The missing link to the Dixie Mafia they wanted so badly. The ones that could tell them something, anything, about the man in Mississippi trying to collect money from Paul before he died. If so, then both L.T. and Boyd had underestimated Junior.

Maybe they were even Dixie Mafia themselves. Junior was a brute, for sure. But Jackson, Boyd could see him as the type of man in charge of a criminal enterprise of some sort. Boyd could feel himself smile at the irony of the possibility. The smile was short-lived though as he as mulled over the possible impact that might have on his current situation. L.T. was convinced that the Dixie Mafia had killed Paul over a gambling debt. How were they going to treat someone who invaded their turf?

A chill ran down his back at the prospect. For the second time in his life, he had underestimated his opponent, and now he hoped L.T. was going to save his bacon again.

He thought back to the last time L.T. had saved his life after he made a huge mistake. For five days, Lt. McCain, Sergeant Dallas, Admiral Buie, and Lt. Gehrke had been evading Vietnamese soldiers that were tracking them through the Cambodian jungle. Boyd was using a makeshift crutch to alleviate the pressure on his fractured left ankle. Admiral Buie was able to walk unaided sometimes, other times he had to be guided by the arm as if he had no concept of where, or who, he was. He was suffering from a concussion and a dislocated shoulder. Lt. Gehrke hobbled along with severe back pain. Unbeknown to them at the time, Gehrke had multiple compression fractures in his spine. Not life threatening, but extremely painful. Lt. McCain had a long shallow cut across his abdomen from the crash but was otherwise uninjured.

Boyd could not figure out how McCain did it. He had no survival training, no experience in the jungle; he did not even hunt as a kid, but he managed to keep them one step ahead of the Vietnamese soldiers at every turn. On their fifth day, they were faced with a dilemma: they had run out of jungle. They were going to have to cross some open fields, traverse a river, and then resume hiking through open fields again. That, or cross a mountain, which was not an option for the injured gang of men.

As they bedded down near the river in the middle of the day to rest and avoid trekking across open ground during daylight, Boyd was assigned the first watch. He found a crook in a low-lying tree limb to rest on that gave him great cover while providing a reasonable view of the area around their camp. Boyd was armed with an M16A2 rifle. He prayed he would not need it; they were down to 25 rounds of ammo. Lt. Gerhke did have his Colt M1911 pistol, but he was also down to one full magazine.

Boyd had been on watch for a little over an hour when he saw the movement. A little over a hundred yards out. Two soldiers were fanned out looking for any tracks that might lead them to Boyd's group. It would have been an easy shot for Boyd, but so far, staying hidden had done a great job keeping them alive. The problem was the men were getting closer, and he could not be sure there were only two of them. Boyd decided to change his position for a better look.

Maybe his plan would have worked if he had not been using a makeshift crutch out of a tree limb, maybe not. Boyd would never know. Instead, while placing weight on the crutch to move up a tiny rise, the crutch broke sending Boyd crashing into the ground alerting a soldier that Boyd had not seen. One that was much closer.

The Vietnamese soldier yelled loudly giving away Boyd's location shortly before firing his AK-47 at him. Boyd was pinned down behind the small rise. His only option was to slide down the bank toward the river. Thankfully, the Vietnamese soldier was inexperienced, or scared, because he did not try to modify his position. He just fired wildly in Boyd's direction and waited for reinforcements from the other two soldiers. Boyd glanced over the small rise and saw the other soldiers advancing. If he did not make it to the river, he was a dead man.

Out of the corner of his eye, he saw one of the advancing soldiers aiming at him from 40 yards out. Unless the soldier flunked every aspect of shooting instruction, Boyd knew he was going to get hit. He swung the M16A2 into position, ready to fire, but never had to pull the trigger. What he saw was unbelievable, the kind of stuff you would only expect to see in movies. Lt. McCain was running through the jungle from the soldier's right side brandishing a survival knife. He moved like greased lightning; Boyd could not believe a man the Lieutenant's size could move that fast. The soldier turned toward the sound of Lt. McCain crashing through the vegetation. From 40 yards out, Boyd could see the look of surprise on the Vietnamese soldier's face. It probably matched the look on Boyd's. All he could think of was who brings a knife to a gun fight.

The soldier never had a chance. The Lieutenant was too fast. He plunged the survival knife into the soldier's right side to the hilt. In one fluid motion, McCain had the rifle out of the soldier's hands before he even hit the ground and aimed it at the second advancing soldier.

Boyd saw McCain pull the trigger on the AK-47, but nothing happened. Then he watched McCain pull the charging handle back. An unfired round was ejected and another round was charged as he allowed the bolt to seat. Boyd realized the Lieutenant could not find the safety. "The lever on your right! Push down!" he yelled as McCain dropped to the ground to avoid incoming fire from the second soldier. Dirt was flying up all around McCain as the bullets impacted the earth. McCain finally depressed the lever down and pulled the trigger. The rifle fired on full auto. The Lieutenant let off the trigger, took aim and fired again. Boyd was still pinned down, which prevented him from seeing the second soldier, but he knew McCain had killed him when he stood up and meekly smiled in Boyd's direction.

He was still smiling when he was struck in the left thigh by a single 122-grain bullet fired by the original soldier that fired on Boyd. It seemed like it happened in slow motion; Boyd actually saw the blood splatter exit the back of L.T.'s thigh. The rest of the story is foggy in Boyd's brain. He remembers firing at the soldier, who dropped to the ground now that bullets were coming his way. The next thing he remembered was watching Lt. McCain drown the soldier in the river with his bare hands. In less than 45 seconds, a Navy officer who could not even find the safety switch on an AK-47 had killed all three Vietnamese soldiers. He had saved all their asses that day.

Ten years later and Boyd was hoping that L.T. still had the same killer instinct.

CHAPTER 26

Friday morning marked the fourth day of my unpaid leave. Originally, I had been scheduled to work the night shift that Friday. Instead, I was sitting in my kitchen trying to figure out what my inner voice kept saying last night when it told me to work the clues. What clues? The visit to the library had been educational, but I had not found it particularly illuminating? I still didn't know where to look next. It looked as if my hopes were resting on my original plan involving Boyd.

Frustration was setting in, so I grabbed a quick workout before driving over to a local automobile dealership. I was thinking of selling the Mercedes. It ran great; it looked fabulous, but I was not convinced it was my type of car. The dealership offered $15,000 more than I had in the car; a nice return on my investment. If I got fired from the hospital, maybe I could fix up wrecked cars for a living. I seemed to have a knack for it. But I didn't sell it right then. I wanted a couple of days to think it over. Even though it did not have a manual transmission, even though it was not exactly nimble through the corners, it was still the smoothest riding vehicle I had ever ridden it. And gorgeous.

When I got back to my apartment, I saw that Chief Parker had left me a message. I called him back immediately and found out he had a preliminary report from the Tennessee Bureau of Investigation. Cause of death was a .22 to the back of the head. It was unknown whether the shot came from a pistol or a revolver as no spent shell casings were found. Stomach contents revealed he was killed within two hours of eating. The lack of rigor meant he died at least 48 hours before his body was found, yet body decomposition put the time of death as less than four days.

In other words, he was killed the night he went missing. And they were sure he was not killed in the car. No blood splatter in the car and blood pooling suggested he was lying on his back for a little while before the killer put Paul in the car. The Bureau also discovered that the killer had wiped the car for fingerprints. The steering wheel, the door handles, the gear shift, the mirror, were all wiped clean. Even the back door handles.

I said, "So the killer was probably in the car at one time, and he was smart enough to wipe things down. Also smart enough to know what he had touched and what he hadn't. What about the position of the seat, had it been changed?"

"I don't know."

"Paul was average height, average build. If the killer had been anything other average, he might have changed the seat position out of habit. Might have even left a print. Have them check it."

"Will do. Anything else?"

"At the moment, I got nothing to report."

"No reports about whether I watched Letterman or Leno? Or whether I bought another cabin?"

"No."

Chief Parker responded in an irritated voice. "Admit it; you were watching me the other night."

"I'll admit to nothing, except to tell you that you and your son were both suspects at one time. Once Paul's body was found, you both fell off my radar. Get over it, Chief. It was nothing personal. Right now, I've got something in the works to flush out anyone in your town even remotely affiliated with the Dixie Mafia."

"Dixie Mafia? What the hell is that?"

My pager went off while talking with the Chief. There was no number associated with the page, but the message was clear and simple. 911. An emergency signal from Boyd.

"Chief, I wish I had time to explain, but I don't. You have a cute librarian in your town that gave me some books to read. Head down there and have her show you them books. Maybe it will jog your brain. At the very least, it will enlighten you."

"I call to give you the preliminary report findings, and you direct me to read some books in the library. Somehow I feel like I just got the raw end of this deal."

"Sorry, Chief. Read the books, trust me."

The Chief protested a few more times, but in the end, he agreed to try the books. I didn't know what he was so upset about; it was not like he told me anything I did not already know. Plus, he did not give me any additional information to help me find the killer.

After getting off the phone with Chief Parker, I immediately paged Boyd to let him know where he could reach me. Within a couple of minutes, my phone rang. I did not recognize the number on my caller ID, but the area code and prefix signified it was from Emmettsville. I grabbed the phone wondering what Boyd had found out.

Before I could even say hello, Boyd's voice came booming out at me. "Hey, Tofu, we got ourselves a pro—."

Boyd was interrupted by a man with a gruff Southern accent. "What your friend was getting ready to say is that he has a problem.

Right now he is tied to a chair insisting he ain't got any boss but tells me you might be someone who might want him back in one piece."

The voice sounded strangely familiar. Like I should recognize it from somewhere. Nothing came to mind, but I realized he might think the same thing about me. I was no good at voices or accents, so I tried to sound hoarse. "I think you is looking for my boss. He ain't here, but I can get him. Twenty minutes." In addition to my horrible English, I added a cough for good measure.

"You better. I'll call back in twenty. For Graham's sake, make sure your boss is ready to talk," he replied and hung up.

The man had called him Graham, which meant his legend was still intact. I immediately called LeClair's. It was the only thing I could think of. I was short and to the point; Boyd was being held captive, and I needed him on my phone in less than 20 minutes. He agreed to meet me at the corner of Fourth Street and Beale, just east of the WC Handy House Museum. I picked him up in the Mercedes, and we made it back to my apartment with five minutes to spare. It was enough time to tell him about the call and why I needed his help.

LeClair looked calm. Not one ounce of nervousness was evident. That is, until the 20 minutes came and went with no return call. At that point, both of us were more than a little nervous. The call came in two minutes late. The same number flashed across my caller ID.

I hit the speaker phone button and let LeClair do his thing. "I heard you want to talk to me."

"If you are the man in charge, then yes." It was the same voice as before.

"Graham does his own thing, I do mine, but we're close."

"Let's get to the point. Felton County is ours. Has been for as long as anyone can remember. Since I can appreciate Graham's entrepreneurial spirit, I'm willing to let him go with a warning."

"Okay, so why call me then?" asked LeClair.

"Cause I needed to make sure his story was straight. Make sure he really is operating alone. So far, your stories match. Good. There's a fella that has been trying to invade my turf. A real dick. The kind of guy that would sell his momma for a profit."

LeClair said, "I know the type. What about him."

"I want to make sure you ain't him."

"Need me to send you a picture?"

"No smart ass. I just need you to be willing to give me the money Graham made selling liquor in my county. If lieu of an itemized receipt, I'm thinking two grand is about right. If you're willing to buy your friend back, then I know you've got nothing to do with that asshole. Catch my drift?"

LeClair answered, "I'm followin' ya."

"Good. And you'll have to come get him, because I've taken a liking to his car as well."

LeClair immediately replied, "As long as Graham is undamaged, otherwise the deal is off. The boy is like a son to me. Anything happens to him, me and my boys will come in guns blazin'. Are we clear?"

The man said, "I hear ya, if that's what ya mean. But don't go thinking we're scared or anything, 'cuz we ain't. You can pick Graham up tonight at the second bridge out of town on Route P. If ya don't know where that's at, tough, buy a damn map and figure it out. Be there at eleven. Bring the money and come alone." Then he hung up.

* * *

LeClair managed to keep his composure until after the man on the other line hung up the phone. I was impressed with how well he performed under pressure with so little preparation. Immediately after hanging up the phone he started asking me what I had planned. I pointed to the caller ID screen. LeClair did not seem to understand immediately. In December 1988 in Memphis, BellSouth became the first telephone company in the US to deploy caller ID. The feature cost extra each month. Thankfully, I had opted in. "What's that?" he asked.

"The idiot did not realize I had caller ID."

"Caller ID?"

"Yeah, it tells me in real time who is calling me."

"You mean you have their damn phone number. Holy shit. Wait a minute; it's just a number. How do we figure out who it belongs to?"

"A reverse directory. Police departments have them. So do public libraries, usually. I'll call the Chief and get him to tell the address associated with that number. You know what this means, don't you? My idea worked."

"Yeah, just a little too good, it seems. So, how we going to do this?"

"*We* aren't going to do anything if I can help it. I'm going to find out where that call came from and track down the A-holes and get Boyd back. I'm not waiting around to see how things go down on that bridge unless I can't find them in time."

"Hey, you can't drag me out of my bar and have me play the big bad boss, then send me home. Besides, you need me to go with you in case you don't find him."

I could not argue with his logic. Even if the phone number led me to an address, it did not mean Boyd was there. I had to plan for all contingencies.

All I wanted was to flush out some organized crime members so I could watch them and see if they led me to anyone of particular interest. Things were getting out of hand. Sure, Boyd and I flushed out some fellow bootleggers, but there was no guarantee they were part of an organization. The man had said that Felton County was promised to him. Maybe that was as far as their involvement went. One thing was for sure; Charles had been right. There were men in this town that were willing to protect their interests. With force. And for only $2000 and an old car.

I nearly called Chief Parker first, and then I thought better of it. He would want answers to questions. Questions I might not feel like answering. I dialed 411 and got the number for the Felton County Public Library. Jenny answered. The library had a reverse directory, but the number was not listed. She could hear the disappointment in my voice as I thanked her for her trouble.

"Dr. McCain, this is really important to you, isn't it?"

"You have no idea."

"Give me your number and let me call you right back. This directory is a few years old. Maybe it is a new number."

"How are you planning on getting it?"

"I have a master's degree in library science, remember. I'll get it. Trust me."

I had no choice but to trust her. I started preparing for my plan while I waited; loading my Glock 21along with both extra magazines. LeClair watched me in silence until I was finished, then he pointed at my pistol. "You think it might come to that?"

Without answering him, I left the room and returned with my Glock 17. "If you're coming with me, then you might need this. It's a 9 mm. Here is an extra magazine for it. Load up."

"This damn gun is made of plastic. You expect me to shoot a gun made of plastic?"

"That plastic gun, as you call it, is the most widely used pistol by law enforcement the world over. You remember how to shoot a pistol, old man?"

"If I have to, I can handle it, but, for the record, I'd rather have an M16."

I was getting ready to respond when the phone rang. It was Jenny. She had my number as promised. "As expected, it is a new number. It belongs to a junkyard outside of town. I think they use it as their second line."

"Let me guess, E's Salvage Yard?"

"Yeah, you know the place, or do you need an address?"

"No, I know the place. Do me a favor, forget I ever called you. Please. And don't ask why." I hung up without waiting for an answer.

I hated to admit it to myself, but I was surprised to find out the call originated from the Estes brothers. I probably should not have been; it seemed everywhere I turned in that blasted town, Junior Estes was in my face. Now he had my friend hostage. Probably tied to a chair somewhere in the junkyard office. Or maybe to an engine block out in the yard. Either way, Junior was going to pay. I was going to do more than just bounce his head off a window this time.

LeClair immediately asked me about the call. He smiled widely when I explained where the call came from. I asked him what he was smiling about.

"Junior is one of the assholes that's so fond of the n-word, right?"

I understood why he was smiling. "You sure you want to come along?" He nodded. "What about the bar?"

"What about it? It ain't goin' anywhere." He cut me off before I could respond. "I know what you mean. Let me tell you a little secret, the only hard part about runnin' the place is bookin' new bands. The day-to-day operations are simple. I got it so it almost runs itself."

"It's not that, man. I mean, how the hell is the umbilical cord going to reach 45 miles to Emmettsville? You do realize this is the first time I have seen you outside the bar. You are like conjoined twins."

"Whatever, Doc. I don't sleep there" I looked at him with mock amazement. "Most nights anyway. And I do date once in awhile."

"Alright, you can help, but if you turn to ash or something worse when you leave the Memphis city limits, I'm not stopping to clean up the mess; I'm on a timetable."

LeClair waved me off and called me a jive turkey. I finished loading the three 13 round .45 caliber magazines and both of the 17 round 9mm magazines and tossed them into a small bag. I holstered my Glock and headed down the stairs carrying the other pistol in the bag. I motioned for LeClair to wait while I swapped the Mercedes for my Jeep. The first stop I made before heading out of town was to a local gun store to buy an extra magazine for each pistol. During the drive, LeClair questioned me about my plan once we got to Emmettsville.

"Find Boyd. Get him out safe and sound. Hope we don't have to shoot someone, but pray we don't miss if we do."

LeClair shook his head in disbelief at my plan. I guessed he was looking for more details. Details I would not have until we performed some reconnaissance. Then I would make it up as I went along. My thoughts drifted back to Cambodia. Eleven days hiking through Cambodia trying to evade hostile Vietnamese soldiers. My plan had been simple then as well. Travel west into Thailand. Don't get killed. KISS: keep it simple stupid.

I was going to rescue my friend. Again.

* * *

LeClair was getting antsy. Or maybe he was just hot. It was 95 degrees out, and for nearly two hours, we had been watching E's Salvage Yard, but still had no idea if Boyd was inside the facility. We had parked in the woods about a half mile past the salvage yard and hiked through the timber until we had a good view. Unfortunately, I had not brought any binoculars. One of the disadvantages of making it up as you go along is poor planning. I doubted that Boyd would have made that mistake. Of course, he probably would have been watching the whole thing through a high powered scope and listening with a directional microphone.

From what I could tell, the place looked like business as usual. One thing I observed was that customers were not allowed in the salvage yard. In some junkyards, the customers are allowed to walk through the automobiles and pull their own parts. For a premium, they can pay the salvage yard to pull the parts they need for them. At E's Salvage Yard, apparently, all parts were pulled by employees.

The junkyard was split up into two main sections. Directly behind the office building was a small section that was surrounded by an eight-foot high chain link fence topped with barb wired. A good looking security fence. The second, larger section of the junkyard was behind the smaller section. It looked like it was easily five times the size of the front section. It was also surrounded by an older looking chain link fence, minus the barbed wire. Inside sat hundreds of older vehicles. Many of the cars had been sitting there so long that grass could be seen growing up through the cars in places. A few employees could be seen pulling parts in that section. I could hear tools being used within the smaller, newer section of the yard, but I could not tell the exact amount of activity since the entire perimeter of the fence surrounding the smaller section was fitted with a green privacy shield.

I looked over at LeClair who was studying me wondering what I was going to do next. Two hours of watching at a safe distance had yielded us nothing. That is the problem with safe distances; they are often worthless distances as well. LeClair was advised to stay put while I geared up. My Glock was securely holstered on my right hip under my loose shirt. An extra magazine was in my left back pocket. From my earlier visit to the salvage yard, I had noticed security cameras at various locations along the front. It seemed reasonable that surveillance might be utilized along the sides, so I decided to approach from the back. The back side of the older lot had tree cover to within 15 feet of the fence. I used that cover to scout out the lot before climbing the chain link fence.

Once inside, everything got a little easier. The old cars provided plenty of cover and within a couple of minutes I had traversed the entire older section of the junkyard. But the older section was separated from the smaller, newer section by the same fence outfitted with a privacy shield. The Estes brothers definitely valued their privacy. I found myself referring to the private area as their inner sanctum. Even the rolling gate had a privacy shield.

I heard voices on the other side of the fence, along with tools being used. It sounded like four or five employees were in the process of removing parts for customers. There was one employee in the older section using a cutting torch to remove a part off an old Buick. He had left the rolling gate ajar, but he was also working within twenty feet from the gate.

The wait was agonizing. Several times I thought the man was done, only to hear him cuss up a blue streak and resume cutting. After what seemed a small eternity, the man got up and walked through the gate yelling for someone to help him lift "the damn quarter panel." Someone responded that he would help him in a minute. The man with the cutting torch got tired of waiting and walked off mumbling something under his breath. The gate was still partially open. It probably always was during the day. I was not planning on waiting for the man to return with help, so I quietly moved over to the gate and peeked inside.

No sign of Boyd. Not a surprise. I knew it wouldn't be that easy. But the trip had not been a waste of time. Near the door of a metal shed about the size of a two car garage sat Boyd's Mustang.

CHAPTER 27

They had used a lot of duct tape. With time, if he had been unsupervised, he could have escaped, but Boyd got the opinion that they were more interested in scaring him than doing any actual damage, so he let them have their way with him. That did not mean he was completely idle. Junior and Jackson left the room to call L.T. while Tyler was left to guard him. He was not a good guard. Boyd could not help think there was something wrong with Tyler. He seemed to have the attention span of a goldfish.

During stretches of time when Tyler was not watching him, Boyd had stressed the tape holding his wrists until the wrists were loose. It had been painful, but he wanted to be able to achieve his own success if needed. Junior returned a few times. Each time he only stayed for a few minutes, and he never rechecked the tape. After nearly an hour, Junior returned again. "Looks like your boss wants you back. He also wants you back undamaged, so I won't be hittin' you anymore. Course

I wouldn't of hit you at all if you had been more cooperative in the beginning."

Boyd figured it was not a good time to remind Junior that he had hit him in the face before the questioning actually began. "Sorry to have inconvenienced you so much. I hope your fists have recovered."

Junior said, "You're a smart ass. I like you, Graham. I hope you realize it was nothing personal, just business."

"It felt a little personal."

"Yeah, I guess a punch in the face always feels that way, no matter how you try to spin it. Why didn't you just tell us how to reach your boss in the beginning? Some kind of macho thing, trying to see if you could get out of this on your own?"

"Well, I am a former Marine. Oorah, and all that."

Junior smiled. "Like I said, Graham, I like you. I'll tell you what, if you still have anything left after we take your cash and your car, you might try the county west of us. We don't venture over that way. Too close to Memphis for our tastes, and closer to home for you since I noticed that was a Memphis number we called to reach your boss."

Boyd had tried to hold out against giving them L.T.'s home number. He knew L.T.'s number was unlisted, but he kept thinking that Jackson might be able to figure out the man on the other line was L.T. And that would not have been good. The blow torch had been the tipping point. Besides, how was L.T. going to save him if he didn't know he needed saving. He only hoped L.T. had a plan. What was he thinking; L.T. always had a plan.

"You're planning on keeping the Mustang?"

"Yeah, my brother has taken a likin' to it. Says he always wanted one. Do you object?"

"No, go ahead. It's not my car," he said with a big smile. "I've never been a big Mustang fan. Too slow."

"See, that's what I was tellin' Jackson. What the hell do you want with a stupid Mustang, I said. Get a real car. Somethin' with a Hemi in it. A Superbee, maybe a 'Cuda."

"A Chevelle SS with a 454," said Boyd.

"That's what I'm talkin' about. Did I tell you I like you, Graham?"

"You did."

"Just for you, I'll try to get my brother to leave you the car."

Boyd said, "You'd do that for me? Be careful, people are going to think we are going steady."

Tyler laughed so hard that he snorted. Junior watched Boyd trying to appraise if he should be offended or not. In the end, he joined in the laughter. "Na, I like my girls with tits, and your face is kind of smushed in. No offense."

"None taken. Besides, I like men that can hit a little harder. You hit like a girl."

"Damn man, you're a funny son of a bitch. I could go on like this for hours."

"Let me loose, and I'll buy you a Corona over at Falco's. Wait. Apparently, you're taking all my money, so you might have to buy." Junior and Tyler were both laughing at Boyd. He was thinking about something L.T. had said a few days ago about information. Something about all information being helpful. Earlier Jackson mentioned someone named Dunham. He wondered if that was important, or was it just another dead end. "So who's this Dunham guy you mentioned?"

Jackson said, "He's some big deal over in Memphis. Seems like he is always trying to branch out. We've run into his boys a few times around here, but we've both agreed not to step on the other's toes."

"Different products?"

"No, he bootlegs too, but just not on our turf. Over here, he's more interested in hillbilly heroin, and we don't want anywhere near that shit. How about you, Graham, you mess with that crap?"

Boyd had no idea what hillbilly heroin was, but it was obviously a drug. "No, ATF is bad enough; I never want to give the DEA a reason to come looking for me."

Junior said, "No shit, those boys are relentless, but ATF is stupid. We've been running liquor for years and have never heard of them pokin' around here. Not ever."

"Under the radar." It was a statement, not a question, but Junior nodded in agreement nonetheless. "Hey, I noticed you were trying to send me west. Since Dunham is out of Memphis, am I going to run into him over there?"

"Probably."

"So you weren't doing me any favors sending me over there."

Jackson said, "Sure I am. If you stay over here, we're gonna have to hit you some more and Jackson might want another car." That time Tyler laughed at Junior's remark.

Boyd was able to get a little more information on Dunham before Junior left the shed again. Apparently, he had been in the game for over 30 years and initially made his money with alcohol and marijuana. In the last few years, he realized the enormous earning potential of OxyContin, a synthetic form of morphine, often referred to as hillbilly heroin, that is twice as strong and equally addictive. Dunham also sounded like the type of man who did his own enforcing, and not the type that would be interested in contracting his services for some extra cash.

Once Junior left the room, Boyd tried his luck with Tyler, asking him some general questions. Tyler was initially reluctant to talk, but Boyd's gentle persistence eventually caused Tyler to soften and start answering back. After several minutes of give and take, Boyd decided to pry a little deeper.

"So, Tyler, I've noticed no one up here seems to be doing any type of gambling."

"Not in this county. Jackson says you have to have dirty cops to pull off gambling on any kind of decent level to make it worthwhile."

"And you got no dirty cops?"

"Na, the Chief in this county is clean as a whistle. You want to gamble, get down near Tupelo."

Boyd tried to get some more information, but Tyler seemed to lose interest in carrying on the conversation. Yet Boyd felt good about what he had learned. For starters, it appeared that the Chief was an honest man. L.T. would be happy to hear that. He also learned that even though the Estes brothers were simple bootleggers they were still in the know when it came to organized crime in the region. And Tyler mentioned Tupelo. That was in Mississippi. It might be a place to start.

* * *

Sneaking out of the junk yard was easy, and within a few minutes, I was standing next to LeClair explaining that I had found the Mustang. We both decided that the presence of the car near the metal shed was probably not a coincidence. It was possible that he was not inside the shed, but it seemed the most likely place to start looking. We decided to start looking after the junkyard closed for business.

The wait was hot. With the high humidity, the heat index was easily over a hundred. Even in the shade of the trees around me, my clothes were sticking to me uncomfortably. And we had another three hours before the junkyard closed. I gave LeClair the keys to my Jeep and sent him out to get water and lunch. While he was gone, I climbed the fence for another scouting mission. Through the open sliding gate, I could see Junior going into the shed a couple of times, although I did not notice anything suspicious about his behavior. When I saw my Jeep return from town, I exited the junk yard and joined LeClair for a late lunch.

LeClair was not impressed with my plan, but he was not able to come up with an alternative, so we were stuck with mine. As usual, it was simple. I would break into the *inner sanctum* while LeClair waited outside with the Jeep. I hated the idea of heading into the shed blind, but I had no other choice. I did not have any cool spy gadgets like Boyd.

Fifteen minutes before five o'clock I climbed the fence to enter the junkyard covertly for the third time. The back sliding gate was still open. Like before, I had a good view of the smaller section of the junkyard. A few employees could be seen carrying tools, obviously putting them away for the evening. However, none of them were carrying those tools into the shed near the Mustang. Instead, they were carrying them into the back of the main building that contained the front offices and customer service area.

The wire atop the fence was not razor wire, it was simple barb wire, but I still did not relish the idea of climbing it. I decided to slip through the sliding gate and find a place to hide before someone shut the gate for the evening. Keeping low, I approached the gate. My heart nearly stopped when I saw the gate start to move. Quickly, I flattened myself up against the privacy fence hoping I had not been spotted. Someone had closed the gate and padlocked it in place; however, there were no cries of alarm. No evidence that anyone had seen me. How, I didn't know; I was only a couple of yards from the gate when it started to close. I could not see the person that closed the fence, but I did hear his footsteps. My breathing returned to normal as he walked away.

A few minutes later the employees started driving away from the salvage yard. Nine vehicles in all. I realized I had not counted how many vehicles were stationed outside. Poor reconnaissance on my part once again. Even with my view completely blocked by the privacy fence and the office building, I knew there was at least one vehicle that did not leave: the two-toned Ford pickup that Junior drove. I knew the sound of that vehicle too well. So unless he left with someone else, Junior was still in the salvage yard somewhere.

A small crack existed in the privacy shield where the sliding gate joined the rest of the fence. I was able to see through the crack into the smaller junk yard. Boyd's Mustang was still exactly where I had last seen it. Maybe he was not in the shed at all. Maybe the car was the only thing in the yard, and they were keeping Boyd somewhere else. Maybe. But I would never know just peeking through a crack.

I knew what I needed to do. The closed gate and barbed wire were not going to be a deterrence; it was simply a complication. I spent a few minutes rummaging through some junk cars before I found what I needed. Two old floor mats. I peered through the crack to look for anyone that might spot me. The yard was empty. With the old floor mats draped over one shoulder, I started to climb where the fence met the gate. The latch on the gate provided an excellent foothold while climbing. Once halfway up the fence, I draped the floor mats over the top of the barb wire and then waited to make sure no one had noticed. The coast was still clear. The rubber floor mats allowed me to climb over the top strand of barb wire safely. The wire barely supported my weight, which made the climb over slow and tedious. I managed to get over the fence unseen with only one small scratch on my left forearm.

Once over the fence, I walked to the shed and looked for a window. I found one on the back side of the building, but it was completely black like someone had painted over it. There was a garage door and a regular door on the front of the building, neither of which had a built-in window. No matter how hard I tried, it appeared I was still going to have to walk into that building blind.

With my ear placed against the door, I listened for any sounds emanating from inside. It was quiet. Maybe nothing was in there. I turned the door knob slowly, pushing the door open just as slowly. Instinctively, my right hand drifted down to my hip, finding reassurance in the form of my .45 caliber handgun. The door was cracked a little, yet I could not see anything inside. I could not hear anything either. The door let out a small squeak. I stopped, wondering if anyone inside had heard it too.

A voice yelled from inside, “Damn man, you back with my dinner already?”

It sounded like whoever was inside was alone. I could hear him walking toward the door. My hand was perched on the butt of my Glock. Tyler opened the door. His eyes bugged out in absolute surprise. Without hesitation, I pulled my right hand off my gun and hit him in the face with everything I had. His body flew backward through the air, landing on his butt. If he was not unconscious before he hit the floor, then his head bouncing off the concrete floor finished him off. The meaty thud sounded painful, but Tyler did not feel it; he was out cold.

A quick survey of the room told me all I needed to know. I had found Boyd, alone and sitting in a chair with his ankles duct taped to the legs of the chair. His hands were free, and he had a small knife in one hand. There was dried blood around his eye from a cut on his left brow. Both eyes were black and swollen. I suddenly felt no sympathy for knocking Tyler out for the second time in less than a week, even though I was completely aware of the possible repercussions of two concussions spaced so close together. The look of confusion on Boyd's face quickly turned into a large grin.

"I'll be doggone," I said, "You are in here after all. Anyone one else in here?"

"No."

"Good. Let's get you out of here."

I heard the thud before I actually felt it. A dull, heavy sound, like someone beating a big stick against a hollow log. When my head shot violently forward, I knew I had been hit from behind. Instinctively, my hand shot to the back of my head. I felt the warm liquid. When I brought my hand forward, it was covered in blood.

I turned to face my attacker, but it seemed like I was moving in slow motion. My reaction speed was diminished. My vision was a little hazy. It was like someone had found a dimmer switch in my brain and had used it. *Holy crap, how hard have I been hit.*

I was almost unaware of the long metal rod, a car part, probably a stabilizer bar, that came arcing through the air at me. There was no way to avoid being hit. My response was not a conscious one. My brain was not functioning at full speed yet. It was not even an instinctual fight for survival that guided me. Instead, years of training, years of forming and honing the neural pathways inside my brain and body took over. I stepped toward my attacker, thus minimizing the impact of the blow I could not escape. I twisted my body and braced.

The blow to my left shoulder hurt, but there was no actual damage. I grabbed the metal object with my right hand and jerked it violently towards me, pulling my attacker, Junior Estes, into the room. Junior released his grip on his weapon and bull rushed me driving me backward into the wall of the shed. We crashed to the floor with Junior on top. He was throwing blows down on me. None of them were landing with any real effect.

I was on my back, my legs around Junior's torso in a classic closed guard position. My head was still bleeding, yet I was strangely aware that I was now smiling because Junior thought he had the advantage. Without his weapon, the tide of the fight had shifted. I knew he was not going to be able to pass my closed guard position. Too many hours of wrestling and Jiu-Jitsu had prepared me for this moment. Junior must have seen my smile because his lips pursed, brows furrowed, and eyes narrowed in a look of extreme anger. He wound up a big punch with his right hand but missed. I deflected it across the midline of my body. His forward momentum carried him across my body. A classic mistake. I pulled his arm over further while crunching him forward, bringing his head down near my chest. From there, all I had to do was open my legs, move them higher, one up over his head and hook them together. His shoulder was locked in an armbar, a move that makes an opponent's elbow or shoulder bend unnaturally. With some upward pressure from my hips, I had Junior writhing in pain.

Junior was tapping my leg with his free hand. "Stop! Stop!"

"Are you trying to tap out? This is a fight, dumbass. I should just break your arm and be done with it."

"Don't break my arm. Please."

I don't know why, but I didn't break his arm. Maybe it was Boyd standing over me watching in a state of awe at the whole thing. Maybe it was because now that he was loose from the tape I simply didn't have to break the arm.

"Shut up, Fireplug. Graham, grab my Glock from my hip and point it at this dickhead." Boyd complied. "If he even thinks about getting up, put one in his knee, okay?"

"Gladly."

Junior stayed on his back while I released him from the armbar and stood up. Tyler was still where I last saw him. Breathing, but not moving. Hopefully, it was not going to be another Tom Harty type situation.

Quickly, I pulled the shirt off my back and placed it on the back of my head, applying direct pressure to my wound. Boyd and I had similar expressions when we saw the amount of blood on the floor where I went down.

"Keys!" I yelled. Junior just stared at me. "Read my lips. Keys. Where are they? I need the gate open, and I'm taking the Mustang. Got it?" More staring. "Don't look at me like that. Graham's never shot anyone. I have. Got no qualms about it, in fact. So, once again. Keys."

Something about my tone must have scared Boyd; I could see it. He must have thought I might shoot Junior if I did not get my way. Junior must have felt it too because he immediately handed over the keys to the Mustang. He also led us to the switch that opened the gate.

Boyd said, "By the way, where's my Sig?"

"In my brother's office, on the desk."

Boyd handed me my Glock and walked down the hall to retrieve his gun. Junior was telling the truth; Boyd returned carrying his Sig. He said to me, "You okay? That was a lot of blood back there."

"It's just a simple laceration. And head wounds often bleed like that. I will probably need stitches, though."

We climbed into the Mustang, Boyd in the driver's seat while I sat in the front passenger seat. Before leaving, I turned to Junior. "This is the second time I let you off easy. I could have snapped your elbow in half, but I didn't. You know why? Because you're not the person I am looking for. You're just the dickhead that keeps getting in my way. Don't make that mistake again. My goodwill is all used up. I'm going to find out who killed my friend's son. No matter what. So stay the hell out of my way."

It must have been the blood on my hand that made me do it. Blood that made me realize the A-hole standing in front of me tried to kill me with a metal bar. Because after seeing the blood, I pointed my Glock at Junior. He looked remarkably unfazed until I pulled the trigger and fired a shot into the ground between his feet. He could not hide the surprise that I actually fired a shot in his direction, nor could he disguise his relief at not being shot. Hopefully, my point had been made. I closed the door and motioned for Boyd to drive.

CHAPTER 28

Boyd and I were recovering in my apartment after being treated at Memphis Memorial. My laceration needed eleven stitches, Boyd's eye needed four. Other than the cut on my head, I was uninjured. Boyd had two black eyes to go with the stitches but was otherwise uninjured. Although he helped kidnap my friend, I prayed that Tyler was alright. He had most likely suffered his second concussion within a week and from what Boyd said it sounded like he was still suffering from post-concussion syndrome following the first one. Junior might have a sore shoulder for a few days; I had torqued it pretty hard, but he was lucky Boyd had been able to cut himself free. If he hadn't, my plan was to dislocate either the shoulder or the elbow. Jackson missed the whole thing. Boyd guessed he had left to get dinner for the group.

Boyd and I had both apologized to each other more than once. He was sorry that he had given up his firearm so easily, thus putting himself in a position that he needed to be saved from. I apologized for not giving him more direction on selling the illegal alcohol. By selling all of it in one day, he had made the Estes brothers feel threatened by his presence. I had not wanted that. I had meant for him to sell a little bit at a time, just enough to draw attention but not ire. What was done, was done, Boyd had said, but I could not help thinking that we had missed our opportunity for Boyd to have an effective dialog with the Estes brothers.

Boyd looked up from his beer and said, "You know, it's not a complete loss."

"Yeah, how so?"

"Now we have someone we can watch or listen to. We could see if they lead us to anyone else, or maybe we could figure out who this Dunham guy is they were talking about. Plus, Tyler did mention that you have to go down to Mississippi to find any good gambling. Maybe what happened today was just a speed bump in the road heading in the direction we wanted to go in the first place."

"Hell of a speed bump, but you got a point. You're no longer any good undercover anymore, though."

"So what. I still have listening devices. I could bug the hell out of that junkyard. They are bound to be talking about what happened. Maybe we'll hear something good."

"They got a lot of cameras around that place. You might be seen getting them in place."

"Okay, the laser mic then. They are a pain in the butt to set up, but I can be miles away if need be. Unless you want me to blind the cameras with a powerful laser. Wait, I don't have one of those with me. Damn. Laser mic is the best bet then."

"You could use the woods LeClair and I were hiding in. Perfect view of the building with plenty of cover. I don't recommend using the Mustang anymore, though."

Boyd said, "Probably not a good idea. I could drive to Huntsville tomorrow and get my truck."

"No, would take too long and your truck could always be traced back to you. I still want no record that Boyd Dallas was ever in Felton County. I'll buy another car tomorrow. Black out the windows."

"L.T., I can't let you do that. I'll get my truck. You spent enough money on this investigation so far. Especially since you might lose your job at the hospital, and you're driving a $100,000 car and live in the biggest damn apartment I have ever seen. You can't even afford to put up walls and finish the upstairs of your building."

I smiled and laughed a friendly laugh at Boyd. "That's sweet. You think I'm broke. The car…it's paid for. This apartment…it's paid for. And it's not finished because I haven't figured out what I want to do with it yet. I'm not sure I want neighbors."

"How much damn money do they pay ER doctors?"

"Not enough to do all that. My dad left me some money. Quite a bit. I use that money to invest in real estate and flipping cars for a profit. My Mercedes, I almost sold it yesterday for a $15,000 profit. Not bad for part-time work over a couple of months, if I say so myself."

"You're a trust fund kid? Why'd you join the Navy?"

"Long story." Boyd stared at me for a few seconds before shrugging it off. Once again, I had deflected answering questions about my past, even with my friends. It was not a healthy habit; I knew that. It was time to start a new habit. "Fortunately, we got the time."

I told Boyd about my parents, the professional football player, the prima ballerina. My sports accolades. The drunk driver, and my lost dreams. Boyd was a pretty darn good listener.

"So you were depressed. Makes sense."

"I was not depressed," I replied, "I was angry."

"Bullshit. You were depressed, which is why you were angry. If you had just been angry, you would have gone on to play professional football or go to the Olympics in wrestling. Anger would have motivated you, L.T., not held you back. You were friggin' depressed, and nobody helped you with it. What a crying shame."

"You don't know what you're talking about. You weren't there."

"I don't need to have been there. Everyone probably looked at this 6'4" man-child who can beat up men twice his size, and thought, hey, he'll be okay. But you weren't okay, and you weren't a man. You were a 16-year-old kid." I opened my mouth to protest, yet no words came out. "Look, I may not be a doctor, but don't bother telling me I'm wrong because we both know I'm not."

I did not argue with him. I couldn't. Because deep down inside, I knew he was right. Which kind of pissed me off, especially when I thought about the fact that not dealing with the depression had caused me to build up emotional walls. Virgil, my best friend for the last 20 years, had hinted at it before and chastised me for living in the past, but he never mentioned depression. Maybe even Virgil liked to think of me as unbreakable. The man who conquers anything that gets in his way.

"Wow, save a guy's butt twice, and this is how he repays me," I said in an obvious facetious tone.

Boyd stood up and walked over to the windows, looking out at nothing in particular. "That's how I roll, don't ya know," he said. We were both quiet for a couple of minutes. Boyd was at the window staring off into space; I was lying back on my couch. "Hey, does Ellie drive a little red car with 4CASTR on the license plate?"

"Yeah, why?"

"Because she just pulled up." Just what we needed I thought. Not that I didn't want to see her, but we were trying to keep Boyd's presence a secret. Boyd read my face. He could see my indecision. "Hey, don't worry. It's a big apartment. I got a feeling I'm going to want to get up real early, so I'll take a nap in the other bedroom."

Boyd was walking towards the other bedroom when we both heard a key in the door to my apartment. He did not let his bad ankle stop him from running into the bedroom just before the front door opened. It was close, but he managed to stay unseen.

Ellie entered the room smiling as she saw my head peering at her over the back of the couch. "So this is how my currently unemployed boyfriend spends his time."

She was joking around. That was a good sign. Our relationship had been tense ever since I got involved with investigating Paul's disappearance, even more so once I got arrested, and Paul was found murdered. I joked back, telling her that I was just trying to figure out the best spot for a TV. Ellie crossed the room to give me a kiss. One of her hands started to go to the back of my head. Immediately, I grabbed her hand and held it in mine. Surely, she would have felt the shaved spot on my head, maybe even felt the stitches. We spent several minutes sitting on the couch while I asked about her day. She sounded happy and willingly to answer my questions about her day.

"Okay, sailor, now that we both know I had a typical day in the life of a weather girl, how has your day gone?"

"Meteorologist," I corrected. "I think I have a good lead on organized crime."

"Really. Already? So where did you get the lead?"

"Can't tell you."

"Why not?"

"Plausible deniability."

Ellie huffed. "Just tell me it's not my dad."

"Seriously? This is a boots-on-the-ground operation. You dad wouldn't even qualify as an adviser; he told me he wouldn't know a prostitute if it bit him on the butt." Ellie chuckled. "So, he probably wouldn't be a great source of information."

"Can you, at least, tell me who you are looking at?"

"Best if I don't."

"It's like I'm dating a damn spy or something. So, what can you tell me?"

"I'm making progress. In fact, I would say I have more than one person of interest."

Ellie asked, "And you have managed to get all this information without putting yourself in danger?" Her tone made it difficult to tell if the question was rhetorical or not.

Serious question or not, I could not bring myself to tell her the truth. I was not sure how she would react to reports of another fight, especially given that the one with Junior might have been a life-or-death struggle. "Nothing dangerous. Just asking questions. Even talked to Junior Estes' brother, Jackson. It looks like he is going to talk some sense into Junior and have him leave me alone."

"But you won't tell me who the person of interest is?"

"Plau—."

"Plausible deniability," she interrupted. Her tone made me feel that she was not buying the plausible deniability excuse, but she stopped trying to press for more information regardless. Our conversation turned to more mundane matters. Her work. My future at the hospital. How my other building was coming. After several minutes, I offered to get her some tea. I walked with my head turned back towards her so she could not see the back of my head, then realized I was being stupid. My bushy hair would cover the shaved area to all but the most scrutinizing observer.

I handed her an iced tea and sat down. She wrinkled her eyes and nose in thought.

"What?" I asked.

"You're acting weird."

"I am?"

"Yes, you are. You're moving stiffly. Did you spar at the gym today?" I shook my head no. "Your neck still hurt from your night in jail?"

Once again, I shook my head. I was actively lying to my girlfriend. Not a good relationship building activity. Opening up and talking to Boyd earlier had been beneficial. Maybe I should try to do the same with my girlfriend.

"I need to come clean about something, Ellie. My head has eleven stitches in it right now from another run in with Junior Estes. He hit me in the head with a steel bar when I wasn't looking. Then, I kicked his butt again."

Ellie quietly mulled over my confession for nearly half a minute standing up and walking into my bedroom. Not exactly the response I had anticipated. Several minutes later she returned. "Is Junior Estes your suspect? I mean your person of interest?"

"Sort of. I mean, I'm looking for someone down in Mississippi, but I don't know who. So, instead, I started looking for anyone with ties to organized crime in Emmettsville who might be able to direct me to the guy in Mississippi. At first, I kept thinking he was just some racist prick, or some friend of Eric's, that was getting in my way. Now I know Junior and his brother run booze."

Ellie said, "In other words, he might be the link you have been looking for all along."

"Exactly."

"Seems like a pretty indirect way of finding the guy in Mississippi."

"Well, I don't have access to a crime database telling me who's involved with illegal gambling in the area. If I knew for 100 percent that Chief Parker could be trusted, I could have used him."

"No, I understand why you didn't ask the Chief. I'm just wondering why you didn't have John make a partial payment to whoever has been calling him and then follow that guy back to where ever it is that you guys have to follow them back to. But I'm just a meteorologist, so what do I know."

"Well, damn," I said. "That would have been a lot easier and a lot faster. Shit." I wondered if I looked as stupid right then as I felt. Her plan was a good plan. Undoubtedly, it would have worked, and in less than half the time. And it would have been cheaper.

Ellie said, "Once you have this link you are looking for, what next?"

"I plan on handing it over to a law enforcement official, hopefully with enough compelling evidence that they can, and will, run with it on their own."

"But not Chief Parker?"

I said, "Possibly Chief Parker, but preferably someone on the state level."

"L.T., I'm not sure what he does there, but I do know someone who works for the State Police. I could call him and see if he knows anyone that could help."

"That would be awesome. Ellie, thank you."

"For what?"

"For being such a peach about things. I know you would prefer that I drop things."

"Yeah, well, I'm being self-serving. If my friend can help you, then it would, in turn, help me. I might not have to worry about you."

"Either way, thanks."

"You're welcome. Now when are you going to get me that TV?"

* * *

Ellie called the next morning with good news. Her law enforcement friend was interested in talking to me. Even better, he was no longer with the State Police. Her friend was Special Agent Mark Sande, a Criminal Investigator with the Tennessee Bureau of Investigation, who, as luck would have it, was stationed in Memphis. Special Agent Sande had blocked out some time for me near the lunch hour. Ellie arranged all this for me by 7:00 a.m. I forgot to ask her how she pulled that off so fast.

Boyd seemed excited when I gave him the news. "We needed this," said Boyd, "To make it all legit, but if this means I don't get to shoot at anyone then I'm going to be a little disappointed." I told him that I would see what I could do while teasing him that he had his opportunity yesterday, but passed. Boyd did not want to wait for me to get back from visiting Agent Sande; he wanted to try out his laser microphone on the Estes brothers.

"I haven't got you a different car yet, so take my Jeep. Nobody in Emmettsville knows it. Wear a cap and sunglasses, and you should be fine."

Boyd had a quick breakfast and left. The meeting was for later in the morning, which gave me nearly three hours to kill. Plenty of time for a good workout and a visit to a used car lot. I hated most cars from the Eighties. No handling, no horsepower. I couldn't find anything I wanted.

I arrived a little early to the local TBI office, which allowed me time to consider how I should approach asking for help. Lay it on too hard, and it would make Chief Parker and his office look corrupt. If his office was clean, I did not want to do that to him. Play it too casual, and Mr. Sande might wonder why I was even bothering him.

I had been sitting outside the nondescript office building for about 15 minutes when a knock on my car window startled me. I whipped my head to my left to discover a tall, lean man in his late twenties dressed in casual business attire — khakis and a short-sleeved, white button-down shirt. Real clean cut. Looked fit, athletic. Friendly smile. Blue eyes. Probably did well with the ladies.

He was moving his hand in a circular fashion indicating for me to crank the window down. He was wearing a Glock 19 on his left hip in a cross draw holster. A plainclothes police officer. "Dr. McCain?" he asked. I nodded. "Special Agent Sande, come on in."

We passed two more tall, lean men dressed in casual business attire on the way back to his office.

"You guys come off a factory line somewhere?" He shook his head indicating he had no idea what I was talking about. "Just making a joke. You guys all kind of look alike."

"Oh. Yeah, I noticed that once too. No, were just inbred down here don't ya know." A playful smirk appeared on his face, the smile reached his eyes. "Come on in and have a seat."

So far, I liked Mark Sande.

"Ellie tells me you are having some trouble back in Emmettsville. Something that I might be able to help you with."

"Back in Emmettsville?"

"She didn't tell you; I grew up there. Went to high school with Ellie. How is Ellie doing these days? I see her on TV but haven't spoken to her in months, maybe a year. Come to think of it, probably about the time you two started dating. You are the same doctor she started dating a year ago, aren't you?"

Interesting, Special Agent Sande had heard about me. Lloyd had told him about me, all good, or so Sande said. He questioned me about Ellie and our relationship for several more minutes. Special Agent Sande was obviously a good friend. My suspicion is that the two of them might have been more than friends at one time. My inner voice also told me that the breakup had not been his idea.

He eventually turned to conversation towards the reason for my visit. "Ellie didn't tell me what was going on. She just said I would be doing her a favor, a favor for a friend."

"Special Agent Sande..."

"Mark," he interjected.

"Okay, Mark. Did you hear anything about a homicide in your hometown earlier this week?"

"Sure did. Emmettsville PD found a body in a car Tuesday morning." He gave me a surprised look. "You tangled up in that mess somehow?"

"Yeah."

"Oh, shit. Ellie didn't tell me it was that kind of favor."

"Well, she didn't tell me that you were an ex-boyfriend, so I guess we both want to give her some crap about now."

"I never said..." He paused. "Oh, forget it. Ellie and I dated our senior year of high school and first couple of years of college. And you're right; we both got a bone to pick with her." He was not angry with her. Nor was I. In fact, both of us were smiling at the prospect that Ellie had pulled a fast one on us. "You better tell me what's going on. Ellie went to a lot of work setting this up."

The best place to start a story of that magnitude is the beginning, all the way back to the night Paul Deland went missing. I explained how the initial confrontation with Eric led me to believe that Eric was involved. Jackson and Agent Sande were in high school at the same time, but he knew Junior as well. So he seemed particularly interested in my first confrontation with Junior and his five friends, and in the fight that got me arrested. Mark's ears perked up when I mentioned Paul's gambling debt. I did not want to influence his reasoning process, so I did not mention my suspicion that organized crime existed in Emmettsville. I also left out the conversation with Chief Parker when he asked for my help, and also about my run-in with Junior and his brother yesterday.

"Damn, you have had an interesting week." He drew out the sentence emphasizing each word for a more dramatic effect. He leaned back in his chair; his hands interlocked behind his head. He looked relaxed, yet deep in thought.

"So, I've told you everything I know, what do you think?"

He was disappointed with Chief Parker, going so far as to say that the Chief needed to pursue charges against his son and the other two. I did not bother telling him that kidnapping and another assault charge could be added to the list of charges against the other Tyler and Junior.

"Doc, I was just wondering if you still think he sent those guys after you?"

"Probably not, but someone in his office did, or at least said something to someone."

"No doubt about that. If it were me, I would look for someone about Eric's age, maybe a friend of his on the force."

"Makes sense," I said. "But I'm more interested in finding out what happened to Paul. What do you think about how the gambling debt ties into the equation, Mark?"

"Could be a coincidence."

"Sure, but what does your gut tell you?"

"Not sure."

"Let me ask you this. If the crime did not happen in Emmettsville, say it happened here in Memphis, and you knew about the phone calls and the gambling debt, what would you think?"

"Organized crime."

"So the reason you are entertaining the idea that it might be a coincidence is because it happened in Emmettsville?"

"Yeah, I guess."

Now we were getting to the real reason I came to ask for his help. I hoped he would have come to the conclusion on his own, but then he did grow up in the town and maybe even knew some of the men that attacked me; maybe it was too much of a stretch for him to consider an organized criminal element in his sleepy little hometown.

I said, "What if I told you that I know for sure that organized crime exists in Emmettsville? Would that change your mind?"

"Probably. Sure. Why, what have you got?"

"Junior and Jackson Estes are selling illegal liquor throughout Felton County."

"You know this how?"

"I've personally witnessed it." I lied out of necessity; Boyd's involvement had to remain a secret. "And I've seen automobiles being delivered to their junkyard that were not junk. I'm telling you, those boys are dirty."

The relaxed demeanor he had throughout our conversation was gone. He was brooding, his elbows up on his desk, his chin resting on his interlocked fingers. I had probably shattered his image of Emmettsville, maybe Chief Parker as well. I gave him time to digest everything I had just thrown at him. "So you think they had something to do with your friend's death?"

"Actually, no," I said. Agent Sande wanted to know why I was watching them then, so I explained how I was looking for a link to organized crime. Specifically, for someone that could direct me to the man down in Mississippi that Paul owed the money to.

Standing suddenly, he looked like a man with an idea. "You mind if I talk to someone else about this real quick? Someone with his finger on the pulse of organized crime in Tennessee?"

"No. That would be great."

And that would be great. I asked John for help on the law enforcement side, but so far he had not come through. I would never have thought that Ellie was the one that would provide the help that I needed. If all went well, I could even turn the case over completely to the TBI and wash my hands of the whole thing. Ellie would be happy, for sure. I would not complain either. Justice was my goal. I did not care who delivered that justice. Boyd would be crushed. I think he wanted to bust this case wide open himself. At the very least, I was going to have to listen to him give me crap that I cheated him out of being able to shoot at someone.

It was easily 10 minutes before Special Agent Sande returned to the room. Another tall, lean man, this one in his late forties, accompanied him. He introduced himself as Captain Morgan Evans. Evans looked angry. Mark looked upset. I had a feeling the discussion did not go well for Special Agent Sande. I also had a sinking feeling it was not going to go well for me either.

I stood up and shook his outstretched hand, but said nothing. "Special Agent Sande has given me quite a report."

I guessed right; this was not going to go well. Condescension dripped off of him like syrup off pancakes. Sitting back down almost seemed like a waste of time, but Captain Evans sat. Therefore, I followed his lead. I was trying to decide how to proceed when Captain Evans started talking again.

"You've reached out to Special Agent Sande for help. What exactly are you hoping for?"

"I was hoping someone would listen to my story and would want to take over my investigation. Someone who would take my information and run with it."

Evans said, "So you were expecting the Tennessee Bureau of Investigation to listen to the report of an amateur detective and then assign one of our Special Agents to your case?"

I stood up. "Sorry for wasting your time."

"Wait, Dr. McCain. I'm just trying to determine your intention on coming here."

"It's okay, Captain Evans. Ellie Carmichael told me that Special Agent Sande might be able to help me. However, you seem to be in charge, and you are obviously unwilling to help."

"You are right; I am the Special Agent in Charge of the West Tennessee Field Unit. I'm in charge of 12 Special Agents, and we service 21 counties and seven judicial districts. I can't send one of my men to Emmettsville simply because you found a lost wallet and got into a fight with some local yokels while playing amateur sleuth."

That cemented it for me; this man was a dick. It was time to be the one asking the questions. "Captain Evans, what's the motto of the TBI?" I knew the answer; I had seen it written on a plaque in the lobby.

Captain Evans was surprised by the question. Maybe even a little annoyed. He paused, and then said, "That guilt shall not escape, nor innocence suffer."

"It's a good motto, don't you think?"

"Sure…"

"Like my pastor says, 'That could preach.' Good words to live by. Sounds like a good motto for a law enforcement agency. You happy with the motto?"

Captain Evans said, "I see where you are going with this Dr. McCain, it's just th—"

"That's awesome, Captain Evans. I'm so glad you understand my intention for coming here. I like your motto too. I don't want the guilty to escape either."

"That's not what I was going to say."

"So, it's not a philosophical problem. Must be more practical then. Maybe you think my hypothesis does not hold water. Fine, I can accept that. But before you dismiss me completely, you should know I am not an amateur detective. The United States Navy paid me to investigate crime years ago. I even got a medal because they thought I had done a good job. Would you like to see it?"

Captain Evans eyes squinted while looking at me. You could cut the tension in the room with a knife. I found that I did not care.

"So, hear me when I say that the wallet was not lost. It was found in an unlikely location under suspicious circumstances. I was not amateur sleuthing; I was investigating. And whether I'm right or wrong about Jackson and Junior Estes having anything to do with Paul Deland's homicide, you still have organized crime in Emmettsville, Tennessee. Which, I imagine, falls well within the jurisdiction of the Tennessee Bureau of Investigation."

"Dr, McCain, I don't appreciate..."

"I don't care what you appreciate, sir," I interrupted. "I only care about justice." Captain Evans cast me a blank stare. "Justice for a murdered man."

Special Agent Sande was watching the exchange with a look of pure trepidation. He looked like a kid in a wagon with a loose wheel, just wondering when that wheel was going to fall off. He was Ellie's friend, ex-boyfriend to be exact, and I hated putting him in the middle of an argument with his superior.

Captain Evans stood to his full height and leaned in towards me. His hand came up, and he started pointing at me. A lecture or a scolding was coming. "Listen here, Dr. McCain. I pride myself on being a part of an organization that has faithfully served the people of the Volunteer State every day since 1951."

"Congratulations," I interrupted, the mocking tone coming out so strong it even surprised me a little bit.

"I was not finished! Even if I wanted to help you, and I'm not saying I do, the Bureau could not investigate in Emmettsville without a request from the Attorney General within that judicial district. Are you an Attorney General, Dr. McCain?"

"You know what, Captain, you should have lead with that. I could have done without the condescension. Just because I don't have a Southern accent does not mean that I'm not also a citizen of the Volunteer State. I love Memphis. It's home to me. I have a question for you, Captain." He did not answer, but the look on his face indicated he was willing to hear my question. "Do you still need a request from the Attorney General to investigate organized crime, or does that fall under original jurisdiction?"

His eyes narrowed, a scowl spread across his face. I had asked the right question.

"I'm not going to help you, Dr. McCain. And my advice for you is that you leave the investigating to Chief Parker and his police force. Special Agent Sande will see you out."

CHAPTER 29

"If at first you don't succeed…" The popular proverb came to mind as Agent Sande escorted me from the building. Maybe all Captain Evans needed was more convincing evidence. Something strong enough that he felt compelled to investigate. I was not going to give up just yet. I would give the TBI one more chance to help, but only one more, because W. C. Fields had been right when he said, "If at first you don't succeed, try, try again. Then quit. There's no point in being a damn fool about it."

Agent Sande was very apologetic on the way out to my car. He informed me that I had been right concerning my assumption of original jurisdiction concerning organized crime and that he would love to help; however, his hands were tied. I knew that and told him not to worry. I would be back. He would be impressed. I did not know what I meant by that, but it sounded good at the time. I thanked him for coming in on a Saturday for me, but he informed me that it was his weekend to work anyway.

Maybe Boyd would come back with something. Maybe I could pay another visit to Jackson at the junk yard to prime the conversation. I could only imagine that conversation, especially a day after breaking into their salvage yard and rescuing Boyd. If that did not work, then I was going to have to pull out my backup plan, which was not something I wanted.

My pager, which I left in the car while visiting Special Agent Sande, had been very busy. Ellie paged me. The hospital paged me. Boyd paged me. Twice. He did not use our predetermined emergency code; instead, he had typed 411, which signified he had information, important information and that I should call him immediately. I drove back to my apartment and called Boyd at the Traveler's Inn.

Boyd answered on the first ring. "Hot damn, Lieutenant, I am about to make your day. Are you sitting down?"

I sat down. "Let me have it, Boyd."

"So you know how my laser microphone is a prototype and does not have recording capability?"

"Yeah."

"Well, I fixed it so it does."

"Boyd, are you playing around in my head. I was just thinking how it would be nice if we could record."

"Great minds think alike. You are going to bow down at my feet when you hear what I got for you. On tape, no doubt."

"So what do you got?"

"The missing piece of the puzzle, my good man. Early this morning, I lined up the laser mic so that it is aimed directly at the office at the junk yard. It took a couple of hours to get a good spot and get the laser all lined up, but I did it. Just in time, I might add."

"Just in time for what?"

"Junior was opening up the junkyard and his friend Tyler was with him when they had a couple of visitors. The visitors did not have names, but they were there to talk to Junior about you know who."

"Paul?"

"Yep."

"Let me guess," I said, "They were sent by the man that Paul owed the money to. The guy in Mississippi."

"His name is Strasser, by the way, and he's not happy to hear that Paul is dead. He sent his men to get the money that Junior was supposed to collect from Paul. His men accused Junior of collecting the money and keeping it for themselves, and now Strasser wants what belongs to him."

"Hell, yeah! We have our connection. Way to go, Bird Dog! So, how did it play out?"

Boyd said, "I thought there was going to be a shootout in that office. That Junior is a damn hot head. I couldn't see it, but I heard the action of a pump shotgun, and then Junior started yelling at them. Told them to get the you know what out of there and tell their boss they had nothing to do with Paul's death. Junior told them they didn't have the money, but they were still trying to collect from the father. Something about making more threats on the father. Lots of yelling. It came real close to being a blood bath in there."

"Whoa."

"No shit."

"How did it end up?" I asked.

"Strasser's men left, but not before telling Junior they would be back. They made a point of telling Junior that Strasser was not going to be happy."

"So did you hear anything good from Junior and Tyler after Strasser's men left?"

"Just a lot of cussing from Junior. Basically, who the fuck does Strasser think he is kind of stuff. And that he still plans on collecting the money."

"And you got this all on tape?"

"Yeah. I had to use a cheap Dictaphone placed next to the speaker, but I played it back, and you can hear everything just fine."

"I don't know what to say, except good job, Sergeant."

Boyd said, "Did I happen to mention that I like this sneaky stuff?"

"You did. Several times."

I could hear him chuckling over the phone.

* * *

I praised Boyd a few more times before describing my visit with Special Agent Sande and his boss. He was as surprised as I was by the surly reception I received by Captain Evans. Both us agreed that the tape should get the response from the TBI that we wanted, the response that we needed to make the whole process legitimate.

I was going to visit Special Agent Sande for the second time in the same day, but first I needed to warn John that Junior was still planning on collecting the money that Paul owed. John took the news better than I had expected. It was obvious that he felt guilty for not simply paying the debt; but ultimately, I think he knew he had done the right thing. If he paid anything now, Junior could make up any amount he wanted and squeeze as much out of John as he wanted. Which was also the reason I had not thought of using Ellie's idea initially, although I still had to admit it would have been a lot easier. John had to stay tough. I hoped he had the fortitude.

Twenty minutes after hanging up with John, I was sitting in the lobby of the Tennessee Bureau of Investigation. Special Agent Mark Sande entered the lobby with a wry smile on his face.

I said, "I'm sorry to keep bothering you on a Saturday."

"Don't worry about it; it's my weekend to work. I'm more surprised to see you back so soon. I seem to remember something about being impressed."

I shook hands with the tall, lean Special Agent casting him a big smile. "Oh yeah, you will be. Why don't you go and get Captain Evans, if he's still here."

"He's not normally here on a Saturday, so he might be gone. He was finishing up a report; let me check if he's still here."

Agent Sande escorted me back to his office gesturing for me to have a seat. "Cross your fingers, Doc." He was gone for about 90 seconds. He returned alone bearing a sheepish grin. "You didn't cross your fingers, did you?"

"He's dismissing me without actually listening to what I have to say. Fine, I'll tell you what I have. You can deliver it to him and see if that don't bring him out of his office."

"You sound pretty confident."

"Confident is too weak a word."

Detailing the recorded conversation between Junior and Strasser's men only took a couple of minutes. When I finished, I reclined back in my chair, crossed my legs, and locked my hands behind my back in a gesture of pure confidence.

"Fuck me," said Special Agent Sande, "You said I would be impressed. I'm impressed. You haven't even been gone two hours."

"What can I say, sometimes us amateurs just get lucky."

"No shit."

"So, you ready to get Captain Morgan in here now?"

"You bet your ass, I am. Don't call him Captain Morgan, though. He hates that."

Special Agent Sande was gone nearly five minutes before returning. This time he was not alone. Captain Evans burst into the room in a frenzy. "What the hell do you think you are doing, Dr. McCain? I thought I told you to leave the investigating to Chief Parker."

"No, you advised me, not directed me. There is a difference, you know. I thought about it for, say a split second, then decided to investigate even harder."

"Well, let me tell you now that you are being directed to stop all investigating of organized crime in Emmettsville and the surrounding area. In all of Tennessee for that matter."

"Aha, so you admit that organized crime exists in Emmettsville."

Captain Evans squinted his eyes at me, a look of absolute anger emanating from his face. "Look here, mister."

Someone else calling me mister.

"I was with CIU for eleven years, and I'm telling you that you are a civilian and are not authorized to..."

"It's doctor, not mister, or you can call me L.T., and I was with NIS, a division of the ONI, part of the USN."

"What the hell are you talking about, Doctor ?" yelled Captain Evans.

"You are throwing out some alphabet soup; I can throw out some of my own. What is CIU?"

"Criminal Intelligence Unit. We handle organized crime and gang activity in the state. What was that shit you were throwing at me?"

"Before I was a doctor, I was a Lieutenant in the United States Navy assigned to the Naval Investigative Service, NIS, a division of the Office of Naval Intelligence. I became somewhat of a big deal in a short time for my ability to investigate undercover."

"Ok, so you are a veteran, big friggin' deal. You are a civilian now, and you need to stop your investigation."

"No."

"Are you dense?"

"No, just stubborn. And I am the only one doing anything in the murder of Paul Deland. So, I will stop when I am finished. I was hoping that someone like you was willing to help, but..."

"Shut up, Dr. McCain!" he interrupted. "Listen carefully. If you go anywhere near Darwin Strasser, I will have you arrested for interfering with a police investigation. Do I make myself clear?"

"I can hear you loud and clear."

"As for your dead friend, without a request from the DA in that county, I cannot, and will not help investigate. Am I still clear?"

"Crystal, Captain Morgan."

I shouldn't have called him that, but the temptation was too great. His face reddened.

"Have your fun, Dr. McCain. You had better tread lightly around me. You don't get to the position I'm in without knowing people that can make your life hell."

He was probably right about that one.

"Sir, I can assure you that you do not want to go down that path with me. You might want to dust off your investigative skills and look into who you are dealing with here. I'm sure you will find that I have some pretty amazing political connections of my own. Food for thought." The redness in his face was spreading into his neck and a small vein was bulging in his right temple. "Since you are not going to help me, Captain Morgan, I guess I am done here. I'll see myself out."

I got up, turned, and left the office. I could hear shuffling behind me. Someone was following me out of the room.

"Doctor, you didn't let me finish. I need you to bring me that tape you made."

I kept on walking, waving my hand flippantly towards him. "Then you better get yourself a subpoena or a warrant. And hope I haven't lost it by then."

I never looked back.

* * *

Although I had not known what to expect from the Tennessee Bureau of Investigation, Captain Evans' response was still a surprise. It was a surprise to LeClair as well, who was pacing around his office running his hands over his head in disbelief after listening to my account of both visits. Reluctantly, I had to admit that I might need Chief Parker's help after all. I did not want to do that. I was convinced he had nothing to do with Paul's death, but I still did not trust him completely. Or, more accurately, I did not trust his department. Too many coincidences had made me wary. Junior and his friends knowing Virgil's name and John's profession. Officer Crane's fortuitous arrival immediately after winning the fight with Eric and company.

LeClair and I were both impressed with Boyd's performance so far. His one mistake — selling the liquor too quickly — seemed to be more my fault than his. And it was his performance today that discovered that the Estes brothers had been hired by Strasser to collect the money from Paul. It seemed like all I had done so far was beat people up. Of course, they had it coming.

Neither of us had ever heard of Strasser, although LeClair stated he could ask around. It was outside his element, but he did know a guy who might know a guy if I knew what he meant. At first, I thought what difference did it make if we found Strasser or not. It was not like Strasser harmed Paul. He only wanted his money. From Junior and Jackson. The same men I was going to focus my entire investigation on. Which meant Boyd and I might be bumping into his men along the way. I changed my mind; it was best that we knew what we might be up against.

Strasser would have to wait until tomorrow. Earlier the hospital had called. It seemed they finally realized I had been the victim of a crime in Emmettsville and not the perpetrator. It was not a requirement, but they were wondering if I wanted to work tonight and I had agreed.

CHAPTER 30

911.

It was a little after nine at night, two hours into my first shift back in the ER since before Paul had gone missing. It was relatively slow, the quiet before the storm, which was not atypical for a Saturday night in Memphis before it got into full swing. Memphis Memorial Hospital was a Level 1 Trauma Center, the only one with that designation within 150 miles. Thus, the mundane world of stomach aches, whiplash patients, COPD complaints, and the like, would soon have to share time with those who fell victim to the nightlife in a city with such a historically high crime rate.

For my part, I just finished placing sutures in the arch of a nine-year-old girl's foot. She had dropped a plate on the floor while climbing on her counter top at home, then accidentally stepped on the broken plate when she jumped down off the counter. The girl had been a real trouper; a small grimace when I injected the lidocaine.

After that, she watched me place each suture. Her squeamish father had to look away.

It was during the lull in the action that I saw the 911 on my pager. Boyd needed me to call ASAP. I grabbed a phone in the nurses' station and called Boyd at his hotel room. He answered on the first ring.

"Dude, I hate to bother you at work, but we might have a problem."

"It figures that my first day back at work in a week and you have to pull out the bat signal. What's up?"

"I only saw Ellie's car briefly the other day." Boyd's impassioned tone did not correspond to his normal relaxed demeanor. "Red, sporty American car is all I remember. That is, except the license plate: 4CASTR. Cute, I thought, so it stuck in my head."

"What are you leading up to, Boyd?" My voice quavered, my palms began to sweat.

"Might be nothing, but in case no one has called you, I just saw a tow truck dumping off her car in front of the police station. It was super muddy and had weeds sticking out all over from under the car. It had definitely been in a ditch."

"How did the car look otherwise? Any extensive damage? Any way it looked like someone could have been hurt inside? Tell me, man. Now!"

"That's just it. It looked like it simply went off the road and got stuck in the mud. No obvious damage except to that plastic spoiler on the front of the car. It was completely ripped off."

"She was driving out to her folk's house. Her sister was visiting from Nashville. Sorry, Boyd, I'm rambling a little. So, it didn't look like it had hit anything?"

"Nope, but I was wondering why it was at the police station. The tow truck left it there. If she simply drove off into a ditch, wouldn't you expect the car to be towed to her father's house or a garage?"

"Stay by the phone, Boyd. I'm going to call her parent's house."

I hung up and dialed 411 for information. Within a couple of minutes, I was dialing the Carmichael house. My palms felt a little sweaty holding the phone. The phone rang four times and went to an answering machine. I did not leave a message. Instead, I hung up and dialed again. My hands were trembling slightly as I held the phone to my ear. The result was the same; I got the answering machine. The sound of the handset being slammed into the receiver echoed throughout the nurses' station. Heads turned in shock.

"So someone just told you about your car?" I turned just in time to see Dr. Pratt leaning in to talk to me. His palm was resting on my shoulder.

"What about my car?" I asked.

"You seem upset. I just figured security told you about your car."

"You lost me, Dr. Pratt. I have no idea what you are talking about."

"You own a red 500SL, don't you?"

"Yeah?" There was a questioning urgency to my voice that did not go unnoticed by Dr. Pratt.

"Sorry to be the one to tell you, Dr. McCain, but someone trashed your car. Security found it in the parking lot with four slashed tires, and it looks like someone threw a brick through the driver side window."

"Dr. Pratt, I know I am scheduled until seven, but I got to go. Now! It's important!"

Dr. Pratt said, "Hey, were slow right now. Call a tow truck and report the car to the police. We can spare you for a few minutes."

"Trust me. It's not the car. It's just a stupid car." I was no longer talking to just Dr. Pratt. I was talking to everyone within earshot. "I'm afraid Ellie might be in danger. Sorry, but I have to go."

* * *

The six-minute run to my apartment gave me plenty of time to think. My first thoughts were dark, unpleasant thoughts. Images of an injured Ellie ran through my mind. The images my mind conjured concerning what I would do to someone if she were injured were downright scary, providing a horrific insight into the lengths the human mind can go once the blinders of human decency have been removed. Retribution, if required, would be gruesome.

Maybe the six-minute sprint had a calming effect, by the time I reached my apartment, I started thinking like a civilized man again, not one hell bent on revenge for a crime that he was not even sure had been committed.

Once inside my apartment, I phoned the Carmichael house again. I got the same result. I did not leave a message.

Holy crap, I forgot to call Boyd back from the hospital.

He answered again on the first ring. "L.T., what the hell is going on?"

"Sorry, I called Ellie's parent's house and got the answering machine. More than once. Oh, and someone trashed the Mercedes. Four slashed tires and a brick through the window. I'm thinking that both cars being damaged on the same night is not a coincidence."

"Probably not, but why attack Ellie? If that's what you're thinking."

"I don't know. My inner voice just tells me they are related somehow. I can't explain. But I also can't explain why no one is answering the phone at her parent's house. That is, unless she were injured and they are over at the hospital. But if that was the case, someone would have called me."

"Good point. Can I help in anyway?"

"Yeah, get over to her parent's house and watch over it. Just in case. Maybe my imagination is getting the better of me, but I got a bad feeling about this one. The little voice in my head is in overdrive right now."

"You got it, L.T. What are you going to do?"

"I already left the hospital. I'm loading my guns, getting in the Cobra, and driving over as fast as I can. She better be okay, or..."

The gruesome images of retribution re-entered my mind as I hung up the phone.

CHAPTER 31

Boyd was worried. Worried what L.T. might do to someone if he discovered that same someone had harmed Ellie. He had seen firsthand the depths that L.T. was willing to go to when he was protecting someone, especially someone he cared about.

Boyd had been through hell and high water with L.T. and had never heard him sound the way he just did on the phone. If it had been panic he had heard in the former Lieutenant's voice, he would be less worried. Instead, he had reminded Boyd of the man he remembered from the Cambodian jungle, only he sounded even more resolute now. No, Boyd thought, L.T. sounded completely hell-bent, with an unhealthy dose of crazy. It was the crazy that scared Boyd.

The drive to Ellie's parent's house was short, only a few minutes. L.T.'s directions had been spot on. He even described a good location to scout the house from. Boyd parked his car in a field 200 yards short of the house, then walked another 40 yards in the dark to gain a vantage point of the old farmhouse.

Boyd breathed a sigh of relief. Ellie, along with the rest of her family, could easily be seen through the bay window in the living room with his powerful Vortex binoculars. The discussion appeared lively and animated with lots of large gestures, yet Ellie appeared unharmed. There was finger pointing from a man he assumed to be Ellie's father. Another man, tall and lean, short, light brown hair, late twenties or early thirties was pacing around the room. The conversation seemed centered around him.

The tall, lean man seemed to be answering questions from Ellie's father, who appeared agitated. Boyd found himself wishing he had some microphones on the window. L.T. was always saying that all information is useful and Boyd was wondering what was being discussed. Furthermore, Ellie was standing close enough to the tall, lean man that it implied a certain degree of familiarity. More than once the man placed his hand on Ellie's arm in a reassuring manner. Boyd turned to walk back to his car and grab a window microphone and then thought better of himself. Just because you can do something, doesn't mean you should. Their business was their business.

Boyd glanced at his watch. Probably every Marine in the history of the Marines, from infantry to helicopter mechanics, has stood watch at some time in his career, so waiting 45 minutes for L.T. to arrive was going to be child's play. It should be the easiest sentry duty he could remember. Boyd mentally worked his way through the 11 General Orders he learned verbatim during recruit training.

First General Order: To take charge of this post and all government property in view.

Check. He had a good view of the beautiful two-story brick farmhouse, the metal building to the left of the house, and the long driveway.

Second General Order: To walk my post in a military manner, keeping always on the alert and observing everything that takes place within sight or hearing.

Check. No one would slip through without being seen.

Many of the rest of the General Orders did not apply in this situation, but it pleased him when he realized he could still recite them verbatim. His DI would be pleased. Well, maybe not. Are DIs ever pleased?

Boyd was mentally discussing the hell that must be involved trying to mow such a large yard when he spotted headlights coming down the road. As expected, the vehicle slowed to successfully navigate a sharp corner located shortly before the Carmichael's driveway. However, this car slowed down even more after the corner, almost coming to a stop as it passed the driveway. Boyd could make out the silhouette of a full-size sedan, probably an older model. Definitely not L.T. He was beginning to walk towards the driveway for a better look, but the car suddenly accelerated away from the corner. He leaned against the closest tree and relaxed.

Maybe the car had slowed down to avoid an animal.

Intermittent traces of the red taillights were visible through the trees as the car continued on its path away from the house. The engine was barely discernible; a noise that would have been lost in the captivating cacophony of crickets, katydids, and cicadas if a person was not intentionally focused on it. The automobile was easily a quarter of a mile away when Boyd noticed an increase in the intensity of the taillights. The car was braking.

The taillights cut out a strange arc in the distance as the undeniable whine of a power steering pump reaching its end limits reached Boyd. It was hard to tell, but it appeared that the car was turning around in the middle of the road.

Was this why L.T. wanted him to watch the house? Boyd had agreed as a favor for L.T., never thinking that his presence would be needed. If the Lieutenant were right, if Boyd's presence were needed outside the Carmichael house, he would never doubt L.T.'s inner voice ever again.

The strange car's headlights became visible as the car completed its three-point turn in the middle of the country blacktop road. The car appeared to be returning as slowly as it left. One hundred yards from the driveway entrance the headlights vanished. Boyd strained to hear the motor; however, as if on cue, the katydid and cicada orchestra seemed to actually get louder, thus drowning out any chance of hearing the motor.

A dim light became visible near the spot he last saw the automobile. Most likely an interior dome light, which meant someone might be exiting the car. Some bushes were blocking his view of the car. Boyd repositioned himself for a better view. Although he was easily 150 yards from the vehicle, the full moon gave him a great view of two men standing near the vehicle clearly engaged in conversation. The conversation was completely unintelligible, yet one of them pointed to the Carmichael house more than once. There was a break in the conversation as one man moved to the back of the vehicle and opened the trunk. The other man was leaning against the front fender of the vehicle.

The trunk lid completely blocked Boyd's view; however, Boyd did not need a visual to know what the man was doing. The unmistakable sound of someone chambering a shell in a pump shotgun resonated above the nighttime din. Damn, he thought to himself, these rednecks really love their shotguns. "Let's do this." It was the man with the shotgun. After he had closed the trunk lid, the other man shushed the one holding the shotgun.

The Eleventh General Order immediately came to Boyd's mind: To be especially watchful at night and during the time for challenging, to challenge all persons on or near my post, and to allow no one to pass without proper authority.

The last part of the order stuck in his mind. These bastards did not have proper authority, and there was no way in hell he was going to let them pass. It looked like he might have to shoot someone after all.

Shit, L.T. had been right to send me.

Boyd quickly ran over to the Jeep. After yesterday, he had decided that his weapons, all of them, were going wherever he went. Boyd pulled his Remington Model 700 .300 Win Mag out of its hard case. It was his favorite gun. He loved long range shooting. In fact, he frequently competed in 600-yard competitions, winning most of them. Boyd had signed up early on in the Marines to be a Military Policeman. His second choice as an MOS would have been a Marine Corps Scout Sniper.

Boyd had not spared any expense on the rifle. A tried and true Leupold 3.5-10 Vari-X Police Standard Scope, one frequently used by SWAT snipers, sat atop the rifle. He used a quick adjust tactical sling, and the barrel was threaded to accept a suppressor, commonly called a silencer in the movies. Boyd was particularly happy with the suppressor attached to his rifle. It was built in Huntsville by a small startup company that aimed at providing the highest quality suppressors on the market. Boyd's suppressor, a prototype, did not even have a make or model number yet. Boyd completed the package by only shooting hand loaded ammo specifically matched to his rifle. He was particularly proud of the fact that he could consistently get half inch groupings at 200 yards.

Boyd watched as the two men finished their conversation. Both turned towards the house, one holding the shotgun, the other holding a handgun. Decision time. Boyd did not want to let them get any closer to the house, yet he did not want to shoot anyone until he was sure of the men's intent. An idea entered Boyd's head. It was going to require a difficult shot. One hundred fifty yards in the dark from a standing unsupported stance, not exactly providing the three elements of a good shooting position as taught in the Marines. He had no choice.

Boyd pulled the rifle up. The rifle rested on his left hand with the sling intricately wrapped up in the left arm to provide proper bone support. He placed the butt of the rifle into the pocket of his shoulder and welded his cheek against the stock. He located his target down the side of the barrel before finding it in the scope. Boyd preferred extending his natural respiratory pause over the decreased breathing technique. He exhaled.

He applied slow, steady pressure to the trigger. Trigger control is the most difficult marksmanship skill for most shooters. Boyd had no flaws in his technique. No jerking of the trigger. No flinching as he anticipated the recoil. Just a perfect follow through. When the pressure reached exactly two pounds on the highly modified trigger, the gun fired. At roughly 3000 feet per second, the 180-grain bullet left the gun and hit the target exactly as Boyd had planned.

The target responded exactly as he expected. It exploded. The explosion was heard easily at 200 yards. It brought a smile to Boyd's face. His shooting instructors would have been proud.

The man with the shotgun shouted something while whipping his entire body around towards the sound of the explosion. Boyd was too far away to make out facial features in the dark, but he could tell the man was nervous and twitchy. The man with the handgun chastised the other man for being too loud. He also turned around towards the sound. His handgun was out in front, ready to engage.

The two men were about 10 yards from the car when Boyd shot the front driver's side tire. Even though the driver's side tire had been a more difficult shot, he chose the tire since it was on the far side of the car thus preventing the bullet from ricocheting off the pavement up through the undercarriage of the vehicle. He wanted it to look like a freak coincidence. It had been a truly wonderful shot. Boyd was even more pleased with the reaction. Neither of the two men had heard the report of the rifle; the suppressor had done its job. All they heard was the tire exploding. It also stopped both men from advancing on the Carmichael house.

Although it was night time, the moon was full, and the sky was clear. Thus, Boyd was cautious as he moved closer. He probably could have run up to them without them noticing, though; they were so focused on looking for the origin of the noise. Boyd stopped when he got close enough to hear most of their conversation. Now if he could just avoid giggling.

The man with the handgun was circling the car. "Holy shit, I was fuckin' right. It's a blown tire."

"You got to be fucking kidding me. The fucking car was just sitting there."

"Do I look like I'm kiddin' you? You think I don't know what a flat tire looks like?" He was angry, even the katydids and cicadas seem to go quiet in his general vicinity.

"Brent, we can't risk shooting into the house now. We got no way to get away."

Brent, the man with the handgun, said, "I'm aware of our fuckin' predicament. The boss is gonna be pissed. We got to change this tire and fast. Maybe if we get it fixed in time, we can still go through with it. Get the jack and the spare and let's get this changed."

The man with the shotgun moved to the trunk and came back rolling the spare towards the front of the vehicle. He returned again carrying the jack. "Here, loosen up the lug nuts while I get this cheap ass scissor jack in place."

Brent accepted the tire wrench. "I know how to change a fuckin' tire."

"What crawled up your ass, man? I never said you didn't know how. It'll just go faster if you friggin' help me."

"Sorry, Daryl. It's just that the boss is gonna be pissed. And I really hadn't planned on a getaway involvin' a fuckin' tiny ass spare tire. You're not supposed to go over 50 on these damn things."

"So we'll buy a full sized tire when this is all over. Look, we're only supposed to scare 'em. Once we get this fixed, I will run up and fire a couple of shots into the house and run back. We'll be out of here before they know what hit 'em."

Brent said, "I don't like it, but it's better than failin'. Lug nuts are all loose. Here's the tire iron."

Boyd was smiling to himself. If they thought there was any chance they were going to shoot up the Carmichael house, they were going to be in for a big disappointment. Boyd decided that the rear passenger tire needed to blow up as well. *I'm not sure if this counts as shooting at someone, but damn, it's fun.*

Suppressors are not silencers. If the tire had not exploded, Brent and Daryl would have heard the crack of the .300 Win Mag. A good suppressor is fantastic at eliminating muzzle flash, though. If Boyd had to shoot another tire, he could do it without fear of being discovered even though he was easily 70 yards closer than before.

Changing the tire did not take long, and within a few minutes the spare was in place, and Daryl was carrying the flat back to the trunk. Brent was leaning up against the front fender, getting ready to light a cigarette while Daryl tidied up. Boyd waited until Daryl had his shotgun in hand before lining up and taking aim on the rear passenger tire. Two pounds on the trigger. One more flying projectile. Another exploding tire. A perfectly suppressed shot.

A barely suppressed bout of laughter.

At the sound of the tire exploding, Daryl dropped the flat tire he was carrying. "You've got to be fucking kidding me! What the hell is going on here?"

Brent whipped his body around towards Daryl. His gun was no longer in his waistband. "Get in the fuckin' car, Daryl." Brent was looking in all directions, peering into the dark for the unseen adversary that he now suspected.

"But we only got thr—"

"I know we only got three good tires. We also got someone out there in the dark fuckin' with us. I ain't heard a mother fuckin' shot, but someone is shootin' out our tires."

"How? We'd have heard the shots!"

"I don't know how, and I don't care. They ain't blowin' up on their own; that's for damn sure."

Daryl walked around the front of the vehicle on the passenger side holding his shotgun at the low ready. Brent reached in and turned on the headlights while Daryl walked to the edge of the woods, trying to see anything.

Boyd had a great view of the events as they unfolded. He knew shooting out the second tire would arouse suspicion, but he did not care. Let them be suspicious; the important thing was that they leave before L.T. get there. Boyd doubted L.T. would show them any leniency if he knew what these two were up to, and he did not feel like digging any graves tonight.

"Daryl! Just get in the damn car, man. We're gettin' the hell out of here."

"It's like a three-mile drive into town. We only got three good tires."

"You want to walk into town and leave our car right in front of the weather girl's house, dumb ass?"

"No."

"Then get in the damn car. We'll drive into town and find a hotel and fix it in the mornin'. Fuckin' sucks, but, hey, we ain't dead, and I want to keep it that way."

"Dead?"

"Yeah, dead. You think that's the Boogie Man out there? I don't. The bastard is dickin' with us."

Brent opened the driver side door and starting climbing in. He was half in, half out, when he paused to stare at Daryl, who was still standing at the edge of the road peering into the woods. Brent cleared his throat, getting Daryl's attention. He gestured for Daryl to get in the car. Daryl walked back to the car, pausing just before opening the passenger door. Both men were staring at each other across the roof of the American sedan. "Brent?"

"Yeah."

Boyd could barely make out their voices.

"How the hell did a doctor do this to us? He should still be in Memphis."

"I have no fuckin' idea, but the boss might want to rethink his fuckin' strategy 'cuz this guy walks around beatin' up people three at a time, and now he is fuckin' teleportin' through space and time. If he showed up wearing a damn Star Trek suit carrying a ray gun saying 'Beam me up, Scotty,' I wouldn't be fuckin' surprised. Now get in the damn car, fucktard!"

Daryl got in without an argument and the car drove off. Slowly. The unmistakable sound of the flat tire walloping and flapping on the blacktop could be heard for several minutes.

Boyd nearly laughed his butt clean off.

CHAPTER 32

To say that Dad's Cobra was fast was a major understatement. Powered by Ford's famous 427 'side oiler' FE engine, a 500-plus horsepower racing engine, Dad's 1966 Shelby 427 Cobra was basically a street legal race car. Top speed over 160 mph, 0-60 in under 4 seconds. Not to mention that Dad's Cobra was not exactly stock; he had purchased the car from a man in Minnesota that had converted it for competition racing.

Carroll Shelby, a legend in his own time, created the 427 Cobra Shelby for the sole purpose of humiliating anything in its path. His creation was enormously successful. The car was so powerful, so wickedly quick, that more than one buyer had returned his 427 Cobra to trade it for a Cobra with Ford's less powerful 289 motor. My father loved the car. He never mastered it, but he loved it. It was his one extravagance.

Personally, I had a love-hate relationship with the car. On the one hand, it was truly the most amazing car I had ever had the pleasure of driving. On the other hand, it reminded me of Dad. While I was growing up, Mom and I used to watch Dad drive the 427 Cobra during various Autocross events across the Midwest. When I became old enough, Dad even let me drive the car in a few Autocross rallies. He took it pretty well when his 15-year-old son beat his track times. Dad said it was because I was just like the car — the perfect combination of brawn, power, and speed. I teased him back, telling him that some men were born to go fast; some were born to watch men go fast. He was the latter.

Now, the truly spectacular vehicle was mine, and I was driving it at breakneck speeds towards Emmettsville, Tennessee. Shelby Cobra speedometers are unique, a circular gauge with a needle that travels counterclockwise as the speed increases. The top of the gauge corresponds to 90 mph. I kept the gauge to the left of 90 for the whole trip once I left Memphis city limits. Normally, a 45 to 50-minute drive, I pulled into the Carmichael driveway in 25 minutes.

Holy crap, if my math was right, I had averaged over 100 mph from doorstep to driveway.

I jumped from the vehicle and ran to the front door, pounding, rather than knocking on the front door. Although it was only a few seconds, it seemed like a small eternity before the front door opened. When it did, I was speechless as I stared at the man in the doorway with a dumb look on my face.

He was slightly less surprised and gestured for me to enter. "You better come in; we got a lot to talk about."

* * *

I stepped into the foyer eying the man who invited me in. He did not look overly worried. Hectic, earnest, but not worried. That was a good sign. Confusion abounded; I was speechless. I stammered out a weak hello as he closed the door behind me.

"Dr. McCain, didn't expect to see you here so soon."

"I didn't expect to see you here at all, Special Agent Sande."

"No, I guess you probably didn't?"

"What the..." I stammered. "What are you..." More stammering. "Is she alright?"

Agent Sande put a reassuring hand on my shoulder. "God yes. She's fine. Come into the living room; everyone is in there."

During the run to my house, I had assumed the worst. During the drive, no the race, over, I had continued to assume the worst. I'm not a pessimistic person normally, more of a realist actually, but for some reason, I could not shake the idea that something bad had happened to Ellie. I leaned over putting my hands on my knees catching my breath.

Agent Sande put his hand on my shoulder again. "Shit, man. What did you think happened?"

"I didn't know. I just knew that her car had been towed to the police station and no one was returning my calls."

"Dr. McCain..."

"L.T."

"L.T., I do believe you are somewhat smitten with Ellie. You look like shit."

"Who's at the door, Mark?" It was Lloyd calling from further inside the house.

"Be right there," Mark replied. "You okay, man?"

"Yeah, just sick to my stomach from the last 30 minutes of constant adrenaline."

"You drove here in 30 minutes? Surely, you jest." I shook my head no. His jaw dropped in amazement.

"What's this about 30 minutes?" I whipped my head towards the voice. Ellie had just entered the foyer. She looked beautiful. Confused, a little worried, but beautiful, and completely uninjured.

"Ellie, I would have been here sooner, but I had to run home from the hospital, get in the car and drive over. I violated a few traffic ordinances. Maybe all of them."

Ellie ran to me and wrapped her arms tightly around me. We held each other in an affirming embrace for nearly a minute. Her head rested against the side of my face. I craned my head to try and cradle her head with mine.

"Okay, you lovebirds. Let's get into the living room. We need to get L.T. up to speed."

Ellie's parents, Lloyd and Virginia, were seated on a love seat in the living room. Ellie's younger sister, Jessica, was standing near the bay window. Despite the muted reception, Lloyd and Virginia seemed happy to see me. Jessica, on the other hand, lit up like a Christmas tree, a warm, welcoming smile on her face, then crossed the room to give me a big hug. "Hey, big guy, didn't know you were coming?"

I had a great relationship with Jessica. Physically, she looked like a blonde mirror image of Ellie, same height, same build, same smile, same graceful movements. The differences in their personalities made it difficult to believe they had been raised by the same parents. Everything about Ellie made her perfect for television and the public eye. She was friendly and approachable, yet formal and dignified. Always cautious with her word choices and actions. Jessica, on the other hand, was loud, fun, care-free, never cautious, and smart as hell. She nearly aced her ACT in high school, already had a bachelor's degree in secondary education and was months away from finishing another degree in environmental engineering from Vanderbilt University in Nashville. All by age 24.

"Heard from a little birdie that my girlfriend's car was sitting down at the police station with dirt and grass sticking out from under it."

"Ah, that's sweet. So you rushed right over, still in your scrubs, no doubt, which by the way, damn, you look good in scrubs, to see how my sis is doing?" Jessica turned to address the rest of the room, "But I thought no one had called L.T. yet?"

Ellie said, "No one had called him that I know of. L.T., you said it took you 30 minutes to get here, but how did you know you needed to be here?"

I explained that I found out about her car, leaving out any reference of Boyd, while working in the ER. Told them I called three or four times, panicked, and then drove over as fast as I could. Special Agent Sande was particularly interested in how I found out about the car to begin with.

"I have spies in the town who tell me stuff," I said.

"No really, how?" repeated Mark.

"No really, I have spies in the town who tell me stuff."

Tell him the truth while still telling him nothing; it seemed like the best way to go.

"Okay, so you got spies, as you call it. But why the panic?"

I told them about my Mercedes and the brick through John Deland's office window. It seemed like someone was sending me a message. Then, when I heard about Ellie's car showing up at the police station and no one was answering their phone, I needed to know what was happening immediately. What if the two events were related?

Ellie said, "I'm sorry we didn't answer. We ignored the phone when it rang; Mark was explaining quite a bit of stuff to us." Ellie was studying me with a look of concern mingled with confusion. "If I had known that you had people *watching* me, I would have called you. You do believe me, don't you?"

"Of course. FYI, I didn't have anyone watching you, just a few people keeping an eye on things around Emmettsville for me. Mark, you mentioned something about catching me up. So what happened tonight? Why is my girlfriend's car sitting at the police station? Why are you here?"

Mark stared long and hard at me. "You really got spies in this town?"

"Yes."

"Care to tell me who."

"Sorry, Mark. I was in the intelligence business in the Navy. You don't give up your sources."

"Can I at least ask if it is someone in law enforcement?"

"It's not."

"Would you lie to me?"

"To protect the identity of a source? Of course." Mark smiled and nodded as if to say he had to try. I smiled back to let him I had no hard feelings for trying. "Look, guys and girls, I would like to know how my girlfriend's car ended up at the police station looking like it's been run off the road. Who's going to tell me?" I was quickly reaching the limit of my patience.

Jessica said, "Somebody tell the poor guy what happened." She scanned the room to see who was going to start talking. "Okay, I'll tell him."

Ellie said, "No, Jessie, let Mark tell him. Mark, tell him what you told me."

"Yeah, Mark," I said, "Tell me what you told her."

"You the kind of guy who needs to sit down to hear bad news?"

"No, but I think I'll sit anyway." I picked out a spot on the couch next to Ellie. She placed her hand in mine; each of us gave the other a loving squeeze. Jessica smiled at me holding her sister's hand, then reached over and tousled my hair. It was something she did the first time I met her nearly a year ago, and it was something she had done every time I saw her since. I had come to expect it.

Mark remained standing. "I don't know how to say this other than just to come right out and tell you that shit has hit the fan big time, my friend. I'm talking out of the frying pan, into the fire kind of stuff."

"Do tell, please."

"I could get in trouble for telling you this."

"You already told them from the looks of things," I said. "So you already broke the rules."

Mark shrugged his shoulders before letting out a resigned sigh. He started off by giving me a little history about Darwin Strasser, a crime boss in the Dixie Mafia out of Mississippi. Strasser was known to have a little over a dozen men directly under him, and he had the money and influence to hire others to do his bidding for him. This was something I had already guessed, although I had not expected him to have that many men on his unofficial payroll. Mark went on to tell me that Strasser thought I had a tape potentially implicating him in the murder of Paul Deland. Mark finished, "He's not happy, and he wants that tape."

"But I never implied anything of the sort. I only said he hired the Estes brothers to collect money from Paul, nothing more. What the..." My eyes bugged as a realization hit me.

Mark picked up on the change in my countenance. "What?" he asked.

"You got a problem, Mark. Your office has a mole. And a stupid one at that."

"What? My office...wait, the problem has to be on your end. One of your spies talked."

"Impossible."

"Nothing's impossible."

"Yeah, no offense, but bite me, Agent Sande. I can guarantee the problem is not on my end. Only three people knew about the tape before you, and I mentioned it to Captain Evans. I know I am not the leak. I know the person holding the microphone for me was not the leak. And I know you are not the leak."

Agent Sande said, "Thanks for the vote of confidence."

"You're welcome."

"So where's the leak?" asked Agent Sande.

"Could be Captain Evans, of course, but I find it unlikely. He's a dickhead, but I don't think he's dirty for no other reason than he would still be in CIU if he were. It would be easier for him to know what's going on in organized crime that way. Besides, finding the mole is your job. I've limited my search to finding murderers only. How many did you talk to about our conversation?"

"One."

"The same one that tipped you off about the threat on Ellie."

"How do you know I was tipped off?" Maybe I found out another way."

"Not likely."

"Why not, if you don't mind me asking?"

"I don't mind at all. I'm not sure what department you work in, Mark, but I know it's not CIU, which means that in a need-to-know work environment, you don't have a need to know what goes on in there. So, you wouldn't have overheard something on your own. However, you called a friend in CIU and told him about an interesting conversation you had with your ex-girlfriend's current boyfriend."

Ellie's head jerked towards me with wide, surprised eyes. "Yeah, Ellie, that took me all of maybe five minutes." Mark and I both feigned irritation.

Jessica said, "Ellie, you can drop the I got caught with my hand in the cookie jar look; they are jerking your chain."

Smiling, I resumed, "Luckily, this same friend, having been made aware of Ellie and me, overhears something that makes him suspicious, so he returns the favor. And here you are. Voila." I made a small flourish with my hands for added effect.

Mark broke out in a huge smile. He was impressed.

Ellie asked, "Is he right."

Mark said, "Yes."

She turned to me, looking bewildered. "Are you spying on Mark, too?"

Mark answered for me. "No, he's not spying on me. Your boyfriend just has a gift. I'll bet you are one hell of a doctor. I ever get an ailment no one can figure out, I'm coming to see you."

"Thanks for your vote of confidence, Mark."

"You're welcome."

Mark went on to describe how the Tennessee Bureau of Investigation had been watching Darwin Strasser for over a year. The

Bureau was having little success with informants or other leads in an attempt to build a case against him.

"Let me guess," I said, "Nothing ever sticks on Strasser, your attempts at infiltrating the Dixie Mafia have all failed, and you have been forced to rely on COMINT."

Ellie said, "COMINT?"

"Communications Intelligence. Probably in the form of wiretaps. Once again, this has been mostly ineffective, especially since a lot of his business is across state lines, but, hey, it's the best you got right now."

Agent Sande was still staring at me, a telling smirk on his face. "My friend, who will remain nameless at this time, intercepted an incoming call to one of Strasser's underlings that lives on this side of the Tennessee border. Something about a reference concerning scaring the weather girl. The message never mentioned Ellie by name, but what other weather girl has a boyfriend kicking the hornet's nest. He wouldn't have even known about Ellie's involvement if I had not called him a few hours earlier asking if he knew anything about the Estes boys."

"No mention of the tape?" I asked.

"No, I worded it as you overheard a conversation. To be honest, I wasn't sure the tape actually existed. I mentioned you, but not by name, Doc, and that you were an acquaintance of Ellie's."

Jessica was the first to point out what I was already thinking. "So, some idiot in the Dixie damn Mafia decides to scare my sister by running her off the road, and the only reason Mark was there to help was because we were lucky enough that you called him a few hours earlier. Damn."

Mark said, "Yep, that's about right."

Jessica asked, "You told us that you followed Ellie from her apartment to here. Why didn't you just tell her what you knew?"

"I don't know. I guess, in hindsight, I should have. It seemed unnecessary to make her worry if it wasn't a viable threat."

Ellie interjected, "Don't blame Mark. He was there for me. That's all that matters."

I said, "Which gets me back to my original question. Why the h-e-double hockey sticks is my girlfriend's car down at the police station?"

Mark said, "It's kind of like this. My friend mentioned that the plan was to scare her tonight. I left work a little early and decided to keep an eye on Ellie. I tailed her. Shortly outside of Emmettsville, a four-door sedan, I believe a Mercury, probably a Marquis, passed me and got between us. Nothing seemed suspicious. It looked like they were getting ready to pass Ellie when the car rammed hers from behind instead and sent her off the road. Luckily there was no ditch along that stretch of road."

Ellie interjected, "Yeah, thank God no ditch there. I still got a major crick in my neck. Probably got whiplash."

Mark said, "The car that hit her stopped. At first, it just seemed like an accident. But when the guys in the car, there were two of them, just sat in the car while their headlights aimed on her, I knew they were the guys sent to scare her. I pulled up behind them, got out of my car and yelled for them to get out. Obviously, they didn't get out. I did manage to get the first four numbers on the license plate before they sped off."

Ellie said, "I had no idea what was going on, then next thing I knew Mark was opening my car door. He made sure I was alright, got in touch with the Emmettsville police department, helped with the report to the officer, and gave me a ride here."

"Thank you, Mark. If I was a jealous man, I guess I would be more worried that an ex-boyfriend plays knight in shining armor to my girl. I'm opting more for grateful."

Mark continued, "I got Ellie home. Told her what I knew. She told me to tell her family, so we did. We were discussing whether we should call you at the hospital and leave you a message when you showed up here."

* * *

Mark and Ellie filled me in on a few more minor details about the crash. Ellie and I exchanged a few more hugs. Jessica gave Ellie and me a simultaneous hug and tousled my hair again. And Ellie's family asked Mark and me some questions. The cat was out of the bag, so both of us answered as honestly as we could. The general mood in the room was one of gratitude and thankfulness. Both Lloyd and Jessica made a point of telling me they knew it was not my fault. I really cared for both of them and appreciated the sentiment, but they were dead wrong.

It was my fault.

A lot of trouble was made to set Boyd up undercover in the town, yet I continued to be out in front of the investigation drawing undue attention to myself. Boyd was supposed to take over the investigation while I supplied support. However, I had screwed that up as well. I did not give Boyd enough direction. He should have only sold a little of the alcohol. Just enough to draw their attention, not their wrath. I got Boyd kidnapped, then had to rescue him. Not exactly hiding in the shadows. If I had, then the Estes brothers would have thought I had let things drop. There would not have been any reason for anyone to go after Ellie.

It was all my damn fault.

Lloyd's voice interrupted my personal pity party. He was asking Mark if Ellie could count on police protection. I could see the color drain out of Mark's face at the question. He opened his mouth to speak, even stammered a few words, but never started an actual sentence. I offered to answer the question for him. Mark just nodded, embarrassed by Lloyd's question.

I explained that Mark was not in their house in an official police capacity; he was a friend of the family that just happens to be a cop. He broke the chain of command when he called his friend, and his friend definitely broke the rules when he called Mark back. It could mean trouble for both of them. Mark added that even if they came clean, it still would not guarantee that the Bureau would help. The whole thing made no sense to Lloyd, but he accepted it.

Mark added, "I might be able to get the Bureau involved after I talk to my friend. He will have to be the one that initiates things. I can't do it without it blowing up in our face. It's going to look fishy enough that my name is on the accident report filed by the Emmettsville PD."

My pager went off. It was from Boyd. He had typed "911-411." I guessed that was his way of saying emergency and information simultaneously.

Mark waited for me to finish checking my pager. "Do you need to respond to that?"

"Yeah, but it can wait a minute more."

Mark said, "Look, I can talk to him tomorrow, but it will need to be face to face. We should be able to come up with a good idea. In the meantime, L.T., can you get Chief Parker to send anyone over and watch the house?"

"You know what, I just might. Right now I need to use the phone. In the other room, preferably. Duty calls."

Ellie motioned towards the kitchen. I excused myself and hurried to the kitchen anxious to hear what now constituted an emergency. Boyd answered on the first right and wasted no time getting to the point. He had tried to flag me down before I entered the house, but I was moving too fast. He apologized for not waiting until later to call, but he could not wait any longer. He yelled, "We got a big damn problem!"

I tried to tell him I would call him later. He insisted and quickly explained that he had run off two gunmen outside the Carmichael house before I got there. I wanted to stay, but I knew I couldn't. Boyd needed me.

"Give me a few minutes to finish things here. I'm coming by the hotel. No, better yet meet me in the clearing in ten."

"Sure thing, Lieutenant."

"And, Sergeant, thank you."

I walked back into the living room. It was getting late, but everyone was still too keyed up to sleep. I was probably not going to get any sleep tonight at all, but then I was scheduled at the ER until seven the next morning, so nothing much had changed there. Now, I just needed a good excuse to get out of there. Ellie quickly observed the change in my demeanor when I returned. She wanted to know if everything was alright. Lying to her was getting too easy. I told her the hospital was still expecting me to come back. I gestured to the scrubs I was still wearing. Ellie said, "It's only a little after ten. If you go back now, you could be there by eleven. You could finish your shift. Everything is okay here."

Good, Ellie was giving me permission to leave. Now, I just needed to talk to Mark. I addressed the whole room, apologized again, and then asked if I could borrow Mark in private. Only Ellie voiced any objection. I asked her to trust me. She reluctantly agreed. A curt "fine." It was hard to make eye contact with her; the lies were adding up.

Mark followed me to the foyer, but I did not stop there. I made him follow me all the way outside. What I had to say was for his ears only.

"Damn, Doc, how bad is it that we need to take it outside."

"Bad. Mark, you got to get busy on the police protection thing. Pronto. I have it on good authority that two men with guns were outside this house tonight. I don't know their intention, just that they were here."

"Your spies?" I nodded. "I take it that was not the hospital that called?" I shook my head in a dramatic no. "Shit, this is getting out of hand. Strasser's men?"

"Don't know yet, most likely, though, don't you think? Finishing the job of scaring the weather girl. Either way, I aim to find out. Can you do me a favor, Mark?"

"Name it."

"Stay with them. Make sure everyone stays safe."

"You don't even need to ask. I was planning on it anyway."

"Thanks. You armed?"

"I'm good." He was pacing around with hands on his head, rubbing them through his hair in nervous thought. He turned to me nervously. "What are you going to do?"

"They shouldn't have called her a weather girl; she's a meteorologist. You know that hornet's nest you mentioned, well, I'm done kicking it. It's time to pull out the bug spray."

CHAPTER 33

Mark never even asked what I meant by my comment. He offered no warnings against vigilante justice. He didn't even tell me to be careful. All I got was a knowing nod of the head and a smile before he turned and started back towards the house. I did not follow him back inside. Instead, I ran to the Cobra. I was pulling the keys from my pocket when Mark said, "By the way, nice damn car." I wondered why things didn't work out between Ellie and Mark because I had only known him for one day and I already liked him.

Boyd was reclining in the front seat of my Jeep staring up at the stars as I pulled into the clearing. He didn't get up. He simply lifted his head and looked my direction before saying, "Nice damn car."

"Yeah, thanks. The Mercedes was indisposed, and I couldn't find the key to the Mustang. I made do."

"Yeah, slumming in a quarter million dollar car. Pardon me if I don't feel your pain, butthead."

"You know that car you've been driving is identical to the one Steve McQueen drove in the movie *Bullitt*, right?"

"Never saw it. So, you saying you want to trade?"

I replied, "Not on your life. Shut up about the car, Sergeant. Tell me what happened."

Boyd wasted no time telling me what he saw. I laughed out loud when he described how he shot out both tires. I laughed even harder when Boyd described how the two men thought I was the one that shot them out.

"Boyd, I knew this doctor while in med school that had built an enormous private practice before retiring and becoming a teacher. Someone once asked him about the secret of his success. He said it was simple: he always tried to exceed his patient's expectations. Boyd, you have exceeded my expectations. Thank you!"

"Geez, you are going to make me blush," he said in mock amazement. "So, do I get a raise?"

"Yeah, double what I'm paying you."

"Bite me. I'm worth at least ten times what you're paying me." He was kidding; we both knew ten times zero was still zero. Boyd finally stopped reclining and turned to face me. "Alright, Lieutenant, what's the plan? Because things are getting heated, and I still haven't shot at anyone. Tires don't count."

"Hey, you had your opportunity twice now, and you passed, chicken dick. Wait a minute, would you recognize the car those idiots were driving if you saw it again?"

"Yeah, it is sitting a little low on the right and it sounds like the tire is out of balance, or maybe it just has a flat spot in it. Why?"

I chuckled at the visual. "You think they might be stupid enough to get a hotel in Emmettsville tonight?"

Boyd cast me a playful, knowing glance. He liked where I was going, but I could tell he was a little worried what I might do to them once I found them. He asked me twice what I was planning to do with them if we found them.

"Same thing they did to Ellie."

"Run them off the road?"

"No, I plan on scaring the living hell out of them. And since they are criminals, I'm assuming it is going to be a little harder to scare them. We will have to be creative."

"How creative?"

"Boyd, are you worried I might hurt them?"

"Maybe."

"Maybe? I'll be, you're going soft on me. I would think after yesterday you would realize what we're dealing with here. You're investigating organized crime."

"I'm not going soft. Just wondering how far you want to take this?"

"You okay with some broken bones as long as they are still breathing?"

Boyd said, "And you are accusing *me* of going soft." Although he was smiling, Boyd did a poor job of hiding his relief that I was not going to take matters further with Daryl and Brent.

* * *

Boyd informed me there were only a handful of motels in the town, along with The Travelers' Inn and one nationally recognized full-service hotel near the edge of town. Boyd had been smart to avoid it when he decided to become Graham, my undercover bootlegger. There would be too much red tape and too many people. We assumed Strasser's lackeys would feel the same.

Boyd directed me to the closest two motels first. No evidence of a three-wheeled four door sedan. The Travelers' Inn was next on the list. Boyd wanted to know if he was still supposed to be undercover. He was riding shotgun in a classic roadster that would stick out like a sore thumb in Miami, let alone Podunk, Tennessee. I realized we probably should have taken the Jeep. I threw him my ball cap. Told him to pull it down and hide his features. Boyd's services as Graham were no longer necessary; regardless, I wanted him to remain unidentified.

He wanted to know what my next step was now that the undercover portion was over. I told him his tape changed everything. When he overheard Junior with Strasser's men, I knew we were on the right path. Deep down, my gut told me that one of the Estes brothers either killed Paul or had him killed. However, it made no sense for them to kill Paul. They were being paid to collect money, not kill him. Killing Paul meant no money for Strasser, which in turn, would create problems with the more powerful crime boss. Even so, my inner voice still insisted that one, or both, of the brothers were murderers.

Boyd agreed with my logic. He said, "So the Estes boys hired someone to run you out of town for good by scaring Ellie, someone she would not recognize, while they probably drove into Memphis and trashed your car."

"Boyd, I told you I had bad news. Those men you chased off, they weren't friends of the Estes boys. Those men belonged to Strasser. He ordered them to scare Ellie to get to me."

"That's was a dickhead thing to do."

"Stupid too. I didn't give two cents about Strasser before tonight. He hired Junior and company to collect some money. Big deal; he didn't kill Paul. It was just business. But there is no way I'm going to forgive them for what they did today."

Boyd said, "Since he didn't kill Paul, why the hell would Strasser go after Ellie? Makes no sense."

"You told me about your day, sweetheart, now let me tell you about mine. It all starts with my remarkable visit to the Tennessee Bureau of Investigation, and an asshole called Captain Morgan." I spent the next five minutes detailing my visits at the Bureau and another five minutes after that describing my time inside the Carmichael house. Boyd mumbled a few expletives but otherwise seemed unfazed.

"He orders his men to go after Ellie because of a misunderstanding. Wow, that's priceless."

"It looks that way. And now they went and pissed me off. Question for you. Were the men outside Ellie's the same that visited Junior earlier?"

"No, two different groups. I didn't get a good look at either group of guys, but I heard their voices, and they were not the same guys. Plus, they had different cars. I think the guys tonight were driving a beat up Mercury. The guys this morning were definitely in a nice looking Lincoln."

That meant Strasser sent one group of guys up here to deal with the Estes brothers and then sent another up here to scare Ellie. Which meant he had a crew. Agent Sande had told me he had over a dozen men. At least four of them were in Felton County. How many more would he send? What would I do if he sent more?

Boyd said, "Well, Lieutenant, you got a plan?"

"No, I'm making this up as I go. I do have a plan name, though, Operation Stromboli."

"Stromboli? What the hell is a Stromboli?"

"Not what, but who."

"Who then?"

"Pinocchio's puppet master. The angry one that locked Pinocchio in a cage."

"I saw that cartoon as a kid. Stromboli was a bad guy."

I smiled, a devilish smile, one so big Boyd had no trouble seeing it in the dark. "Exactly," I said.

We finished checking the third motel parking lot. Still no luck finding the crippled car. The fourth motel on Boyd's list was near Falco's. My eye spotted a car with a strange lean in Falco's parking lot. It was a Mercury. I tapped Boyd on the shoulder and pointed.

"Fitting," I said, "Seems like I can never get away from this cockamamie restaurant."

"Cockamamie. Really? You must be the only person under 90 that says cockamamie."

"Bite me. My mother raised me not to curse. Get moving, toe jam."

I doubted if either of us could set foot in Falco's without causing a ruckus, but we had to know if Brent and Daryl were in there. Either way, I did not know what they looked like, so it was up to Boyd. After five minutes inside, Boyd returned, climbing in the Cobra with a satisfied smile. The men who most likely ran my girlfriend off the road, the same ones that planned on shooting up her family's house, were eating a burger in the same restaurant where the trouble began. I slid my right hand down my side. Felt the reassuring weight of the gun holstered on my hip. Out of the corner of my eye, I could see Boyd staring at my hand.

"You know," I said, "I got an idea." I started up the car and headed out of the parking lot. "Don't worry, Boyd, I'm not going to shoot anybody…just yet. I'm taking you back to your car. You are going to come back and watch Butch and Sundance like a hawk. Wherever they go, you go. Let me know where they bed down for the night."

"Okay, so I'm no longer on sentry duty, now I'm a spy. Where are you going to be?"

"Memphis. I need a vehicle with some storage space, and I want out of these scrubs. I might not be back until after two or three. This is going to be a long night."

* * *

The drive back to Memphis was considerably slower than the drive from Memphis earlier. A classic high-performance roadster, a full moon, no clouds, a winding blacktop with little traffic. If Ellie had been sitting next to me, if I was able to catch the even the faintest smell of her perfume or the hint of her smile, then it could have been a great date night.

Instead, she was bunkered in her parent's house with her ex-boyfriend standing guard duty. Boyd asked me earlier if it bothered me. I had said no, but I was lying to myself. The roles should have been reversed. He was the criminal investigator. He should be out here catching the bad guys while I stood guard duty.

I was so mad I could spit. What was that quote by Mark Twain? I remembered it, "When angry, count to four; when very angry, swear."

Out loud, I counted, "One. Two. Three. Four." Not working.

"Fuck it all to hell." I followed that up with a few more profane sentences. The curse words literally exploded from my mouth. The string of profanity is probably still circling in the ether above Southern Tennessee to this day. Now that felt good. Sure, no one was there to hear it, but it had felt good just the same. Mark Twain was a genius.

Looming over me was the realization that I was now being forced to fight a war on multiple fronts. Strasser had come after me. He shouldn't have, but he did. Junior was probably the one that trashed my car; it seemed like his style. He also promised he was still trying to collect money from Paul's father, something that might include another brick through another window, but would more likely involve threats of violence. There was no way a two-man operation could defend the Carmichael family and the Deland family while still launching an investigation. More people would be needed.

Too bad I could not count on help from the Tennessee Bureau of Investigation; that relationship seemed totally FUBAR. I could ask Chief Parker for help watching Ellie, although I doubted his level of competence. No, I doubted his resolve more than his competence. I needed someone I could trust unwaveringly. Shit, I had no choice but to clone Boyd.

Or call Virgil. He was the only other person I could trust. This would be completely outside his comfort zone, but he would do it without question. No doubt. If Operation Stromboli worked as planned, his presence would only be required for a couple of days.

Operation Stromboli. Just thinking about it made me smile.

My father told me that as an offensive lineman, he loved running plays where he got to be a lead blocker. It was one of the few times offensive lineman felt like they were truly part of the offense, helping the team move the ball, instead of just defending the quarterback. They got to hit someone for a change, to bowl someone over, and it felt good. I played tight end in high school, a truly hybrid position that sometimes requires the blocking skills of an offensive lineman, at other times requiring that the player line up as a wide receiver. I was good, making All-State my freshman, sophomore, and junior years before quitting football when my father died. One of the things I loved most about playing tight end was sometimes the best way to take pressure off your quarterback was to give him good targets quickly down field. In other words, sometimes the best way to defend your quarterback was to be even more aggressive on offense.

That is how I thought of Operation Stromboli. To hell with focusing solely on defense, it was time to launch my own version of a counteroffensive on the damn Dixie Mafia. It was time to make them play defense. It was time to call Virgil in to guard Ellie. It was time to arm John if he was not armed already. It was time to get a car with a bigger trunk. And it was time to borrow a truck.

LeClair called me a devious SOB. We were sitting in his office off the kitchen. It was small. A desk, couple of filing cabinets, a small fireproof safe, some old chairs, and a couch that looked like it had been slept on a few hundred times. When I asked him if he had a truck I could borrow, he had invited me back to hear the whole story. That is when he called a devious SOB.

He agreed to loan me a vehicle on one condition: he got to help. I thought about arguing with him and then realized that after yesterday he was already involved. And another set of hands would come in handy for my plan. Earlier, I had dropped off the Cobra and changed clothes before calling John and warning him to take special care over the next few days. I also let him know that I might not be able to attend the funeral tomorrow. I was trying Virgil again; he did not answer earlier.

This time he answered with his trademark exuberance, "Hey, L.T., what's up?"

"How did you know it was me?"

"Only two people would call at this hour, and the other one is sitting next to me sipping a nice Cabernet."

"I don't have time to explain much, but I need your help."

"What can I do?"

"Drive to Emmettsville and watch over Ellie and her parents."

"This is related to you investigating Paul's death, isn't it?"

"Yeah. I would only need you for the weekend, maybe only tomorrow. Boyd can't do it. I'll have him busy with part of my plan. LeClair and I are doing another part. I'm short one person. Ellie's ex-boyfriend, who happens to belong to the Tennessee Bureau of Investigation, is there now, but he will have to leave tomorrow at some time."

"I'll do it. What do I need to bring?"

"A bag big enough to hide an SMG."

Virgil asked, "Boyd's H&K?"

"Yeah."

"Okay, I can sneak that in, no problem."

"I'm sorry to ask, Virgil. I know this is not your kind of thing, but I need someone I can trust. Unfortunately, for you, you were on the top of the list. I'll call you later to tell you where and when to meet Boyd, but be ready to be in Emmettsville by ten, okay?"

"Don't apologize. You're like family to me."

LeClair entered the office twirling a set of keys on his finger as I was finishing my conversation with Virgil. I followed LeClair out the back kitchen door into the alley, smiling as I realized it was only the second time I had ever seen my friend outside of the bar. I was following him through the alley to the nearby parking garage. He looked different already. More dangerous somehow. Maybe it was anticipation, or excitement, or a case of the nerves, but his very gait was different. He was treading lightly, moving fluidly, moving like a man on the prowl, moving like a former Marine in the face of possible danger. Asking to borrow his truck had been a great idea, especially since LeClair insisted on coming along with the truck.

LeClair led me to a late model silver Cadillac Eldorado, a large two-door coupe. The trunk looked large. Perfect. LeClair's house was on the way, not too far off Poplar a little north of the Botanical Gardens. I had not known what to expect, let's face it, he was always in the bar. The house was nice. It looked like a home where a married couple with 2.3 kids would live. He pushed his garage door opener revealing a small orange and white panel van. It was an old U-Haul van. If you looked close, you could still see the letters on the side.

I gave LeClair one last time to change his mind. He gave me a dirty look. "Keys are in it; let's go mess with some rednecks."

LeClair stayed in the Cadillac. We needed two vehicles, one with a trunk and one that could hold lots of boxes. I got the van. Operation Stromboli was officially underway.

A little over an hour later I was back in Falco's parking lot. The Mercury with the flat tire was still there. So was my Jeep. I pulled alongside Boyd, who smiled when he saw the van, got out of his car and walked around to get in next to me.

"Where in the hell did you get this piece of shit?"

"LeClair." The passenger door of the van suddenly opened. "Move over and let him in, will ya?"

Boyd was a little surprised to see LeClair and was even more surprised when I told him that he was going to have to loan Virgil his H&K in the morning. But that surprise paled in comparison when I explained my plan. His mouth was hanging open in shock.

"What," I said, "No comment? LeClair called me a devious SOB when he heard the plan."

Boyd nodded in agreement. "No shit." His nodding turned into a large grin as he replayed the plan over in his head. "Alright, I did what you asked; I found out where they are staying. The motel across the street. First floor. Even got the room number."

I thanked Boyd and told LeClair to drive his Caddy across the street. I had him back the Caddy up to the hotel as close to the room as he could and told him to stay in the car.

"Keep it running, in case this does not go as planned." He nodded. I motioned to Boyd to see if he was ready. He put his hand inside his jacket where his Sig would be resting in the shoulder holster. I walked up to the door, checked my pockets for the stuff I brought along. Crap, I thought. I almost forgot something. I jogged across the street to the U-Haul, returning with a large role of duct tape. "Now, we're ready."

I had decided against kicking the door in. Sure, shock and awe is a great technique, but stealth has its charm as well. Now, if I could just pick the lock without making too much noise. I pulled out my pick and tension wrench. Placed it in the bottom of the keyhole and determined the correct direction to move the lock. That was the easy part. The rest required patience and a feel. A little more practice would have been nice as well. With the pick, I felt around clumsily for the pins I needed to depress. With each metallic click, I kept wondering if I had woken up the two assholes in the room. It took me over a minute, I was sweating when I finished, but eventually I successfully picked the lock.

I slowly started to open the door. The hinges squeaked a little, but it opened freely; Brent and Daryl had not used the door chain. I slipped the Glock 21 from my holster and walked through the door. Boyd followed, his Sig P226 in his right hand, ready at a moment's notice.

The door opened into an old motel room. There was actual paneling on the walls, probably left over from the Seventies. Just like the lock. I could not help but think we had been lucky the motel had not had the newer electronic card reader locks present in most newer hotels. A dresser was on the right side of the room, along with a TV. Two queen beds were on the left. Both men were asleep on top of the covers. Both were fully dressed except for their shoes. Neither man had a gun near him that I could see.

I motioned for Boyd to take the man on the left; I took the one on the right. Pointed my gun at his head, just out of arms reach. Boyd did the same. I counted down from three with my fingers. No turning back now.

On three, I threw a pillow at the man's face. Boyd did the same with the other man. They both woke up to the sight of a handgun aimed at their face. It had the desired effect: a look of pure shock on both of their faces. My guy started to open his mouth. I quickly shushed him with a finger across my lips.

"Brent, Daryl, look at me. Don't talk. You assholes know who I am? Just nod." They both nodded. "So then, you know why I'm here. No need to answer that question. No one, and I mean, no one, can do what you two did to my girlfriend tonight and get away with it."

The man on the right opened his mouth. "What do y—."

I punched him hard in the face. Shushed him once more. Then hit him in the face again, a little harder. His nose started to bleed. "The first one was for talking when I told you not to talk. The second one for was for calling my girlfriend a weather girl. She's a meteorologist, asshole." I punched him again in the stomach. "That one is because, well, that is just because."

Boyd was smiling. I could not tell if he was happy I had not shot anyone yet or if he was simply pleased with my performance so far.

"Now that I have your attention, I need to let you know that if you follow my instructions, then you stand a good chance of making it through this evening with all your pieces still attached. Nod if you understand." They both nodded. "Good, now I need you both face down on your beds, arms behind your head."

They both complied, trying to play it cool, although the look of dread on their faces was giving them away. I tossed Boyd a large zip tie. Covered him while he pulled the man's arms behind his back and used the zip tie as our version of handcuffs, and then sat him up on the side of the bed. I continued to cover him while he repeated the same procedure with the man I hit in the face.

I addressed the men again in an eerily calm voice. "Got a question for you. Answer honestly, because I will know when you are lying. SEC football, who do you root for?" Neither man answered right away. They were both trying to figure out what I wanted to hear, but it would not be any use. I did not care what their answer was to my question.

The one sitting closest to me said, "Tennessee."

"So you are a Vol? How about that. And you?"

The other one said, "Ole Miss."

"Good for you," I said. "You actually answered honestly. So, neither of you like Bama?" Both shook their head. Boyd was looking at me strangely trying to figure out where the questioning was going. "It's okay. I hate football. My daddy played it professionally and ever since he died, well, the game just leaves a sour taste in my mouth. Graham, here, he is a different story. He loves the Crimson Tide. Bama fan through and through. You know, he actually gets depressed when Bama loses. Depressed over a stupid game." I paused for dramatic effect. "Now, the good news is that neither of you are Auburn fans. Otherwise, he would probably shoot you out of principle. Wait, you guys are probably wondering where I'm going with this. Sorry, I digress. In a minute or so, Graham and I are going to load you into the back of a car; then he's going to drive you somewhere. During that time, you are not going to give Graham a hard time. Nothing should come out of your mouth during that time. Not even a Roll Tide, because we all know it wouldn't be sincere. Remember, you guys have admitted to rooting for the wrong team. And you ran my girlfriend off the road and planned on shooting up her house. Graham is the one that shot out your tires before. That's before he found out you aren't Bama fans. Give him any trouble, any lip, so much as bang your knee on the back of his seat funny, and, well, don't be surprised if the crimson you see is your blood oozing out a bullet hole. Nod if you understand." They both nodded earnestly, eyes wide with fear.

I had Boyd cover me as I used duct tape on the first one's mouth. I did not tear off a strip and place it over his mouth. Instead, I wrapped the entire roll around his head covering his mouth. Wrapped it twice. Then I did the same with his eyes. It was probably going to hurt when we pulled the tape off later. I did not give a shit. I taped up the second man the same way, and then we escorted the men outside. LeClair must have seen us exiting the motel room because the trunk suddenly opened. I pushed the men into the trunk, quickly zip tied their ankles together, and closed the lid. LeClair handed Boyd the keys. I smiled as Boyd drove off.

No one had seen a damn thing. Part one of Operation Stromboli was over.

* * *

Strasser's men were on their way to Memphis in the back of LeClair's car. Boyd was taking them to my apartment. The loading dock to be more exact. They were going to see me again, but, first, LeClair and I had work to do. By kidnapping Strasser's men, I had launched an offensive against Strasser. The second part of the plan was still waiting. Now I was going to launch an offensive against the Estes brothers as well.

When Boyd followed Junior around, he discovered where they stored their illegal liquor: the building they bought for the pawn shop. Within minutes, LeClair and I were sitting outside the back door of the building with the van. There was a padlock on the back door, which I was able to pick. However, I could not pick the deadbolt. After three failed attempts, I turned to LeClair. "Screw this. I'm busting out a window, and I'll open it from the inside."

Liquor was stacked in boxes along one wall. Lots of it. Maybe more than the van would hold. Forty-five minutes later the van was full. There were only a dozen boxes left over. I took great pleasure smashing the remaining boxes.

I was surveying the damage trying to imagine Junior's face when he realized all their booze was gone. The image brought a smile to my face. LeClair must have noticed. "Feelin' pretty good about yourself right now, huh, Doc?"

"Not yet, first I have to leave a note." I grabbed a Sharpie out of my back pocket. I had brought it from home. I realized I had not brought any paper, so I broke open a box and laid it out flat on the floor, and then wrote in big, bold letters, all caps: I WANT MY MONEY. NO EXCUSES. "Now I'm feeling pretty good."

We wasted no time getting out of there after I left the note. We were not going to have to unload the van tonight, but Boyd still had two kidnapped men in the back of LeClair's Caddy that required my attention. LeClair asked me what I was planning on doing with them. It was a good question. Not one I had an answer for yet. I could not kill them; that would be murder. I could not let them go either. At least, not with their gun hands still intact.

From the beginning, I had planned Operation Stromboli as a two-pronged offensive against both the Estes gang and Strasser. I was framing Strasser for the missing liquor, and I was planning on implicating the Estes boys in the disappearance of Strasser's men. If I were successful, then neither side would trust the other side, thus preventing them from being able to launch a united front against Boyd and me. I figured that if we were going to have to fight a battle on two fronts, then they might as well too.

One positive about driving an old U-Haul van that maxed out at 50 mph, it gave you plenty of time to think, and I needed the extra time. We were over half way back to Memphis. and I still had not figured out what to do with Brent and Daryl. I had figured out what I was going to do with the stolen alcohol. I was giving it to LeClair, along with the liquor I bought for Boyd to use when he was undercover. LeClair would not accept my offer. He kept telling me that there was easily $20,000 in booze in the van, and I had already spent $2,000 on Boyd. But Boyd had paid me back about $1500 on the liquor he sold. So, I agreed that he could buy Boyd's liquor from me. For $500. LeClair started to argue with me, but he soon realized I would not budge. "I'll tell you what, LeClair, you can throw in a year's supply of burgers, and you have to keep some broccoli for me in the back."

"Deal," he said. "You know, I might have an idea on what to do with your new redneck friends."

"Cut them up and serve them as barbecue like I saw in a movie last year?"

"Damn, Doc, what kind of movies are you watchin'?"

"*Fried Green Tomatoes.* Kind of a chick flick, but I enjoyed it. Anyway, I was kidding. So, what's your idea?"

"Put them in the van, then put the van in the woods for a couple of days."

"I want you to know that I hate you, LeClair."

"Why?"

"Because now we have to unload this van tonight after all. And I have to drive this piece of shit back to Emmettsville to stash it in the woods around there. I think I have just the place."

CHAPTER 34

Boyd was sitting on a stool in my loading dock when LeClair and I arrived. Brent and Daryl were still in the trunk, although the trunk lid was open. It smelled of urine in the trunk. One of them had obviously pissed himself during the ride over. I closed the trunk and told Boyd our plan. He seemed to like it. What he liked best was that he was not going to have to help unload the liquor.

LeClair and I returned after nearly two hours from emptying the truck at his house. It took a little longer to unload because he wanted the boxes in his basement instead of his garage. We also had to stop by a grocery store and buy bottled water and energy bars. It was a little after 5 a.m. when we returned to my apartment. During that time, Boyd had taken the men up to my apartment in the freight elevator and let them use the bathroom. They were sitting on the floor of the loading dock, still cuffed, still blindfolded, and still gagged. I suppose I should have felt sorry for them.

I didn't. Not in the slightest.

LeClair loaded the water and energy bars into the back of the van. I grabbed some other supplies. A couple of blankets, two log chains that I used when pulling motors from cars, and a five-gallon bucket with a lid. Everything I needed for their makeshift prison for the next couple of days. I was not sure what I was going to do with them after that. Probably break their fingers after all and let them go.

I only had one last thing to do before driving back to Emmettsville. I needed directions to Chief Parker's cabin. Shortly before six in the morning, I called him and asked him if I could park a van on his property. I did not tell him why. I merely told him it had supplies I needed and that if possible, I preferred to park it in the shade. He readily agreed, especially when I told him that I had an extremely viable lead on who was trying to frame his son. I had to tell him that I had evidence that some local boys involved in the Dixie Mafia had been hired to collect money from Paul. He pressed me to tell him their names, but I resisted.

"Why won't you tell me who it is? You afraid of retaliation on my part?"

"No. Chief, for reasons I can't get into right now, I just can't tell you. Not yet. Trust me. Remember, you are a necessary cog in the wheel; you are the law. Which brings me to another request. Two more men have gone missing in your town, Brent and Daryl. You can find their car in Falco's parking lot. It's the one with only three good tires. I need you to report them missing to the Tennessee Bureau of Investigation, Criminal Intelligence Unit."

"Why in the world would I do that?"

I did not answer him. I just kept right on talking like I never heard the question. "Brent and Daryl are members of organized crime. They were last seen last night arguing in the parking lot with a short, stocky man who drives a two-toned Ford F-250 Ranger XLT. Picture it with large mud tires and a lift kit. Can you think of a person with a truck like that?"

"Junior Estes."

"Exactly. Last seen talking to Junior Estes, the owner of the two-toned green pickup mentioned by the anonymous caller. You got that?"

"I got it. I just don't know what the heck you are up to."

"I know you don't, Chief. And I know it's frustrating to be kept out of the loop, but, for now at least, the less you know, the better. When you call, someone is going to wonder why you called CIU. Tell them the anonymous caller said he heard them arguing about illegal gambling. And since there was a homicide involving a man in your town that had gambling debts, you thought that CIU was the best place to call. Before you call, though, I need you to go over to the motel across from Falco's and get their last names and the room number they were staying in."

"Can't you just give me their names and room number."

"I could, but I'm not going to. To sell this, I need you to do the investigating yourself. Take another officer with you even. Once you got at least one of their last names, then call it in. Mention the truck, and for the love of God, please make sure that you mention Junior Estes being the only one with a truck like that. CIU may, or may not, tell you how to proceed. If they do give you any direction, follow it. Chief?"

"Yes," he said.

"This is important. It will get the heat off Eric, I promise. I know you are confused. Just know this; you know that saying about kicking a hornet's nest? Well, you are helping me kick the ever-loving crap out of it."

The Chief promised he would start on my little project for him as soon as he got to work and then hung up. I turned to Boyd and LeClair and gave each of them a big thumbs up. With any luck, by noon Chief Parker would be calling CIU and implicating Junior Estes in the disappearance of Brent and Daryl. Once the mole inside the Bureau called Strasser, my ruse would be complete. Jackson and Junior Estes would think Strasser declared a personal war on them when he stole their liquor, and Strasser would think the Estes brothers did something to two of his men.

It felt good to be the puppet master.

For the third time in the last twelve hours, I was driving back to Emmettsville. It was the second time in a piece of crap panel van that could not hit 60 mph going downhill with a tail wind. Boyd was following me in my Jeep, so I had plenty of time to think. I was wondering if my ruse was going to work, at least for a couple of days. Hopefully, by that time I would have a confession from Jackson or Junior concerning Paul.

Why did they kill him?

I had no actual evidence at the moment that they did kill him, just a hunch. I did not like coincidences, and it was the only thing that made sense. Strasser would not have done it. Why hire them to collect the money in the first place if he planned on killing Paul? And why would he still be trying to collect the money from the Estes brothers if he had killed him? But why would they kill Paul? Dead men don't pay bills. My guess is they were going to get 20 percent, maybe 25. Should have been an easy three to four thousand.

I needed to get them to confess somehow. Preferably on tape, or in front of someone in law enforcement. The problem was that I had no idea how to trick them into hanging themselves out to dry. Nothing came to mind. I thought of a few ideas, but I quickly dismissed them. Each idea seemed a little more farfetched than the previous one. I think the lack of sleep was affecting my judgment. I had been awake for over 24 hours. Not a record by any means, but apparently enough to affect my focus.

Finding the murder weapon made more sense. But even if I found it, how would I get it into police hands in a legal manner. Breaking and entering to steal the gun would not work. No, if I were going to go that route I would need to come up with a reason for the police to get a search warrant. Maybe I could bait Junior into coming after me. If he had an attempted murder charge against him, then it seems the cops would likely get a search warrant for his property. Maybe they would find the gun he used on Paul. Maybe he would use the same gun when he came after me. Maybe. Too many maybes.

Maybe I needed some sleep.

Chief Parker's directions to his cabin were a little hard to follow, but we eventually found it. I parked the van where it would get shade during the hottest part of the day. The van was going to be Brent and Daryl's home for the next couple of days; I did not want them to die of heat exhaustion. I grabbed my supplies from the front seat and had Boyd cover me while I opened the sliding door on the back of the van. The two men were sitting pretty much where I left them, wrists and ankles still bound. We had removed the duct tape from around their eyes but left the tape on their mouths. Their eyes were wide with fright as they realized the van had stopped in the middle of nowhere. Their fear changed to confusion as I threw the five-gallon bucket into the back, followed by the energy bars and water.

"Good news, boys, you are going to live through this after all. Bad news, you are going to have to live in this van for the next couple of days. There's your food, there's your water, and the bucket is for you to, well, you know, what it's for, don't you. I will take the tape off your mouths. You can talk all you want once we leave. Scream if you like. Won't do you any good, but, hey, if it makes you feel better, then be my guest. If, after two days, this is not all over, then I will come back, break the fingers on your gun hands into little pieces, and let you go. There is potential for a plan B. Anyone want to hear it?"

Both nodded. I motioned for Boyd to cover me while I removed the tape from their mouths. I still did not know which one was Daryl or Brent, but the one I hit earlier started yelling as soon as I removed the tape. "Do you know who the fuck you are mess—."

I knew what he was getting ready to say. I did not care, and I had warned him before about talking out of turn, so I punched him in the mouth. His lip started bleeding. "You Daryl or Brent?" He did not answer, which made sense. He probably thought I was going to hit him again.

The other guy spoke up, "I'm Brent."

"Thanks." I turned back to address Daryl. "I know exactly who I'm messing with. You belong to Strasser. Supposedly a real big wig in the Dixie Mafia. But he hired you, and you, my boy, are about as dumb as a box of rocks, so my opinion of him is slipping just a bit. The real problem is that you idiots don't know who you are messing with. I'm Captain Frigging Kirk." I couldn't resist the Star Trek reference.

"You mentioned a plan B," said Brent.

"Right, plan B. It's simple. Tell me how to get a hold of Strasser. If he calls off any attempts to harm me or any of my friends, then I can let you guys go, and we're good. If not, you guys get broken fingers and then I have to sic Graham on Strasser. He has been begging me for an opportunity to shoot someone since I hired him. You see, I was Navy Intelligence in a former life. Graham was the Marine Sniper we used to send in to take out high-value targets behind enemy lines. He never failed. Over 70 confirmed kills. Now he's a mercenary. Expensive, unless he owes you a favor. Lucky for me, he owes me a favor."

It was a lie, but it seemed like a good lie. I know it would have scared me if the tables had been turned. Brent must have thought it was pretty scary as well. He gave us Strasser's location down in Mississippi. A small bar just south of Tupelo. I congratulated Brent on his wise decision to cooperate while telling him I would do everything in my power to ensure a positive outcome for him. Apparently, I had a trip to Tupelo coming up soon. I had never been to the birthplace of Elvis. I thought if I ever did, it would be under different circumstances.

* * *

Nearly 26 hours without sleep, and still no sleep in sight. I knew it would have to come before I made the trip to Tupelo. Boyd and I had a brief conversation. He wanted to go with me to Tupelo, apparently to watch my back. Personally, I thought he wanted to make sure I didn't do something bad to Strasser. We only had one car for the two of us, so I agreed he could go. After securing the lift door of the van with the log chains, I had Boyd drop me off at the Carmichael house. Everyone was awake. The smell of breakfast still lingered in the air as Ellie let me in.

She greeted me with a big hug. "Whatever are you doing here so early? Didn't you get off at seven?"

"They let me out early."

More lies. The lies were getting easier and easier. That had to be a bad sign. And how much longer could I claim plausible deniability? Could I even claim it now? The poor girl had been attacked because of me. Shouldn't I just tell her the truth? I realized I was no longer protecting her from me; I was protecting me from her. I was kidnapping people, threatening them with bodily harm, and getting ready to visit an organized crime boss. Not to mention the breaking and entering and theft of thousands of dollars of liquor. Of course, it was illegal alcohol. What would she think of me if she knew all that? It probably would not have been positive.

She asked me if I had eaten. I readily accepted her offer to cook me some breakfast. It seemed remarkable to me, but her family still welcomed me into their home. No one seemed to be blaming me for last night. Jessica even tousled my hair again while I was eating breakfast. None of them suspected that I was the type of man that could chain men inside a van and make them relieve themselves into a five-gallon bucket. I was able to hide that part of myself from them. I could not hide the fact that I was tired. Ellie offered a chance to get some sleep in the guest room, which I readily accepted. Not before I had a chance to talk to Mark, though.

We excused ourselves outside after I finished eating. I got right to the point. "Mark, I found the guys that ran Ellie off the road. They were also planning on shooting at the house last night, but that attempt was foiled."

"One of your spies again?"

"Yes.

"You must have some great friends."

I smiled. Mark was right. I did have some great friends. Two of them had gone above and beyond the call of duty of being a normal friend. One more was on his way here to watch over Ellie for me. It felt good to have friends like that. "I do. I also have the tag number of the car that ran Ellie off the road and the names of the men inside. And I have made things much easier for you to get that protection for Ellie."

"Oh, do tell."

I explained what I had ordered Chief Parker to do earlier this morning. How he was to call in the missing men, the abandoned car, and the fact that they were last seen arguing with Junior Estes. Next, I wanted Mark to visit Chief Parker to tell the Chief what happened with Ellie last night. I told him to leave out the part about the men being outside the Carmichael house.

Special Agent Sande said, "I think I understand what you're doing here. You're paving the way for me to ask for protection for Ellie since the tag number you are giving me also matches the tag number on the abandoned car, which belongs to two men involved in illegal activity. You want the Chief to make the initial contact with CIU. Then, when I talk to the Chief, because of my knowledge of Ellie's boyfriend having problems with the Dixie Mafia, I realize she is in danger from the same people. Thus I can ask for protection."

"Yep. So now you don't have to ask your friend for help. He will not have to get involved. No chance of this blowing back on him, or you for that matter."

Mark said, “They teach you this stuff in spy school or something?” I gave him a big exaggerated smile. “I’m afraid to ask. Where are the two ‘missing’ men?”

“Chained inside an old U-Haul parked in the woods.”

“No, really.”

“Really.”

“Oh, shit.”

“Don’t worry; they will be fine.” I explained the energy bars, the water, and the bucket. Mark actually laughed at the prospect. He wanted to know how long I planned on keeping them hostage. “If I can’t resolve this in the next couple of days, I will break all the fingers on their gun hands, and let them go.” He did not laugh at that prospect. Because I could tell that deep down, really deep in that area of the brain that none us want to admit we have, he agreed with me.

CHAPTER 35

I took Ellie up on her offer to use the guest room. Nearly six hours later, I woke up refreshed and ready for my drive to Tupelo, Mississippi. Ellie informed me that lunch was sitting on the table on a plate with a towel over it. Virgil walked into the kitchen while I was devouring cold country fried steak, green beans, and corn bread. "Chew your food, my mom always said."

"I know, I know. But I'm in a major hurry."

"So you aren't planning on staying, I take it?"

I told him my plan. His wrinkled brow said it all. He started telling me how much I needed to stick around and smooth things over with Ellie. She was scared. Not so much for herself, she felt safe sitting in her family home. *If she only knew.* No, she was scared for us. Virgil said she was confused about her feelings toward me, mostly because she no longer felt she knew the man she had been dating for the last year. She did not understand my current obsession. She did not understand my reaction, or lack of reaction, to fear. She did not understand how I could risk everything just for the sake of justice. At first, she thought she understood me and my desire for justice, but as everything became more dangerous, riskier, she could no longer see things from my point of view. I seemed foreign to her.

"Funny thing, Virgil. The night I stopped Tom Harty in the hospital, she admitted to me that she knew I had a dangerous side, and she also admitted that no one ever made her feel safer than me. Now that the stakes are higher, she is questioning things. She does not realize that it is my dangerous side that enabled her to feel so safe with me in the first place." Virgil was absently nodding in agreement. "Which means she would never understand what I have to do next. I am going to walk into the face of danger because doing so will guarantee her safety. So, you can talk to her if you want. Try to explain it to her if you can, but, for me, I'm going to Tupelo, Mississippi to talk to the man that involved her in the first place. He will agree to leave her alone, or I will make him agree. That's my damn solution."

Immediately after my conversation with Virgil, I started looking for an excuse to leave. I settled on pretending I needed to attend to my Mercedes. A partial lie; I did need to attend to my car, but I had no intention of doing it just then. Within the hour, Boyd and I were on our way to Tupelo to meet Darwin Strasser. We did stop by to check on Brent and Daryl. They were where we had left them.

An hour and fifteen minutes later, we pulled up in front of Strasser's bar. According to Brent, Strasser had an office in the back. He did all his Dixie Mafia business out of that office. It was the middle of the day on a Sunday in August. A beautiful, sunny, hot, summer day in the South. The kind of day that my colleagues spent outdoors playing golf, working in the yard, swimming in their pools. I was going to visit a crime boss. I had a Glock 21 holstered on my right side in case I needed it. My colleagues probably had barbecue utensils holstered in an apron while trying to grill the family meal.

I ordered Boyd to wait by the car and watch the front door. From the outside, the bar looked like a dive. Poor signage, grass growing up through the multitude of cracks in the driveway, faded exterior paint. Inside, my suspicions were confirmed; the place was an absolute dive. It reeked of disinfectant trying to cover up the odor of stale beer that had probably seeped into the wooden floor one too many times. Dimly lit. No attempt at any type of decor. It did have a pool table, a regular pool table, not a coin operated table. The felt was threadbare in places. I was definitely in the right place. No way a bar like that was run by a competent, hard-working business man. It looked exactly like what it was: a money laundering operation for a two-bit crime boss in the Dixie Mafia.

Three men lounged at the bar. Lazy looking guys in jeans and cheap tee shirts. One wore a ball cap advertising Peterbilt trucks. None of the men were drinking. No one was working behind the bar. If the bar did any actual business, I had arrived before the evening crowd. All three turned lazily to look my direction as I entered the front door. One informed me the bar was closed.

I replied, "Fine with me, I don't drink." The man replied back, informing me that solicitors were not welcome. "Not here to sell anything, either," I said. "I have something for Strasser, something I hear he is looking for." The man glanced quickly towards a door in the back before informing that there was no one there by that name. A poor liar. I could teach him a thing or two.

I pulled out a small cassette tape Boyd had given before entering the bar, cleared my throat and started again once I saw all three men look at me. "I can see you are all busy testing the integrity of Mr. Strasser's bar stools, but I need one of you to relay a message to him. Tell him a doctor from Memphis is standing in his bar holding a tape that he has gone to great trouble to find."

That got their attention. All three of them instantly got to their feet and faced me in an aggressive stance. One started to reach behind his back. I quickly unholstered the Glock and pointed it at him, an average looking man in his thirties that looked twice his age in the eyes. Life had been hard for the man; it was easy to see that. "Whoa there, cowboy. I'm here to give Strasser something he wants. I'm not here to give you something you don't." The man brought his hands slowly forward. I thanked him and asked them again if Strasser was in the building. Two of them nodded yes. "Now yell back there and tell him he has a visitor."

The man who had reached behind his back said, "We usually just use the intercom on the phone behind the bar."

"Okay, but not you." I examined the other two men and tried to pick the one who looked scared. They both looked scared, so I picked the one that seemed twitchy. I figured it would be best if I gave him something to do before his ADHD took over and made him do something he regretted later. I told him to summon Strasser, and to keep his hands in clear view while doing it. He nodded his acknowledgment.

"Before you make that call, I need you," I was looking at the man who reached behind his back, "To keep your hands up high where I can see them and turn around. Slowly."

He glared at me, yet readily complied. I moved forward and patted him down finding a small handgun in his right back pocket. A Raven Arms HP25. I almost laughed out loud. I was probably safer with the gun pointed at me than he was with it in his back pocket. Raven Arms was a notorious gun manufacturer that started producing guns in the early Seventies. It was considered the original "Ring of Fire" company. The Ring of Fire companies were a list of gun manufacturers that specialized in cheap, poor quality semi-automatic pistols commonly known as Saturday Night Specials. The gun probably sold for less than $30.00. It was worth less than that.

"Were you seriously thinking about trying to shoot me with this piece of crap? I should probably hand it back to you and let you take your chances firing it at me. FYI though, the last time a gun was pointed at me it was an AK-47. The owner of that gun shot me in the thigh. He isn't around anymore to tell his side of the story if you catch my drift."

I motioned for the twitchy man to call Strasser over the intercom while advising the other two to sit with their hands where I could see them. They complied without an argument. Strasser readily answered the intercom indicating he would be up in a moment. Nothing in his voice over the loudspeaker indicated any sense of alarm. He was true to his word; Strasser strolled into the bar nearly a minute later, oblivious to the danger waiting for him. He was a very cool customer. No sense of alarm on his part when he spotted me holding my Glock. He just stood where he was in the hallway leading into the bar and waited for me to motion him in. He puts his hands out in front before I had to ask and smiled as he took a seat on one of the bar stools.

"Dr. McCain, I presume."

I had not known what to expect from a Dixie Mafia crime boss. Some toothless, tobacco chewing redneck. A good ole boy with a winsome smile. A charming Southern gentleman dressed like Colonel Sanders. Those were a couple of images I had formed on the drive to Tupelo. I had not expected to see a well-tailored man in a black suit, white shirt, no tie, who looked as if he was George C. Scott's forty-five-year-old twin brother. Intelligence gleamed in his eyes. This man was not stupid. Not like the three men he had sitting out front. Not like Brent or Daryl. He was crafty; it was easy to see it about him, especially if you knew what to look for. And I did.

"What gives it away?" I asked.

"You fit the general description. Big fella with a surfer dude haircut. What brings you to Tupelo, Doctor?"

"Heard you were looking for a tape. Is that true?" I was not going to allow him to dictate the conversation by asking me questions. That was my thing. He nodded. "There has been some kind of misunderstanding." He raised his eyebrows to query me to continue. Clever bugger, he was asking me questions without actually talking. "The tape in question does not exist. There is a tape involving some men asking about some money owed to you, but that's it. No mention of you being involved in Paul Deland's murder, although the men asking about that money seem to think that Junior might have had something to do with it. Your man on the inside, your police informant, got his story wrong."

"Is that so?"

I was really starting to dislike this guy. I had the gun. I ask the questions. What part did he not understand? I pulled the tape out of my pocket again. Held it up for him to look at. Then, I dropped it on the floor and smashed it with the heel of my shoe.

"And now even that tape no longer exists. Strasser, you got no beef with me. You want no beef with me. I will let your little show of force last night slide. Once. Not twice. I am asking for a truce while I nail one, or both, of the Estes boys for the murder of Paul Deland. If I find 15K sitting around during my investigation, I won't even pick it up; that is, unless you want me to set it aside for you before the cops show up to haul them away. Would you find that satisfactory, Mr. Strasser?"

He studied me. I could tell he was wondering how far I would take things if he refused. I wondered if he could tell that I was not sure how far I would take things either. I could kill in self-defense. I already had, years ago. More than once in a jungle in Cambodia. More recently in a hospital in Memphis in defense of a fellow doctor. Possibly, shortly, if anyone in Strasser's gang even looked at Ellie cross-eyed now that I had delivered my ultimatum.

Strasser seemed to sense the change in my resolve. "Jackson Estes and his nit-wit of a brother were hired to do a job for me; they do not work for me. Thus I owe them no loyalty. I find your offer completely satisfactory, Dr. McCain."

I nodded at his declaration of acceptance of my offer and holstered my Glock. Reaching into my back pocket, I grabbed the cheap handgun I pulled of Strasser's man. I hit the magazine release and checked to make sure the gun was empty before throwing the magazine to the man I took the gun from earlier. Turning to Strasser, I said, "You really should pay your men a little better. Raven Arms makes their guns out of cheap zinc alloy, basically a type of pot metal." I grabbed the cheap handgun with both hands and brought the gun down hard across my knee. The gun literally broke in half in my hands. I tossed the pieces to the man, smiled, and backed out the front door.

CHAPTER 36

"Holy cow," said Boyd, "You actually broke the gun in half with your bare hands? That must have left an impression." I smiled to myself as I recalled the look on their faces when I broke the gun in half. "So, you think we have a truce with him?"

I wasn't sure. There was no guarantee that Strasser would keep his word. However, for now, he appeared to be a man of reason. There was also no way of knowing if he believed that the tape I destroyed was the real thing. It wasn't, but it didn't matter. I broke the blank tape as a visual aid to help Strasser realize I was not his enemy. Unless he went after me or one of my friends. If he made that mistake again, then I would probably shoot him, plain and simple.

Even if Strasser decided not to call off his men, I could not help thinking that the last 24 hours had been fruitful. I had successfully pulled off my plan, aptly named Operation Stromboli, which pitted the Emmettsville faction and the Tupelo faction against each other. The pressure on Jackson and Junior should be twice as strong as they felt a double squeeze from Strasser on one side, Boyd and me on the other side. I wanted those two to squirm, to feel the heat. Get them nervous and jumpy, they would eventually screw up; the average person usually succumbs to extreme pressure.

But was the pressure extreme enough? I was not sure. Suddenly, my inner voice spoke up, giving me another idea. It was time for a triple play on the Estes brothers. It was time to get the Emmettsville PD involved, and I had the perfect plan.

We were only five minutes from my apartment when I realized I had not checked my pager all day. There were five separate pages from the hospital. Not a good sign. If I did not change my actions, I was probably going to lose my job. I needed to get to work on time and finish a shift. I also needed to get my car out of their parking lot if the hospital had not already had it towed for me.

We parked the Jeep and went inside. Surprisingly, there were no messages on the machine. I couldn't believe it. Maybe they were waiting for me to show up at work to fire me. I stir fried some chicken and vegetables, my version of Gai Pad Khing, a Thai ginger chicken stir-fry with oyster and fish sauce, while I explained the next step in Operation Stromboli. Once again, Boyd was impressed. With the Gai Pad Khing and my plan.

I never did buy another vehicle for Boyd, so he left for Emmettsville with my Jeep while I prepared for work. I arrived at the hospital by 6:30. As expected, my Mercedes was no longer in the parking lot. Security informed me which towing company had my car. I wanted to be early for work, and I was. Not to make myself look good, but to see if I was even expected to work that night's shift. Remarkably, my name was added to the control board shortly after I walked into the ER. I received a few stares from the nurses. A few were bold enough to ask me if Ellie was alright. Dr. Pratt also asked about Ellie. He was remarkably understanding about the whole thing.

The evening was chaotic. The type of evening that often accompanies being a Level 1 Trauma Center in a large city. We had six people with gunshot wounds that evening. More than usual, but, unfortunately, business as usual in all other regards. One did not make it; a poor young woman that happened to be collateral damage in a drive-by shooting between rival youth gangs. I was exhausted when I crawled into bed at eight the next morning.

I woke up Monday a little after two in the afternoon. Six hours of sleep. Not enough, but all I was going to get. I cooked some more stir fry for lunch and jumped in the shower. I checked my pager, no messages. There were two on my answering machine. The first one was from my mother. As usual, I skipped over it. The second was from Virgil. "Hey, L.T. I'm back in Huntsville. Boyd followed Ellie all the way to Memphis. No problems. Mark followed her in as well. By the way, Happy Belated Birthday."

Yesterday, Sunday, was my birthday. I had forgotten all about it while driving all over God's creation, threatening a Dixie Mafia crime boss, and watching a young woman die a senseless death from gang violence. I was 34.

For some reason, after calling my insurance company and reporting the damage to the Mercedes, I decided to listen to the message from my mother. It was from yesterday. She had called to wish me a Happy Birthday, the only person who called me on my birthday. There was genuine love in her voice. She also sounded better somehow. It was hard to explain.

Her only son had locked her out of his life for the last 14 years. During the time, she had called numerous times. Her tone always had a degree of anxiety and yearning to it. I replayed the message. She sounded older. I replayed it again. The anxiety, the yearning, it was gone. That's why she sounded better. Nothing but untempered love in her message. Even with increased age in her voice, she sounded like the mother I had known before Scott Oswald Beyers came into her life. Maybe she had finally left the SOB.

My right hand absently started to drift toward the phone as I contemplated calling my mother for the first time since I joined the Navy. My phone ringing jolted me out of the moment. I answered, half expecting it to be Mom. "Hello," I said.

"Hey, sleepy head, I did what you asked," roared Boyd. "I called Jackson and told him he might want to check his pawn shop out. When he went inside, I called Chief Parker and said what you told me to say. He flew right over, just like we figured. Jackson was still inside when the Chief arrived."

"And?"

"I don't know."

"What do you mean by you don't know?"

"Just that. Parker went in. They were both in there about ten minutes, then they both left separately. I followed Jackson, and I'll be damned if he didn't drive over to the police station and spend another 30 minutes in there."

Boyd and I were confused. It seemed that the third part of Operation Stromboli had not gone as expected. We were hoping that law enforcement would want to know why a bunch of broken alcohol bottles was found in Jackson's future pawn shop. That was supposed to be the third part of the squeeze on them, yet Boyd said Jackson acted like he hadn't a care in the world when the Chief caught him in there. If Tyler himself had not confirmed to Boyd that the Chief was clean as a whistle, we both might have thought the Chief was dirty.

"I'll bet we screwed this one up," I said.

"How so?"

"LeClair and I took too much alcohol. With what little we left behind, Jackson could have easily come up with some story about why it was there. He could even admit it was there and report it stolen. Crap, I didn't think of that. Well, at least he knows his alcohol is gone. And as long as Chief Parker called in Brent and Daryl going missing, Strasser should think the Estes boys did something to his men. Still not a total failure."

"Oh, you are right about that. At the junkyard, I was listening to Jackson yell at Junior about the missing booze. They definitely think Strasser took it. Junior wants to kill Strasser, and Jackson is thinking about letting him."

"You're kidding me, right? And you got this all on tape?"

"I do. Don't get me wrong, they're not planning anything. Junior is venting, and Jackson keeps telling him that it will all happen in due time. Whatever that means."

Boyd played the tape back for me through the phone. He was right; there was nothing overly incriminating on the tape. Boyd also informed me that he had checked on Brent and Daryl. They were quite sullen, and the smell from the back of the truck was less than agreeable, but they were otherwise okay.

"So what's next, Lieutenant?"

"I got an idea. It's a lot more direct." Boyd sounded intrigued. "How about I drive over to their stupid junkyard, walk right in, and tell them I know they killed Paul?"

"Shit. That's pretty direct. What do you think that will do? They're just going to deny it."

"Of course they will to our face. But they don't seem to know we have been recording them. It seems that only Strasser knows. They are bound to walk into their office and start talking about it as soon as I leave. If we're lucky, one of them will say something incriminating."

Boyd spent a good time playing devil's advocate to my plan. What if they didn't have anything to do with Paul's death? What if they decided to come after us? Did I realize that the cops would not be able to use our tape in court?

"I've thought about all that, Boyd. But I got to know if we are chasing the right guys. My inner voice tells me we are. Even if we can't use the tape in court against them, it might be enough to convince someone like the Tennessee Bureau to go after them finally. If not, I do have federal connections. I've purposefully avoided using them, but they are there if we need them. Besides, we want these guys busted for murder, not some damn RICO charges."

We both tried to poke holes in the plan, but neither of us could find enough negatives with the plan to decide against it. What was the worst that could happen? Could they get even more mad at us? Big frigging deal. I welcomed their hate.

Boyd said, "After all the sneaking around, you are just going to walk up to them and flat accuse them. It seems so anticlimactic. We could have done that at any time."

"Hey, without all the subterfuge we would not have known who to accuse in the first place."

It was decided. I was going to walk right into E's Salvage Yard and tell them I knew they had killed Paul and see what transpired afterward. Keep it simple stupid.

* * *

I wanted to get to Emmettsville before the junkyard closed for business, so I packed my Glock 21 and extra magazines and jumped in the Mustang. Boyd still had my Jeep, which was enabling him to drive around Emmettsville without drawing attention while he prowled around in the background. The same level of concern did not apply to my situation. Once Strasser's men attacked Ellie, I decided to take the gloves off from there on out. Anyone stupid enough to cross me was going to get busted up bad. I was not sure if I was the unstoppable force or the immovable object. I was not sure it mattered. If anyone got in my way, I was going to mow them down. If anyone tried to push me around, they would bust themselves up like ships on an iceberg.

I pulled up to the junk yard 45 minutes before closing time. Boyd was right; the whole idea seemed like such a cliché. A plot line pulled from nearly every cop and detective movie. Shrugging off the notion, I stepped out and walked up to the front door. Jackson was working the service counter. His eyes nearly bugged out in surprise when he saw me stroll up to the counter. He recovered a normal composure relatively quickly, yet it was easy to see that he was undecided about his next step.

Earlier I had decided against doing any talking inside the office building. There were two men in front of me, both of which turned in my direction when Jackson's eyes bugged out. I shouldered past them and placed a piece of paper on the counter. Slid it across. Jackson's eyes never left mine while he reached down and retrieved the paper. Mine never left his while I backed out of the building.

It took me nearly 15 minutes to find Boyd in the woods near the junk yard. He had set up the laser microphone 100 yards from the edge of the timber line. As a joke, I tried sneaking up on him. I failed.

"Now you know why all the Special Forces guys aren't built like football players. Damn, did you step on every twig on your way in?"

I knew he was teasing me; I had not been that loud. "I figured I better let you know it was me since you are so itching to shoot someone."

"Shoot *at* someone. *At,* is the key word."

"Well?" I asked.

"Well, what?"

"You heard anything yet?"

"No, you kind of have to go in there and accuse them first, don't you?"

"Been there, done that?" Boyd wrinkled his brow in confusion. "I wrote it all down on a note, and I slid it across the counter." He shrugged his shoulders indicating me to continue with my story. "I wrote down what I told you I was going to say. 'I know you did it. Once I find the .22 your ass is mine.'"

"Just like that?" I shook my head yes. "Then, no, I got nothing?"

We listened for another half hour but heard nothing of any importance. It sounded like business as usual in E's Salvage Yard. The microphone performed flawlessly, so that was not the problem. We were easily 300 yards from the window Boyd had targeted, yet we could hear everything going on inside the building. The whole thing seemed sort of surreal to me. Light carrying sound waves back. Boyd explained that was not exactly how it worked. The whole thing was a type of optical interferometer. Invisible infrared light traveled through the air and struck the window. Some of the light was reflected from the outside window pane back to the device. Boyd referred to it as a reference beam. Some more light bounced off the inside window pane back to the device — the modulated beam. When the two beams traveled back to the device, the light waves combined and interfered with each other, causing peaks and dips in intensity as one beam was modulated more than the other by the sounds hitting the panes of glass. The electronics turned the intensity variations back into audio.

I said, "So the windows vibrate as sound waves hit them, the laser picks up those vibrations, and then this doohickey turns the light back into sound. Fascinating. It makes no sense, but fascinating."

Boyd said it made no sense to him either except when the optical engineer at work explained it. A laser microphone does have its drawbacks. The worst was setting it up. Bouncing invisible light over long distances and being able to recapture that light in the device is understandably difficult. Plus, I noticed that the microphone also picked up noises occurring outside the building. Something that was unavoidable. Finally, apparently they are not too hard to defeat. Just place something that vibrates on the window, like a small speaker taped to the window or even something like an electric toothbrush or shaver, and you can't hear a darn thing.

It also did not automatically make the people you want to eavesdrop on say something you wanted to hear, which was becoming more and more apparent as we could hear people milling around inside getting the business closed up for the day.

Boyd said, "You sure you gave him the right note? You didn't give him your grocery list or something? Maybe Jackson is just sitting in there scratching his head in bewilderment." I told him to give it time. Maybe the brothers would discuss the problem after all the employees left. "That ain't going to happen, my friend. Jackson is not in there. He left about 20 minutes before you got here."

That was not what I wanted to hear, and to our chagrin, Jackson left about ten minutes later without giving any indication that he had even read my note. We loaded up in the Jeep and decided to follow him. Within in a few minutes, Jackson pulled into the driveway of an old two-story farmhouse. Turn of the century, and not exactly well maintained. It needed a new roof and a paint job. The yard needed mowing. Junior's two-toned Ford was parked in the yard. A well-worn path of dead grass revealed he often parked there. Probably too lazy to walk the ten extra steps from the driveway.

"Damn," I said, "I think it's safe to say these boys are not in the real estate business; that is one ugly house. The sofa out on the front porch takes the cake. Even Northern rednecks don't do that."

"Hey, living room furniture out on the front porch, that's practically a Southern redneck tradition. Now what?"

I wasn't sure. The brothers were most likely inside discussing my little note. I had wanted to hear that conversation. See if one of them admitted to anything. My inner voice screamed they were guilty, but that's not exactly the kind of evidence one can use in court. We needed to hear what was going on. I volunteered to run up and place a microphone on one of the windows. Boyd talked me out of it. There was not one tree, not one bush of any kind in the yard. Nothing I could use as cover. It was too risky. I would have to wait for the cover of darkness.

Our wait did not last as long as expected. Junior and Jackson came out of the house and piled into Jackson's car, a nondescript blue four-door Buick. Even from our safe distance, we could see that Jackson had a handgun in his waistband.

Boyd turned to me to see if I had seen the handgun. I nodded. "We following them?" I nodded again. Even though neither Junior nor Jackson had ever seen the Jeep, it did not mean following them was easy. Jeep CJ-7s were not exactly common vehicles, and traffic was not exactly heavy on the country roads. Not to mention, my windows were not tinted.

Jackson was heading south into Mississippi traveling just slightly above the 55 mph speed limit. We had been following them for 15 minutes when I noticed Jackson slowing down to make a left-hand turn an empty field. The car stopped at the entrance into the field. They were waiting for something.

"Crap," I said, "I think they are pulling over to see if we are tailing them. Quick, turn away from them."

If Jackson was just sitting there in an open field looking for a tail, then he was a crafty son-of-a-gun. I pulled the cap I was wearing down harder on my head and floored the Jeep, driving past the parked car as quickly as possible. Once past them, I noticed in the rear view mirror that both men had their heads turned in our direction.

"Boyd, I'm beginning to think Jackson is smart. That was how to spot a tail 101. Don't drive fast, just do the unexpected. If we had done anything other than blow on by them, they would have known someone was following them."

"Yeah, and now we have lost them."

"Maybe not. I'm starting to get a sneaking suspicion I know where they are going. We'll drive on ahead and get in place."

Another 15 minutes later, Boyd realized where we were heading. We did not know for sure where Jackson was headed, but in light of recent events, it made the most sense. An hour later, Boyd and I were trying to find an inconspicuous place to park the Jeep outside our target location. I could not hide the Jeep, so I dropped Boyd off and continued driving another half mile before finding a suitable location to park the Jeep. In high school, I could run the 40-yard dash faster than all but one player on our football team, but that did not mean I enjoyed the half-mile sprint back to Boyd's location. I arrived out of breath and perched behind a foul smelling dumpster. Six cars were in the parking lot. Boyd was not visible. He was probably hiding on the other side of the lot.

I had guessed correctly. The Estes brothers arrived shortly. How were they going to play this? It was a Monday evening, so although the bar was not busy, neither was it empty. Yesterday, when I did the same thing, Strasser's bar was closed.

Neither brother wasted anytime exiting the car. From my vantage point, it was evident Jackson still had the handgun in his waistband. Junior appeared unarmed, which seemed highly unlikely. Maybe I injured his shoulder too much for him to hold a gun. One could always hope.

The brothers strode into the bar, out of my sight. Unless I wanted to crash the party, it was anyone's guess what was going to happen inside. Hopefully, I would not need to call 911. Then again, maybe that wouldn't have been so bad.

I spotted Boyd perched behind a car in the parking lot. He looked my way and shrugged his shoulders questioningly. I returned the gesture. Boyd did not sit long, though. Instead, he walked over to Jackson's Buick and opened the driver's side rear door, fumbled through his pocket, then bent over and reached inside the vehicle. He closed the rear door and started to walk away when Jackson and Junior came back out the front door of Strasser's bar. Fortunately, the brothers were preoccupied, or else they would have spotted him.

The brothers were exiting the bar walking backward. Jackson had his arm around a man's neck, the same man I took the cheap handgun from. Jackson's gun was pointed at the man's head, while Junior had a small handgun pointed towards the front door. From the look of things, Jackson's visit had not gone as planned.

The man was scared. He didn't even try to struggle loose. Jackson opened the driver's door and pushed the man across the front seat with his gun still trained on him. Junior crawled in the rear passenger door while Jackson turned to watch the front door. Once Junior was situated with his gun aimed at the man's head, Jackson got into the car and sped out of the parking lot. That was the third one of Strasser's men to have been taken captive in as many days; Boyd and I had the other two trapped in a panel van in the woods.

I kept an eye on the front door of the bar expecting to see Strasser's men exiting in hot pursuit. But they didn't. Boyd must have expected the same the thing because he remained hidden behind some cars and motioned for me to get the Jeep and pick him up. This meant another half-mile sprint. I was still out of breath when I pulled up in front of Strasser's a few minutes later.

Boyd immediately climbed in and starting barking orders. "Gun it, man. If they are heading back the same way they came, then you might be able to catch them."

"I don't give a crap about saving Strasser's man."

"Me neither. I threw a bug up under their seat. If we get close enough, we will be able to listen to what's going on inside their car."

That explained why Boyd had walked up and opened the back door. Boyd was coming through again. Now I just had to hope I could push the top heavy Jeep fast enough on the winding road to catch up with Jackson. Horsepower was not the problem. I had made modifications to the AMC 258 engine, an inline six known for having decent torque at low RPMs; the year before I rebuilt the engine and squeezed an extra 60 horsepower out of it. The problem was that no one in their right mind thinks of a Jeep CJ7 with a four-inch lift kit as being particularly well suited for a high-speed chase on a curvy, winding road. In every curve, the tires squalled and squealed as I pushed the Jeep to its handling limits. After the first ten miles, I decided I would never complain about the handling in the Mercedes ever again.

Thirty minutes went by before I gave up. If we were going to catch them, we would have done it by then. Jackson was probably pushing his Buick just as hard as I was, or he had taken a different route. Boyd was disappointed, but he understood why I slowed down to a safer speed.

"Well, look on the bright side," I said, "Now that the Estes boys have kidnapped one of Strasser's men, we don't have to hold Brent and Daryl any longer."

"So we just let them go?"

"After I break their fingers on their gun hands?"

"Do you think that is necessary? It would be a show of good faith to Strasser if you let them go unharmed. Keep Strasser's wrath focused on the Estes boys."

Boyd had a great point. I kidnapped them because they attacked Ellie. No doubt Strasser would understand that. But if I broke their fingers after I had called a truce, then maybe he might not be so understanding. On the flip side, someone still needed to pay for running Ellie off the road in the first place. Maybe I would just break one finger a piece. Trigger fingers only. Better yet, thumbs. Take the opposable digit away, and that would render them useless in a gunfight.

Boyd was watching me mull it over. "You don't agree?" he asked.

"You make a great point. It's just that, you know when you watch a movie, and the good guy has a chance to take the bad guy out, but he goes all soft. So the bad guy gets away only to attack the good guy again later, and the good guy has to kill him after all. Well, if I break their thumbs now, then they shouldn't have to be killed later."

"So, you're thinking of Brent and Daryl's safety?"

"Of course, I am a doctor. Think of this as an ounce of prevention is worth a pound of cure."

"I can never quite tell if you are serious or not."

I informed Boyd that I was quite serious, but my mind was not made up yet. We were about an hour out of Emmettsville, which gave me plenty of time to decide and to listen to Boyd's side of the story. Boyd had the skill set to be a top-notch investigator. He was clever and insightful. He made good deductions. He had access to some wonderful toys. The only thing I questioned was his ability to make tough decisions. I would never have given up my gun when Tyler and Junior approached me. I probably would have shot Brent or Daryl, or both. And now he was worried about breaking their little fingers. Maybe he still had too much cop left in him.

* * *

We were 20 minutes from Emmettsville when I noticed a set of headlights approaching quickly from behind. It was too dark to tell for sure, but my inner voice was yelling at me regardless. "Hey, what's the range on that microphone you put in Jackson's car?"

"Probably a quarter mile. Why?"

"Humor me. Turn it on?"

"Sure."

Boyd pushed some buttons, twisted a dial or two. A voice came across the speaker. "That fucking Jeep up ahead look familiar to you?"

I looked at Boyd, gave him a big thumbs up and warned him about looking back. Jackson and Junior were directly behind us. I loved my inner voice. At times it almost made me feel clairvoyant. "You know, Boyd, sometimes it's even better to be lucky than smart." He just smiled.

Once again, the sound quality from Boyd's tiny microphones was superb. The company he worked for made excellent equipment. Junior answered his brother, "Yeah, that's the same damn Jeep we thought was followin' us on the way to Tupelo. Look at it, white CJ7, chrome package, brown hardtop, lift kit. No doubt about it, same Jeep."

"So we agree it's the same Jeep, then. Seems strange to run into it twice on the same day, don't you think?"

"Yeah, but we both agreed it wasn't followin' us earlier, and we came up behind it just now, not the other way around. Same Jeep, but has to be a coincidence. Maybe they were headin' to Holly Springs in that thing earlier, and we just happen to catch them again on the way home. Why, what you thinkin'? Strasser's men?"

Jackson said, “Hell no.”

“Then what?”

“Ten to one, it’s that fucking doctor. He’s smart. Too smart. I think the deal with that Graham fella was all part of his master plan. Although, for the life of me, I can’t figure out why he had him selling liquor in our county. Seriously, what did he hope to gain by that?”

“Why you askin’ me? I’m still not convinced he’s actually a doctor.”

Jackson said, “Really? So you think he just parks his pretty red sports car outside the hospital for fun? Besides, how else do you think he can afford a car like that?”

“Okay, okay. You made your damn point, bro. It’s just that he told us that he used to arrest Marines, which meant he must have been a military cop, and now he’s some kind of bad ass doctor. Kind of a stretch, don’t ya think? Hell, he even went all Kung Fu on my ass in the shed. He could have ripped my shoulder out; I know it. And you know me, bro, I don’t lose fights. Ever.”

“Sorry for getting all smart assy with you. Everything is just getting out of control. Strasser steals our booze. Even leaves a note, then denies it when we show up in his bar. Instead, he starts accusing us of kidnapping two of his guys. You ran them out of our office, but we didn’t kidnap them. Strasser is acting weird, man. Plus, he mentioned something about meeting our doctor friend. What the hell did he mean by that?”

Junior must not have had an answer to his brother’s questions because all conversation ceased for a couple of minutes before Jackson resumed the conversation. “I’m still wondering if that’s the doctor up ahead of us. Maybe he knew we were on to him on the way down to Tupelo. Maybe he knew we were heading to Strasser’s, or, at least, guessed. Don’t look at me like that. I know it doesn’t explain why he’s in front of us right now.”

The two brothers argued for the next couple of minutes concerning the coincidence of seeing the same Jeep on the same stretch of road a couple of hours apart. Neither was able to convince the other of their viewpoint. Both brothers were yelling after a couple of minutes of arguing. It sounded like the stress of their situation was getting to them.

"You know," yelled Jackson, "If you had handled things with Deland like I told you to, none of this would be happening."

Junior replied, "Brother, I told you to stop bringin' that up. I shot the son of a bitch. He's dead. I didn't mean to, but there's nothin' we can do about it now."

Boyd and I whipped our heads towards each other in amazement. Over the last ten days, I had run into Junior on three different occasions, each time I had seen Junior as a hindrance, not a suspect. Not once had I suspected Junior's involvement in Paul disappearance and death; that is, until Boyd overheard him talking with Strasser's men two days ago. Only then had I started to suspect anything. It was why I had delivered the note to Jackson. By telling them that I knew they did it, I hoped they would talk about my note while Boyd taped them. However, that had not worked. Instead, they were following us with a bug under their seat talking away while we heard the whole thing. No tape, but we now knew everything we needed to know. Boyd and I had found our man.

The irony of the situation was not lost on me. If Junior had left me alone from the beginning, maybe I never would have suspected him in the first place. If he had not kidnapped Boyd, then we probably would not have set up the laser microphone outside their office. They could have laid low, and my investigation might have gone right over them. But that's not what happened. Over and over, they brought attention to themselves. I doubt Boyd could have slapped the smile off my face as I contemplated our success.

Boyd said, "We frigging got 'em. You hear that. We got them. Hot damn!"

"We find the gun Junior used, and they are screwed. To hell with us finding it; let's tell the Chief and let him get a warrant, and he can find it. Our part is nearly over, Boyd. Way to go, Bird Dog, I never could have done this without you."

Our celebration was cut short as Junior's voice started over the microphone again. "What we gonna do about Strasser?"

"Since we didn't hurt his man, I say we just give him 15 grand and move on. We'll admit to nothing, of course, and tell him it's worth it to us to just put it all behind us. Then one day, when he least suspects it, bam, I'll make sure he pays for stealing our booze."

Junior yelled, "I don't like it, bro. We had 10,000 in liquor in there, at least. We're out 25,000 if we pay him. Not good, bro. Not good at all."

"We'll only be out 10, Junior, because you're still gonna collect from the little twerp's family. I'm not eating 25,000. Hell, I'm not eating 10. We'll just get that from Strasser at a later date. If we don't get it, then fuck it, I'll blow up his bar and call it even. That piece of shit bar couldn't have been worth much more than that."

"Okay, I'm followin' you. But what about the doctor? He ain't gonna let us just waltz in there and collect from Paul's old man."

Jackson said, "How about I just pass them on the next straight away and if it's them, we take care of him and his friend once and for all." Junior liked the idea.

"Well, shit," I said. "It looks like things are going to get all climactic here in a second."

"You think?" Boyd's voice had the tiniest tinge of nervousness in it. "You going to let them pass?"

"Sure. Boyd, you got your MP5?"

"Yeah. Why?"

"Set that thing to full auto and let me have it." Boyd wanted to know why. "Because I'm going to hang it out the window and shoot their car all to hell. They think they got the element of surprise. Well, 30 rounds of 9mm Parabellum flying their way should rid them of any notion they have about being in control."

"I got a better idea," said Boyd. "You can drive better than me; I can shoot better than you. Stop them in the middle of the road, and I will jump out and shoot their tires and radiator. Leave them sitting there while we go see the Chief and tell him what we found out."

Now that was a plan I could not argue with. My driving, his shooting. The element of surprise. They were screwed. Boyd grabbed his H&K MP5. I saw him set the selector switch to 3-round burst mode. Boyd must have had some excellent connections to get his MP5. His model was an MP5-N, a version developed for the United States Navy in 1986. The ambidextrous Navy trigger group included the 3-round burst mode. The MP5-N also had a collapsible stock, a tritium illuminated front sight, and a threaded barrel to outfit it with a suppressor. It was one heck of a gun.

Boyd looked a little nervous as he turned his hat around backward. For all his talk about shooting at someone, he did not seem too keen on the idea of firing on Jackson's Buick. Secretly, I think he just wanted the keep the gun out of my hands. "Ready!" he yelled. I jammed the brakes while steering towards the left side of the road. Before coming to a complete stop, I turned the wheel hard right, twisting the Jeep sideways in the middle of the road. Boyd jumped out and began firing. The first burst went directly into the front of the Buick.

"Oh shit, oh shit. Back up! That son of a bitch has a machine gun. Shit!"

From the speaker, we could hear Junior yelling. Both men were yelling a string of obscenities as Boyd fired off another round of shots. The second 3-round burst hit the front tire on the passenger side. The Buick lurched backward as Jackson threw the car into reverse. With the front tire blown out, he was losing control of the vehicle, although he did not let up on the gas. The front end of Buick was violently swaying back and forth. Boyd fired off another 3-round burst. I could not tell if he hit anything.

Suddenly, the car fishtailed off the road, jumped the short ditch bordering the road, and struck a tree. The Buick was easily 100 yards away, yet I could hear the impact of the collision with the tree as if it happened right in front of me. Boyd fired off two more 3-round bursts into the side of the car. I noticed he was shooting into the rear of the car to avoid hitting them. It probably was better that he was doing the shooting; I was going to spray the whole car. If one of them got hit, so be it.

The collision with the tree must have shaken both of them up because it was easily 15 seconds before we saw Junior's door open and Junior climbed out. Jackson also exited Junior's door and started shooting at us with his handgun. It would have taken a very impressive shot for him to hit anything at that distance, but that did not mean that sometimes a person still gets lucky. Boyd fired off another volley of shots, and both men ducked into cover. "And that, my man, is how it's done," he said as he climbed into the Jeep. As I speed off towards Emmettsville, I saw multiple muzzle flashes in the rear view mirror as Jackson must have emptied his pistol.

CHAPTER 37

Junior Estes killed Paul Deland.

Boyd and I both heard him confess. He claimed he did not mean to kill him, whatever that meant. It was an execution-style shooting. A .22 into the back of the head at close range. How would someone accidentally shoot someone in that manner? Murder. No doubt about that. Death was not an unintentional consequence of firing a gun into the back of someone's head.

We did not have a recording of the confession, but that did not matter. We knew. No more searching for who did it. Now we could concentrate on gathering evidence. Or better yet, letting Chief Parker gather the evidence in a legal manner. Emmettsville was a small town. Boyd and I were not even sure Chief Parker could get a search warrant at ten o'clock at night. Some judge would probably have to be woken up for that. Something that was most likely not a common experience in Felton County. I could already see the fumbling around as Chief Parker tried to figure out how best to get a warrant before morning.

Boyd could not understand why I was so adamant that Chief Parker get the warrant that night. The Estes brothers did not know that we had thrown a microphone in the back seat of their car, so they would not necessarily know they needed to get rid of the murder weapon. Of course, maybe they already had. Junior might have used a cheap Saturday night special like the idiot in Strasser's bar. No one gets attached to a $20 gun. Boyd was probably right, but my inner voice was still telling me to find the Chief and get him to act as soon as possible. I could not explain the urgency inside me either, but, like always, I trusted my inner voice.

Boyd and I were still in the Jeep. We had already called the police station from a pay phone and asked for the Chief. He was not there. We called his home. He did not answer. We went by his home. He was not there. We tried Eric's house and cruised by several of the bars and restaurants. No sign of him.

"Boyd, this whole thing is just weird as hell."

"How so?"

"Think about the circumstances, the timing, on the night of Paul's murder." Boyd urged me to continue. "Paul knows he owes Strasser money. He knows some guys are trying to collect. I think he even knew it was Junior, and that Junior lived in Emmettsville. But, on the day we all go hiking, he plans a dinner in Emmettsville on the way back. You've eaten at Falco's, was the food anything special?"

"No, not really. Just food."

"Exactly. Which means that Paul must have planned on meeting Junior at Falco's that night. It's probably why he went out to his car when he did. Maybe he was going to make a payment. Or he had all the money. But something went wrong out in that parking lot, or wherever Paul met with Junior. You heard Junior. He had not planned on killing Paul."

Boyd was staring at me, digesting everything I had just said. "This Paul guy, a friend of yours?"

"No. Until that day I had only met him at his parent's house a couple of times. Why?"

"Because, I think you are right. He planned on meeting Junior, or Jackson, or whomever, to either pay off his debt or negotiate for more time. Which makes him a fucking dick?" My head snapped towards Boyd as I arched my brows questioningly. "What kind of asshole plans on meeting with members of organized crime while out for dinner with a bunch of friends? A selfish, unthinking dick, that's who. His ass was in a sling because he had a gambling problem. No need to include others in his problem."

Boyd's revelation created an awkward silence. He was right. It was a dickhead thing to do. Paul should never have brought us into Emmettsville on the evening he was planning on meeting with members of the Dixie Mafia. My nostrils flared as I contemplated how I would have reacted if I had known Paul was meeting with the Dixie Mafia that night. I would have wanted to kick his ass for potentially endangering my friends.

Boyd finally broke the silence. "That doesn't mean I regret helping you, L.T. Nobody deserves to die over $15,000. And maybe this is callous to say, but this is the most fun I had since leaving the Marines. I mean it. I've screwed up a few times. I know that, but I could see myself doing this for a living."

"Investigating murders?"

"Investigating anything. No police force is ever going to touch me with this ankle. Best I could ever do would probably be a rent-a-cop security guard. No way. Private investigator, though. I'd be my own boss. Call my own shots. It wouldn't all be like this, I'm sure. Probably do divorces and crap like that to pay the bills, but I'm definitely going to look into being a private investigator when I get back to Huntsville."

Boyd Dallas, private investigator. It had a ring to it.

We were tired of looking for the Chief and decided to swing by the police station one last time. Officer Willis was working inside the station. He eyed me warily as he approached the front door. He opened an inner door into the glassed off foyer, but did not open the outer door. Instead, he yelled through the glass to ask me what I wanted. There was no use explaining anything to a man like Willis, so I told him to have the Chief call me as soon as possible.

My inner voice was grumbling as it realized it was not going to get its way. Boyd and I drove over to the Traveler's Inn and checked him out of the hotel. Boyd's job was done. My job was done. We had found Paul's killer exactly as I had promised my friend John. Ellie would be pleased. From here on out, it was all up to Chief Parker.

The next morning I woke up to the delightful smell of ham and eggs. The clatter of cookware emanated from outside my room along with the soft murmur of more than one voice. I looked at the time. A little after eight in the morning on a Tuesday. I donned some shorts and plodded out into the kitchen area. Boyd and Ellie were talking at the kitchen table. Ellie turned towards the sound of my footsteps. Boyd cast me a quick "I'm sorry" kind of look.

"Good morning, Ellie. What a pleasant surprise." I leaned in to give her a good morning kiss. She turned at the last moment and let me kiss her cheek. Probably didn't want me messing up her lipstick. Or maybe it was my morning breath. I need a quick cover story to explain Boyd's presence. "I see you've met Boyd again. He came up last night to deliver a car I bought from Huntsville. A 1968 Ford Mustang GT fastback. 390 cubic inch V8. Just like the one Steve McQueen drove in *Bullitt.*"

"Boys and their toys," said Ellie. "Three cars are not enough for a guy who walks almost everywhere?"

"Oh, I'll be selling it when I'm done. Should make a pretty penny. Going to sell the Mercedes too when I get it fixed up again."

Lying to my girlfriend yet again. But I had decided from the beginning that only Virgil and LeClair would know Boyd had helped me with my investigation. It was not a girlfriend thing. It was a civilian thing. Every one of us that sat at that table in LeClair's bar was former military. We all knew the importance of secrets. And we all knew that they were often unavoidable.

Maybe I was being silly. Maybe I was being stupid. But it was the way I wanted it, so it was the way it was going to be. At least until Junior was locked away. Then, maybe, I would let the cat out of the bag.

"Ellie, you will be glad to know that I'm officially done with the investigation."

"You're quitting?" Her mouth was agape.

"No, I'm done. I know who killed Paul."

The look on her face was priceless. "Who?"

"Junior Estes. And before you ask if I'm sure, let me tell you that I heard him confess with my own ears. He was talking to his brother and didn't know I was listening. He was the one hired to collect Paul's gambling debt, and something went wrong. I don't know why it went wrong, and I don't care. He did it. Now it's up to the Chief now to make sure justice is served. It was something he promised."

"So you aren't going to get Junior yourself?"

"No, I'm done. I did the Chief's investigation for him. It's up to him to make it all legal. Get a warrant, find the murder weapon. All that kind of stuff. I wrapped it up for him and put a ribbon on it for him."

"What about John? Didn't he want you to avenge Paul for him?"

"I don't do revenge. I do justice. Which reminds me, Strasser shouldn't be bothering you anymore either."

"Why not? What did you do?"

"I had a talk with him, face to face." Ellie's eyes bugged open. "Don't worry; it was no big deal. I was able to convince him that I knew he had nothing to do with Paul's murder and that he did not want me as an enemy. He was remarkably receptive to the idea."

"You threatened a crime boss? My god, L.T. Are you crazy?"

In my heart of heart, I always knew I would find Paul's killer. Maybe not in a week and a half, but I knew I would solve the case. Then I would put it all behind me and lead a normal life again. Somewhere along the line, investigating Paul's death had started to feel more *normal* than abnormal. If felt right. It felt just. It felt righteous. I liked the feeling. My girlfriend did not share my feelings. Not once had she congratulated me. No "job well done." Not even a trace of elation that it was all over.

The night after stopping Tom Harty, I had warned her that I was not a nice guy. I was not benign. Sometimes, true altruism requires a departure from the niceties of life. Sometimes in life, the gloves have to come off. Sacrifices have to be made. At times, the nicest thing you can do for one person is to hit another person over the head. Or threaten a crime boss.

I answered the best way I knew how. "Well, crazy about you, so it was worth the risk."

Nothing. No smile. No thank you. She was stone-faced. Ellie asked a few more questions, some I was able to answer, the ones that might have implicated Boyd, I sidestepped. Worry crossed her face when I told her that I had not been able to reach Chief Parker yet, although I expected him to call soon.

After a few more minutes she got up to leave for work. I walked her to the front door and opened my arms for a hug, which she returned. Once again, she allowed me to kiss her on the cheek. "By the way," she said, "I notice you still haven't got that TV." Unlike the last time she said that to me, this time there was no teasing tone to her voice. She left for work without looking back once.

When I returned to the kitchen table, Boyd apologized. Ellie had let herself in with her key caught Boyd. He told her that he was just visiting, which she seemed to accept. "We were having a pretty friendly conversation until you came out here. After that, you could cut the tension in the room with a knife."

"So you noticed it too, huh?"

"Notice it? You could feel it, dude. It permeated the room like a bad fart. I don't envy you; you have your work cut out."

"No shit, Sherlock."

"Don't Sherlock me. You're Sherlock; I'm Watson."

"Watson was a doctor, you know."

"Yeah, I know, but it also says he was a *good* doctor," he said with a mocking tone. "Besides, you can't be both Sherlock and Watson, and I say you are Sherlock."

I said, "I won't argue with you. Just know I couldn't have done this without you."

"Oh, I know that. You still be fumbling around trying to—."

The telephone interrupted Boyd. It was Chief Parker. We exchanged hellos.

"I understand you were trying to reach me last night."

"I was."

"What's up?"

"I found Paul's killer last night. Eric is off the hook."

"Let me guess, someone who works for Darwin Strasser, a Dixie Mafia boss down in Tupelo."

"No. Where did you ever get that idea?"

"Jackson Estes called me early this morning and told me that he figured out who killed Mr. Deland. He told me that everywhere he turns, he keeps running into you and that you keep harassing him and his brother. So, to get you off his back, he did his own little investigation and found the killer himself. The guy was hired by Strasser to collect the gambling debt, and he got carried away and killed him instead."

What in the world is Jackson up to now? That was the first thing that came to mind. Jackson, the brains of the outfit, was trying to find a way to work the angles. He was getting squeezed on two sides, and he needed to try and get Chief Parker on his side. A nice counter-move on his part. Too bad I knew he was bluffing.

"Chief, one of Strasser's men didn't kill Paul. Junior killed Paul. I heard him say it with my own ears. I threw a bug in the back of their car last night and listened to their entire conversation. Junior said it was an accident, but he said it out loud. No doubt about it."

"A bug?"

"You know, a small covert listening device."

"I know what a bug is. You threw one in the back of their car? And you overheard Junior admit it?"

"You bet your ass, I did. And I have a witness. Someone that was in the car with me. Chief, I followed the brothers down to Tupelo last night and watched them kidnap one of Strasser's men. When I caught up with them later, they didn't have the man with them anymore. My guess is he is the one they are going to try and pin this on. Just like they tried with Eric."

Complete silence on the other end of the phone. He was obviously trying to digest all the new information.

"You have a witness, you say? This witness own a machine gun?"

"Not that I'm aware of." It was a true statement. An MP5 uses pistol ammunition, which makes it a submachine gun; machine guns use rifle ammunition. I was always amazed at how many people were not aware of the distinction. Regardless, I was a little surprised that Jackson told the Chief about our little encounter last night.

"So no one shot up their car last night just south of the Tennessee border?"

"I didn't say that. You asked about a machine gun. If one were to study Jackson's Buick forensically, I'm positive they would only find 9mm bullets. Don't believe everything you hear, Chief. Let's get to the brass tacks of the situation, Chief. Junior killed Paul. It's a damn fact. I wrapped this all up for you; now it's your job to find the murder weapon and other evidence. I'm done. If you need help, I suggest you call Mark Sande of the Tennessee Bureau of Investigation in Memphis and ask for their help. They can't help without you asking. Trust me, I know."

"Just like that, you're done?"

"What else you want me to do? I can't arrest them. Me doctor, you cop. That's how this works, remember."

"But what about proof of what you're saying. Jackson swears it was some guy named Raymond that works for Strasser."

"Chief, I didn't promise you proof, at least not proof that will stand up in court. I promised you I would find the killer, which I did. Junior Estes. Besides, this Raymond fellow you are talking about. I pulled a Raven HP25 off of him a couple of days ago. Anyone stupid enough to be carrying a .25 caliber Ring of Fire Handgun is not smart enough to pull off an execution-style shooting and remember to wipe the car down and not leave any prints. Regardless, I'm still done. Get a warrant. Tap their phones. You will find what you need, trust me."

"So you didn't tape it?"

There was something strange in the Chief's voice, some queer aspect in his voice inflection. He knew Boyd, and I had recorded the conversation Junior had with Strasser's goons. But I never told him about that tape. And neither Junior nor Jackson knew of the tape either. Only Strasser knew. And some agents down at the TBI.

"Oh, I taped it. I always tape everything. I was a Navy spy, remember." I was lying my ass off about the tape. "Of course, the tape would not be admissible in court. So you would still have to get your own evidence."

Chief Parker went quiet again. It was nearly a full minute before he started speaking again.

"I guess this is where we part ways then, huh?"

"Unless you are going to deputize me and get me a warrant to record them, then there is nothing more I can do within the confines of the law."

"Why let the law confine you now? You, or your friend, shot up their car last night, and you've been illegally recording people all over Felton County."

"I am neither confirming nor denying what you say, Chief. I can tell you are irritated with me, and I'm sorry I wasn't able to give you a murder weapon. But you have to admit, I fulfilled my end of the bargain. Plus, things have heated up between the Estes boys and me to the point that it's best we not run into each other again."

"I'm sorry, Doc. You are right. Thanks for everything. I'll let you know when I've busted Junior. Bye."

We both hung up. It was obvious Chief Parker was not happy. I couldn't understand why. Unless he was so far in over his head that he didn't know how to investigate a case even when pointed in the right direction. That was not my problem, though. Maybe John was not going to be happy either. Once again, not my problem. Like I told Ellie; I don't do revenge. If I could forgive the drunk that killed my dad, then John would have to settle for justice himself, not revenge.

"Boyd, it's time to get you home. I don't have to work today, so why don't we pack you up and I'll drive you back to Huntsville."

"You're forgetting something."

"What?"

"Brent and Daryl."

"Crap, I forgot all about those two douchebags. I guess we'll give them a ride down to Tupelo. Seems like the right thing to do. Man, they are going to stink to high heaven."

Boyd and I both laughed at the image of Brent and Daryl stuck inside a panel van with a bunch of power bars, bottled water, and a smelly five-gallon bucket. My smile disappeared as I contemplated the thought of cleaning up the van before returning it to LeClair. *If they tipped over that bucket, I might break their fingers after all.*

It took a little over an hour to shower and pack Boyd's stuff into the Mustang. While locking my door, I heard my phone ring. I almost decided not to answer it. I was glad I did; it was Chief Parker again.

"Doc, I've talked to Jackson. I told him about the tape you have of him and Junior. It didn't scare him at all. He knows it is worthless, legally speaking."

"Okay, so Jackson is smart. Be smarter, Chief, and remember you got the law on your side."

"I wasn't finished, McCain. It's worse than you think. They have decided to stop implicating Raymond, and are going back to framing Eric. Somehow, I don't know how exactly, they have planted Eric's DNA on the gun used to kill Paul Deland. They have hidden the gun and are going to call the State Police and tell them they saw Eric burying it. We are right back where we started. They can mess up my son's life real bad."

"Why do I get the impression there is a great big 'but' at the end of this?"

"They are willing to call a truce. If I give them $15,000 to give to Strasser to keep him off their back, they will tell me where they buried the gun."

"That's a stupid plan. Once you have the gun, there's nothing to keep you from going after them again."

"Yeah, that's what I thought. You said Jackson is smart. He knows how fond you are of taping things, so he wants both of us there when he tells us where it's at. He also wants you to tape the entire conversation and give him the tape."

Well, shit, Jackson might be smarter than I thought. He was up to something. He was probably planning on directing the conversation in such a manner that we might say something that could implicate us in criminal activity. We could take him down, but he would make sure he could take us down as well. Mutual annihilation can be a wonderful deterrent. The United States and the Soviet Union both based their nuclear weapon policies on the same prospect.

Of course, I could just avoid the problem by not meeting with Jackson. The problem was that if I sat out on the meeting, Jackson would make sure Eric was framed for the crime. Eric's DNA was already on the tee shirt used to tie Paul to the steering wheel. And now they had DNA evidence linking the gun used on Paul to Eric as well. I was faced with a dilemma. Promises had been made to John and Chief Parker to find the killer, which naturally implied the killer would be brought to justice, not someone else taking the blame for something they didn't do. I was not sure I was willing to take more chances, make more sacrifices to the cause.

CHAPTER 38

In the end, I decided to go along with the Chief to meet with Jackson, but I was adamant about picking the time and the place. No one in their right mind should ever agree to meet with someone they don't trust on their terms. Control the time and location. One of the things they taught me in Naval Intelligence. And if you can't control both, then at least control the location. We had decided to meet at the Chief's cabin at 7:00 p.m. Chief Parker called back later and informed me that Jackson agreed to both. I know I should have been happy about that, but, truth be told, it left me a little unsettled.

Boyd, on the other hand, seemed almost happy we were back in the fray of things. He kept insisting he had a good feeling about today. I did not share his optimism, and neither did my inner voice. *It's a trap.* I kept hearing the words over and over inside my head. I was of the same opinion; I had learned long ago not to argue with my inner voice.

Boyd was already packed, so preparations for the evening were easy. I grabbed both Glocks and the extra magazines and jumped into my Jeep. Boyd followed me in the Mustang. An hour later we pulled up to the Chief's cabin, seven hours before my scheduled meeting. The U-Haul panel van was still parked in the shade. The log chains holding the back lift door were still in place.

I motioned for Boyd to cover me while I unlocked the lift door. "Brent, Daryl, I'm letting you guys go, so don't try anything. Graham will have a 9mm trained in your direction just in case. Please acknowledge."

Brent answered, informing me that both of them were away from the door. As expected, the horrific smell of human feces and ammonia hit my nostrils like a freight train as I lifted the door. Brent and Daryl were sitting near the front of the truck away from the door squinting as their eyes tried to acclimate to the overabundance of light. I suppose I should have pitied them. I didn't.

The two men staggered towards the front of the truck. They were stiff, their movements slow and guarded. Spending two days and nights in the back of a U-Haul was not like staying at the Ritz. Both men plopped out of the back of the van onto the awaiting ground, their eyes still acclimating.

"You're really letting us go?" Daryl must have learned to keep his mouth shut around me; he was letting Brent do all the talking.

"Yep, with your fingers still intact. Your boss and I have called a truce. Not only that, but Graham is going to give you a ride down to Tupelo and drop you off at the front door of that horrible looking bar. Now, I need both of you to look at me for a second. Brent Stephens of 649 Oriole Street, Daryl McGregor of 181 Route P, I never, ever want to see either of you again. I don't want to accidentally run into you two down on Beale Street having a good time. I don't want to pull over to help a stranded motorist and find out it's one of you two douchebags. I don't want to be vacationing on Borneo and see you playing in the surf. If you're going to retrieve your car, send someone else to pick it up for you. You catching my drift?"

Daryl nodded, Brent answered in the affirmative.

Boyd and I let them stretch their legs while I contemplated how I was going to restrain the two men in the back of the car. Life in the back of a van for two days had been pretty hard on them, so I tried to find a comfortable arrangement for them. However, with no partition separating the front from the back, I eventually settled on lots of zip ties in numerous places. *Safety first, I always say.*

Once I finished restraining the men inside the Mustang, Boyd took me out of ear's reach and argued against meeting with Jackson alone tonight. I reminded him that the Chief would also be there, which did little to allay his concerns. Boyd reminded me that Tupelo was only about an hour and a half away; he could be back in plenty of time to watch my back. I told him to go home. He had done a fantastic job. One worthy of praise. He really should look into being a private investigator, especially if the company he worked for would still let him play with their wonderful toys. It was not an easy argument, but one that I won in the end.

Another thing they taught during my time with the Office of Naval Intelligence was to arrive early to any meeting location and properly scope it out ahead of time. I had over six hours until the meeting. More than enough time.

Chief Parker's cabin was, in fact, a log cabin. It looked like the real thing. A thick, sturdy, attractive one story cabin with plenty of windows and an inviting front porch. The cabin was large for a weekend getaway hunting cabin, probably 1600 square feet, with electricity running to the cabin. A TV satellite dish sat atop the building. Chief Parker had splurged and went in for gray sheet metal roofing that added a nice touch. The cabin sat on flat ground surrounded by forest on all four sides. On the west side, the ground rose slowly, yet substantially, forming a large, long hill. I walked off approximately 40 yards of clearing around the house on all four sides.

If my math was correct, that meant the cabin sat in the middle of a little over an acre and a quarter. One small building sat around the back of the cabin that I assumed was the well house. There was only one entrance, a quarter mile long, winding, sparsely graveled driveway cut through the forest on the front. I'd never hunted a day in my life, but if I did, Chief Parker's cabin looked like the way to do it right.

My reconnaissance took a little over 45 minutes. Not even two in the afternoon yet. I saw no reason to sit for over five hours, so I drove into town and grabbed lunch at Ray's diner. If all went well, it would be quite some time before I came to Emmettsville again, and I looked forward to seeing the pleasant gentleman once again. I took my time. Ordered another apple pie and ice cream. Drank three large teas. And I still got back to Chief Parker's cabin by four. Three hours to kill, which I spent cleaning out the back of the van. I even found a hose around the back of the cabin.

Boyd did not like anything about L.T.'s plan, which involved sending him home before his meeting with Jackson. The Estes brothers were backed into a corner trying to fend off a three-pronged attack. It appeared to Boyd that they might have fought off the Chief for now and were maneuvering to get Strasser and L.T. off their back as well. They were desperate, and desperate times call for desperate measures. That's what worried Boyd. Even a cornered mouse will try and fight when it's left with no other options.

L.T's solution to the problem: have him deliver the Stinky Brothers, Brent and Daryl, back to Tupelo. *Screw them; they could find their own way home.* Boyd had half a mind to ignore L.T.'s orders and let them out right then and there and let them hitch it the rest of the way. Of course, who in their right mind would pick up two scruffy, stinking rednecks.

He was roughly 15 minutes outside of Tupelo when he heard Daryl whisper, "Where the fuck do you think they're going?"

Brent answered, "Shut up, man. I don't know. Who cares? We're almost there."

Boyd said, "What are you two talking about? Who did you just see? Someone in those two cars I just saw?"

Daryl said, "I don't know what you're talking about. I didn't see anyone."

"Yeah, right. You're a terrible liar, dipshit. How about you, Brent, you standing by your dimwitted friend's answer? Remember, 70 kills, Brent Stephens."

Boyd allowed Brent a few extra seconds to ponder over his last statement

"Those were our guys that just passed us goin' the other direction. The second car was Strasser's."

Boyd looked at his watch and checked the time. "See, that wasn't so hard. As a reward, I'm going to take you guys all the way to the bar instead of making you walk the next 15 miles."

Strasser's parking lot was empty when Boyd arrived 15 minutes later. He snipped Brent's right hand loose with a pair of diagonal cutters, then handed him the pliers. "Cut yourself loose. Then cut your idiot friend loose. Then get the hell out of my car. Remember, what Dr. McCain told you; he doesn't want to see you ever again. Me, you won't ever see me again, because if I see you, then I'll make sure you never see anything ever again."

L.T. had told them that Boyd was a contract killer. It seemed like a good idea to keep the legend going. It took over five minutes for Brent to cut both of them loose. Boyd's fixed his SIG on them as they slowly exited the car. Once they were away from the car, he jumped in the Mustang and sped off toward Emmettsville. Sometimes a Sergeant has to disobey his Lieutenant; this seemed like one of those times.

* * *

Cleaning the U-Haul was dirty work. It reminded me a visit to my grandfather's farm as a kid. Smelly. I was cooling off resting on the porch swing sipping from one of my water bottles when Chief Parker arrived in his official Sheriff Department vehicle. He was in uniform. Crisp creases in the olive colored pants and khaki shirt. No tie or hat, but otherwise real official looking. Usually, he just had on dark jeans, a khaki shirt, and his badge. Another new feature was his duty belt. It was the first time I had seen him wear one. The duty belt was simple. There was no baton, no chemical spray, no flashlight, no radio, no taser. Just a black leather belt equipped with two sets of handcuffs and a couple of Speedloaders for the Smith & Wesson .357 N-frame revolver he was wearing. The .357 was a surprise. Especially since a man of his slight build was carrying the large N-frame. Regardless, it was a great gun. I did not own any revolvers, but if I did, a Smith & Wesson N-frame .357 would have been my second choice, right after the Colt Python.

"First time I've seen you with a gun, Chief. You thinking this might go poorly?"

"Honestly, I don't know what to expect, other than expecting the unexpected seems like a good rule of thumb. Remember, until a couple of days ago I didn't even know we had organized crime in our town. By the way, you're early."

"You have no idea, Chief. I was here at noon."

"Holy cow, I thought a half hour was early."

"Navy spy, remember. By the way, I've seen nothing suspicious in the whole time I've been here. No sign of the Estes A-holes. Or anyone else for that matter."

Chief Parker pulled out a key and opened the front door of the cabin. "I would offer you a drink, but you don't look like you need one. Need to use the facilities?"

"No, I'm good. I've been watering your lawn all afternoon."

"Glad to know it was only watering. Give a quick tour, then?"

"Sure. Nice looking place on the outside; it would be nice to see what the inside looks like."

Chief Parker escorted me in and gave me a guided tour. It was an attractive three bedroom, two bath log cabin. Rustic decor, fireplace, elevated ceilings. I liked it. Right up until I heard the unmistakable sound of a revolver hammer being cocked into place while I was examining the kitchen. Maybe I should have been surprised, but with all the twists and turns of the last few days, the whole thing seemed almost natural. I turned to see the Chief pointing the .357 directly at me. The hammer was cocked. His finger was on the trigger.

"This is how it's going to play out, huh, Chief? So my original assumption that you were a dirty cop was…?"

"False." The look on his face said it all. Sorrow mixed with fear. He was not a dirty cop, but he was a desperate man. "You don't have kids. You don't know how it is. What lengths you will go to, to keep them safe."

"Whatever is going to help you sleep at night, Chief. You won't get away with it, you know. No offense, you just lack the temerity and expertise to pull this off without getting caught, even if you are a good liar. Plus, you have to realize by now, since you talked with both Strasser and Jackson, that I have not been acting alone."

"What makes you think I've been talking to Strasser?"

"You knew I taped Strasser's men talking with Junior. I never told you that. Jackson didn't know either. Care to tell me how this is going down?"

"Sure, I guess. After you and your friend shot up Jackson's car last night, they were stranded. Strasser and his men were planning on coming into Emmettsville and finishing them when they came across them just sitting by their car. Instead of a firefight, cooler heads prevailed, and they reached an agreement. They were no longer going to attack each other and instead were going to focus everything on eliminating you. The only problem was that they weren't exactly sure how. You kept outsmarting them."

"Yeah, I'm smart, they're dumb. Can we just fast forward to why you're pointing a gun at me?"

"I'm here because they aren't as dumb as you think. Jackson approached me telling me that they had the DNA evidence I told you about earlier. If I didn't go along with setting you up, then Eric would be framed for murder. Plain and simple. Sorry, but family is family, and my son is innocent. I can't let him take the fall for something he didn't do." He actually looked remorseful.

"They will own you, Chief. You will be their bitch from here on out."

"I don't care. It's all about my son."

"Well, shit. You sound convinced. Do it, then."

Chief Parker still had the gun extended in his right hand. It had been for the last couple of minutes, which meant it had to be getting tired. And tired makes for sloppy. I could already see the front end of the gun dropping a little.

"Not here."

"That's where you're wrong, Chief. You're going to have to shoot me right here in your own damn kitchen. No way am I going to make this easier on you. Forensically, you'll never get the blood out of the cracks in this floor. If you were going to kill someone in your kitchen, you should have put down tile." The Chief's confidence was slipping. "And before you say, no big deal, remember, I still have associates who know I'm here, and I've been keeping Special Agent Sande abreast of my comings and goings."

It was a lie; however, it was a good one. Whatever confidence remained inside Chief Parker was completely eroded at the mention of Agent Sande. His head hung low, possibly in shame. The front of the gun dropped a little further.

Without warning, I sprung into action, stepping forward with my left foot while pivoting and ducking at the same time to add both a vertical and lateral component to my evasive maneuver, making it twice as hard for the Chief to track me with his revolver. For a split second, my back was to the Chief as I was closing the 15-foot gap between us. When I spun back around, now seven feet closer, I noticed the Chief had reflexively raised his right arm. His tired right arm over compensated. His aim was too high. Plus, I was still ducked. The high-pitched crack of the .357 reverberated through the cabin stinging my ears. His shot was not even close. Bewilderment spread across his face as I grabbed the revolver with my left hand and pushed the revolver even further away from my body. The Chief's left hand came up to help wrestle with the gun. Just like Tom Harty, all his attention was focused on the gun.

My right hand smashed into his face. I both felt and heard the crunch of cartilage as his nose broke. He did not go down, though; instead, he managed to pull off another shot with his revolver. Although the bullet was nowhere near me, I felt the heat from the blast on my hand. Instinct told me to let go, but I ignored my instinct. Training told me to hold on tight to the gun to prevent the cylinder from turning so that he could fire another shot. My right arm cocked back to prepare for another blow; however, in what must have been a delayed reaction, Chief Parker let go of his revolver and his eyes rolled up into the back of his head before falling to the ground. I easily had 80 pounds on the Chief, and I had let him have every ounce of my weight. His adrenaline must have kept him standing a few seconds longer after his brain function got interrupted, because, ultimately, a concussion is a concussion, and Chief Parker's brain could not do anything to help fight off the disabling effects of being knocked unconscious.

CHAPTER 39

Chief Parker regained consciousness approximately 20 seconds after hitting the floor. More than enough time for me to pat him down for any other hidden weapons. The Smith & Wesson was his only gun. Chief Parker lifted his head and then dropped it back down onto the floor in despair. He had played his cards. He had come up short. The only thing left was to wait and see what I had in store for him.

"I'm sorry," he said, "I had to try."

I waved off his apology. I was not in the mood. "Well, you failed. You know why?" He shook his head no. "Just like your son, you lacked commitment and conviction. You were wrong, and you knew it." The realization was all over his face. "So, what's the contingency plan? Smart guy like Jackson would have a contingency plan?"

"Why would I tell you?"

"Because you are sorry. Truly sorry. However, you still hope to come out of this with your son not going to jail, and you've suddenly realized I am your best hope."

"I have, have I?"

"Yes, you have."

He sat up and leaned against a table leg of the large kitchen table. His wheels were spinning as he weighed and reweighed his options and counter-options. It looked like he was having one hell of an internal struggle.

"Funny thing about truth, Chief. It always wins in the end. Be on the side of truth. You can still wear the white hat in this story. You know, be a good guy. Help me he—."

My sentence was cut short by the sight and sound of breaking glass slightly to my right, followed by the report of a high-powered rifle. Chief Parker didn't need to speak; I had just discovered the contingency plan. Instinctively, I flattened myself against the floor and crawled over to the window. Tried to spy around and see where the shot came from without getting my head blown off. Another shot hit the wood just below the window frame. In a regular frame house, I probably would have been shot as the bullet traveled through the exterior siding, insulation, and interior drywall. I smiled as I realized that bullets would have very little chance of penetrating the thick exterior logs.

Once the men outside realized their bullets were not penetrating, the next logical step would be to breach the house. Entrances needed to be secured. The deadbolt on the back kitchen door was still in place. Regardless, I shoved the heavy kitchen table against the door. It would not prevent them from entering, but it would slow them down enough that I should be able to pick off anyone that tried.

"Chief! You on my side or not? Help me with the front door. Let's get that sofa over there."

Chief Parker stood up, yet hesitated, still unsure if he should help the man he tried to shoot a few minutes ago. *Screw it; I'll get the couch over there myself.* I bolted for the front door. Too late. The front door flew open. A man holding a pistol was standing just outside the doorway. He was prepared to shoot. I dropped onto my belly to get out of the line of fire. At the same time, a grimace appeared on the man's face as he jerked his right foot. Instead of shooting, he howled in pain. For some reason, it looked as if the man's right foot had partially exploded.

Contemplating his foot for more than a split second would have been a waste of time. The man was still standing. He was still holding the gun. Still on my belly, I pulled my Glock from my holster, aimed, and squeezed off four quick successive shots. Each shot landed center mass. Momentum equals mass times velocity, and what the .45 ACP lacks in velocity, it more than makes up for in bullet mass. A fact impressively displayed as the man was knocked off the front porch into the yard.

Panic started to creep in as I realized the man I just shot was one of Strasser's men from the bar. Chief Parker had said that Jackson and Strasser had reached an agreement; however, I expected the Estes boys to be the ones attacking me, not Strasser. Maybe Jackson and his crew were out there as well. Either way, I was not sure how many men were outside waiting for me. I showed up seven hours early, and I still got played. *Damn it.*

I rushed to the front door and locked it, then pushed the couch in front of the door. The open layout of the house allowed me to see both the front door and rear door simultaneously, as well as all windows in that half of the house. However, I was going to be vulnerable to anyone that climbed through a bedroom window. Once again, I created a barricade, this time between the hallway to the bedrooms and myself. I threw the Chief's recliners on top of each other as well as using his kitchen chairs and a coffee table. To my surprise, nobody fired any shots through the window during that time.

"Chief, if you're not going to help, at least throw me those Speedloaders." He just stared ahead. "Chief, the damn Speedloaders. Now!"

Without a word, he handed over three Speedloaders. Eighteen rounds, plus the four remaining in his revolver. Nine left in the Glock, along with 13 rounds in an extra magazine, 44 rounds total. Half in a gun that I had never fired before. *Great.* Unfortunately, the other two magazines for my .45 were in the Jeep, along with my 9mm and its two extra magazines.

It was quiet. Too quiet. They were planning something out there. I just knew it. Unlike in the stupid movies where the bad guys simply shoot into the house from every direction with automatic weapons, it never happens like that. They would try to breach the perimeter somewhere.

❋ ❋ ❋

For the first time in his life, Boyd shot someone.

Before getting set up in the woods above Chief Parker's cabin, Boyd sped back to Emmettsville in time to witness Strasser and his men getting a room at the hotel across from Falco's. Strasser checked into Room 119. The rest of his seven men filled various other rooms. He had no idea what they were doing in Emmettsville. It didn't matter. They needed to be watched. So he watched them. Around six, all the men except Strasser loaded up into two of the three cars and headed out. Within minutes, it became obvious that the men were heading to Chief Parker's cabin. He wished he could say he had been surprised.

When they stopped at the entrance to Parker's driveway, Boyd drove on past. At the first available turnout, he parked the car and unloaded his .300 Win Mag and H&K. He loaded ammunition into a backpack and ran off into the woods. The house was to his east. Exact distance was unknown. Running on the leaf-covered, uneven ground reminded him why no police force would ever hire him. His fused ankle made it difficult to compensate for the tiny surface variations. It did not hurt; it simply made running difficult and slow. His doctor said the fusion would always affect his proprioception. Boyd had to look that term up to fully understand it. It simply meant the fusion made it difficult for his brain to interpret where his foot was in space. He never really noticed when walking on even ground, but after his first trip to the white sandy beaches of Gulf Shores, he understood what the doctor meant.

It wasn't pretty, and he nearly fell twice, but Boyd managed to find the cabin. From the top of the long hill to the west of the cabin, he had a great view of the front side of the cabin and a portion of the back yard. L.T.'s Jeep was parked near the front, but no sign of L.T. Boyd noticed a small flicker of movement on the front porch. A small animal maybe. The movement disappeared and reappeared a second later. He set the binoculars to the maximum magnification. Something small disappeared and reappeared again. Boyd laughed when he realized what he was seeing. L.T. was swinging on a porch swing, seemingly without a care in the world. The overhang of the porch had blocked Boyd's view. What he was seeing was L.T.'s foot disappear and reappear as he swung.

Boyd guessed he was about 250 yards from the house. Getter closer had not crossed his mind until he realized his view of the front door was blocked. It only took a few minutes to reposition himself a little further down the hill with a slightly better view of the front door.

The sound of tires crunching on gravel reached Boyd while he was scanning the woods around the cabin for other signs of human life. It was a police cruiser. Boyd watched it travel along the winding driveway and stop near L.T.'s Jeep. A small, wiry man exited the car alone. Chief Parker. In full-service uniform. Wearing a duty belt. Interesting.

And odd. Boyd had secretly observed Chief Parker before and noticed he never wore a gun. Boyd could not help but wonder if the Chief was expecting trouble of some sort. Which made sense. What didn't make sense was how the Chief drove directly past Strasser's men without any apparent problems. Something fishy was going on.

The Chief walked up to L.T., who stopped swinging but did not stand up. There was a minute or two of conversation before Boyd observed both men enter the front door of the beautiful log cabin.

Boyd set up his observation area as a potential sniper position. He extended the bipod on the Win Mag and inserted a magazine while placing two extra, fully loaded magazines on the ground to the right of the rifle. His laser range finder verified he was 227 yards from the front door. He put on his tactical belt and loaded two thirty round magazines for the H&K and four magazines for his SIG.

He didn't have a ghillie suit, but he did have a camouflage blanket in his backpack, which he extracted and placed over his back before assuming a prone firing position. All in all, Boyd realized he had a pretty good shooting position. Plenty of trees for cover, yet the woods were thin enough to allow him multiple shooting lanes through the trees. Elevated position with a good view of the front of the building. No brush that needed to be cut back in front of him. Sun was behind him. The wind was coming from behind him as well. And 227 yards was an easy shot, even with the changing elevation from position to target.

He was ready. Hopefully, all his firepower would not be needed, but he wasn't getting a warm fuzzy about those chances. All that was left to do was wait. Something he was damn good at.

Movement in the timber on the back side of the house caught Boyd's eye. He panned his scope in that direction. Two men were standing just outside of the perimeter of the yard. They were not standing together. *Shit, it's Tyler and Junior.* Both had rifles slung over the shoulders. Junior was smoking a cigarette. Tyler was resting against a tree. The civilian method of waiting, but what were they waiting for?

Things just kept getting more interesting. Chief Parker and L.T. were inside the cabin. Junior and Tyler were in the timber behind the cabin. Jackson was nowhere to be found. And Strasser's men had parked at the entrance to the driveway, although Boyd highly doubted they were still sitting there.

Boyd started panning his rifle on the woods in front of the house. His suspicions were correct; he spotted five different men fanned out in front of the house a few yards inside the line of trees. They were also waiting. Two men were unaccounted for.

Boyd mentally tagged the location of the men he spotted, including Junior and Tyler. He frequently shifted his attention looking for any sign of a change in the status quo. Any sign of aggression. Strasser and the Estes brothers had probably declared war on each other, and Boyd's friend was in the middle. When the Hatfields and McCoys started shooting at each other, hopefully L.T. would remember to duck and let them take themselves out.

More movement at the back of the house. Through the Leupold scope, Boyd observed Junior finishing his cigarette and readying his rifle. Tyler pushed himself away from the tree and unslung his rifle. They glanced at each other. As if on cue, both men raised their rifles and aimed them at the cabin, or so it seemed from his angle. A couple of seconds later, Junior fired. A 30-06, no doubt about it. A popular hunting round among whitetail deer hunters. A second shot rang out.

Boyd was preparing to fire at Junior when a man holding a handgun bolted from the woods and ran to the front door of the cabin. The man reached out and opened the front door, then raised his pistol. The son of a bitch was getting ready to shoot inside the cabin. Maybe he was aiming at L.T. The man took one step forward, which due to the angle of the roof overhanging the porch meant the only thing Boyd could see was the man's feet. He did the only thing he could think of. He shot the man in the right foot.

For the first time in his life, Boyd shot someone.

The man jerked his right foot in an obvious reaction to the pain he must have felt as the large 180-grain bullet tore through the tiny, fragile bones in his foot. Boyd had no time to contemplate the pain the man must have been feeling because less than a second later the man was thrown backward off the porch into the front yard. A split second after that, Boyd heard the sound of four quick bursts of gunfire.

Oh shit, this is getting real. Boyd realized L.T. must have shot the man. The ten times magnification on his scope enabled him to see blood oozing from the man's chest from four different holes. Relief washed over Boyd as he realized that meant all four shots he heard came from inside the cabin.

The man on the ground was as good as dead. His limbs were moving, which meant his brain was still functioning, but he would bleed out and die of exsanguination. Focusing on the dead or dying was a waste of time, so Boyd started scanning the front of the house for other immediate threats.

He spotted five of Strasser's men, six if he included the one dying, which meant one was still unaccounted for. The five men were all hiding behind trees. None were looking in his direction. They were whipping their heads around trying to find where Boyd's shot came from, but none were focusing their attention in his direction. Contrary to popular belief, suppressors do not completely silence a gun, especially when the gun is a high-powered rifle. It's basically impossible to do that, especially considering because a supersonic bullet still causes a crack as it breaks the sound barrier. The "whoosh" sound a person hears in the movies is bullshit. But it still masks the location of the shot, which was good enough for Boyd. He really, really loved his suppressor.

Boyd directed his attention to the back of the cabin again. Junior was no longer visible. Tyler was standing up against a tree with his rifle aimed at the house, probably covering the windows as Junior or Jackson advanced. It was time to provide L.T. some more help. The tree prevented a kill shot into the body, but Tyler had one knee jutting out from behind the tree. 270 plus yards and his target was a knee. Well, he hit a foot earlier with no time to line up the shot like he wanted, so the knee seemed like a piece of cake.

Aim. Relax. Breathe. Squeeze. Fire. An 180-grain bullet hitting a human knee at over 3000 feet per second is truly disastrous. With over five times the energy of a bullet fired from a pistol, even an extremity wound caused by a rifle can be deadly. Bone can turn to dust. Arteries completely severed. Luckily for Tyler, the bullet ripped through the tissue a couple of inches above the knee. Any lower and he might have lost his right leg. Either way, he ran the risk of dying due to rapid blood loss; Boyd got the impression his shot hit Tyler's femoral artery.

Tyler seemed to no longer be a threat, so Boyd panned his rifle to the front of the cabin again. The suppressor was still doing its job. Strasser's men were looking around for the source of the crack. He could hear them yelling, asking each other where the shots were coming from. None of them were moving from their perceived safe spots.

He panned the rifle to the right once more trying to find Junior. He was still not visible, although Boyd noticed Tyler was on the ground holding his leg trying to stop the rapid flow of blood from his leg. An arterial wound, and a bad one at that. If he did not get medical care soon, he was probably as good as dead within a couple of minutes.

For the moment, all was quiet. Boyd was unsure how to proceed. Should he shoot some of Strasser's men and force them to leave the current battle zone? Or should he wait until one of them became aggressive again, which would force him to shoot? He was pretty sure he was going to be responsible for Tyler's death soon. The idea of more bloodshed was not appealing. Waiting seemed like the best option, except he realized that three men, Junior, Jackson, and one of Strasser's men were still unaccounted for. That realization was unsettling.

* * *

Something strange was going on. I knew it. I saw that man's foot explode before I shot him. It made no sense. It also made no sense that no one was trying to get inside. I crawled to the front window and peeked around one of the edges fully expecting to have shots fired at me. However, that was not what happened, so I grew a little bolder and took a longer look. The man I shot was twitching. Not dead. Yet.

I stared a little longer, just long enough to see two more men standing about 50 yards away whipping their heads around looking for something. Or someone.

"I just killed one of Strasser's men, Chief. How many more are there, do you know?"

Numbly, flatly, he responded, "All of them."

"What the hell does that mean? A number. I need a number. Five! Six! Seven?"

He lit up a little at the mention of number seven. "Seven. Plus, three more."

"Let me guess: Junior, Jackson, and Tyler."

The Chief simply nodded. *Great, nine more guys.* I probably would not have to kill them all; I figured the fight should drain out of them pretty quickly if I managed to get three or four more. Still, that meant there were still a lot of people who could throw hot lead my direction.

"You do realize they were going to kill you too, don't you Chief? They didn't wait to see if you were successful before shooting at us. You notice that? Damn, Chief. You had no leverage. What the hell were you thinking?"

Browbeating the Chief was a waste of time, and I knew it. I walked into a trap just the same as he did. A pretty clever trap at that. Convince the Chief to double cross me, then double cross him and remove both threats. Jackson was smarter than I had expected. I had underestimated him.

Only the Chief failed, and they were down one man. And somebody shot the dead man's foot shortly before I shot him. Maybe Estes and Strasser called off their apparent truce.

I spotted one of Strasser's goons approximately 50 yards away moving toward the cabin. Hitting him from that distance seemed unlikely, so I grabbed the .357 and quickly fired off two rounds through the front window, forcing him to rush back into cover. Better to waste rounds with the unfamiliar gun.

"You wouldn't happen to have a phone in here, would you, Chief?"

"No."

"And your radio is in the car?"

"Yep."

'And you came alone?"

"Uh-huh." My look said of course. "Doc, I can help."

""Forgive me if I don't hand you a gun. You want to help, watch the back of the cabin. Let me know if anyone is coming."

Chief Parker moved to the back window and peered out. "Doc, did you shoot Tyler Shriver? I don't remember you firing out the back side."

"That's because I didn't. Why, what do you see?"

"Tyler's on the ground about 40 yards out. Looks like someone blew a big damn hole in his leg. He's bleeding like a stuck pig. That boy ain't looking so good. It looks like Jackson is trying to wrap a belt around his leg."

"They must have turned on themselves out there. Funny I didn't hear anything. These walls are thick enough to stop bullets, but it seems we still would have heard something…unless…"

Boyd. He must have come back. It would explain the foot exploding on the front porch without an apparent rifle report. It also explained why the men outside were whipping their heads around looking for something they couldn't find. Apparently, he finally got to shot someone.

"Unless what?" asked the Chief.

"Nothing."

"You were going to say something. What was it?"

"You don't think a bunch of rednecks would be using silencers, do you?"

I let Chief Parker mull over that one while I looked for a way to see if Boyd was out there. I didn't know why he didn't just shoot a couple of more guys so we could all go home. But I did know why. Even though Boyd was a former Marine, he had been an MP. A cop, basically. Not a soldier. Not really. And cops don't draw first blood. It's just not in their nature, or their training.

I glanced out one of the back windows. The Chief was right; Tyler was bleeding profusely while Jackson tried to place a tourniquet in the wrong place. Tyler was going to die. Too bad. He had poor taste in friends, but I never felt he was truly an evil person.

An idea came to mind. One that might save Tyler's life and forfeit Jackson's instead, which was okay with me. Jackson was the brains on the Estes side of this little battle and cutting the head off the snake seemed like a smart move.

Moving the kitchen table only took a few seconds. Carefully, and while still in cover, I slowly pulled the back door open. No shots were fired. A good sign. From the doorway, I spotted Jackson still trying to figure out the tourniquet. *Now or never.* I bolted through the front door sprinting toward Jackson and Tyler like my life depended on it, which it probably did. I extended my .45 as I ran, ready if needed. Jackson spotted me at the last moment, dropping the belt he was using as a tourniquet and reaching for the rifle at his feet. His hands never reached the rifle; the concussive force of two successive .45 caliber bullets knocked Jackson onto his back. Center mass once again.

Tyler's eyes were wide with fright. Or maybe pain. His hands went up to his face, seemingly hoping it would protect him from me. He need not worry; I was there to help. Two rifles were sitting on the ground. Hunting rifles of an unknown caliber outfitted with simple 3 x 9 scopes. I popped the magazine out of one of the rifles and threw it into the woods as far as I could before examining Tyler's gunshot wound. It was bad. Blood littered the ground all around him.

"Tyler, I'm here to help." He seemed doubtful. Who could blame him; I had just killed his friend. "Hold still man." Once he complied, I wrapped the belt around his thigh in the proper place to compress the femoral artery. The belt was obviously not the right size for his thigh, so I tied the belt in place, then stuck the barrel of the empty rifle under the belt and started twisting it. It took 3 revolutions of the rifle to tighten the belt around his thigh to compress the femoral artery properly, but the blood flow finally slowed down. "Tyler, listen to me, I can't stay here. You will have to keep this tight yourself. Do you understand?" He nodded. "Good. Good luck."

I grabbed the other hunting rifle and sprinted back towards the cabin hoping Boyd would cover my retreat. The back door of the cabin was closed. I didn't remember closing it. It was also dead bolt locked. *Damn it, Chief; I'm on your side.* I could hear furniture crashing and breaking on the other side. Someone breached the interior. Maybe I should have left the Chief a gun. The door was thick; the deadbolt was strong. In the movies, all it takes is a shot at the lock and the door just flies open. Yeah, that's the damn movies, because after two shots from my Glock, the door was still locked. More crashing emanated from inside. Apparently, the Chief was putting up a fight. Hopefully, the door frame was not a solid as the rest of the house. I lowered my shoulder and hit the door with my full force. The jolt traveled through my body. My shoulder hurt but the wood splintered enough that I was able to kick the door open the rest of the way.

Chief Parker was yelling at someone on the other side of the kitchen wall, apparently near the hallway barricade. The meaty thuds of fists repeatedly hitting flesh echoed throughout the cabin. Rounding the corner, I found Junior straddling the Chief while throwing repeated punches toward his face. He was also pistol whipping him with a small handgun. Chief Parker was blocking some of the blows, but the lacerations on his face were evidence that more than one blow had landed.

"You stubborn son of a bitch, Chief, for the last time, where the hell is the fucking doctor?" yelled Junior.

I grabbed the hunting rifle by the barrel and prepared to swing it. "Right here, asshole," I yelled. Junior whipped his head around just in time to see the wooden stock of the rifle smash into his face. I never played baseball. Never had the temperament for it, but I understood what batters meant by the sweet spot when the rifle struck Junior's face.

Junior's body slumped forward atop Chief Parker. Glancing around revealed the front door barricade was still intact. As I guessed, Junior came through the hallway and crashed through the barricade. Obviously, while I was outside killing his brother.

"Are you going to get this asshole off me?" asked the Chief.

"Depends."

"Depends on what?"

"We on the same side yet?"

"Yes."

"Then you shouldn't have locked the back door. Damn you, Chief. You keep screwing this all up."

"I know, I know! I'm sorry!"

"Sorry enough that you are willing to do something about it?"

"Sure. What?"

"This is a hunting cabin, right? So, you're a hunter. Think you can hit a couple of Strasser's men with this rifle? Honestly, I'm not much good with these things."

I pushed Junior's limp body off Chief Parker and held out the rifle I took off Jackson. The Chief grabbed the rifle, and I used it to pull him to his feet.

"I've never shot anyone. Over 35 years in law enforcement and I've only pulled my gun once in the line of duty."

"You're saying you can't do it?"

"No. I'm saying give me a second to wrap my head around this."

"Wrap your head around it later, Chief. Better to ask your conscience for forgiveness than for permission. Besides, if you were right about Strasser having seven men, that means he still has six outside the cabin. Tyler is outside hopefully not bleeding to death, and Jackson is dead, or will be soon." The Chief's eyes bugged open. "He pulled that rifle on me," I said in a matter of fact tone. "So I shot him."

His shoulders slumped as he weighed the ramifications of my statement. "Should you check on Junior? Make sure he's not dead?"

I bent over and picked up the .22 pistol Junior dropped on the floor when I hit him with the rifle. I crammed it into my back pocket. "He's breathing. I'll look at him later if we make it through this. You ready for this? Or am I going to have to save your bacon again?"

Chief Parker's face transformed from fear and worry to dogged determination in the blink of an eye. "Give me that damn rifle, McCain."

He studied the rifle, narrating to me that it was a Remington semi-automatic 30-06 hunting rifle. He had the same model at home. I stopped him from walking up and simply pointing the rifle right out the front window. Sniping was not in my skill set, but one thing I knew was don't stand in the window. Stand back in the shadows if you can. From a safer distance, Chief Parker started scanning outside the cabin with the rifle scope.

"Chief, take the dog out of the fight or the fight out of the dog, that's up to you."

"Speak English!"

"Kill them or wound them. But shoot enough of them that the rest lose the will to stay and fight, got it? And pick your shots wisely because we got no more bullets after for the rifle."

"Got it. Now shut up and let me do this."

More than once, the Chief lowered the rifle without shooting, rested his arms, and then started scanning again. It was never going to work. He was too unsteady. Probably from all the blows to his head. "Hold on, Chief; I got an idea." I dragged Junior's body over to a spot in the middle of the floor in front of the door. The A-hole was still breathing. Labored, but I didn't give a damn. "Over here, Chief. Use this dipshit's body as a gun rest."

Chief Parker complied without reservation, lying alongside Junior with his rifle across his chest while I opened the front door. "His breathing is too ragged. I found a guy out there, but this gun is bouncing too much."

"Don't waste the shot. Let me think of something." I scurried around for a few seconds before getting an idea. "Here, couch cushions." Chief Parker smiled; he liked the idea. I threw one to the Chief and was carrying the other over to him when a shot fired out. Instinct caused me to duck even though the thick exterior logs protected me. When I looked up, Chief Parker was patting himself down. Blood splatter covered his face, but there were no obvious injuries. It took a second or two to realize what happened. Someone had fired a shot through the open door and shot Junior in the chest. Blood was oozing from an entrance and an exit wound. It was Junior's blood on the Chief's face. Somehow, the bullet completely missed the Chief.

"Oops, maybe not such a good idea," I said.

"Junior just got shot, and you say 'oops.' What the hell is wrong with you?"

They say timing is everything in comedy, and Chief Parker obviously did not appreciate my sense of timing.

"What are you waiting for, Chief? Shoot the SOB. Now!"

The rifle came up across Junior's body while Chief Parker went prone. He tucked the stock tight against his shoulder, took aim, and released the safety. After a long sigh, he fired, moved the gun so that he was aiming a little more to the left and quickly fired again. Probably too quickly. I was getting ready to remind him there was no additional ammunition when he sat up and said, "There. Two down."

"Good job, Chief."

"Yeah, well, excuse me for saying so, but fuck you, McCain."

I took the rifle from him before he changed his mind about shooting me and then used it to look for myself. Two different men were lying on the ground, completely immobile. Apparently, he decided to take the dog out of the fight and not the other way around. Good for him. A faint cracking sound from outside caught my attention. Followed by someone yelling that they were getting the hell out of there. Another man yelled his agreement. Through the trees, I observed three men running back towards the road. Assuming Boyd just shot another one of Strasser's men, that left four shot, presumably dead, and three retreating.

"Chief, you sure there were seven of Strasser's goons out there?"

"Yes, I'm positive. Why?"

"Because I think we did it. We made it through this in one piece."

CHAPTER 40

I doubt anyone in their right mind celebrates after something like what the Chief and I just went through, but I would be lying if the thought did not cross my mind. Outnumbered ten to one, eleven to one if I counted the Chief as an adversary, and I was still in one piece. Not even a scratch. Just a bruised shoulder. Of course, I had not been alone. Thankfully, Boyd disobeyed my wishes and returned to help.

The body count was high enough that the State Police showed up to help the tiny Emmettsville police department process all the evidence. Chief Parker and I practiced our story that we were ambushed by both Strasser's men and the Estes brothers, which was true. In fact, everything we told the State Police was true. We simply and conveniently left out the part about the Chief attempting to double-cross me. If anyone doubted our story, they never let on. Chief Parker and I proved to be very adept at lying just enough.

Boyd managed to get away unseen. If the Chief suspected Boyd's presence, then he never mentioned it to me. He shot three men total, not killing anyone. The crack I heard near the end of the standoff was the sound of a shot proficiently placed into the calf musculature of one of Strasser's men. Boyd opted to take the fight out of the dog and did so with complete efficiency.

Jackson died exactly where I left him. Junior was killed by the shot that came through the open door, although an autopsy implied he might have died anyway from the blow to the head I delivered with the rifle. Tyler was the only survivor from the Estes gang, and he kept the leg.

Unfortunately, with both Junior and Jackson dead, we never knew for sure why Junior had killed Paul. Tyler verified that Junior had told him he did not plan to kill Paul. Apparently, Paul, still upset from being decked by Eric in the parking lot, had decided to get mouthy with Junior. He even put up a fight. Junior became enraged and shot Paul. The story did not make sense, but Tyler's story never changed, so it became the official story nonetheless. It also helped that ballistics proved that the .22 pistol I took from Junior in the cabin was the same gun used to kill Paul.

Strasser. He was a different story. Four of his men got away, although one of the men was obviously missing a huge chunk of calf muscle. He was apprehended nearly a week later trying to get medical care for his injured leg. Despite the lack of structure within the Dixie Mafia, there still existed a strict policy against snitching that all members were expected to follow. He never peeped a word about the other three men.

Which meant Strasser remained the one loose end. Although he was basically scot-free, neither Chief Parker nor I trusted that he would let things drop. Evidence gathering and questioning lasted until the wee hours of the mornings. More than once we managed to steal some time away together on how best to handle Strasser.

Our planning turned out to be a waste of time and worry; Strasser was found dead inside the hotel near Falco's the next day. Room 119. Killed by a .22 to the head. Days later, forensic experts proved that ballistics matched the gun belonging to Junior Estes. Apparently, Jackson planned on double-crossing everyone involved. I had to admit to myself that Jackson outsmarted me. He had covered nearly every angle and managed to get both Strasser and the Chief to come after me. Boyd had been the great equalizer. I shuddered to think what might have happened if he had gone back to Huntsville as I had advised.

Sometime around three in the morning, Chief Parker and I found ourselves sitting on the sidewalk outside the police station. Chief Parker was sure his career was ruined, yet it was worth it to save his son.

"Don't worry about your career, Chief; I'll never tell anyone you planned on double-crossing me."

"I don't deserve to wear the badge."

"Maybe, maybe not. My advice, though, is to wear it proudly until this is all over. Spin everything that happened here tonight in your favor. If the indignity you are feeling right now won't let you be an effective lawman again, then let someone else take over."

"You know what?" I looked at him to continue. "You're alright…for a damn Yankee."

Chief Parker gave me his office so I could take a nap around 3:30 a.m. At seven, he woke me up and told me that I was no longer needed. I could go home. He would call me when I could pick up my Glock 21, which was being kept temporarily as evidence.

The ride home gave me time to reflect on the last couple of weeks.

I did it. I found Paul's killer.

There would be no trial. No confessions. Because the killer was dead. Shot by one of Strasser's men as we used him as a rifle rest. An anti-climatic end, if I said so myself, but still an ending. One I could live with. Justice had been served.

Whether or not Ellie would be happy with my success was a mystery. She was never a fan of my involvement in bringing Paul's murderer to justice to begin with, and when she did help me, it was admittedly self-serving. Time would tell, I guessed. Not to mention I would have to explain killing two men. I was not looking forward to that conversation. It was the same reason I avoided telling her any more than I had to about my time in the Navy.

When I arrived home, I unplugged my phone, turned off my pager, and went directly to bed. I slept for twelve hours and still woke up groggy. It was a little after nine in the evening before I had showered and cooked a bite to eat. Something flashing from the kitchen caught my eye. It was the message light flashing on my answering machine. Weird, I thought, I had unplugged the phone. But it was plugged in, and one of my apartment keys was sitting next to the machine.

I hit play. The first message was from Ellie. She had entered my apartment while I was sleeping and plugged in my machine so she could leave a message. It wasn't a *Dear John* message, not really, but it might as well as been. Plus, she had returned my apartment key. Well, that cleared up one more mystery. It seemed my dangerous side proved to be too dangerous for her after all.

The next message was from John Deland. Chief Parker had called him before he heard about yesterday's activities over the phone. John was thankful and apologetic all at the same time. John left two more short messages. He needed to talk.

The last message was from my mom calling from Chicago again. Like before, she sounded great. She wanted to talk and hoped I would return the call. *Now here is someone who would appreciate what I've accomplished in the last few days.* Mom. Sure, she misquoted Edmund Burke, but she would understand regardless. Tears welled up in my eyes, but I would not allow them to fall. I could not let them fall. If the tears fell, I would not be able to stop them. I didn't have time. It was nearly 10 o'clock at night on a Wednesday. Late, but not too late. Besides, I had something I had to do, and in my world procrastination was a four letter word.

I grabbed my wallet and the keys to the Cobra and headed out. The trip took longer than expected. Upon reaching my destination, I realized I had arrived ahead of schedule. Funny thing about time. It is a constant, something that "flows equably without relation to anything external" according to Newton. Apparently, Newton knew nothing about how fear and anticipation can affect time.

I had gotten as far as the driveway of my destination, yet my rear end seemed glued to the seat. The courage that had enabled me to get that far seemed to have evaporated as soon as I arrived. How could I run towards someone who wanted to kill me to save a dying man, yet lack the courage to get out of the car and ring a doorbell? It was ludicrous.

My mind could not seem to handle the concept of what I was preparing to do. *What do you say in a situation like this?* No words would ever seem adequate. My annoying and tireless inner voice told me to *just do it.* At times, my inner voice is eloquent, at times practically clairvoyant, and the best it could come up with was *just do it.*

It was enough, though. My courage reinstated, I crossed the driveway, hoping someone would be awake, and rang the front doorbell. Nothing for a full minute, so I rang it again. An interior light came on. I heard the faint pit-pat of bare feet approaching the door. The light from the peephole went dark. Too late to turn back now.

Please, let the right person answer the door. I might lose it otherwise.

Someone unlocked the doorknob followed by the deadbolt. The door swung open. Even though the face of the person in the door was backlit, the expression was evident. I instantly knew I had done the right thing.

"Hey, Mom, remember me, Legend."

About the Author

BRIAN CRAWFORD had a brief stint in the U.S. Navy before working as an optical scientist in Huntsville, Alabama designing fiber optic sensors used primarily in security and surveillance applications. He is particularly proud of one invention: a fiber optic microphone that is completely invisible to ALL electronic detection devices, much to the chagrin of the "undisclosed" government agency that witnessed it in action. For the last 17 years, he has gone by the title of Dr. Brian Crawford, a practicing chiropractor in Central Illinois, where he lives with his wife and four daughters.